One

Forbidden Attraction

So much is left unsaid.
So many emotions to unravel.

Two stories of a couple
overcoming the odds to be
together—for ever!

Dear Reader,

Welcome to Desire.

We have three stupendous volumes for you this month, starting with **Millionaire Marriages** which includes the final MILLION DOLLAR MEN story from best-selling author Leanne Banks—*The Millionaire's Secret Wish*—and a rich tale from Peggy Moreland entitled *Millionaire Boss*.

Next we have **Forbidden Attraction**, a volume that contains the deeply moving *Gabriel's Gift* by popular author Cait London and the passionately intense *Victoria's Conquest* by the always-wonderful Laurie Paige.

Our third volume is just as fantastic. **Heiress in His Arms**, where the title says it all, includes Bronwyn Jameson's sensuous *In Bed with the Boss's Daughter* and *The Heiress & the Bodyguard* by Ryanne Corey.

We hope you enjoy them all!

The Editors

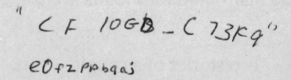

Forbidden Attraction

CAIT LONDON
LAURIE PAIGE

SILHOUETTE®
DESIRE™

First published in Great Britain 2002
Silhouette Books, Eton House, 18-24 Paradise Road,
Richmond, Surrey TW9 1SR

FORBIDDEN ATTRACTION © Harlequin Books S.A. 2002

The publisher acknowledges the copyright holders of the individual works as follows:

Gabriel's Gift © Lois Kleinsasser 2001
Victoria's Conquest © Olivia M Hall 1993

ISBN 0 373 04745 2

51-0402

Printed and bound in Spain
by Litografia Rosés S.A., Barcelona

GABRIEL'S GIFT

by
Cait London

CAIT LONDON

lives in the Missouri Ozarks but loves to travel the Northwest's gold rush/cattle drive trails every summer. She enjoys research trips, meeting people and going to Native American dances. She is an avid reader who loves to paint, play with computers and grow herbs (particularly scented geraniums). She's a national best-selling and award-winning author, and she has also written historical romances under another pseudonym. Three is her lucky number; she has three daughters, and the events in her life have always been in threes. 'I love writing for Silhouette,' Cait says. 'One of the best perks about all this hard work is the thrilling reader response and the warm, snug sense that I have given readers an enjoyable, entertaining gift.'

To Stella

Prologue

———

From the Journal of Magda Claas, Montana 1881

This beautiful valley, in the land the Indians call "Montana," and the women who have become my sisters, have given me peace and comfort. In the heat of that hot, dry summer, ten women came together in this beautiful valley with towering mountains on one side, a lake filled with fish, and lush green grass for our stock.

The land is wild and rough with men, who would take us as they would a cow or a horse, caring little for our pride. Who would protect us? we wondered by our campfire and wagons and stock, women without menfolk in a harsh land. We wanted husbands, of course, but we

wanted the freedom to choose good men who
would treat us well.

Fleur Arnaud, Anastasia Duscha, Beatrice
Avril, Jasmine Dupree, China Belle Ruppurt,
and Fancy Benjamin had already been treated
poorly by their men. They would not settle for
less than their rightful due again. Margaret Ger-
traud, Cynthia Whitehall and myself had not
suffered so, but we were determined to keep
ourselves free of unjoyful and painful bondage,
such as they had suffered. We know little of the
woman known as LaRue, except that she is most
helpful and inventive. She has loved, she said,
and she has lost. Yet her quiet, secret smile tells
more.

So it was that women with strong minds decided to become a family, to protect one another, to weigh marriage offers as a father or
brother would have done in the Old World, to
see that men courted as was proper and that they
kept their marriage promises. We decided that
our family would protect the brides men would
have, inspecting the men's qualifications as future husbands. At first, we laughed, and then the
idea grew into our dream.

Jasmine Dupree had been berry picking when
her baby decided to come, and an Indian man,
Mr. Deerhorn, came to her rescue. He fashioned
a *travois,* two long poles with a blanket between
them, which dragged behind his horse, and
brought her back to our camp. He was most
shocked when Cynthia Whitehall of Boston society thanked him by kissing his cheek.

I am a midwife, and when Jasmine's baby

came into my hands, we cried. That night, we decided to name our valley Freedom, and our town, too. With the fine big boy nursing at Jasmine's breast, and joy in our hearts, we sat down to decide the Rules for Bride Courting. By next summer, we will have a town called Freedom.

Mr. Deerhorn came the next morning with a reed basket of herbs from his mother. He explained the uses to us, but his warm gaze followed Cynthia. A bold woman, she has become suddenly quiet.

Magda Claas, Midwife and Healer and
Butter Maker
Freedom Valley, Montana

One

My children are my joy. A widow with three young children, I feared I would fail them. Yet now Tanner, the oldest at twenty, is already off to college and has his heart set on Gwyneth Smith. At sixteen, Kylie is the youngest, and tosses herself into life. She is determined to bring down one Michael Cusack. My oldest daughter, Miranda, is just eighteen and furious with Gabriel Deerhorn. It has been months since he called or came to our house. Always controlled and keeping her secrets, Miranda will say nothing. I think she dreamed of marrying him, and now she is grimly determined to leave Freedom.

—from the journal of Anna Bennett,
descendant of Magda Claas

The woman stood in the night, campfire smoke curling around her and Gabriel's baby nestling in her rounded belly. Filled with promises and love, her hair swept back from her face by the mountain wind, her eyes were warm upon Gabriel. The joy that she gave him swirled through the tops of the pines, settled deeply within him. She had his heart and together they had made a child—

Gabriel awoke suddenly, his heart racing, his mind trying to hold the dream close to him. Yet it swirled off into the mountain's December snow, torn from him too soon. It was always the same, the woman who came to him in sleep, his child nestled within her. He sat up, his hands shaking as he stirred his campfire into life—not for the warmth, but to do something, anything. Gabriel lifted his face to the slashing mountain snow, then turned to study his evening campfire. The snowflakes blended with the smoke and disappeared, just as the woman always left him. Without her, he carried the cold ache of loneliness.

His people believed in dreams, in the meanings they held. Gabriel breathed deeply, and glanced at his horse in the pine bough shelter. The Appaloosa's mottled coat blended with the veil of snowflakes as the gelding returned Gabriel's study. Once the woman had come to Gabriel when he was cold and alone, curling warmly against him, placing his hand on her full breast. Milk for the coming child had dampened his palm and gave him peace; he knew that his blood would live on, his heritage and pride. He had dreamed of her riding in front of him, wrapped snugly in his arms. Turning slightly, she would lean against him, her breath warm upon his throat, their baby pressing against his stomach.

Gabriel shook his head and dusted the snowflakes from his face. Perhaps it was Michael Cusack and Kylie Bennett's approaching church wedding that had stirred the dreams, like dying embers brought back to life. Perhaps it was Tanner and Gwyneth's announcement of a coming baby. Gabriel hadn't thought of his need to have a child for years. At thirty-seven, he had settled into his mountain ranch, tending his horses and cattle and occasionally serving as a guide for tourists.

He shoved a stick into the fire, prodding it, and watched the coals spring into flame. He'd been too lonely at his cabin, and he'd known the woman would come to him where his Native American blood called to him and the dreams came more freely—in the high untamed mountains overlooking Freedom Valley.

He rose and walked to the rock bluff overlooking the valley with its twinkling lights. His ancestor had helped the women who founded their dream, a land and a town where they could choose their lives.

Just there was the Bennett farm, a tiny complete twenty acres. Mother of three children and a widow, Anna Bennett had lost her life almost a year ago, when her car collided with a semitruck. A midwife and healer, she was loved in Freedom Valley, respected by Gabriel's mother, also a midwife and healer. First Tanner Bennett had come home to claim his ex-wife, and then Kylie to clash with Michael Cusack. Miranda would be coming soon, Kylie's matron of honor.

Miranda. Gabriel breathed unsteadily, hunching down into his shearling coat, as her name curled in the wind. He was only nineteen to her seventeen when they started dating. In another year, Miranda had finished high school and colleges were courting her. Gabriel saw then that their lives were not meant to be entwined. For he was a part of this life, these high mountains, the livestock, the land and his blood.

For Miranda's good, he had torn her from him, never to hold that sweet scent of her close, those soft innocent lips against his.

He'd told her he didn't want her. The lie had hurt, because back then, he had wanted to go before the Women's Council and speak for her. He'd wanted to court her in the traditional way of his ancestors, to offer horses as a bridal price. But Miranda was meant for a different life, one apart from his. Intelligent, creative, and at the top of her class, Miranda would have resented him eventually.

When she'd visited Anna, Gabriel had seen her and the ache returned. She'd said she was happy, and that a few years ago she began living with a man she intended to marry. Gabriel lifted his face to the icy mountain wind. At thirty-five, Miranda was now probably married and a mother. He frowned slightly. Anna had been so proud of her children, and yet she had said nothing of Miranda's wedding or of grandchildren. A sensitive woman, perhaps Anna had known that information would trouble him.

He wasn't looking forward to seeing Miranda and her husband at Kylie's wedding. Gabriel stood suddenly and tore off his coat and the layers of clothing beneath it, giving himself to the freezing, cleansing winds. The wind tore at his hair, swirling it around his face in a storm of snowflakes, and he thought he heard the song of her low, soft voice.

He pushed her from his heart and still she clung to him—soft, warm, beckoning.

The first week of January, Miranda came down the wedding aisle before Kylie, the bride. Standing with the other men beside the groom—Michael Cusack— Gabriel held his breath. With a coronet of daisies in her sleek black hair, bound into a fashionable knot, Miranda caught his heart—just that easily, after all those years.

Taller than Kylie, Miranda moved with the same lithe grace, her flowing feminine gown of mauve emphasizing the blush on her cheeks. Those green eyes were just as startling, highlighted by the magic of makeup. Framed by those long sweeping lashes, her eyes still reminded him of the summer meadows in the mountains. Her brows, finely arched, were like that of the wings of the raven. The new softness in her face, much like Anna's, said she had found peace.

But her mouth— Gabriel tensed, pushing away the soft, haunting memory of it against his, the sweet hunger of seventeen-year-old Miranda.

Then she turned, taking the traditional matron-of-honor's place beside Kylie, and Gabriel's gaze locked on Miranda's gown, clinging to the slight mound of her belly.

There was no time like the present, Miranda thought, as she moved through the dancers, making her way to Gabriel. If she were going to make a home in Freedom Valley for her and her baby, she had to grapple with her "ghosts" first. Gabriel was definitely a man no woman could forget.

As a teenager, she'd had a crush on most of her brother's friends—some of them had married, but those who remained were called "the Bachelor Club" by the matrons of Freedom Valley. Those men who did not conform to the time-honored customs of the Founding Mothers of Freedom Valley were condemned as "Culls."

Gabriel was definitely not a "Cull." He was quiet, thoughtful and lived peacefully on his mountain ranch. He had never married and had been her first real love. At times, the sweetness of those memories caught her, wrapped carefully before she stored them again in the past. Standing with the other men at the altar, Gabriel had been just as tall and fierce and lean as she remembered. His dark suit emphasized that hawkish look, his hair in a rough, long cut and just touching his shoulders. His face was harder, more weathered and angular, tension humming from him. He wouldn't be comfortable in a suit, of course, but he had made the sacrifice for his friends.

She'd felt the burn of those black hunter's eyes, the narrowing of them on her rounded belly. Had his hard mouth tightened then, or had she just imagined that reaction? Gabriel always held his emotions tightly, even at nineteen, when his body ran warm and taut with the need to take more....

Miranda fought the tremble moving through her, and stopped her hand from nervously fidgeting with her hair. She wouldn't be nervous of Gabriel Deerhorn, no matter how fiercely he'd scowled at her.

Again—had she just imagined his reaction? Or was it a reflection of her own shaken emotions?

Standing in front of him now, Miranda looked up. His black eyes were flat, shielded now, deep set beneath those fierce brows. The lights gleamed on his high cheekbones, the planes and shadows of his face cruising along an unrelenting jaw and a chin with a magical little dimple. For just a heartbeat, the memory of his unsteady breath sweeping across her cheek, the open hot furnace of that mouth, startled her.

There had been no softness in that long, well-shaped mouth the day he told her that he didn't want her.

Miranda pushed away that slicing memory and decided to keep their meeting light. "I've danced with all the other men in the Bachelor Club. You're next and it's the last dance."

Gabriel looked over her head, ignoring her. Then those black eyes pounced upon her, tearing at her, though his deep voice still held that magical lilt. She didn't understand that slashing glance, battering her, and it was quickly shielded into a bland expression. "Sure."

He took her stiffly in his arms, in the traditional way she remembered, and eased her into the waltz. She'd forgotten that he was so tall—six foot three—and with the added height of his polished Western boots, she barely reached his shoulder. He had that ramrod-straight look of a lean working man, and for just a moment, she imagined him on horseback, his body flowing easily with the animal's.

As a teenager, he'd been so careful of her sensibilities. The first time she saw him playing field foot-

ball without his shirt, she'd been entranced by the
beauty of his smooth, dark skin rippling over the muscles and cords.

Now his hand was rough against hers, his shoulders
even wider, and she felt feminine and delicate within
his very proper embrace. She wondered what had
happened to that sense of being a woman—had it
been stripped away by her career, in the push-push to
succeed? She dressed and acted like a woman, but
inside she felt so empty—except for the wonder of
her coming baby. Miranda glanced up at Gabriel,
dancing as if forced to do his duty. He'd given her
the only wildflower bouquet she'd ever had, but now
those high, sharp cheekbones and that jaw looked as
if none of the boy's softness remained. She wondered
what bitterness had happened to him, to make those
lines upon his brow, the brackets beside his lips.
Strength ran through his body, though he held her
lightly. She could sense the vibrations of emotions
circling him, that taut hoarding of his thoughts, the
control she always associated with him. "Michael and
Kylie are so perfect for each other, don't you think?"
she asked, just to hear him speak.

"Sure." A man obligated to dance with his friend's
sister, Gabriel looked over her head, studying the
other dancers.

Gabriel was simply doing his duty, dancing with
her, and Miranda gave in to the impish need to prick
that cool shield. "I hear you have a ranch now, and
that you guide like your father did."

"Sure. He's retired now." He looked down at her,
and his hard face softened momentarily. "I'm sorry
about your mother. I liked Anna."

Suddenly he seemed so safe, even after all the years between. She couldn't resist placing her forehead against his shoulder and resting there for just a moment, her hand clenching his large calloused one as an anchor. Gabriel tensed, his hand at her back opening, digging in slightly. Was he afraid she'd cry? That a pregnant woman's moods would embarrass him? Unpredictable emotions seemed to be the effect of her pregnancy, so unlike Miranda's usual control. She was too vulnerable now because she'd fought reality and lost. The man she'd thought she would marry didn't want her or their baby.

Only Kylie and Tanner, her brother, knew that she wasn't married, that her child was unwanted by its father. She'd come to Freedom to protect her baby, to surround it with love and family. She'd stay in her mother's home, find work and nurture her child. Freedom Valley was where she belonged; somehow she'd find a way to explain the missing husband, and in two months she'd be holding her baby. She'd only been back two days, but amid the hustle of the traditional wedding Michael Cusack wanted for Kylie, Miranda knew she had made the right choice—to come back home. She'd sold everything of her past life, wanting a new one for herself and her baby.

After living together for three years and finally planning a wedding, Scott wasn't prepared for the changes in her body, her brief morning sickness had repelled him. He'd wanted a family earlier, but then suddenly—with the wedding a month away—he explained how trapped he felt by her and the impending marriage, and the child he didn't want. He blamed her nesting urges for ruining a "good setup."

"Do you want to rest?" Gabriel asked softly above her head. That liquid deep voice was the same, calming, gentling...

Unwilling to leave the safety of his shoulder, Miranda shook her head. "I'm sorry. I wish Mom could have been here."

Her mother's fatal accident had stirred her need to marry, to have children, to carry on with life. She couldn't blame Scott. He was clearly surprised by his own fears. They'd had a good relationship, blending their work and lives. It wasn't a blinding love affair, but she had settled for a workable and pleasant one with Scott. Yet, there it was—a solid lump of the ugly unexpected. Scott did not want to be a father; he couldn't bear to look at her, or touch her, after the six-weeks' pregnancy test proved positive. He'd been almost physically ill at the news.

The plain gold band on her finger was a lie, and looking back, so was her life with Scott. She'd desperately needed her mother's home in which to mend, to be strong for her baby. With Tanner and Kylie living nearby, Miranda's baby would always have a family and safety.

The music ended and still Gabriel held her, unmoving. She caught the scent of wood smoke and horses and leather and man, all safe and good. Slowly she lifted her head to meet those searching black eyes. "I'm fine," she managed to say and forced herself to ease away from the first safety she'd felt in months. "Thank you."

"Sure." Gabriel stood very still, watching her, and Miranda couldn't bear to meet his gaze.

Then Sadie McGinnis, a member of the Women's

Council, came to her side. "Your husband couldn't get away for the wedding, hmm?"

Miranda shook her head no, and hated the lie. "Excuse me. It's time to catch Kylie's bouquet."

"But, honey. That's for the unmarried girls," Sadie said firmly.

"Oh, yes. Of course. But I want to see better." Miranda moved away quickly. Did anyone suspect? Amid the cheers, she glanced at the people she'd known all of her life. She found only joy and warmth in their expressions. Gabriel stood apart, his face unreadable, and she wondered if he knew that she was alone.

Somehow, she'd get through her unsteady emotions, Miranda thought in the silence of her mother's home. In Seattle, she'd used her analytical mind to dissect statistics, to determine potential markets. A high-paid executive with a magna cum laude degree, she'd plunged through daily routines, gauging her life by clocks and corporate demands. Scott had been a comfortable part of that life, those routines.

Who was she? Where was that cool reasoning power now? she wondered, as she foundered in her emotions. She sat by the opened hope chest she'd filled all those years ago. She'd dreamed of being Gabriel's wife, of having his children. Hope chests were a requirement of the brides in Freedom Valley, and her mother had helped her fill this one. Miranda smoothed the tiny hand-stitched quilt her mother had made, the note pinned to it. "With love, Grandma."

Miranda scrubbed the tears from her face, then

gave way to crying. "I need you, Mom. Why did that accident have to happen?"

The house she'd grown up in was too quiet, the shadows echoing with Tanner's outraged shouts as he tore after two younger sisters. Kylie's giggles curled through the years, and their mother's soothing voice: "You'll be fine. Just do what's right and everything else will follow."

Miranda smoothed the baby blanket Juanita Deerhorn, Gabriel's mother, had stitched long ago. When Gabriel and Miranda were teenagers, Juanita simply came to Anna's house one morning with a wrapped present for Miranda. One of Juanita's famous saucer-size red roses had been tucked into the ribbon binding the gift. A Southern woman of grace and charm, Juanita's birth name had been Lillian. But the elder Deerhorns affectionately referred to her in a name more familiar to them—"Juanita."

Juanita had been unusually serious that morning. "My mother-in-law, Gabriel's grandmother, White Fawn, told me to make this for you. I always do what she tells me, for she usually has a reason. I hope you like it."

The baby blanket was for Miranda's hope chest, dainty hand stitching fashioning a Celtic-looking design of interwoven circles with no beginning and no end. Juanita's smile had been soft as she traced them. "The batting was from White Fawn's sheep. She hand-carded it and drew the design for me to use. Don't make too much of this, honey. White Fawn often tells me these small things to do, and because you are such a lovely girl, and I love your dear mother, this is a gift of the heart, not because I exactly expect you to be toting my grandchild someday.''

The blanket had remained in Miranda's hope chest, the rose carefully pressed with it.... She pressed her hand against the small kick in her womb. The baby seemed weaker in the past few days, but perhaps that was the stress of leaving her old life. Easing downstairs, Miranda suddenly felt very old and worn, as though she'd crossed centuries, not a hectic month of making arrangements to move to Freedom Valley.

She brewed a cup of tea and settled comfortably under the afghan on her mother's couch. Her mother was still here, in the scents and herbs, though Gwyneth and Kylie and Tanner had tended and cleaned the house. In the spring, the yellow tulips and irises and lavender beds would sprout, the tender herbs scenting the air.

Tanner and Kylie had each returned to Freedom Valley, and each had lived in Anna's home. Its warmth circled Miranda now, giving her the shelter she needed. But one day, the contents would have to be separated, each sister and Tanner taking a bit home with them.

"My doctor said the baby is perfectly healthy," Miranda quietly reassured herself amid the still shadows of the house. *"But oh, Mom. I wish you were here."* Miranda decided to rest before checking in with Freedom Valley's doctor and tried not to cry, a brief release for all the emotions storming her. She was simply too tired to drag herself into the reality of her new life in Freedom Valley just yet.

Tanner and Gwyneth's baby would arrive after hers, and the cousins would be family. Kylie and Michael wouldn't wait to start a family, because Kylie never waited, forever leaping into life. Her brother and sister were blissfully happy in their new lives and their mother would have loved keeping her grandchildren.

Her mother's death had pricked Miranda's biological need for a child, a new life to replace a dear one that had been cut short. The continuity of Anna's life was important, and so, safe in the knowledge that Scott would want their child, Miranda had conceived. Looking back, while she was grieving over her mother was not the best time to make a decision to have a baby. Miranda smoothed her belly and knew that she had enough love for two parents.

"Mother? Where are you?" Miranda whispered, and ached when no answer returned from the shadows. She looked outside to the snow slashing across her mother's front porch. Anna had always fed the birds early in the morning, and filling the many bird feeders would be a start for Miranda's routine. Day by day, she'd build a life for her child that was safe and good. Just now, she wasn't ready to expose herself to anyone but Kylie and Tanner. But eventually she would have to deal with gossip. A younger, more vulnerable Miranda had already handled rumors and sympathetic looks by Freedom Valley's townfolk.

All those years ago, teenage Gabriel had hurt her terribly. "I don't want you. Don't even think of marriage between us, or anything else," he'd said grimly. She'd cried horribly, hiding from her family, trying not to show her pain. *He'd torn away her heart and deep inside she'd hated him, vowing never to forgive him.*

Years later, another man's confession had jolted her. She'd been startled by Scott's reaction and rejection, but not hurt. It was as if her emotions with him hadn't been deep enough to wound. He'd been truthful, though, and she admired that more than a man who forced himself to submit to a life he didn't want.

Miranda slid down on the couch, snuggling into the familiar warmth of her homecoming. She closed her eyes and wondered why she could not remember the Nordic texture of Scott's crisp waving blond hair, and yet the coarse, straight texture of Gabriel's black shaggy mane seemed so familiar.

Was he happy? Gossip said he hadn't married, that he kept to himself and his mountains. Miranda frowned and closed her eyes wearily, her hand smoothing the baby nestled within her. Why did he seem so uncomfortable with her? Did those sweet days of their teenage years still curl around him as they did her? *Gabriel, you look so hard and lonely. What happened to you?* Then, a tiny kick beneath her hand claimed her thoughts of the future.

Two

The most gentle of hearts can be found in un-suspecting places. Women tend to think that only another woman can give comfort, but men—given the chance—can offer kindness to a troubled heart.

Anna Bennett's Journal

Gabriel followed the snowplow as it passed Anna's small farm, leaving small mountains of snow on either side of the road. Departing immediately after their wedding for their honeymoon, Kylie and Michael had missed the heavy snow that now bent the trees and blocked some roads and airports. The light lacy snow-flakes hit Gabriel's windshield and the *clack-clack* of his wipers created the pattern for his thoughts.

After the wedding, he had packed a two-week supply of groceries into his battered Jeep. Then he had settled down with his friends at the Silver Dollar Tavern, the site of the wedding reception. He was more comfortable there, with the loud country music and the smells, than in the church, with a tie tight around his neck. The sounds had vibrated in the tavern's smoky room, a jarring contrast to his very quiet, solitary log home. Though he visited Tanner and his life-long friends throughout the year, Gabriel was always glad to get back to his mountains. The Bachelor Club—Koby, Fletcher, Dylan, Brody and the rest of his friends—had toasted their "dying breed." Because Dakota Jones's little sister, Karolina, alias "Super Snoop," had been in a snit, mourning her "old maid" status, the men had taken turns dancing with her. But Gabriel had danced the last dance with Miranda. Another time, when a woman would ask a man for the last dance, it would mean she chose him for her future husband. Gabriel wasn't likely to follow the local customs—love had passed him by, and he'd settled for peace in the mountains.

Later, only a little of the tension remained from holding Miranda in his arms. He'd stayed the night at Michael's house, the newlyweds bound for a sunny, tropical honeymoon.

Filled with thoughts of yesterday's wedding and seeing Miranda again, he kept his four-wheel-drive Jeep a respectable distance behind the snowplow. At six o'clock in the morning, the flashing red light of the snowplow shot off into the darkness. Behind the wheel of the charging beast, Mac Reno would be in an evil mood, pained by a Saturday night hangover. Mac had once gotten in an argument with Willa, the owner of the Wagon Wheel Café and the mayor of Freedom; he'd used the snowplow to bury her car.

After the joy of Kylie and Michael yesterday, and Gwyneth and Tanner's delight in their coming baby, Gabriel's solitary life seemed as gray as the morning. The woman in the smoke—her eyes warm upon him, and her body rounded with his child—was only a dream he used to fill the ache inside him, a self-induced medicine to give him momentary peace. He'd made the right decision when they were teenagers—

Gabriel ran his hand over his jaw, the sound of the scrape as raw as his emotions. He didn't like being unsettled, tossed back into the past when Miranda danced close and sweet against him. She wore another man's ring, and now she carried his child— Why had that shadow crossed her face when asked about her husband?

Gabriel's hands tightened on the steering wheel. If she had been mistreated— He pushed away that ugly thought. She looked as if she were blooming, the pregnancy sitting well on her.

But she had leaned against him in the old way, when troubles came too deeply upon her. As a boy, he'd been stunned that she would give so much to him, letting him see her doubts and trusting him with her thoughts. She'd grieved then for her father, Paul, a good man who had died of a terminal disease.

Miranda smelled the same—of sun and wind brushing across the lush sweet-grass meadows. Her eyes were still the shining green of new grass, clear and bright and happy—she'd looked that way when he'd given her that wildflower bouquet all those years ago. Now she was a woman, preparing for her child, and

*yet she seemed so fragile, light and willowy in his
arms. He feared holding her too close, keeping his
distance, for just then, he was uncertain of himself.*

Gabriel glanced at Anna's driveway, at the snow
the plow had piled high, barring the entrance. Out of
habit, he eased the Jeep over the snow and reached
to the back to push aside the snowshoes resting over
his shovel. Anna had always been good to him, and
he was only one of many who would clear her driveway. In no hurry to return to his empty house, Gabriel
glanced at Anna's home and found light streaming
from all the windows, creating golden patches into
the gray dawn. The house was much like Anna had
left it a year ago, though both Tanner and Kylie had
taken turns living in it. Tanner had explained that
none of Anna's children could bear separating her
things. Filled with warm scents and Anna's tender
presence, the house would be a ghost to Miranda now.
She would be doing her prowling, missing her
mother, and that wound would be slow to heal. How
could her husband not see to her at such a time, not
come with her? To know such a woman and not care
for her was unthinkable.

But then Miranda was her own woman, very independent, and it wasn't for Gabriel to mull her life.

When he opened the Jeep's door, the freezing temperatures hit him. He sucked in the icy air, letting it
cleanse him, and then began to shovel the snow. The
earth needed snow for nourishment, and to make the
grass grow lush and green— Miranda's eyes were still
as green, softer now with her coming baby nestled
inside her. The thought jarred him, how easily she

stepped into his mind after all those years. Perhaps she had always been there.

The image of her teenage disbelief slashed across him. In curt terms, he'd told her that they weren't meant for each other and that she should take the scholarship offers coming to her, that she should leave Freedom Valley. He'd told her that their paths were not meant to be one—that his life's path was not for her—and the shock in those green eyes had shamed him. Her slender body had recoiled as if taking a physical blow. Though his heart had been tearing, he tried not to show his anguish and how much her tears hurt him. The memory added force to his shovel's blow against a shrub, shaking the branches and dislodging the heavy snow before it could break them. He tempered the other blows, pushing the shattering image into the past for a time.

The birds began to chirp and he smiled briefly. Anna's feeders were always kept well filled and suet balls hung from the trees. Coming from a close family, Miranda would honor her mother's desires. When would she leave? Would he see her again?

Gabriel thrust the unseemly thoughts from him. She was another man's woman, and it was not his way to— In the stillness of morning, a soft moan sounded amid the chirping birds, and there at the base of Anna's front steps was—

Gabriel ran toward Miranda, curled into a ball. Birdseed was scattered on the snow, and the skid mark on the icy top step told the story. Tearing off his leather gloves, he crouched to her side. He eased away the corner of her shawl and found her face too white, a thin trickle of blood at her forehead.

How long had she lain in the freezing temperatures? Trembling, Gabriel eased his arm beneath her head. "Miranda?"

His heart stopped beating while he waited for her to answer. "Miranda?"

This time she moaned slightly and tensed, as if in pain. When she moved, Gabriel saw the blood soaking the white snow. He eased away her long, heavy coat and grimly acknowledged the likelihood that Miranda had lost her baby. "Shh, Miranda," he whispered as he began to work quickly.

Through the pain tearing at her body, Miranda looked up at Gabriel's darkly weathered face. He looked so tired and worried, his black eyes soft and warm upon her. "Miranda?"

Her head throbbed, and the cold cloth on her forehead came away with her blood. She remembered falling, trying to protect her baby and icy terror leaped into her. *"My baby?"*

"Miranda, you're in Anna's house. Upstairs in your bedroom—"

She reached to snag his flannel shirt, to fist it with both hands. "Tell me."

"Miranda, you have to help me. The roads are closed and the doctor can't get here soon. You have to tell me what to do. Mother is a midwife, but I can't reach her. You helped your mother at times like this. You've got to think—"

"My baby?" she cried again and knew from the emptiness inside her that the baby had come too soon.

Gabriel took her hands in his and shook his head. "I tried. He was a fine boy."

Her wail ripped through the still shadows. Or was that the sound of her heart and soul tearing apart? *Oh my little love, wait for me…Mommy will take care of you…wait for me…*

"Miranda, come back to me," Gabriel said firmly. "Tell me what to do. The doctor told me some of it, but you know what your mother would have done. Where are Tanner and Gwyneth? They're not answering their telephone."

She shook her head, fighting against reality and pain. Tears burned her eyes and she remembered how cold she'd been, how the baby— *The fall was her fault.* Her baby would have lived except for her need to start a daily routine, to feed the birds. Her voice was rusty, thin and seemed to come from someone else. "They decided to spend the night in a resort hotel."

It wasn't true. Her baby was still… The pain slapped at her, no worse than her grief, her heart and body crying for that little, precious life.

"Tell me what to do," Gabriel repeated softly, firmly. "You need attention."

Tiredly, without emotion, her voice coming from far away, she instructed Gabriel how to help her. He drew off her soiled clothing, replacing her pajamas with a warm soft flannel shirt and nothing else. In her grief, she felt no shame. Gabriel spoke to her softly, soothingly, his manner impersonal as he changed her toweling and lifted her hips. His callused hand laid on her forehead, anchoring her as she grieved. "I will bring your son to you. Do you want to see him?"

"Yes," she whispered, the emptiness of her womb aching. She wanted just one moment before the doctor arrived and officially declared the medical reality. How could this tiny, perfect life be torn from her? *Oh, my little baby—*

Gabriel had cleansed her baby, holding the tiny body close against him. "His father will want to know. Do you want me to call him?"

"No! My baby is mine alone." She couldn't bear to share anything of her baby with the man who didn't want him. She met Gabriel's frown and the truth tore from her. "I'm not married. Scott couldn't bear the thought of marriage or children. The changes in my body repulsed him. He tried not to show it, but he couldn't bear to touch me. I couldn't bear the thought of a baby raised by a father who resented being trapped. I came home to Freedom Valley to keep my baby safe—"

She tugged the wedding band she'd purchased from her finger, hurling it against the wall. It bounced and fell, rolling across the floor as empty as her life now.

She tensed as Gabriel sat, holding the tiny baby close and safe against him. "He's a fine son. A man would be honored to know that you carried his child."

Miranda turned her face away from the tender sight. Gabriel was a man meant to hold and love children; he wouldn't understand Scott's fear.

"A fine son... For a man's blood to continue gives him greatness. To have a woman give him such a child is a treasure most men would honor. I have longed for a son, or a daughter," he added as a gentle afterthought. "My arms need a child in them. I know this in my heart, but yet I cannot—"

She turned suddenly to him, rage and pain searing

her. She didn't hide her torment from Gabriel, a man she'd known all her life. Tossed by her emotions, she was angry with him, for tearing them apart. Gabriel would have been a perfect father and yet he hadn't wanted her, either. "Did you hear me? Scott did *not* want me, or my baby."

"Who do you grieve for—yourself, or your child?" The quiet, thoughtful challenge took her back and she turned away again. "A woman carrying a child is beautiful. I thought at the wedding how you glowed, how you seemed to have the sunlight inside you."

Gabriel pushed away the rage within him. How could any man not be at the side of the woman carrying his child? Yet he forced himself to calm, for Miranda was too pale and vulnerable now. Her eyes were shadowed, dark circles beneath them. Her mouth quivered, those beautiful eyes brimming with tears and the pulse in her throat beating heavily with emotion. She held her child for a while, and then he eased it away.

She looked outside at the snowstorm, too silent, her grief etched in her pale features, the tears dripping from her cheeks. "I don't blame Scott. He was as surprised at his reaction as I was."

Gabriel damned the weakness of her lover. Holding him blameless, she must still love him. Perhaps she wanted him still, wishing for him to come claim her. Gabriel pushed away that slight, unexpected burn of jealousy; Miranda needed his strength now. "Your mother would want you here, Miranda. Can you feel her?"

"Yes," she said tiredly. "I can. I hurt, Gabriel. Every part of me and I feel so empty and so cold."

"You're badly bruised, Miranda. You must have fallen from the top step, and you were lying in the snow for a time. The cold probably slowed the loss of blood." Gabriel inhaled sharply. He placed his hand over her forehead, testing its warmth, and then he took her pulse. "I'm going to call the doctor to see what else I can do. Then would you like me to lie with you, to hold you?"

In her pain, she'd lost all sense of modesty and she was feeling too weak, too vulnerable now. Where was the strong controlled woman she'd always been, always—? Now she only felt the need for life. "Just for a little bit. I need to feel—a heartbeat other than mine."

Miranda gave herself to the warmth of Gabriel's gentle hands and voice and when he settled beside her, she slid off into a welcoming darkness. Then someone was shaking her lightly, and Gabriel was bending over her, cupping her face with his big, callused hands. His voice was low and urgent. "Miranda, listen to me. The doctor is almost here. Will you trust me? I am only thinking of you now and your baby and of your mother. I want to smooth this road for you."

She shook her head, unwilling to agree to anything but the truth. Then Gabriel took her hand, wrapping it in his warm, strong one. "It is in my heart to protect you and your baby. Do you trust me?"

His eyes were kind and concerned and she had nowhere else to go, nothing— She gripped his hand, nodded slowly and slid back into sleep.

* * *

Gabriel. Through a window in her mother's house, Miranda watched the birds feed outside, gay in the dazzling midmorning light. Gabriel had been in the ambulance with her, staying in the small room at Freedom's clinic with her. "She carried my baby," she'd heard him say. "A fine son.... We had an argument and were working on our problems...."

The elderly nurse, Sarah, had been a friend of Anna's and hadn't spared Gabriel in her searing denouncement of "irresponsible males." He'd nodded solemnly, taking the tongue-lashing without comment. "I see she's not wearing her ring. She probably only purchased it to prevent gossip about her baby. Women have a sense of honor, even if *some* men do not," Sarah had stated pointedly.

Gabriel's plan was so old-fashioned, Miranda mused, giving his protection to her. Yet just then, she'd needed someone to lean on, the months of struggling with her failure—her misplaced trust in a man frightened so badly by marriage and children—and it was only too easy to let Gabriel handle everything. While the Bennetts were well respected in Freedom, Miranda didn't feel like explaining her past life, or the reason she was in Freedom now, without a husband. With Gabriel, Tanner and Kylie's solid fronts, she was well insulated against those who would gossip.

As the birds outside flitted around the feeders, swooping to the snow to pick at the fallen seeds, she pushed away the teardrop on her cheek. She was weak and uncomfortable and grieving and she didn't like herself now.

How could she have been so wrong about Scott? He'd been the perfect companion, a friend.

Why hadn't she been more careful that morning?

Miranda traced the window, mid-January's temperatures icy upon her fingertip. How strange that Tanner and Kylie would agree that Gabriel's plan was good for her. She shook her head. She was usually so strong and in control and now she seemed without an anchor. Miranda ran her cold fingertip across the tiny fresh scar on her forehead. The doctor's words of two weeks ago kept running through her mind. "A slight concussion... A premature delivery..."

She scrubbed her hands across her face and knew that she had to do something, anything to reclaim herself. Miranda suddenly closed her eyes. *How could she reclaim herself when every time she saw Gwyneth's softly rounded body, she thought of...?*

Her mother's house seemed so empty now, her crocheting basket just as she left it. A smoothly worn hook was still poised in the loop of white thread and anchored into the large spool. The image seemed symbolic, for Miranda was held in a moment of her life, unable to move on. She placed her hand over the spool of crochet thread, the hook and the half-finished doily. Her hand drifted across her body and she forced it to lift away from the emptiness. She had to go on, to make a life, and stop worrying Tanner and Kylie. Miranda inhaled the scent of her mother's lemon and beeswax furniture oil, and knew it was time to get to work. Her mother's pantry was a perfect place to start.

Kylie and Gwyneth could not empty Anna's canning jars, the green beans lined carefully on the shelf. After the thin years of widowhood and bringing up three children alone, Anna wouldn't have liked the waste. But she'd kept a tight eye on dated foodstuffs and the labels proved that the filled jars were past due. Tying on Anna's big work apron over her sweater and jeans, Miranda set out to clean her mother's pantry.

Tanner and Kylie and she had agreed months after Anna's accident that they would return to separate her things. Yet everything, except for the absence of Kylie's hope chest, was the same. Miranda inhaled slowly; the house couldn't remain as it was forever. Nothing was forever.... Kylie and Tanner were deep in their own lives, in the families that would come. She had to have a purpose—she'd always had goals, living her life by fulfilling them—and now she had nothing but her mother's pantry.

Gabriel shoveled the new snow in the driveway and then worked his way up Anna's walkway. He carefully cleaned the front steps and then circled the house, noting the light in the kitchen. After Miranda's family returned, he had eased away, letting them comfort her. But her eyes filled with pain at the sight of Gwyneth's rounded belly, and he knew that the healing would be long and painful. From others, he knew that Miranda hadn't left her mother's house.

Perhaps she mourned the man who couldn't bear the shackles of marriage or children. Perhaps she waited for him to come to her. It wasn't Gabriel's place to stay with her, but he came down from the mountains every two days, trekking the first bit with his snowshoes to shovel snow and tidy the limbs broken by the snow's weight. Miranda's car, a compact hatchback wagon, hadn't left Anna's driveway. The only marks were those by the Boat Shop, the building near Anna's house where Tanner fashioned custom-made wooden boats. Emotionally stripped, Miranda hadn't changed from the silent shadow of herself, and Gabriel wondered how she would react to his offer.

Was it for her welfare, or his own? Was he being selfish? Wanting to care for her, to be with her a little longer, before she left again?

To be truthful, Gabriel admitted to himself, the offer he would propose to Miranda suited his own needs to be close to her, to cherish her.

She didn't want to answer the quiet firm knock at the back porch door. One look through the window and she recognized Gabriel's height and broad shoulders. He'd come to shovel snow before, leaving as silently as he came. Wearily she opened the door to him. He'd seen everything, knew the ugly truth about a man who couldn't bear to look at her. But courtesy in her mother's house had always been observed. Those watchful black eyes traced the circles beneath her eyes, her pale coloring, and the large dampened apron. He knew too much for her to deny her mental state; she felt as if he could see into her mind, the storms battering and draining her. "So I'm depressed. It happens. I'll deal with it. Come in."

Gabriel stamped the snow from his boots and stepped into the back porch. Careful of Anna's floors, he sat on an old chair and unlaced his boots, removing them. In the kitchen, he eased off his coat and draped it methodically, thoughtfully, over the back of a chair. He took in the empty jars on the table, the contents dumped into a five-gallon bucket, the jars in the soapy water and ranging across the counters. Without speaking, he lifted the bucket and carried it to the back. He replaced his boots and carried the bucket outside. Miranda returned to washing jars, meticulously scrubbing them, holding them up to the kitchen window and inspecting them. If she could, she'd wash away the past as easily.

Gabriel returned with the empty bucket and stood watching her. Empty, she thought, comparing the bucket to how she felt. She avoided his gaze; he'd already seen too much of her life. Struggling against crying, Miranda turned to him. "It's an ordinary thing to do, isn't it? Cleaning jars? I have to do something…Gabriel, there was no need for you to feel you had to protect me."

She was angry now, with herself, with Scott, with Gabriel, with life. Her emotions swung from grief, to frustration, to self-pity, and back to anger. "I've always managed. I want to return something to you. Your mother made it for me years ago."

Hurrying upstairs, Miranda tore into her old hope chest, retrieving the baby blanket Juanita had made. She returned and handed it to Gabriel. She wanted him and everything about him stripped from her. "You should have this."

"Is it so hard to give yourself into the care of another?" he asked quietly, smoothing his large, strong fingers across the delicate stitching.

"She isn't here, Gabriel. *My mother was always here, and now she isn't.*" Illogical and grieving and emotional, Miranda served him the truth.

"She has done her work. Let her rest." Gabriel's

voice was deep and soothing, that slight lilt unique
and magical. "Have you eaten?"

"Does it matter?" She was bitter and alone and
detested herself now, for lashing out at a man who
had helped her.

"Come with me to the café, Miranda. Eat with me.
Let people see you are a woman of pride and strength,
for Anna."

"That would only reinforce your lie, that you were
the father of my baby, trying to reclaim me."

"You can tell them it is a lie, if you wish. I wanted
to protect you then. I still do." He smiled softly, his
hand smoothing her rumpled hair. She moved away,
wary of Gabriel, who overpowered her mother's sun-
lit kitchen. "Because if you will allow me, I would
like to ask for you at the Women's Council."

Miranda closed her eyes, his offer echoing in her
head. She gripped the kitchen counter for an anchor.
"I didn't hear that."

He placed his hand on her head and shook it
lightly. The gesture was familiar, one her brother and
his friends had used for a younger sister. "Open your
eyes, little Miranda. It is a logical plan."

Little Miranda. He'd called her that so long ago....

She stared up at him, trying to mentally jump from
a man who'd run from responsibility to the man wanting it. What did Gabriel stand to gain? Why would
he want to protect her so dramatically, creating a lie
that damaged his honor in Freedom Valley? "Tanner
put you up to this. He was always—"

"He's worried. You are only human, Miranda, and
dealing with too much all at once. You need a place

apart from here to heal. I am offering my home. It is quiet and you would have time to adjust."

Adjust? How? She shook her head. "No."

His body stiffened. "Because you do not trust me?"

She met his eyes, fierce and black now with pride, the scowl darkening his hard face, the gleaming skin taut across those sharp, high cheekbones. "I have always trusted you, even when you were such a rat and broke up with me. I could visit you, Gabriel. I would like that. But the Women's Council is for marriage offers and I see no reason to deceive anyone any longer."

"I do. Let me share your burden. Let me give you shelter in all ways while you heal. For the most part, Freedom Valley has kind hearts, but there are tongues who would slice and hurt. Anna would not like that."

Miranda's head began to throb, part of her wanting to leap into Gabriel's offer to let someone else deal with her own affairs. But reality said that she was a woman who could and should manage her life. "The idea is tempting, but I couldn't let you offer for marriage. I have to handle this on my own."

"But my pride will not let me do less. It is only a temporary means to help us both. The custom allows you my protection and my honor would not allow me to do less. I will only live with a woman under the custom of Freedom Valley—the trial marriage gives me a bit of company until spring, and hopefully, you'll relax and think and heal."

Gabriel ruffled her hair slightly, his fingers drawing away a strand before leaving her. A smile lurked around his eyes and lips. "With you in my home, my sister Clarissa would stop nagging me to get married. You'd be my protection.''

''You're offering me a distraction, Gabriel. I'll have to face life sometime.'' Yet his idea warmed her, a temporary reprieve.

''True. While you're thinking about it, let's go down to the Wagon Wheel and eat.''

Three

Even the most levelheaded woman will be shaken by a man's honorable and sweet intentions to claim her. I long for the day my Miranda sees such a man coming for her in the old traditional ways of my mother and her mother before her. She guards her heart well, now that Gabriel is not in her wedding sights. His ancestor would not court Cynthia Whitehall of the Founding Mothers all those years ago. Though they married others, Cynthia was said never to glow again as she had when she looked at Mr. Deerhorn. I want my Miranda to glow and to dream as is any woman's right. It seems that now she has sealed her heart away. I wonder what can bring her back to life and love.

Anna Bennett's Journal

"**I**'d like to handle my own problems," Miranda whispered fiercely as she sat across from Gabriel at the Wagon Wheel Café. Her edges were showing now to a man who already knew too much about her. The falsely admitted father of her baby, Gabriel had stoically taken an amount of verbal battering from the traditional community. Though he seemed undisturbed, Miranda felt guilty, another emotion she couldn't afford. She hated her weakness now, feeling as though one more blow would shatter her like glass. "I know I'm not myself now, but I will be. I don't need your sympathy. You're asking me to live with you and let everyone think that we're trying to work out a nonexistent relationship. This is today, Gabriel, not a century and a half ago. Women have children— and lose them, and tend their own lives. I will...I will when I'm good and ready."

Gabriel nodded and leaned back in the booth, a tall broad-shouldered man, one long leg stretched outside the enclosure. The rich tone of his weathered skin reflected his Native American ancestry. The rough cut of his hair rested on the collar of his dark red sweater, those jarring fierce features locked into an unreadable mask. He'd dressed carefully, his jeans new and pressed into a sharp crease. His big hands framed the café's coffee cup, making the thick porcelain appear delicate. "I am not offering you a fancy resort in which to rest, Miranda. I built my home with few luxuries. You eat little. You can't grow strong without good food. You should eat what Gwyneth and Kylie bring you."

"I'm not hungry." Her stomach ached now, unused to the warm, nourishing "blue plate special" of roast beef, mashed potatoes and green beans. In front of her, a wedge of Willa's famed apple pie stood untouched.

"Are you going to eat that?" he asked and when she shook her head Gabriel ate her serving. "I like to eat with someone," he said quietly. "Do you?"

She shrugged and glanced at Willa, the owner of the café, who was eyeing Luigi of the Pasta Palace down the street. Luigi had once burst into an emotional Italian song that clearly marked his intentions to court Willa, a seasoned widow of many years. Luigi's huge drooping moustache was twitching as he smiled at Willa, his teeth gleaming whitely.

Following Miranda's look, Gabriel noted, "He's got her on the run."

"That's what people will say about you and me, Gabriel." Miranda's tone was hushed and fierce. She didn't want his kindness; she wanted to retreat. "This is all a sham. They'll think you *want* me. I don't feel right about this—my mother believed in the traditional courting customs here. I shouldn't have agreed to the lie about my life. I've managed so far without your protection."

Bitter? Ungrateful? She was all of that and guilty, too. Gabriel didn't deserve her harsh tirade. "I'm not exactly a likable person now. I'm sorry."

"Anna understood a great many things when it came to surviving. She'd understand you need to heal. She'd understand that I am made a certain way and that we have reached a compromise…. *Want* you?" He lifted an eyebrow, his black eyes challenging her. "We'll know differently, won't we?"

She looked away out into the bright January sunlight, to Mr. Collier carefully helping his pregnant forty-year-old wife across street. The child was their first and both were glowing.

Gabriel was right; she wasn't ready to face life just yet, to see Gwyneth's body rounding with a baby. At times, Miranda's grief slipped beyond her tethers and revealed more than she wished. Tanner was too careful not to speak of his joy and hurt her. Michael and Kylie were bursting with excitement, quickly shielded when Miranda was near—she expected that they had their own news of a baby and the ache within her grew. She couldn't bear casting a shadow upon her brother's and sister's happiness. She couldn't bear living in her mother's empty house.

"Only for a time, Miranda. Until you feel better."

She rubbed her throbbing headache. Every part of her now wanted to agree to Gabriel's offer, to take shelter away from everything. "You're pushing me, and I don't like it."

"The offer is mine. The choice is yours." Gabriel looked away as if they weren't discussing the deep traditions of Freedom Valley, where a man declared his intentions in front of the Women's Council.

Miranda traced the rim of her water glass. "I'm in pieces," she said finally. "Not at all like myself, and you know it."

He nodded solemnly, those straight black lashes shielding his gaze. The sunlight passing through the window caught the dark tone of his skin, the angle of his high cheekbones. He seemed timeless as the mountains, his aura that of a man who spent his life outdoors amid the pine and clear water. "I think that your heart is wounded and that you are tired. You will be strong again.''

Long moments passed and then Miranda gave way to the need running within her to escape. ''Okay,'' she whispered bleakly. ''I'd like to get away from everything for a while, and if it's necessary for you to present this deception—a trial marriage—I guess that's okay.''

The smile lurking around his lips matched the tone of his deep voice. ''Ah, the gracious acceptance of the doomed. Do you think you can ride in another week?''

''I don't feel like—'' Then she caught that hard, straight look. The Deerhorns obeyed their own traditions. ''You're coming for me in the old way, aren't you?''

''Yes. It is important to me. But if you prefer—''

''What am I worth?'' she couldn't help asking, slightly surprised by her own humor.

He shrugged, a gesture that said little and yet everything. That black gaze slid down her gray sweater, woolen slacks and boots. ''You're scrawny. Two horses maybe. Not my best ones.''

She smiled at that. Gabriel used to tease her in the same way. ''You'll get them back. This is only for a time.''

He was trying to help her, but there were concessions to Gabriel's traditional-based honor. ''I'll manage. Thank you, Gabriel.''

At the cash register, Willa glared at him and stared pointedly at a jar filled with wrapped roses. Gabriel nodded and selected a tiny perfect yellow bloom.

While Willa watched approvingly, he tore off the long stem and slid the rose into Miranda's hair.

His hand rested warm and hard and callused against her cheek. She wondered why his gaze was so soft and seeking on her; she wondered why it called forth a tenderness she hadn't expected.

She wondered why, at times, he spoke to her in that careful, proper way, his deep voice curling intimately around her.

Later, she would see that Gabriel had not taken the baby blanket, and her senses told her that he was uneasy with returned gifts, especially gifts between women.

In his way, Gabriel was a very traditional man. He was also known to be very private, and Miranda knew it was no light matter for him to open his home to her.

A week later, the blinding morning sun danced across the crust of the snow. Tethered behind him, Gabriel's six best Appaloosa snorted steam into the frigid air. Three horses were his offering for Miranda; the one with the saddle was for her, one was to act as a pack horse, and another for him to ride on the return journey. He glanced at his four-wheeler, parked and ready for use, but today he was bringing Miranda to his home and nothing but the old-fashioned way would settle his heart. He'd cleared the narrow winding road to his home with the blade attached to his vehicle, because he wanted Miranda's journey to be safe. "As the crow flies," his home was not far from Anna's, yet it was over ten road miles. Intermittent horseback trails, passing through woods that a vehicle could not maneuver, closed the distance to five. Clumps of snow fell from the pines bordering the road to his mountain home, making muffled sounds as it hit. Branches cracked beneath the snow's weight and Gabriel's experienced eyes traced the paw prints of a big wolf, running alone and free. The wolves would mate for life and perhaps that was his nature, too, because he'd never wanted another woman. Chiding himself for the traditional ways that had always been within him, springing now to life, Gabriel led his best Appaloosa to Tanner and Gwyneth's ranch.

Miranda was right—he was pushing her. He was hungry for the sight of her, for the sound of her voice. When the wind stirred her hair, sending the blue-black silk swirling around her too pale face, Gabriel wondered about shaman's spells, for he was so enchanted. His hand gripped the saddlehorn and he realized that he had never been nervous of a woman before, except teenage Miranda.

Two days ago, Fidelity Moore's cane had hit the floor at the Women's Council meeting. Her high-pitched voice had run above the women's gossiping. "I want to hear what the boy has to say for himself. You've come here with Tanner Bennett, Miranda's brother, at your side. He approves of the situation? That you've finally decided to do right by Miranda? Well, speak, Mr. Gabriel Deerhorn. It is no light matter to ask for a bride before this Council. We want assurances that you are a rightful candidate for Miranda's future husband. Speak."

In the bright January morning, Gabriel glanced at the cows mulling around the huge round bail of hay in the field. Freedom Valley was warmer than his

mountain ranch, and his horses—except for the six
with him—were staying at his father's place.

He thought of the women's faces, the Council earnest and fiercely protective of Anna's eldest daughter.
Uncomfortable with opening his heart, he had spoken
truthfully, simply. When he'd finished, he did not understand why the women's eyes shimmered with tears
or why they hugged him. It had been no easy matter
to tear away the shields of his heart, to speak to the
women. Before he spoke, they had lashed at him for
not courting Miranda, for giving her his child without
wedlock. Yet as he'd finished, they listened intently.
The words were true—how he had waited for Miranda to come back to him, how he would cherish her
and make her safe, how she filled his life and that the
years without her had been too empty. He'd been approved and the week of preparing his house for a
woman startled Gabriel—the furnishings were plain
and serviceable and probably not appealing to a
woman.

At nineteen, he'd cut the timber for his log home,
furiously planing it with his stormy emotions, his anger at himself for hurting Miranda. He'd tried to concentrate on the building of the cabin, not on the college girl who had taken part of his heart. He'd worked
with ranchers until he dropped, then pushed himself
home and worked more, so that he wouldn't dream
of her, wouldn't miss her, wouldn't think of her sharing his home.

The newspaper had listed the college's honor stu-
dents and Gabriel took pride in Miranda's achieve-
ments. But pride was little comfort when he ached for
that slanted, mysterious green look as she considered

him, the warmth of her body against his. He was a
dreamer, of course, longing for what was not meant
for him.

*And now he had to protect her as she fought
against life's hardships.*

*Did she still love the man who was no man?—the
father of her lost baby.*

Gabriel rubbed his leather glove over his chest, unfamiliar with the tightness there, the uncertainty of
how Miranda-the-woman would greet him, and if she
would like his home. *Would she stay? Would her
lover come for her?* It was only because of his past
with Miranda, he told himself. It was only because
Anna's daughter needed his protection that he would
take her to his home.

A hawk soared high in the sky as Gabriel told himself that he would protect his heart. Could he? Could
he remain detached, unhurt when Miranda left once
more? But then, how could he protect his heart
against Miranda?

Tanner took the horses solemnly and handed Gabriel a small, soft thermal basket. "Gwyneth's warm
milk and hot stew for the trip. When this is over—
and I hope it works because Miranda is tearing the
life out of herself—the horses are yours again. You're
a man who keeps his traditions. I know this bridal
price is important to you, even in this sham to help
Miranda. Take care of my sister," Tanner said as,
heavily clad in a long quilted coat, Gwyneth came to
loop her arm around him.

"I will honor and treasure her, just as I told the
Women's Council." Gabriel nodded and changed his
saddle to another horse, swinging up on it. He reined

the fresh horse toward the field separating Tanner and Gwyneth's land from Anna's.

Gabriel had barely tethered the horses when Miranda came from the house. "I'm ready," she said, as Gabriel took her small suitcase from her.

Dressed in a red down coat with thick insulated pants and winter boots, she looked like a child, her eyes shadowed beneath the red knit cap. She seemed too vulnerable and he'd taken advantage of her— Gabriel didn't like the panic surging through him, and tightened his lips to avoid saying too much. Miranda studied him. "What is it? Have you changed your mind?"

Gabriel nodded to the extra horses, one with an empty saddle, the other with a small canvas pack and dragging two long poles. He was suddenly nervous of her, afraid that she would turn away from his simple life. He had not exposed himself to another woman and he wasn't certain how to handle his fear that she might still reject him—his plan. "Does it look like it?"

His words were too sharp in the crisp freezing air and he tried to soften the impact. "You should take something of your mother's home, Miranda."

She shook her head and Gabriel eased that enticing wisp of black hair back from her cheek. The need to hold her close and soft ruled him, but she loved another man, defended a man who ran from marriage and children. Pushing away the thought, he concerned himself now only with Miranda's recovery. Then he moved into the house, wanting some of Anna's gentleness to help his barren home. He quickly folded a

crocheted afghan from the couch, and moved into
Miranda's feminine room.

When he returned, her arms were tight around his
horse, her face pressed to the warmth. Gabriel ached
to hold her, to warm her, but placing his arms around
her would be too much of a declaration and he
couldn't trust his heart—or his anger—then. What
man could not want her as she carried his child, a
beautiful gift? Why would he not want to give her his
name?

She shook her head at the hope chest he carried,
the afghan and Anna's daintily stitched patchwork
quilt tucked beneath his chin.

"You would come to me without Freedom
Valley's required hope chest?" he asked teasing her
just a little to lessen the tension. When the familiar
shadow crossed her expression, he added, "I removed
the baby things."

"We can't take all that." When the *travois,* quickly
fashioned by the two long poles behind the horse and
wrapped in canvas was finished, she said, "I guess
we can."

Two hours later, Gabriel swung down from his
horse and walked back to Miranda. Through her sunglasses, used to cut the blinding glare of the sun on
the snow, his expression was grim. "You are tired.
This is too much for you. My tradition costs you. I
was foolish in my honor and pride."

"I'm fine. You've been moving more slowly than
you probably would without me. I know you're trying
to be very careful of my…weakened condition. But
I'm enjoying—" Miranda held her breath as Gabriel

reached for her and swung her into his arms. He carried her back to his horse and carefully placed her sideways on the saddle. He tucked her long quilted coat around her legs, then swung up behind her. Gabriel's arms were around her, tugging her back against him, arranging her coat's hood over her knitted cap.

Drained by the day and her emotions, she closed her eyes and gave way to the warmth of his throat against her face, the familiar scents of a boy who had become a man. Snug and warm against him, she gave way to her memories of Gabriel—fishing, laughing, teasing her as Tanner's little "tagalong" sister. At sixteen, she'd had her crush on Michael Cusack, Kylie's new husband, or rather Michael's powerful motorcycle. Then Gabriel had given her wildflowers—

"I can't even remember what Scott looks like," she whispered suddenly, startling herself. Gabriel's body tensed, and against her cheek, his chest did not rise and fall for just that moment. She glanced up at him and found his grim expression, that flat, closed-in look. But she could feel his anger vibrating around her. "Scott was weak, not bad, Gabriel. He was as surprised as I was to find that he couldn't bear the thought of children, or marriage."

Gabriel looked off into the woods. A muscle crossing his jaw contracted and released. His next words were a statement, not an accusation. "He suited you. You lived with him."

"I'm thirty-five now, Gabriel. I wanted a home and children. I seemed so buried in my career and working overtime, that there was no time for anything else. I made time for a life and Scott had come from the same family-oriented background as myself. When

Mother died, something happened inside me and I wanted a baby, a little part of her to carry on. Until then, my thoughts of children and a family were only passing—one of those 'some days.' My biological ticking clock started in fast forward—I can't explain it, really. It just happened and I was terribly happy. But until then, Scott seemed to be a logical choice.''

"Ah. The statistical analysis of backgrounds for the selection of a mate.''

Miranda sat up, away from his strength. The blinding harsh light was no worse than her realization of how smug she'd been, how certain and clinical. "You're mocking me. Isn't that what you did all those years ago? Decided that statistics were against us?''

She hated lashing out at him; it wasn't like her to dredge up the past, to wallow in it, but the old anger and frustration burst into the dapple sunlight.

Gabriel's hard mouth softened slightly. "You feel like fighting? That's good. I've been worried that you'd lost your bristles. You're not going to slap me again, are you?''

The image of teenage Miranda hurled through the adult woman. She'd been hurt and blinded by tears at Gabriel's choice to separate, striking out at him. Tall and lanky, already packing on muscle from hard ranch work, he'd stood under her mother's backyard tree. The summer night had been sweet around them as he accepted her verbal blows and then the final hard slap to his face.

"Snob,'' the adult Miranda muttered now. "You could have gone to college with me. That 'our life paths are different' stuff was just because you didn't want to try.''

"Could be. That was a long time ago. Now shut up and get some rest," he murmured easily, tugging her back against him. His chin fitted over her head and his arm curled securely around her again.

"You're wallowing in this big macho protective male role, aren't you?"

"And you like the last word, don't you?"

Miranda caught his gentle tone and asked, "Are we going to get along, tearing at each other?"

"Sure. You need to tear at something, don't you? It might as well be me." He nodded at the bark torn away from a tree. "Bear."

Gabriel was right. She didn't like her weakness, her vulnerability, nor her uncertain mood now, and she didn't like the dark anger stirring in her. The bear had only marked his territory, yet Miranda wanted to claw and fight and forget. "I don't know what I need. I don't want to feel anything for a long time...."

At four o'clock in the afternoon, the mountain evening crept over the snow, tinting it a soft blue. Made of rock and logs, Gabriel's home nestled in the pines, the windows looking like square mirrors, gleaming in the shadows. The huge barn was weathered gray, the metal roof showing reddish streaks of rust. In the sweep of a snow-covered field, the mountain's shadows and the forests, the colors blended soothingly. Gabriel swung down from the horse and again lifted Miranda, carrying her to his front porch. He placed her to her feet as he opened the door and a dark furry shape hurled itself past them, barreling down the wooden steps and into the snow. The gray striped cat stopped and daintily shook its paws, trying to rid itself of the snow. Gabriel's grunt was of pure disgust and he hurried after the cat as it leaped across the crusted snow. The man's weight, breaking through the snow made his progress slower, but soon Gabriel was scooping up the cat and tucking it against him. She hissed and clawed at him, not a fierce objection, but enough to let him know she wasn't happy.

Miranda hid her smile in her collar, as clearly nettled, Gabriel tromped up the porch's steps. He shoved open the door and lightly tossed the cat into the house. "She's mad at me for leaving her. Meet Jessica."

Jessica was too busy for pleasantries, tearing across the wood and cushion furniture and hiding in a stalking position. Gabriel scowled as the cat tore across the room again. "She'll get over it. I'll up her sardine ration for a few days."

He closed the door and began stoking the banked coals in the big, freestanding heating stove. Miranda noted his tense, dark expression, one he used when closing himself in, and she wondered why he needed to protect himself, what emotions could be troubling him. The house was spacious and filled with the scent of sage. Braids of sweet grass and camas bulbs hung from pegs, a basket of small bundles of sage for burning and purification sat on a high ledge. At his grandmother, White Fawn's home, Miranda had seen the elk horn, used by women to dig camas bulbs.

It seemed like another century since Juanita had brought Miranda to White Fawn's death bed, and the old woman's shaking, work-gnarled hands had

framed her face. Anna had spent many hours with
White Fawn, sipping tea in the makeshift outdoor
kitchen; as children, the Bennetts had sat upon White
Fawn's lap and enjoyed her stories. Approaching
death, the woman's face was dark and lined, but her
eyes still bright as she studied Miranda. "A good
face. Strong. Smart. She will become a woman who
will fight for what is in her heart. She is a warrior
with the need to test herself, too."

Jessica sauntered across the thick braided rug covering the wooden floors to her master; she rubbed up
against him sensuously. As if claiming her exclusive
territory, her yellow eyes found and locked on the
feminine intruder. She rolled over on her stomach,
and without pausing in his fire-building, Gabriel
reached to scratch her belly. He glanced at Miranda.
"Keep your coat on. The house will be warm soon."

The kitchen was at one end of the living room,
separated by a sturdy wooden table and two chairs.
Gabriel disappeared into a small side room off the
kitchen and a motor began to purr. He lifted the tap
of a plastic water container and filled a teakettle, placing it on the kitchen's gas stove. He began turning on
lights, exposing the simplicity of his home. The wide
wooden flooring planks had been varnished, a braided
round rug placed in the living room. The couch was
wood frame with dark brown woven cushions, matching those of a big wooden oak lawn chair. One of
Gwyneth's pottery mugs sat on the wide wooden
arms, and a low flat table clearly served as a footrest.
A table stacked with magazines completed the chair's
comfort.

Bending to the floor, Gabriel picked up a pottery

lamp—one of Gwyneth's—as if he were used to Jessica's antics. He ran his hands over it, checking for damage before straightening the shade. "Break this and you're out of sardines for a century," he noted darkly to the cat and moved to open the two bedroom doors. Jessica ran after him, tail held high, twining around his legs as if the sardine threat had hit home. "Won't work," he said to her, then looked at Miranda. "Open doors let the heat into the bedrooms. The stove provides the only good heat, but I keep a small heater in the bathroom to keep the fixtures from freezing. Oh, yes, no outhouse for me. I'm spoiled. You'll have to sleep with the door open or freeze." He nodded toward one bedroom. "The guest room. Look around. I'll see to the horses."

Miranda stood very still, feeling as if she were caught between the past and the future. She didn't feel a part of either world. The white chinked lines between the logs ran around her, yet she was somewhere else, not herself. The rough wooden beams overhead supported the ceiling, everything had a purpose and place in Gabriel's home. Once she'd known her purpose, known that she'd had to succeed and now she wasn't certain of anything—except she couldn't go backward.

Bookshelves lined one wall, brimming with books and magazines. A line of small, unmatched picture frames ran across one shelf and Miranda moved closer. There was the Bachelor Club, boys now grown into men. Her mother and Gabriel stood close, arms around each other. The picture had been taken within the past few years, her mother's expression one of peace and warmth. Gabriel's mother and father posed

with their son and daughter. Juanita was petite with
curling bright red hair and a pale face that had to be
protected from the sun with a straw hat. Her husband,
Carl, towered over her, angular and lean, long jeaned
legs braced upon the land he loved. He stood hip-
shot, the same knife-edge cheekbones as Gabriel, that
fiercely proud look of a father with his family around
him. Gabriel wore a boyish grin and Clarissa, his
much younger sister, rode her father's hip. Always
serious, Clarissa stared at the camera from behind her
large glasses with the same flat expression Gabriel
used to shield his emotions.

Resting across deer horns was a capture rifle used
to tranquilize animals. The small, high shelf beside it
contained a well-worn book of dosages and several
vials, marked with chemical names, laid in a box.
Tanner had told Miranda that Gabriel tracked poten-
tially dangerous animals, or predators who had taken
stock from the ranchers, helping the wildlife officials
transport or terminate them. The knife in the fringed
leather sheath was big and terrifying, and no doubt
Gabriel was good with it. It was at odds with the
colorful bottles of beads and leather crafting goods in
a large shallow basket.

That array contrasted her life, filled with laptops,
mainframes, conferences, company tension and corporate intrigue. In comparison to her life, long hours
of overtime, stress and company deadlines, Gabriel's
solitary existence seemed so free and clean.

Miranda wandered to a bulletin board, cluttered
with scenic and animal photographs. The close-ups
focused on milkweed pods, the silk and seeds caught
in the wind. She felt like that, tossed by the wind,

letting everyone else make decisions for her. The empty pods reminded her of—

She forced her thoughts away from that too-open wound and looked at the other pictures, carelessly tacked to the board—cattails slightly bent in the wind, grass rippling like an ocean wave, a chickadee perched near blue juniper berries, mule deer in flight, soaring over a fallen log, butterflies on dandelions. Brilliant blue flowers dotted a high camas field where Gabriel's female ancestors had dug for the bulbs years before white settlers. A wide shot caught a herd of white-and-black spotted Appaloosa moving through the mottled shade of a trembling aspen clump. The white bark of the trees blended with the horses as they flowed across the picture. Another photo was that of contrast, of sunlight passing through trees, slanting onto a lush green meadow. The same pictures were on sheets torn from magazines, copies of paychecks carelessly tacked beside them. Gabriel's pictures seemed to focus on life in motion, until she noted the picture of a man, crumpled in death. Shots of footprints in the mud, the victim's wounds and body position were exact.

Gabriel's footsteps sounded outside, followed by the customary *thump-thump* of boots stomped to dislodge snow. He shouldered into the door, carrying her hope chest and found her in the shadows. "Where do you want this?"

She shrugged, wondering how she would know where to put the chest, when she didn't know her own life. He placed it beside the couch and nodded. "I needed an end table there."

"You're a photographer?"

He glanced at the pictures, eyes narrowing critically. "I try. Basically I take the shots and send the film to a friend who takes care of the cropping and sales—it works out for both of us. He visits when the weather is good. I do some forensic shots when needed."

"I see. So you guide, photograph, ranch a bit and occasionally put up needy guests."

"I buy feeder calves and sell them in the fall. It's a living."

Miranda inhaled slowly. She'd been so driven, punching computer keys for hours, steadily building her career. In comparison, her life seemed cold and as inflexible as steel, while the texture of Gabriel's consisted of color and warmth and fulfillment.

A moment later, Miranda followed Gabriel into the guest room. He placed her suitcase on the bed, not a match to the huge dresser. Gabriel drew back the covers of the bed and placed Miranda's patchwork quilt at the foot end. "Open your bed in the evening, letting some of the warmth into it. The flannel sheets are warmer, but if you like, there are cotton ones."

"Everyone is worried about me. They're making decisions for me," Miranda said, her tone hollow and echoing in the still room. She inhaled the sweet-grass scent, braids of it resting in the basket that was White Fawn's design. "What I need, what I want, how to care for myself."

"For now. You're a strong woman. You'll get better. Would you like a cup of tea while I fix supper?"

She turned to him, wondering how he could know so much. Images flipped through her again—Scott's disbelieving, then angry expression, teenage Gabriel handing her the wildflower bouquet, White Fawn's bright, penetrating stare, her mother's funeral, the empty house, her empty body, the tiny body of her baby.... "Why am I here?"

His hand was warm upon her cheek, his thumb cruising along it gently. "To rest. To heal. It's no more than what other people have done and no less. I can take you back anytime you want."

"I didn't love Scott," she said quietly as he drew off her coat. "I settled for less. I simply made up my mind to go with my damned biological ticking clock. That's how I do everything—just make up my mind and do it. I was really wrong that time."

"You'll work it out. You're a woman, not a machine. You simply followed your heart," Gabriel whispered unevenly and for just a moment, his hands tightened on her upper arms, warm and strong through her sweater.

The eerie howl at the front door preceded Gabriel's dark tone. "That's Fletcher. He followed us up the road and he's been waiting until you leave. Clarissa is the only woman to come up here alone."

When Gabriel opened the door, a huge dog—a blend of German shepherd and wolf—entered warily. He padded to the heating stove and plopped down, yellow eyes gleaming. "Fletcher, meet Miranda. She's going to stay with us for a while."

Jessica, who had been napping, curled on the couch, hopped down. She arched and yawned and padded to Fletcher, snuggling up beside him. "Are you frightened of him?" Gabriel asked as Miranda studied the sight.

She shook her head, suddenly feeling too tired to move. "No. They adore you, don't they?"

Gabriel snorted. "I feed them. We understand each other." Then he looked down at her tears, skimming one away on his fingertip. "You're just tired, Miranda. You'll be fine."

Would she ever be "fine"? Right now, she felt as if pieces of her were scattered on the varnished floorboards and none of them fit. "Sure I will," she said, and prayed that somehow all of this pain would make sense.

Four

Healing can be painful, but it is a passage that must be made if one is to be whole.

Anna Bennett's Journal

Did Miranda think of her lover? *Did she still want him, the man who would not marry her?* Gabriel wondered darkly. He didn't trust the temper brewing within him, the stormy emotions. At midnight, Miranda slept restlessly in the next room. Lying dressed only in his jeans, his arms behind his head, Gabriel studied the firelight dancing on the rough wood beams of his room. He'd pushed her too hard, and now guilt and an unfamiliar jealousy rode him. When he'd held her on the ride back, she'd seemed so fragile and light, almost as if the wind would blow her away. Her spirit was wounded now, her face haunted, the fine bones showing too clearly beneath her too-pale skin. She looked like a ghost of the Miranda who had danced with him at Kylie's wedding. He wanted to go to her, to hold her close and safe. He listened for each sound, his body tense.

Her scent filled his senses, her bathroom toiletries dainty beside his few necessary ones. Tonight, taking a shower after hers, the feminine scents had startled him, curling around him. Those damp footprints on the bathroom rug were narrow and small when he placed his naked foot beside them. He'd stood in the small enclosure, breathing unsteadily, unprepared for the sensual need ripping through him. At first he thought the impact was a ghost of his teenage need, but the force was too great and too deep, hardening him.

Now he wasn't prepared for the sight of Miranda, dressed in flannel pajamas and a worn, long flannel robe appearing at his doorway. "I'm awake," he said, thinking how small and vulnerable she looked with the back light washing over her, wedging between her bare feet. He could hold one in the length of his open hand, his fingers could easily overlap her wrists.

Her arms came protectively around her body, the firelight glowing around her black hair. "I've got to get out of this depression, Gabriel. I have to."

"I know. You will."

"You're so certain of everything. How can you know?"

"I know you."

There was a moment's too-still silence and then Miranda erupted. Her temper licked suddenly, furiously at him. "Damn you. You always know every-

thing, don't you? You always know exactly what is
right. How wonderful that must be.''

He was pleased at that, because Miranda was a
strong woman who was beginning to feel, to free her
blocked emotions. Her robe fluttered behind her as
she pivoted and stalked to her room, slamming the
door behind her.

''You'll freeze if you leave that door shut,'' he
called after her, not understanding her tumultuous
mood, but appreciating the fire in it.

When the door didn't open, Gabriel shook his head.
Miranda had always been an independent child and
now she was a stubborn woman. He rose to his feet,
padding to the closed room. He knocked on the door.
''Miranda?''

''It's cold in here,'' she returned sharply.

He smiled at that; independent and stubborn be-
havior had its place, but not in a house with one heating stove. The small bathroom heater, used to keep
the insulated pipes from freezing, wouldn't help the
guest room. ''Told you.''

The bed creaked and then Miranda jerked open the
door, glaring up at him. The fragrance of her hair and
skin curled around him, unsettling in his masculine
house, as she asked, ''Why didn't you ever marry?''

He'd been relaxing a bit, the flash of fire telling
him that Miranda was fighting to reclaim herself. Her
fierce scowl tore through his safety; he wasn't prepared for that attack. He couldn't tell her that she was
still the woman of his heart, that she would always
be. ''You should marry and have children, Gabriel,''
Miranda said firmly. ''You're a man meant to have a
family, to care for them.''

He frowned down at her, not shielding his irritation. Who was she to tell him what he should do with women—when she was the only woman he'd ever wanted.

"Most women don't like it here. They say they do to please their boyfriends and husbands. No shops, no girlfriend chitchat. Too much quiet. Too many animals and itchy, yucky grass." He tossed her a challenge, to test the midnight fire and truth between them. "You'll want to leave, too."

Her finger jabbed his chest. "You don't think I can last, do you?"

"Not really," he lied, pushing her, enjoying life stirring into her.

With a toss of her head, Miranda padded back to bed. She climbed in and sat studying him, her head held in her hands. Jessica leaped up into her lap. Fletcher whined at the side of the bed until she reached to pet him. Clearly Fletcher had lost his wariness of women.

Gabriel leaned against the door frame, studying the sight of Miranda in bed, petting his cat and dog.

Miranda scooted down the bed and patted an empty place for Fletcher. The huge dog, weighing more than Miranda, accepted the invitation easily, plopping down and settling his muzzle over her legs. There was one thing missing in Miranda's bed—himself, Gabriel decided uneasily. "Gabriel? Thank you for bringing me here."

He nodded and turned away, his heart aching to hold her.

A week went by quickly and January became February, one month had lapsed since she'd lost her baby.

Drained by the past months, Miranda settled into Gabriel's home. With Fletcher and Jessica in her bed, warming her, the comfort of life nearby, she slept heavily. When she awoke, Gabriel was always there, his house warm and usually scented of food. Gabriel spoke little, but his presence was comforting. The steady rhythm of the day—his voice in the morning, talking with his animals, the meals they shared—began to soothe and relax her. He was usually gone in the late mornings until the shadows began to crawl over the meadow, but she could see him work with his three horses, feeding them, walking with them. At night, with his animals warm against her, she heard him prowling in the house. More than once, he'd come to her open doorway, a big man, his broad shoulders gleaming in the lamplight.

That old tightness rose, surprising her in a demand. She wanted him to hold her, to wrap her arms around that strong body and see if his kiss—edgy with hunger and sweet with tenderness—tasted the same. She'd fought the need to touch that hard jaw, to skim her fingers over those sleek black brows and ease the creases at the sides of his mouth. Gabriel was only trying to help, and she couldn't focus on the past, or transfer her body's needs so soon to another man. Miranda tried to push away the startling sensuality. She hadn't considered herself to be a sensual woman, but Gabriel was definitely filling her senses. Too masculine to be denied, his presence created unpredictable needs in her healing body.

This morning was bright and Miranda awoke to the scent of freshly baked biscuits. Gabriel and Fletcher had already gone, and she had the house to herself—except for Jessica who lay sleeping on the couch.

Miranda had enough of sleeping. She forced herself to dress in jeans, a sweatshirt and socks. Bracing herself, she sat her morning cup of tea on the floor beside her hope chest. Gabriel had taken more than the chest from her mother's house. Inside were her mother's crochet basket, that hook stuck through the loop of thread, sunk into the spool, as if waiting for completion. The doily was delicate, a pattern Anna had long ago tried to teach Miranda. Colorful lengths of embroidery floss, needles, and a small metal hoop seemed too familiar.

Firmly placing the basket aside, Miranda saw the framed pictures of her family, also taken by Gabriel. She was a part of them still and they a part of her, and she stood to place the frames on the shelf next to Gabriel's family. The box he'd placed in the chest was filled with her old drawing pads and pencils and then her teenage handwork and memories filled the rest of the chest.

An hour later, Gabriel pushed into the house with Fletcher, his boyish grin proof of their play. He stopped and stared at Miranda in the kitchen. "What are you doing?"

She licked the frosting from her finger. To accomplish anything now was to reclaim a small part of herself. "Cooking. Baking a cake and making a casserole for tonight."

He whipped off his knitted cap and jerked off his jacket, sitting down on the chair to unlace his boots. He placed them neatly beside hers. Everything about Gabriel was studied and concise, very controlled. One

dark look seared the house, her family pictures near
his, the afghan folded on the couch, his box of patch-
ing thread and needles lying next to a pile of his jeans
and shirts. In the kitchen, his washer was chugging
away, working on a load of brown nubby curtains.
On the ironing board, a basket of rolled and dampened laundry waited. Then Gabriel's gaze traveled the
length of fishing line, strung near the heating stove
and draped with her panties and bras.

Sweeping his hands through his hair, Gabriel
frowned. "I don't want you to work."

He seemed too rawly masculine, the frigid air
clinging to him, his black hair rumpled and shaggy.
The worn, thick flannel shirt and jeans and his thermal
socks completed the picture. The frosting spatula
seemed to tremble in her hand—or was that the shaking of her heart? "You said to make myself at home.
I have to do something."

He crossed into the kitchen, towering over her. His
tone was low and commanding, and for the first time
a fierce anger leaped from him, trembling in the large
room. "You are doing something. You're healing.
That's enough. I don't want you cooking or cleaning
my house. Tell me what you want done and I will do
it."

"Grump," she said lightly and on impulse slashed
her finger through the frosting bowl and reached to
swipe it across his lips. They opened and caught her
fingertip, and a jolt of electricity skittered over her
skin. The lick of his tongue followed her finger as she
drew it away.

She tried to breathe and couldn't, her senses too
filled with Gabriel, the heat coming from him and

trembling, snagging her own body. She couldn't turn away from that warm dark gaze, stunned by the intimacy of it. Then his head lowered and slanted and his lips brushed hers. The taste was familiar, and yet new and exciting. She stood very still, uncertain she hadn't dreamed the kiss. Gabriel straightened, studying the heat moving up her cheeks. "Your cheeks are turning pink, the color of a wild rose."

"We were compatible. Scott and I were friends," she said breathlessly, the haunting thought bursting into words. She needed Gabriel to understand. With him—the man who knew everything about her—parts of her life unexpectedly erupted, needing explanation. The absolute clarity startled her, and sprung from a need to clear her mind aloud. Her emotions felt as if they had been stored too long, passing through a narrow bottleneck where she dissected them ruthlessly. Why was she shaking so badly, her pulse pounding through her?

"But this is between you and me, isn't it?" he underlined coolly.

But this is between you and me... Miranda slept restlessly, too aware of Gabriel in the next room. The next morning, dressed in a heavy woolen sweater and jeans, he sat in his chair cleaning his camera lenses. Whatever bothered him hummed violently in the wood-smoke-scented air and bounced off the white chinking layered between the logs. Almost palpable, his tension ricocheted off the wooden beams, circling her. The morning shadows caught his taut expression, that rhythmic hardening of his jaw. He suddenly launched himself to his feet and began packing his canvas camera bag. "I'm going out."

"Where?"

"To take some pictures." His usually liquid deep voice held a frustrated, ragged edge she hadn't known. He was impatient, hurrying now to be rid of her, just as he and her brother had done long ago.

"I want to go." Her demand startled her. She wanted to walk and feel the cold, see the glittering sunshine on the pristine snow.

His black eyes ripped down and then up her body. "I'm hiking on snowshoes. You're not up to it."

"Try me. I've been exercising and taking my vitamins. I'm tired of sleeping." Whatever her biorhythms had been, they were spiking now. It was as if she were coming out of hibernation. Miranda felt like layers of darkness were being peeled from her and she wanted to reach out for life. Nettling Gabriel had always been very enjoyable, seeing just how far she could push him. She recognized that dark gleam now, the taunting challenge of a younger, carefree Gabriel. She smiled up at him, feeling warm and young, as if the past had just dropped from her. "Just don't call me a 'tagalong.'"

The nickname brought a smile, so brief she wondered if she had imagined the warm humor in his eyes. There was that lingering look, Gabriel searching her face as if trying to see within her. *Why was her heart trembling and her body heating?*

An hour later, Miranda trudged behind him in the snowshoes he'd made smaller than his own. Strapped to her boots, they'd been his sister's. Gabriel had insisted on bundling her, until only her eyes were to be seen. She'd had to wear sunglasses, while Gabriel moved easily without the confinement of heavy clothing, his face hard and angular in the brilliant light. He seemed so strong, so complete within himself. He spoke little, but those quick penetrating glances back at her told of his concern. "You haven't taken many pictures," she said, breathing heavily and disliking her weakness.

The blinding snowscape swept around her, the air crisp and fresh as though the slate had been wiped clean. Miranda felt life stirring within her, the excitement of being freed from indoors into this bright new world. Despite the weakness of her body, she felt wonderful. Had it only been a month since she'd lost her baby? Was that life calling to her? Had she come so far?

Gabriel's black, glossy hair escaped his knitted cap, the shearling jacket's collar turned up at his throat. He pointed to a winter rabbit, bounding along the snow then huddling beneath brush, sending off a flock of snowbirds into flight. Then he turned, eased off his gloves and lifted his camera to frame her face.

Following an impulse, Miranda didn't hesitate. She reached for snow, formed a ball and hurled it at him. The pleasure came from her childhood, when Freedom Valley children built forts and battled each other with snowballs, most frequently girls against the boys. Gabriel lifted a shoulder, protecting his camera and the snowball glanced off. He packed his camera into the bag, shielding it with his back, which Miranda hit with another snowball. She hit him twice more as he back-walked to her.

Suddenly he turned, placed his snowshoe over hers,

trapping her immobile, and grinned boyishly. Miranda struggled to pull her snowshoes free and couldn't. Off balance, she grabbed for his coat and held him tightly; Gabriel reached to the snow-covered pine branch over her head and tugged. A tiny avalanche of snow fell on her. It was an old familiar game, played as teenagers and Miranda laughed aloud. "That's not fair!"

Gabriel brushed the snow from her cap, propping her sunglasses over it. Then that quiet searching tenseness danced on the brilliant sunlight and he slowly tugged down the scarf protecting her face. Emotions tangled and warmed as he studied her. Then in an uncharacteristic show of affection for Gabriel Deerhorn, he bent to place his cheek against hers. Held in place by the magic of that brief endearment he'd given her long ago as she grieved for her father, Miranda couldn't breathe. She turned her head slightly, resting her face within the warmth of his throat and collar.

The moment was brief and treasured, glittering in her like the life she was beginning to feel.

He turned slightly toward her, just as she was moving away and those deep dark eyes caught her reflection, his breath warm on her face. "Miranda," he whispered so quietly the sound seemed to slip into the glittering day.

His lips were cool and firm against hers, the brush light as a feather before drawing away. Shaken by the kiss, Miranda stared up at him. Gabriel's expression was kind, that of a friend, nothing more. She released the timid smile, uncertain that she had tasted the hunger of long ago in that brief moment. Gabriel gently adjusted her shawl around her throat and lowered her sunglasses into place. Did she imagine the tenderness of his expression?

She reminded herself that he was only a friend, trying to help. She couldn't misread his caring actions. He'd always been her brother's friend, sometimes tormenting her. He was the teenage boyfriend she'd adored and later hated bitterly. He was the man who knew more of her life than anyone. "I don't want your sympathy," she stated quietly.

"You haven't got it."

"Maybe I'll stay up here forever, in this fairyland, and not face my life. That would serve you right for this idiotic plan."

"Think of how boring my life was, how much you can make me suffer and how much gossip we're stirring up." That old charming smile was there, that fascinating roguish tilt to his head. "Feeling better?"

He'd looked like that years ago when he'd asked her to trust him, to jump from the top of an embankment down into his arms. He'd held her tight and safe then, and her instincts said that he was just as safe now. "Yes, thanks. I needed to get out."

Her first visit to the large weathered barn was later that day. She hadn't wanted to intrude upon him more than necessary and accepted his absence as the time he needed away from sharing his home. A heavy-duty, battered farm pickup was parked inside, an aged tractor, a small hay baler, a plow and field mower. The barn smelled of hay, bales stacked in the loft above and on the north wall, buffering the penetrating cold wind.

Gabriel was moving around his horses, talking to them in the airy cold space. They nudged him for the grain held in his hand, and he rubbed their ears. The mottled Appaloosa coats shifted in the dim light, churning slowly around the man standing tall and proud amid them, his deep voice like liquid magic. Gabriel seemed to be a part of them as those dark eyes found her in the shadows. "They're missing the rest of the herd. They're staying at my father's during the winter. It's warmer at his ranch."

"Do you ever get lonely, Gabriel?" she asked, wondering how being with him could be so natural and yet new—except when those long slow appraisals crossed too deep within her and she had to shield herself against him.

He shook his head and glanced at the pigeons entering their barn coop. He'd explained they were carrier pigeons, used to carry messages for the teen members of his extended family. "I have what I want now."

There was that look, that "seeing inside her" look. "What do you want, Miranda?"

As the pigeons cooed and settled for the night, she considered her thoughts. "Peace, I think. Most of all, peace. I hadn't realized how tired I was. Even before I lost the baby."

"You're a strong woman. You're getting better."

She leaned against the mottled throat of the Appaloosa near her. "I know I can't afford a second mistake like the first—assuming too much, wanting something that just wasn't there, wasn't real. This isn't real, either. It's only a resting place, for which I'm grateful."

In Freedom Valley, Tanner's wife would be rounding with his child, due the first part of June. Kylie,

Miranda's sister, would likely be pregnant from her January honeymoon, because Kylie never waited for anything she wanted. Miranda had wanted her child to grow up within her family's love, the cousins playing together.... "I can't stay here forever, Gabriel. We'll have to call the Women's Council and tell them this isn't working out. Or better yet, we should just tell them the truth and be done with it."

"Can't. No phone. You're either here, or I'll take you back. The rest of it, you can handle as you wish. Your choice."

She studied him. At times, Gabriel could nudge her emotions, firing them. "You don't think I'm suited for this—the frontier lifestyle, do you?"

"Nope. Can't see you gardening or canning beans, or—"

"I did all that with Mother, when I lived at home."

His look was too innocent. "You're 'city' now."

"I haven't changed that much. Neither have you."

He didn't answer and she knew that he'd slid into that protective shield where she could not reach him. A shadow crossed his face before he turned away, walking to the pigeons and reaching for one. He untied the band from its leg and frowned. "My mother and father are coming one day soon."

Miranda hadn't wanted to see anyone and yet Juanita and Carl would want to visit with their son. "Do they know of our arrangement? How kind you've been to me?"

Gabriel cradled the gray bird against him, stroking its blue-green iridescent head. "They know."

She didn't trust the dark, ominous tone as if he were dreading the visit. She *knew* she was. The Deerhorns were likely to ask questions she might not want to answer.

Miranda had taken to studying her mother's doily, trying to finish it as though she were trying to see the pattern of her life. She'd begun drawing Celtic patterns, comparing the eternal winding and strength to the doily. The graceful movement of her hands, the way she concentrated on the designs, fascinated Gabriel. Miranda was working her way through her emotions and he had no right to touch her, to kiss her on the mountain. She'd seemed so fresh and young then, her face pink with cold and her eyes lighting with pleasure as she threw snowballs at him.

Give her the peace she needs, he thought and added a reminder to himself, *you have no right to think of holding her, kissing her.* Miranda seemed so soft and fragile; she would turn into smoke if he touched her. Yet she was real, the scent of her clung to him, haunted him. Did she still think of him? The man who had run from her?

During the evenings, she often sat on the floor, the firelight playing on her glossy hair. It shifted like a silky wave around her face as she leaned into her work. She looked up at him and smiled as though just remembering he was in the same room. It was enough, he told himself, even as he clenched his hands to keep from reaching for her.

She turned to him that night, saw what was within him before he could shield himself. "You're brooding again, Gabriel. Why?"

He shrugged and began cleaning his tackle box, one she had thoroughly messed when they went ice fishing. He began straightening the fouled lines methodically as was his way, while he tried to place his thoughts in neat order. With Miranda nearby, his thinking wasn't that clear—it ran more to placing himself over that smooth graceful body and kissing that incredibly soft mouth. She still tasted sweet and innocent as she had long ago. Now with her green eyes dark and mysterious on him, the sharp clench of desire hit him. He could not love her, tell her of his heart, nor could he lie. Instead Gabriel left the cabin and the seduction that was Miranda.

It was mid-February now and Miranda had slept for the most part of that time. She seemed suddenly restless, and when he returned to the house, he found her on the floor, staring at the firelight. He watched her from the shadows and Miranda turned to him in one of those lightning quick moods that startled him. "You really didn't think we were suited, did you?"

"No, I didn't. I thought you should have better." He saw her again, a teenage girl with her future ahead of her, colleges calling her, scholarships waiting.

"You broke my heart, Gabriel Deerhorn. That was a terribly arrogant thing for you to do, to make my decisions for me." Then while he was struggling for words, she turned back to the firelight. Her words came back to him, quiet and firm. "I'm a woman now. Never do that again. Never take away my choices."

Gabriel held very still, aware that the kitten was showing her claws. He hadn't expected the sudden attack, the fierceness of it. "I will try to be very careful of you," he said, meaning it.

"That's just it. You're very careful of me, tiptoeing

around any subject you think might upset me. What subjects upset you, Gabriel? Why do you lock so much inside yourself, your feelings? Do you think it's fair that you know so much of me, and I know so little of you?''

"This isn't about me," he stated cautiously.

"No, it's about me, isn't it?" she asked sharply, clearly set to battle with him.

Uncomfortable with the confrontation, Gabriel stared at her. He couldn't tell her of his heart, how much she pleasured him, just by living with him. He couldn't tell her how much he feared she would leave one day, and his life would be cold and empty again. Instead he rose and left the house.

Two days later, the sound of snowmobiles tore through the mountains' morning silence as Miranda and Gabriel were hiking. Feeding on her growing sense of reclaiming herself, Miranda had wanted to push her strength, building it. Gabriel wouldn't let her take the snowshoe hikes alone and they usually moved in silence, his long legs taking shorter strides to accommodate hers. "My parents," Gabriel announced in a nettled sound like a growl.

"I haven't seen anyone for weeks. I'm going to enjoy visiting with your parents," Miranda said. She had decided that the Deerhorns were sensitive people—they would not press for details.

"They weren't invited," Gabriel reminded her darkly.

"My future in-laws?" she teased, enjoying his frustrated mood. Usually silent and controlled and in-charge, Gabriel settled for a burning glare at her. She smiled brightly at him, enjoying his discomfort.

When they arrived at Gabriel's cabin, Juanita and Carl Deerhorn were already inside, the scent of brewing coffee filling the house. Carl was an older version of Gabriel, tall and lean and weathered. Gray threaded Juanita's dark red curls, her light complexion still bearing freckles from summer sunshine. Slightly rounded now, Juanita hugged her son warmly, then Miranda. Juanita ignored her son's frown and placed a cookie in his mouth. "Brought your favorite. Dad wanted to eat them on the way, but then what reason would I have to come visit my son, hmm?"

"Yes, what reason," Gabriel murmured, eyeing her warily. "No Clarissa? My nosy sister decided to stay at home?"

"You know your mother," Carl said. "I suppose the 'pigeon boys' sent you warning she wanted to come. Those teenagers love their message system."

"What could I do? Run? Hide? She'd find me. I'm a grown man now, and questions about my life aren't appreciated, especially when asked by a nosy sister." Gabriel's grumbling wasn't in anger, rather the sound of doom, as he reached for another cookie. He placed it between his teeth, lifted the plastic container of cookies and his coffee cup and eyed his father. In silent agreement that retreat was safer than arguing with Juanita, the men walked out the door.

"Stop grumbling. Clarissa loves you." Juanita looked around Gabriel's house, clearly noting the items marking Miranda's presence. "It looks like a home now. Not so barren. I see you're working your mother's crochet hook."

"I'm not very good. I miss her."

Juanita's slight Southern drawl softened. "I miss her, too. She was one of my best confidantes when Carl was battling marrying me. He had some notion that we didn't belong together—just as Cynthia Whitehall did not belong with his ancestor. I had to fight for him, though he is certain that he is responsible for our marriage. It's a battle we have often, and one that used to be ferocious in our early days. But I knew from the moment I saw that tough cowboy that he was mine. Don't tell anyone, but he cried when Gabriel and Clarissa were born—simply came apart with pride and happiness. I've never looked back to the arguments my family tossed at us, or the threats of being disinherited from my family. They mellowed with age, especially with their grandchildren on their laps. My parents absolutely doted on them, and Carl was eventually, albeit reluctantly, admitted to be a good husband and a match for me."

Juanita shook her head, her blue eyes softening as she spoke of her husband. "Oh, he was a hard case to break, and I knew that I was just the woman to match him. White Fawn would later tell me that she knew no other woman would do for him, once we'd met and tangled. Your mother listened to me cry and whine and plot to have that stiff-necked, arrogant cowboy. She would want you to go on, and do what you're doing—healing and getting strong. You've always been strong."

"Not now. I've made a lot of mistakes."

"Everyone has, but to put a life back together, to make it stronger, takes a special courage."

"Gabriel was kind enough to offer his home—"

"You think he thinks only of you? I think he's a little selfish, wanting you for himself. My son is very old-fashioned, it seems. To offer for you at the Women's Council, to protect you from gossip in his own fashion," Juanita said, her blue eyes warm with affection. She lifted the whistling teakettle to pour water into a crockery teapot. With experienced hands, she wrapped a dishcloth around it to keep it hot, letting it steep. "Little Miranda. Gabriel's little Miranda. That's how he used to speak of you when you were dating all those years ago, and now you're back."

Miranda took the mug of hot tea from Juanita. She didn't want to mislead his mother. "You know the circumstance. He's explained?"

Juanita turned slowly to her, her expression serious now. "Perhaps he should explain to you. About the woman who has his heart."

Outside, Gabriel's father leaned back against the log wall and said, "I see you cleared more of the pasture. The grass should be perfect for stock this year.... It's a good sound, the women talking. Peaceful, isn't it?"

He smiled, tilting his head closer to the door. "Listen. Your mother's voice has that sound—she's talking about me and how hardheaded I was, determined not to love her. I didn't think a lady, with her soft voice and dainty ways, could fit into a Montana rancher's life. We fought early on, before you came. But I think a woman has steel in her when she wants to change a man's mind and have her way. I was helpless against her."

Gabriel tossed the last of his cookie to Fletcher, who caught it in midair. A midwife, his mother would be talking to Miranda about her body and her moods. The silent weeping was the worst for Gabriel. "Miranda misses her baby. I cannot help her."

"Give her another one. She has always had your heart. You will not give me grandchildren, if not with her. My mother told me that on her deathbed. She was never wrong about such things."

Gabriel tried to dismiss the burn of jealousy. It wasn't his right. "She chose another man."

"Because you denied her. Her woman's time had come upon her, and she wanted a child. Nature puts that in them, the same as in men, who want their song to be carried on long after they are gone. Her mother's death turned Miranda's mind and body to life and how it must go on."

Gabriel shook his head. "She was so young and bright. I could not bear her looking at me years later, feeling trapped and angry that her song had been taken away from her too early."

"She is your vision. If you do nothing but dream of her, life can be long and empty." Carl inhaled the fresh, crisp air. He was silent as Juanita's lilting laughter carried out into the sunshine. "Listen to that. When I first heard that sound, I knew it would be the music of my heart. I knew that I could not be as noble as our ancestor who turned away from Cynthia Whitehall. But I tried."

Carl studied his son. "How long do you think you can keep her here without revealing yourself?"

Five

Most women can draw upon a strength men
know little about.

Anna Bennett's Journal

Gabriel didn't think; he acted. In the barn, with the
third week of February cold and misty, he placed
aside the cup of early-morning coffee Miranda had
brought to him. He threw the lariat he'd been re-
winding toward the loft above him, and the loop slid
smoothly around her. Her arms pinned at her sides,
Miranda stood on the loft above him, her broom in
hand. She frowned down at him and in a restricted
movement sent the broom across the boards. Bits of
straw fell into his face and he blew them away.

Above him now, tethered by his lariat, Miranda had
just served him a notice he didn't like. "What do you

mean, you invited the Women's Council on Bride Courting here—to my ranch?'' he asked very carefully.

The broom swished again, sending more straw bits onto his face. ''It's what they do, inspect how you're treating me and how we're getting along. I've been here almost a month now and that's time enough for us to get settled. Unless you want to call this whole thing off—cancel our supposed arrangement, or tell the truth about why I'm here, it's the custom that the Women's Council visits and inspects.''

Gabriel tried to ignore how her denim jacket had gapped over the lariat. A button slid open on her blue flannel shirt, revealing a beige lace bra. One look at her underwear drying on the shower curtain could wipe his thoughts clean. Now her lingerie was on her and all he could think of was taking it off, pressing his lips to the smooth flesh below. A man used to control, his lack of it where Miranda was concerned disturbed him. In the house this morning, the chill had hardened her nipples beneath the form-fitting thermal top. His mouth had dried instantly and he'd had to turn away to shield his hardening body. Then she'd bent over to take biscuits from the oven, and the curve of her hips... Her soft, feminine scent could distract him too easily, riveting him, blocking everything from his mind but the need to hold and touch her. Unused to his body's instant and obvious reaction to Miranda, the sensuous desire locked in his body, Gabriel was not a happy man. ''I'm not a side of beef for women to inspect. I'm up here for the peace and quiet, not to have women nosing all over my place.''

''Spoken like a true hermit. Pray for a blizzard

then, because I used one of your pigeons to get the message to your cousin, who called Fidelity Moore, president of the Women's Council. According to the returning pigeon, Fidelity accepts our invitation.''

"Our?" he underlined darkly. Still holding the lariat, Gabriel climbed up the wooden ladder to Miranda. He tugged her closer to him. "I asked you to leave the barn alone. It's enough that everything in the house is moved around so I can't find it."

Oh, he knew how to find her well enough—that feminine scent haunted his senses every moment of the day. He'd been stunned at her "getting in shape" exercises, hurriedly excusing himself. Now, he listened at the house door for the music she used, rather than entering at will. That body-clenching exercise and leg lifts carried the impact of a thousand-watt jolt. He'd always controlled himself and his thoughts, but he wasn't certain he could keep his composure when he'd reached to steady her. She'd stood on the kitchen counter, dusting the ceiling beams and Gabriel had seen her lose her balance—his hand had shot straight to that round, soft bottom. The touch burned him, and he mumbled a quick excuse to exit the house for more wood. At night, he heard her stirring on her bed, and hot, sweet images flew into his mind, devastating him.

"Take this rope off me," Miranda ordered fiercely and with her arms tethered, swished the broom at him.

Gabriel held the lariat firmly, not enough to hurt her. He tilted her face up with his fingertip. "Now get this. You are going to cancel."

Fire shot into those green eyes, burning him. "This is all part of the deal, Gabriel. Take it or leave it. My mother treasured these women and the customs of this valley.''

He leaned down to her. ''You're getting awfully bossy lately. You must be feeling better. Have you sent a message to your lover as well? Did you change your mind about him? Is he coming for you?''

Gabriel cursed himself and his fears that Miranda would leave him, returning to the man who left her. Miranda's expression was blank for a moment, and then furious. ''You think I'd want him? *Take this rope off.*''

He shrugged, uneasy with revealing his jealousy into the barn's air. He hadn't been vulnerable, and emotions were tricky and slid from his keeping too easily now. He lifted the lariat from her and she flung herself at him, sending them tumbling back against the wall of hay bales. Gabriel turned, placing his hands on either side of her head. He didn't know how to handle her now, those green eyes lashing at him, her mouth tight with anger—

Her mouth...

Her anger slid into another emotion he could not define. Though they were not touching, he sensed that her body was less tense. She had that curious, soft look, tracing his features, looking too closely into the passion he would shield. With Miranda, he sensed that need would be tender and growing like forest tinder ignited by a lightning bolt.

There with the barn's cold air churning with the scent of horses and hay and leather, golden bits of dust swirling on the shaft of sunlight between them, Miranda slowly lifted her lips to his.

He held very still, fearing a movement would send

her away. Against his, her mouth was soft as a but-
tercup's glossy petal, tasting of curiosity and warmth.
He inhaled her breath, took it into him, just as he
wanted to make her a part of him, of his heart and
soul, so that she could never leave him again.

"I'm sorry," she whispered breathlessly. Before
she hurried away from him, Gabriel took her shy
blush into his heart.

On the floor level, she turned, her legs braced apart
and her fists curled tightly. She slowly looked up at
him. "You were wrong, Gabriel. Admit it. Our paths
could have been the same all those years ago."

"That time is ended," he said, uncertain of her
now. What did that kiss mean? Did her heart beat as
wildly as his?

"You just make certain that you look like a happily
tended man when the committee arrives, Gabriel
Deerhorn. They're coming next week. Work on a real
glow, will you? Meanwhile, I'm going for a ride."

She walked toward the bridles and saddles and fear
leaped into Gabriel. She still seemed too fragile and
tired easily—if she hurt herself... *Do not lift a saddle. If you want to go for a ride, I'll saddle the horses
and ride with you.*

"No, thanks," she returned lightly, shoving open
the barn door to enter the corral. Outlined in the brilliant sunlight, she turned to him again. "You're not
invited and stop giving me orders. Don't forget that
I was raised in this country, too, Gabriel, and I've
saddled horses. I've ridden in snow...I'm smart
enough to know that I shouldn't go too far when I
have an afternoon appointment with the doctor.
You're a snob in your own way, you know."

Snob. The word stopped him cold. That was the second time she'd labeled him with the unattractive name. He opened his mouth, then closed it, too aware that when Miranda chose to fight, she was very effective.

Hormones, Miranda thought late that evening as she sat next to Gabriel. The Jeep's headlamps shafted through the bluish shadows of the narrow road leading to his home. Gabriel was silent, as usual, a man who said little and yet who seemed to have a river of understanding inside him.

She wanted Gabriel to hold her, and to make love to her. This morning, she shouldn't have kissed Gabriel's hard, set mouth, reacting to her unsteady emotions. But just then, suddenly nothing had changed in all those years. He was still Gabriel, tall and strong and safe, and she still adored him. But the underlying current between them had shifted into a primitive beat she didn't understand. Or was that the heavy pounding of her heart? Was it her body changing, coming to life after trauma? Could she trust her emotions now? When she'd taken her lonely ride, she had been so angry with herself. Gabriel hadn't touched her, except in a friendly way. He'd given her no encouragement and yet every nerve in her told her to lift her lips to his and *feel.*

She looked out into the pines bordering the narrow, winding road. She hadn't felt for so long, life moving in fast motion after Scott left. She'd been consumed with making her future baby's life safe and now— A pine bough swished along the window, hissing against the glass. Her thoughts danced between a man whose face she couldn't remember, whose voice she couldn't remember, and the babies rounding Gwyneth's and Kylie's bodies.

In Freedom, Gabriel had made a point of squiring her to the Wagon Wheel for lunch and then to the doctor's office for her checkup. He'd paid for her bill, despite her hushed protest as the nurse looked on with interest. They'd shopped for groceries together and from obligation more than need, she'd visited with Gwyneth and Kylie. Kylie had just happily confirmed that her baby had been created on her January honeymoon. Miranda had tried to be natural, to show them that she felt only happiness for them, but she couldn't help feeling so utterly empty. Later, at her baby's grave, Gabriel had placed his arm around her.

They'd stopped at Anna's house and Gabriel had gathered the bulbs and clay pots and the flat window beds used to start tomato seedlings for her garden. The errand-day had exhausted her, new situations springing at her from every direction. Never far away, Gabriel was quiet as usual, those dark eyes quick to note her uneasiness. He seemed to steer her through the day, deflecting any hardships. At her mother's, she'd leaned her forehead against his shoulder in that old familiar way, using his strength as her anchor.

The flower bouquet Gabriel had purchased at the grocery store rattled within the paper sacks, the scent filling the Jeep's cab. He glanced at her, shifting easily into another gear over a small mound of snow. "Hard day, hmm?"

"Very hard."

"It will get easier."

"Will it?" she asked dully. "I feel as if I'm a robot winding down."

"You're shifting gears is all," Gabriel noted, scanning her face. "Getting ready for the rest of your life." He brushed the hair back from her cheek, his thumb circling her ear. The gesture seemed so intimate, far from sensual, and she leaned her face into his hand. When her lips brushed his palm, Gabriel's indrawn breath hissed through the small enclosure. His hand eased away, clenching the knob on the floor shift until his knuckles were white.

She shook her head. She'd made him uncomfortable, a man who ignored everything to help protect her from gossip. "I never should have involved you. This whole situation—"

"Is what I want."

"You should be role-playing the would-be husband for a woman you love." Miranda didn't like the thought of Gabriel loving another woman, as his mother had said. Yet Miranda had no right to be so curious, to want to know more about the woman he loved.

Gabriel was silent, his profile hard in the dim light. He inhaled roughly. "Is it a hardship, being with me? For only this short time while you heal?"

"It's the first real peace I've had in years," she said honestly, vehemently. "You must know that."

"When the ladies come, how much of a glow are you expecting me to produce?" he asked, reminding her of the happy-husband-to-be image she'd wanted. "A small glow? A medium glow? Or just plain sappy-in-love-with-you glow?"

She stared blankly at him, amazed at the ability he had to distract her.

"You're not going to cuddle against me, and maybe even kiss me when they're around, are you? Yuck." In the dim light, his boyish grin flashed at her.

She recovered enough to lightly punch his shoulder and return the grin. "I'm going to make you suffer just as much as I can. You're enjoying this whole thing, aren't you?"

"Sure. I need a little excitement in my old age. Get me a cookie from Eli's Bakery sack, will you? In the back seat?"

Miranda turned to reach for the cookies and her breast brushed Gabriel's shoulder. He seemed to tense, adjusting his body away from her, allowing her room to sift for Eli's Bakery sack. Was her body still so sensitive that the slight contact burned?

He'd withdrawn again, his expression tight as if he couldn't wait to get out of the Jeep and away from her. That muscle in his jaw contracted and released again as though some inner leash had been tested and denied. Whatever his dark moods were, she ached to step into them and stir them until the truth sprung free. She placed the cookie in his teeth and studied him. "Your mother said you loved a woman. Who is she? Won't she mind me living with you?"

He chewed slowly and took his time answering her. Gabriel's expression was closed, as if he were mulling his thoughts before expressing them. "My mother should keep her thoughts to herself.... The woman in my heart is kind and thinks of others before herself. She would protect them with all her being. She would understand that you need peace. That I have little to offer but that.''

''Where is she? Who is she?'' She knew so little about him, while he knew intimate details she'd never told anyone but her family.

Again, there was that long, thoughtful silence. ''She is always with me, close inside. But to see her, I go to the mountaintop and camp, waiting for her. She comes in the smoke and she's round with a baby—my baby. Everything that I am or will be lies with her. I have tried to be with other women and still she haunts me, her eyes soft in the smoke.''

Miranda stared at him, shocked at the emotion in his deep voice. He had never revealed so much about his feelings. Gabriel's senses had always been tuned to his Native American heritage, and now he spoke of a vision, a dream woman. Miranda settled back in her seat, slightly jealous, ridiculously so, of a woman who was fantasy and smoke.

Later that night, Miranda studied herself in the cabin window's glass, the night freezing and yet damp outside. Then Gabriel's face loomed in the glass above hers, his stark image familiar and yet new. His body heat licked at her skin beneath her pajamas and robe.

She ached for him to touch her, trembled with the need.

He hadn't touched her in a way that said he felt anything for her, other than friendship. Maybe she wasn't— ''Gabriel, do you think I'm...desirable?''

''I think a man would want you,'' he said very slowly, in that deep, liquid voice that curled intimately around her.

She turned to look up at him, to see if there was sensual hunger in those marvelous black eyes, but Gabriel had withdrawn behind his harsh, unreadable expression.

"So it's working out, then," Fidelity Moore said in her high chirpy voice. The last week of February's bright midmorning sunlight shafted into Gabriel's house as Fidelity scanned the mix of Gabriel's and Miranda's possessions. "Just as I knew it would. Your mother would be pleased that you are working with her crochet hook and embroidery hoop. She would have loved to know that you have planted seed in the kitchen window for garden plants, just as she always did. I thought highly of your mother, Miranda. She was a woman of strength and conscience, and not once complained of hard times. I see her in you. Only a strong woman would come back to find herself and her love."

She used her cane to walk to Miranda's bedroom and then to Gabriel's. Gabriel slashed a dark, irritated look down at Miranda as Fidelity said, "Neat as a pin and homey. A little plain, but then a woman needs time to make a home her own. Miranda is simply blooming, young man. You must be treating her well."

"Very well." Miranda glanced at Gabriel, who had stiffened as he stood beside her. A private man, he didn't like his life, nor his home, inspected, and now the Women's Council had invaded it. She leaned against him, to comfort him, because he looked like he'd escape at any moment. His hand went to her waist and then slid fractionally lower, fingers digging in slightly where the women couldn't see. He tugged her closer, fitting her against his lean body. The unfamiliar gesture from Gabriel surprised her.

Fidelity's bright blue eyes warned Miranda. "The boy has a tongue and he's spoken much about his dislike of women inhabiting his mountain retreat. Let him speak for himself and tell us why he accepts you and runs from all the other women chasing him."

Miranda hadn't thought of Gabriel running from anything, anyone. "Other women?"

"Of course, he's been evidently involved with you, visiting you in Seattle, or else you wouldn't have created a child together. You never should have skipped the customs that the Founding Mothers set up to protect and insure a good marriage, my dear. Coming to meet us outside, you two looked perfect together, 'like a good pulling team of horses,' my dear departed Alfonso, used to say."

"Tracked her down and impregnated her," Sadie McGinnis muttered indignantly. "Those Bachelor Club boys…"

Gabriel's smile was nothing less than a roguish smirk and Miranda nudged him with her elbow, tossing him a warning look. He lifted his eyebrows, looking bland and innocent. Dahlia Greer, an experienced and outright sensual woman with several deceased husbands, laughed outright.

Fidelity's stern look focused on Sadie, renowned for her open views on the Bachelor Club "impregnating" any and every available, vulnerable woman. Then Fidelity turned back to Gabriel. "I would have liked to have seen more courting. It is Miranda's option to invite and court you, you know. The Founding

Mothers wanted to make certain that women were active in selecting their future husbands. But with snow and this winding mountain road, I see the difficulty of her courting you. You have no problem with the isolation of Gabriel's home, the farm life, after your career in business, my dear?''

Gabriel tensed again, looking outside the window, pulling himself away from her. His hand eased away from her as if he didn't want to tether her. If there was anything that made Miranda want to claim him, to get his attention, it was *that look.*

On impulse, Miranda stood on tiptoe and kissed his cheek. ''He's nervous,'' she explained gently, delighting in riffling that cool, distant, totally arrogant look.

''We're taking our time working things out,'' Gabriel said smoothly, serving back a bit of her torment. ''But I wish she'd court me. A man should have some romance.''

''Mmm,'' Fidelity murmured thoughtfully. ''Yes, you should. Miranda, do not let it be said that you didn't court your man.''

''If she doesn't nab that gorgeous hunk of man, she doesn't deserve him,'' Dahlia noted.

''I didn't know I was so appealing, Ms. Greer,'' Gabriel returned in that soft, lilting tone, his smile devastating.

''Why, you are just absolutely delicious, Mr. Deerhorn,'' Dahlia returned at ease with the playful flirtation.

Miranda mentally shook her head trying to clear it. Gabriel had unexpected facets and when he wanted to, he dropped the silent leave-me-alone act and reached for the charm.

"I think that went well," Miranda said later, as she stacked the teacups into the sink. "I don't want any of them worrying about me. I couldn't have done this in my mother's home, but now that it's over—I think I can manage. We should talk about ending this, Gabriel, you have to go on with your life, and I have to go on with mine. I'm more comfortable with people now, and I'm going to take pleasure in the broods my brother and sister are creating. You've been so kind. However you want this handled, I will do my best to—"

"'Kind?'" The word cut at her, his expression fierce and angry, surprising her. "I'm checking on the horses," Gabriel stated curtly as though he couldn't wait to escape the house, echoing with the sounds of women's chatter. The sound said he'd had enough of women and of her—

Miranda turned to him and his look took her breath away, staking her hotly as if he wanted— She swallowed, her hands shaking so badly that she dropped the next cup into the dishwater. Gabriel had looked as if he'd wanted her desperately, as if he wanted to make love to her. The air hummed between them and she couldn't move. She wanted to undress, to have him undress her. To feel his lips against her skin... The silence rocked with a primitive sensual beat... and when the fire in the heating stove crackled, she jumped, because the image of his tall body, gleaming and powerful rising over hers had seemed so real. She'd never been looked at like that, as if a man could devour her, claim her, never let her go....

She was misreading him, of course. Her body was coming to life and receiving wrong impressions. Gabriel's actions had been kind and nothing more. He was tense because of the earlier strain, his home invaded. She tried to keep her voice even, concealing her uncertainty. "Yes, you'd better do that."

By late evening, Gabriel hadn't returned. Miranda had prepared dinner, baked bread and had finally admitted she was afraid for him. He was an experienced woodsman, but he'd never been late for dinner. Gabriel was a man who needed his privacy. Perhaps he was using the forest to soothe him. A "chinook," a warm winter wind, howled fiercely around the house, a lonely sound like that of a lost soul. Perhaps it was his "woman in the smoke" calling to him. Perhaps he'd gone to see her.

Fletcher paced the house restlessly, whining and looking at the door, evidently wanting to be freed. He growled, his hackles raised. Once, he lifted his head and an eerie howl that spoke of his wolf's blood iced Miranda's skin, lifting the tiny hairs on her nape.

Leashing Fletcher, making certain he wouldn't tear off into a possible wolf pack, Miranda made several trips down to the barn. As restless as the dog, she watched for Gabriel through the house's windows. His tracks led off into the woods, following those of a horse. On her last trek outside, she noted the big cat's paw prints circling the barn and without expertise, Miranda knew they were that of a mountain lion. Fletcher continued pacing the room as if he sensed Gabriel needed him. If Gabriel were hurt…if a mountain lion… Miranda hurried to make hot tea, pouring it into a thermos. She settled the house, turned down the damper in the heating stove and quickly bundled for the freezing weather outside. With her snowshoes

lashed to her boots, food and a thermos in the backpack, she released Fletcher out into the dim light, following him with a flashlight. "Go, boy! Find Gabriel!"

Six

A dash of temper fuels strength and pride. It's good, sometimes I think, to take temper out of the drawer and let honesty clear the air. Miranda holds too much inside, but one day she'll fight for what she wants, leaving nothing unsaid or undone.

Anna Bennett's Journal

A clump of melting snow slid from a pine bough and plopped down beside Miranda. Fear ruling her, she jumped, the flashlight's beam searing off into the tall pines. Fifteen minutes ago, Fletcher had raced ahead, ignoring her call. She prayed that he had found Gabriel safe. She'd lost his tracks, but continued in the same direction.

An hour in the forest worrying about Gabriel

seemed like an eternity. She'd tied her snowshoes to her backpack; they were good for open country, but not for the forest's dense brush, catching on twigs. She fell, pushed herself up awkwardly and trudged on in the snow, the chinook's winds hurling around her.

The flashlight battery was dimming and finally there was nothing. Weary, terrified for Gabriel, Miranda threw it away and marched on, the shadows seeming to come alive. Her backpack, not that heavy at first, caused her shoulders to ache. In the night's distance, Fletcher barked furiously and then nothing.

She ran toward the sound, dragging breath into her aching lungs. The wind swooped at her, tearing away her woolen scarf as if Gabriel's woman didn't want him to be found.

From behind, something grabbed her coat, immobilizing her. Terror surged through her as she thought of the size of the mountain lion's paw prints. She turned, fists flying and a mitten glanced off Gabriel's face, just as he ordered roughly, "Hold still. Stop fighting."

Because he was Gabriel and she had been both terrified and angry, she hit him again, this time in the chest. He grunted, scowling down at her while Fletcher leaped and played and threw his one-hundred-plus pounds into a friendly bump against her legs. She struggled for balance and Gabriel's fist locked onto her jacket, just beneath her chin. He hauled her up close to him. "It's a hell of a night to be out for a stroll, lady," he said tightly.

She was still fighting terror, her reasoning shooting between it and anger and the need to throw her arms around him. "If you can, I can."

Gabriel raked off his knitted cap and shoved his hand through his hair. "Now that's a childish statement."

She had to know— *"Were you with her?"*

He shook his head and stared blankly at her. "Who? My mare? Yes, I was. She takes a notion to go off into the high meadow once in a while. I left a note in the barn."

Miranda thought back to how frightened she'd been for him, disregarding the paper tacked to the door. *"I was worried about you!"*

"You're tired and freezing and illogical. Did it ever occur to you that you might be that big cat's dinner?"

Gabriel's cool control only made her more angry and frustrated; she tossed fear away and the other two emotions swallowed her now, the chinook wind's howl rising eerily in the night, coursing through the trees and swishing the branches. "I'm trained for logic, remember?"

"You should have stayed put. You're not trained for night hunting in the mountains." Gabriel's leather glove eased her scarf away from her face. "You're in a snit, lady, and this is no time to debate whatever mood you're in now. You need a warm fire—"

She wrestled the backpack from her and hurled it at him. She'd come after him because Gabriel was all that mattered to her. Not because he might be in danger. Not because he had been so supportive, a strong anchor holding her in rough times, but because whatever she felt for him years ago was a shadow of her emotions now. While she stood, buffeted by fear and anger and tearing through layers of what was important in life and what wasn't, Gabriel seemed unaffected. "'Stayed put?' Like in not meeting life and whatever it holds? I won't let you do that to me, Gabriel.... That's a thermos of hot tea in that backpack. For you when you're lying half frozen down some ravine with one broken leg, and a mountain lion gnawing on the other and I'm tired of the subject always being 'what I need.'"

Gabriel closed his eyes and shook his head as if dealing with a child's tantrum. With apparent effort, he kept his uneven tone low. "The mountain lion had more sense. He's back in his den, keeping warm. His tracks veered off mine about a quarter mile back. When I saw Fletcher, I knew you'd—"

"Who do you think you're dealing with? Why can't you show me what I'm showing you? You're angry with me—well, tell me that. Don't—"

That dark flash of anger tore across her like a sword and she reveled in the reality of Gabriel stirring past his self-protective shields. Because her emotions were flying now, out there on the howling wind, Miranda released them full force. She threw her weight into the shove, both her hands on his chest. He didn't move, as unreachable as ever, no reaction. "It's always about me, isn't it, Gabriel? What about you? What is behind all those nice placid remarks, the encouragement, the little you have to say about yourself? Just once, I'd like to hear—"

Gabriel turned from her, shutting her away, and only infuriated her more. Miranda stamped back a distance from him, then turned and retraced her path in the melting snow until she could see his face clearly. She tore off the coat hood covering her knitted cap. "I hate that—when you shut me out and when you run from any situation. Well, you're not running from this one. You used to be so open with me—enough to tell me that 'our life paths are different.' Oh, you could do that well enough. What changed you?"

"It's cold out here," he said too coolly, too logically. "Maybe you could wait to have this tantrum or whatever back at the house."

She jabbed a mitten-covered finger into his heavy coat. Gabriel grunted, but he didn't move. He'd shoved that nick of anger behind his walls, and that knowledge hiked hers a notch higher. "Oh, no. You're not running from this one, buddy."

He smiled a little at that, watching her. "What would you do if I did? Track me down?"

Gabriel as a confident, indulging male, secure that he could protect her wasn't what she wanted. She wanted equal terms now, not patronization. "I did it once, I can do it again. Every time I get too close to a subject you don't want to discuss, you either throw the conversation toward me, or you're gone, tuning me out or running away."

"Miss me, did you? What is this? Some aftermath of staying in the house too long? Maybe you're right. Maybe you have certain rights to know more."

That magical deep lilt coursed through the howling wind, staking Miranda with its sensual tone. Then Gabriel's big hands were framing her face, drawing her lips up to his. Eyes wide-open, she watched his intent expression, the line deepen between his brows, his lashes close. At first his lips were cool and firm, then they opened and played and nibbled and...

Miranda sank into the sweet kiss, tossing away everything but the magic that was Gabriel, that had always been Gabriel. He eased off her knitted cap and his hands dived into her hair, fingers splayed open, holding her as he slanted his open mouth on hers, locking the fit. The heat and hunger tore away the sweet taste and hurled Miranda into her own shaking hunger. She put her arms around his shoulders, opened her lips to his and felt the primitive beat of his passion, tuned into it so strongly that it became her own, trapping her body, pounding at her. She met him out there on that stark plane where shields were ripped away, desire burning bright. His mouth cruised her face, the kisses hard and hot and welcome, tasting of dark nights and skin upon skin. Tasting of eternity and vows and—

Shaking with sensual need, unprepared for Gabriel's own, and with too many layers of bulky clothing between them, Miranda eased away from him. Passion had honed his angular, hard face, his eyes narrowed and sultry, and his mouth rich and soft with the kisses they'd shared. "What was that, Gabriel?" she asked very carefully, wanting to make certain she understood the velocity and heat of that kiss.

"I think it's pretty clear. I want you. I always have." The words didn't come easily…it was as if he'd torn them from his soul. He took a deep unsteady breath and pushed the truth through the howling winds. "*You're* my woman in the smoke."

His statement knocked her back against a sapling and she leaned against it for support, trying to put all the pieces of the puzzle together—trying to make sense of the years wasted between them. He'd just kissed her as if nothing could tear him away. She'd absorbed the heat and impact of his desire, her own body shaking now in reaction.

"What's the matter?" he asked unevenly, clearly unsteady and wrapped in his own emotions. His angular face suddenly seemed so weary and sad, mixed with a frustrated tenderness. He wasn't a man to display emotions, but suddenly the wind whirled them around him. "Don't the statistics add up? I'm just as unsuitable now as I was then, yet it hasn't changed how much I want you. But I am a foolish man and cannot help the dreams that come to me. Sometimes I hunt them. The woman in the smoke is round with child, Miranda. My child. What I am will go on with that child, and what came before from my father and his father before him. But that is not for you—my mind tells me this, not my heart. You belong in another place, not with me."

"Let me get this straight," she whispered huskily as she struggled for reality, sorting through every nuance of his looks, his voice. "You still care?"

He looked at her darkly, a big male used to keeping his distance, prodded into an admission he didn't like. "We aren't a good match and you know it."

Miranda held to sorting the facts, keeping to the facts. She focused on absolute clarity, not wanting one false detail to interfere. "This isn't about careers, or lifestyles, or money, is it? It's about a man and a woman."

"Maybe." He nodded, tilting his head and watching her in that quiet assessing way.

"You coming after me, the bridal price—that was *real* to you, wasn't it?"

He nodded again, and she continued working

through her shocking discovery. "You wanted me here, living with you."

This time a nod wouldn't do; his anger struck through the chinook's howling winds. "Do you have to drag everything out and tear it to pieces?"

"What did you expect to gain?"

"I wanted to give you shelter. I wanted to protect the woman who haunted me, day and night. The way you looked at Gwyneth, at the baby nestling in her— as if it were tearing you apart.... Then for more selfish reasons—I wanted a little bit of you, just a short time to hear your voice, to see you in my home, to smell the perfume of your body—"

"All those years," she murmured, anger simmering like hot coals about to burst into flame. "All those years lost when we could have had—"

"What? For how long before the world called to you? You're smart, Miranda. Your future—"

"Lies where? With a man who ran from responsibility? With my own delusions that I could make life work *my* way? *How dare you, Gabriel. How dare you make my decisions for me and not serve me the truth.* That's what all the silence is about, isn't it? Why you run from any situation that might be considered intimate? Why you don't come too near?"

Gabriel's hand swept through that rich, shaggy hair. Caught by the wind, it swirled around his face. "You're angry, and this isn't the place to discuss—"

"I'm very angry. You're still making decisions for me, big ones. You decide what's safe to talk about and what isn't. *You* decide what is a dangerous area and what isn't, where I should be, and what I should do after losing my baby. You're telling me that you fantasized about me—you wanted me all this time. *And I didn't know it? How was I supposed to know? You kept that from me?''*

"That's a stretch, and you know it. You were vulnerable, I agree. But I wanted to give you protection—'' He frowned and closed his lips as Miranda's green eyes seared him.

"Well. This certainly has been an interesting, but a bit late, little discovery,'' she said briskly, before turning and walking away from him. Furious with Gabriel and herself for letting all those years escape, Miranda didn't want him to see her tears. *I want you. I always have.... You're my woman in the smoke,* he'd said. All those years they could have had...

"Ride the horse. You're exhausted.'' Gabriel frowned at the woman trudging ahead of him. She tossed him an airy wave, dismissing him.

He looked down at her smaller footprints, fitting his boot beside them. He shouldn't have let her tear into him, rip open his heart and take the truth as if it were her right. They couldn't have had a future. She was angry now, but later she'd understand the reality....

Her mouth had tasted like fire and roses and dreams.

Ahead of him, Miranda stumbled and fell, and when Gabriel reached for her, she swatted him away. "Don't you *dare* touch me.''

The fury wrapped in her words shocked him, stayed his hand. "You're tired and cold and too full of pride.''

She launched to her feet as if anger had shoved

through her again, giving her extra strength. Her face was pale and taut, but her eyes were brilliant, lashing at him. *"Leave me alone."*

Uncertain how to handle her in this mood, Gabriel put away the horse as Miranda marched up to the house. It had taken every bit of his strength not to pick her up and place her on the horse. He had seen his petite mother match his father's temper with one dark look, and now Gabriel knew the force of a woman's fury. He decided to give her time to cool down, then try logic again. He shook his head; at this point he wasn't certain about Miranda's surprising flash-fire temper, her ability to take strips off him.

He paused before entering the house, carefully wiping his boots on the heavy outdoor mat. From the look of Miranda, he didn't know what to expect. She'd always been so cool and reasonable, and now temper ruled her.

Maybe his own was simmering, too. *He'd made the right choice for her all those years ago.* She'd gone on to become successful. She'd gone on to a man she'd chosen, a life that she fit into smoothly. Her anger wasn't justified, he reasoned, turning the doorknob and stepping into the firelit room. Miranda usually hung her clothing by the door, her boots placed neatly, side by side. Instead, this time she'd left a trail behind her that led into the kitchen area. There, she was dressed in her thermal underwear, glaring at him as she slapped peanut butter and jelly on bread.

Gabriel carefully removed his heavy winter outerwear, trying not to notice how the thermal silk clung to Miranda's curved body. "I am not in a good mood," she said warningly.

"Neither am I." She'd been crying, the paths still streaked her face. How could he have hurt her so? "What good would it have done to come to you? To tell you what was in my heart? So I left you to move on, into your life away from me and Freedom."

She held up the peanut butter knife to demonstrate her point. "Yet another decision on the part of Gabriel Deerhorn."

"Could we talk about this when you are rested?" To do something, anything, Gabriel picked up her sketchbook, studying the Celtic symbols woven and unending in their design. Miranda's intelligence was like that, sturdy and intricate and restless. She'd weave through everything he'd said, find the pattern of his need for her and lock onto it. He didn't have long to wait for her response.

She swiped the knife through the jam and held it to emphasize a point. "That's one more. You've just decided that I'm not logical enough now to think straight. I'm doing plenty of thinking now and I'm not tired. I'm angry. Boy, you're racking up the decisions here, Mr. Deerhorn. I settled for less than I wanted and I wanted you. *I settled for less because life has to go on and I couldn't spend my life mooning over someone who didn't want me, who didn't care enough to discuss the decision he had made for my welfare.*"

She reached over his shoulder for the bag of chips on the refrigerator. The contact of her soft breast against his chest sucked the breath from Gabriel. Miranda tensed, watching him, her eyes wide.

"You want me now, don't you?" she asked unevenly, her hand lowering to his shoulder, her fingers digging in. That quick green glance down his body locked on the intimate, undeniable thrust against his clothing. Then her eyes were clear, meeting his with a challenge.

There was no denying the effect she could have on him. Held too long, the truth exploded from him in a harsh admission. "Yes. I want to hold you and know that you are safe. I want to feel the beat of your heart against mine. To make you mine. It is in me now to take you, to make you my woman."

"I see. But this is my decision, isn't it?" Her gaze drifted over his lips, studying them, and Gabriel's heart leaped. Her fingertip slid along his brows, lowered down his nose and traced the outline of his mouth. He couldn't breathe as she stood on tiptoe, placing her mouth against his, those dark green eyes watching him. The play, the shared kisses, eyes open, tested Gabriel's resolve not to touch her, to take advantage of her. The flick of her tongue against his lips startled him and he jerked back, wary of her. She wore the look of a woman desiring a man, that closed-in, soft and hunting look.

Uncertain of what she wanted, or what game she now played, Gabriel shivered lightly. "What do you want, Miranda?"

"You," she whispered simply, and lowered her hand to unbutton the top of her silk undershirt. "Now."

Gabriel tried not to look at her body, those soft flowing curves, the flesh revealed in the opening, the shape of her breasts so close, he could— His hand trembled as he touched her, finding the delicate wonder of her breast within his hand, cuddling it gently.

Her sigh was that of pleasure, and desire danced into flame between them. Holding his eyes, Miranda eased off her undershirt, leaving her in the lacy bra that had tormented Gabriel. "I want to hold you, too. To know that you are safe and close against me. To feel you inside me."

The bold erotic statement jarred Gabriel. He wanted her to know that he was uncertain of his control and of how careful he would be of her. "I have not had a woman in a long time."

"I know. That's why you're so nervous around me, isn't it? You speak very properly when you are trying to conceal your emotions. You're afraid of me, in your way. Afraid you'll hurt me. I'm well now, Gabriel, in more than one way. I'm not vulnerable. I'm angry, yes. I haven't decided how to handle that yet as anger isn't something I deal with on a regular basis. But I do know that you're not running from this, from me." She leaned close, her breasts against him, burning him. Her body rested against his, her hips nestled closely. "Just once, for tonight, lose that control, Gabriel, and show me what you feel. *I need to feel.*"

Her open lips on his caused him to tremble, forcing back his need to— Then his hands opened on her hips, tugging her closer, and he knew he was lost.

Miranda closed her eyes when he swung her up into his arms. Somehow she'd always known that Gabriel would let his instincts rule him when he wanted a woman desperately—his woman, the only woman for him. He would move swiftly, claiming her, for that was his hunter's nature. His heart raged against hers, heat pouring from him, his hands holding her close, his body corded with the strength of desire.

His bedroom was cold, and yet she knew that he would take her to his bed, not hers. He lowered her to her feet, his hand circling her throat, a firm possessive touch, not threatening as his mouth came down again, swooping to fuse to hers. "Change your mind," he whispered raggedly, his lips hard against hers, feverish and tasting of desire just as she wanted. But he had stripped away her bra, his hands cupping her breasts, smoothing her trembling body as if researching the woman he would claim for a lifetime. "Leave me."

"No, I've waited too long, a lifetime, and I can't wait longer." She would not let him draw back, finding his mouth, claiming it, feeding upon him. The incredible sense of coming home ruled her, that for a time, she would know who she was, what she was intended to be.... *Gabriel...Gabriel...*

With shaking fingers, she fumbled with the layers of his clothing, his shirt, undershirt and with an impatient hiss of breath, Gabriel shed his clothing, standing before her bold, aroused and so alive. Heat shimmered in the cool air as his hands slid beneath the elastic waistband of her long silk pants and briefs. His rough palms and strong fingers spread over her bottom, holding her tight against him as he nuzzled her throat and gently nipped her earlobe.

He moved quickly, strongly, tugging her closer, as she arched against him. Lowering her to the bed, Gabriel lay over her, watching her. Those black eyes flickered down their bodies, hers pale and soft, tangled with his. There was nothing but the sound of

their hearts now as Gabriel found and nudged her
intimately.

Taking care, he eased slowly within her warmth,
the incredible filling like magic, making her whole
for the first time in her life. He shook against her, the
muscles of his arms standing out in relief. That angular face above her displayed emotions she'd wanted
all of her life—fierce, tender, amazed. There was male
arrogance there, too, as if nothing could keep him
from her. A look questioned her as she moved in the
slow rhythm he had set, a familiar controlled rhythm
with a different meaning. She knew he leashed himself, perspiration gleaming on his harsh face. The
muscles bunched at his throat and shoulders told her
the price he paid for keeping her safe.

"I'm fine," she whispered, fingers digging into his
shoulders as she drew the incredible pleasure deep
inside her. "Make love to me, Gabriel."

Seven

A man's pride is fragile as the petals of my roses. To understand that pride is to peel away the petals and thorns, and to listen to his fears. He makes choices by a different standard than a woman's sturdy heart. But when a woman makes a choice, she is not apt to give it up lightly—if it really matters.

Anna Bennett's Journal

Miranda lay within the cove of Gabriel's big warm body and listened to the wind howling in the predawn. She was exhausted from the trek in the mountains to find him, tired of plodding through his reasoning, and still furious with the years they had lost. Her thoughts churning, she lay very still, her hand over his as it cupped her breast, his thumb smoothing a caress.

He had touched her with reverence and care both times they had made love. His lips had moved over her body slowly, as if placing her in his memory forever. Incredibly sweet and tender, he'd given her everything, shattering her.

His heart beat steadily against her back now, and his thoughts echoed in the bedroom's shadows. "Miranda?"

She wasn't ready for the night to pass, yet a slice of brittle, harsh dawn pierced the window's curtain and reality would soon follow. The empty years that had passed between them slid over her; she shivered in the uncertainty that given the same choice, Gabriel would do the same. *She wouldn't.* She wouldn't settle for half a life again. A fine anger brewed in her now, pricked by his arrogance then and now. *I want you. I always have,* he'd said.

All those years... Miranda shivered, chilled by the thought that she might never have known...

Out there in the snowy mountain wild, he'd lost his temper, anger flying at her, and turned toward himself. The lid containing his emotions had come off for the first time, revealing that he *needed,* he *wanted,* he *dreamed.* Gabriel had kept all that from her, hoarded it for himself.

"Miranda?" he murmured again, this time his lips against her throat.

"I'm leaving," she whispered unevenly and fought the tear sliding down her cheek. The morning after making love with Gabriel she was too emotional. She wanted to compile the facts, sort through his admission that he'd always wanted her. "I need to think."

"I see." He tensed, but he didn't ask her why, or

to stay, and didn't say that he wanted her in his life. His quiet acceptance of what must be tormented her. That he'd expected her to leave angered her, inflamed the knowledge of the wasted years between them.

An hour later, Miranda shifted the gears on Gabriel's Jeep, driving down the mountain. In the rear-view mirror, she saw him standing on the road, legs braced against the wind, hair flying untamed in the morning sun. He'd offered to drive her to Anna's, but she couldn't have that, tears too close to the surface.

Once on the highway, she couldn't drive straight to her mother's empty house. She circled the town, and found the sturdy, comforting familiarity of it.

Gabriel hadn't asked her to stay. He'd withdrawn again, as if their beautiful lovemaking had never happened.

She glanced at the church's white steeple, as the street's cobblestones rhythmically jarred the Jeep. There was Eli's Bakery and he'd be baking the cookies Gabriel loved so much. She drove to the cemetery and visited the gravesites where her mother and father and child were buried. If it hadn't been for the tragedy, her baby would have been due any day.... The chinook that could last for days swept over the valley and she knew she'd come full circle.

Only she could change her life and take what she wanted.

Miranda looked up to the mountains and knew that she wanted the man there.

Was she hurt by him? Yes. Miranda slid into Gabriel's Jeep and knew she was too tired to battle today. But if Gabriel thought he could make all the decisions in *her* life, he was mistaken.

*   *   *

Gabriel rubbed the ache in his chest and glanced at the garden seedlings beginning to sprout in Miranda's window boxes. It was only a few hours since she'd left him and it seemed like a cold eternity. It was for the best, he told himself repeatedly. He shouldn't have let her see into his heart, shouldn't have let her know that she'd haunted him all these years.

He shouldn't have made love to her. That memory could never be buried or washed away. He'd never forget the way she sighed luxuriously as he tasted her body, the way she moved so easily into his touch, opening to him, giving to him. He'd been careful, mindful of that slender, vulnerable, silken body.

She was angry with him now, for keeping his secrets. Given time, she would come to know that when they'd made love he'd been greedy for life, for her. But that their lives couldn't blend—he picked up the intricate Celtic symbols she'd drawn while coming back to herself. Interwoven, they were without end. He drew a fingertip across one design, severing the image of his and Miranda's lives intertwined. Gabriel shook his head. How could he sever the memory of their passion? How could he not remember the sweet yielding of her body, the softness of her sighs?

Gabriel drifted the palm of his hand across the dainty seedlings for a garden Miranda wished to make. For once the mountains did not call to him, the winds still howling her name, and having tasted the woman and the dream, he had never been so empty.

In the new pink dawn, he placed the tomato seedlings on Anna's step, wanting Miranda to have what

she had sowed. The beaded moccasins were products
of his hours, trying to stay away from her in his
house, giving her time to think and heal.

On the window above the porch, Miranda watched
Gabriel's tall body stride through the dawn, moving
quickly away from her and what they could have had,
could have now. Anger quivered within her now, but
also excitement. For she had sowed more than seeds
at Gabriel's house... His lovemaking mixed hunger
with reverence, tenderness with passion, longing with
fulfillment. There was no way she could turn away
from that honest, frightening beauty—the insight Gabriel had given her with each touch, each breath.
She'd glimpsed more in those few hours than she had
in a lifetime and she would grasp it with both fists.
She wanted a resolve between them—an equal resolve. "Like it or not, Mr. Gabriel Deerhorn, we are
not finished yet. This time, I'm going to be included
in the decision-making, whatever it may be."

Gabriel ladled water from the bucket onto the hot
rocks of his sweat house. Midmorning seemed to
hover in the first week of March, tiny slices of day
penetrating the cracks between the small building's
overhead boards; outside, blinding sunlight bounced
off snow. When the snow melted, the nearby stream
would become a small river tumbling down the mountain, feeding Valentina Lake. The weathered gray
building, a distance from his house, was scented of
the sage and sweet grass he had crumbled onto the
coals. Steam slid through the pine boughs placed over
the hot rocks and layered the small enclosure. On a
plain wooden bench, Gabriel lay naked, sweat pour-

ing from his body, his hands folded behind his head. He inhaled the purifying scents, gave himself to them, and still could not rid himself of the need for Miranda. *Miranda.*

She'd been so small and pale, lying in the snow at the foot of her mother's steps. He'd never been so terrified. She'd seemed empty later, too fragile, mourning her child and her mother. Miranda seemed as if her soul would pass through her skin at any moment, escaping her keep.

The agony in her eyes as she saw her sister-in-law's rounding body had been too much for Gabriel. His need to protect Miranda, to keep her from harm, to give her shelter, had been overwhelming.

Perhaps it was his father's blood that told him to claim his woman, to keep her near.

Perhaps his needs were selfish, not only for Miranda's sake, but for the peace she brought him. Perhaps he took advantage of her—just to scrape that small bit of time from the world and treasure it close against him.

Two mornings ago Gabriel had wakened with her in his arms. Was that a dream, the soft fragrance of her haunting him? In her, he'd seen his eternity and his essence, in that flashing pinpoint before his desire came flooding into her keeping. He'd known that he was meant to hold her, to give her his child, to keep her safe until the winds took away their breath—together. She'd burned a path to his heart, and that soft scar hurt him more deeply than those of the flesh.

Flesh? She was more—a part of him now, inside him, moving in his blood, heating it, the fever for her— Gabriel hadn't been aware of the power of a woman's calling to him, and he wasn't certain about his strength against it now—now that he had tasted Miranda. He was angry with himself, and with her. She'd torn away the pretense and exposed his need, his dream of the woman in the smoke.

Bitterness curled from the scented steam into him. He'd reached and taken. He'd tossed away reality and devoured the few hours with her, reveled in them. Perhaps when the winter years came to him, he would know that it was a dream, and that he did not have the right to touch her. Miranda was probably safely on her way now…away from him.

Gabriel rubbed his hands over his damp face. *What had he been thinking?*

Outside, Fletcher barked happily, probably chasing a rabbit. Gabriel frowned; his house was no longer barren, but softened by her woman's touch. The bedroom she had used, carried her fragrance.

He would not expose himself to her again. He would retain what little pride he had left.

Gabriel reached for the ladle and just as he was to pour it on the hot stones, the door of the sweat house jerked open. A shaft of blinding midmorning sunlight hit him, outlining a woman's long legs and curved body.

The steam shifted, and catching the sudden sweeping blast of fresh air, the coals ignited, tiny flames dancing around the pine needles. Then the door closed and Miranda eased onto another bench, lying down on it, her hands behind her head.

The slice of sunshine passing through the boards on the roof softened as it fell on her long, curved body, the dips and curves and fullness that marked her as a woman. Scraps of lace covered her breasts and hips.

Perhaps he was dreaming; Gabriel lifted the ladle and poured the water over his head. He tried to remain calm, to cover his emotions while his heart leaped at the sight of her. "I suppose you think this is funny."

She turned slowly to him. In the half-light, her green eyes burned through the layers of steam to him, her face pale amid that shifting silky black hair. "I saw no reason to disturb your meditation. Please go ahead."

"You've come for your things. I will bring them back for you." He hadn't been able to stand the thought of wrenching her presence away from him.

"Don't you dare…. You talk too much."

Gabriel inhaled, the gentle verbal slap unfamiliar to him. He had always been a quiet man. He had— the steam had dampened the lace covering her, clinging to her, and Gabriel tried to remember what he had been about to say.

Miranda closed her eyes and placed her arms at her side, lying still, breathing slowly. Gabriel tried not to trace that long, soft body, the flow of her breast, the dip of her stomach, the jut of her hipbones and the slender strength of her thighs. He remembered the clamping pressure of them along his hips, the ebb and flow of her body against his, the cries that seemed drawn from her soul—

Gabriel rubbed his head and sat up. He poured water onto the rocks and fought his dancing nerves as the steam hissed. He rummaged for a logical protest and managed, "This is a man's place," he managed finally, firmly, in his best eviction notice.

She squirmed slightly on the wooden bench. The movement was sensuous, feminine and caused Gabriel's throat to tighten. She smiled slightly, drowsily as if settling into the steam and comfort. "Mmm. I know. It feels like you."

She was too quiet and Gabriel resented the question erupting harshly from him. "Why are you here?"

Miranda took her time in answering. "To set the terms."

Again, he was forced to pursue her. His mind cautioned, but he could not resist. "Terms?"

She stirred luxuriously, a strand of black hair clinging damply to her smooth cheek. "I have my pride. You have yours. Mine is no less than yours, Gabriel. It's time you recognized that."

"Pride does not come into this."

"So says you."

Gabriel frowned at the challenge, so unlike sweet teenage Miranda. She had crossed into a woman and he realized from experience with his mother and sister that feminine emotions were as safe as a lake's thin ice, or a wildfire searing the tops of the pines. Her gaze slowly took in his body as he sat, frowning at her. That dancing of his senses told him he wanted her, here and now. That primitive beat pounded him relentlessly.

"There's nothing here now but you and me," she said softly. "There is nothing else to consider. There is no past and no one else involved. Just you and me," she repeated.

"You know this isn't right." Gabriel scrubbed his shaking hands over his face. In another minute, he'd be moving over her, in her, that dark fever escaping his tethers— And where would it lead? Nowhere. Nothing had changed. Miranda was meant for one world, and his path was set for another, just as it was years ago. "What do you want?" he repeated darkly.

"I want the courting time we missed."

Gabriel shook his head and droplets of water sprayed across the layers of steam. Miranda's eyes were narrowed now, pinning him. "I have my pride, too. You took me in, gave me shelter at a time when I needed it. But I'm past that now, Gabriel, and you're going to have to deal with what has happened—will happen—between us. You can't shove me away. You cannot make my decisions for me. If you didn't want me, that would be one thing. But you do. It's in every look and touch—now that I see exactly how much you've withheld from me."

His answer was blunt and from the truth he knew. "It won't work."

"Well, for appearances at least, it's going to work for a while. I've already explained to Fidelity Moore and the ladies that I am handling you gently. In Freedom, you've apparently set an image for yourself as a confirmed bachelor. I simply explained that I wanted to give you more time to adjust to life with me, and that for a time, I wanted to court you, living at my house at times, easing you into a situation—"

"Dammit, I'm not to be trained. *And I am not delicate.*"

Miranda's summation of him was concise and slashed with anger. "No, you're just arrogant, hardheaded and need bringing down a notch. You think you can set terms? You think you can just waltz up to my home at dawn and give me the most beautiful, thoughtful, most romantic gift I've ever had, and then not take the consequences? You think you can come for me in that lovely old-fashioned way that meant so much to you—then discard me?"

"I did not discard you." Gabriel did not like the picture she presented. Freedom Valley had known he'd given the bridal price for her, that he'd come for her in the traditional way of his father's people. "The customs of Freedom Valley allow for a couple who try, but cannot weave their lives together."

"It's difficult to weave when you gave me nothing of yourself. Yes, you gave me a place to heal and the comfort of safety nearby. But you gave me nothing of what runs inside you, all that river of feeling that your eyes express and your body told me was the truth, not some cold excuse. You're afraid of me, Gabriel. You're afraid of intimacy with me, of giving me my due—that which is in your heart."

The challenge spread across the steam to him. Gabriel refused to answer her goad, to clash verbal swords with her.

Miranda sat up, frowning at him and Gabriel tried not to look at the dark, nubby circles outlined by the damp lace of her bra. He stared at the hot stones, which seemed more safe than Miranda just now. Still, he couldn't resist answering her taunt. He slapped the basic facts into the steamy enclosure. "How many degrees do you have, Miranda? How many do I have? What lifestyle suits you? What place? I can't see you living here with me, the hardships and—"

He glanced at her, that shaft of midmorning light cutting through the steam to capture Miranda's pale body, gleaming in the shadows. The need to take her, to claim her was too fierce, pounding at him. Taking a deep breath, Gabriel prepared to leave, and then Miranda's slender hand reached to flatten on his chest.

He trembled with desire, some inner instinct that told him to take her. Without force, that pale feminine hand over his heart tethered him. "I've come to court you, Gabriel," Miranda whispered softly. "Do you refuse me?"

Could he refuse the air coming into his body, sustaining him? Could he refuse the sun that heated the earth, the rain that nurtured it?

Could he refuse the woman he loved as she shed the damp lace and moved sleekly, damply, warmly into his arms?

Then the fever and the hunger that was Miranda took Gabriel Deerhorn, leaving him no defense, no logic. Their bodies slid together as if they were meant to be—

In his house, forty-five minutes later, Gabriel shook his head as Miranda emerged from her shower wearing only his chambray shirt. Folded turban-style, the white towel around her head emphasized her brilliant green eyes. She found him in the shadows of the kitchen area and her brisk efficient movements slowed, her gaze slumberous as it strolled over his bare chest and jeans. "Why, Gabriel. I do believe you're sulking," she murmured.

Gabriel was methodically making sandwiches and trying to assemble what had happened. With one touch, Miranda had destroyed his vow to separate his life from hers, freeing her. He was still stunned at how he'd taken her there in the sweat house, on the floor covered with toweling. This time had been different, for Miranda's fever fed his own, her teeth nipping at his shoulder, her fingers digging into his back. He rolled a shoulder, suspecting the marks she had left, the pleasure that had riveted him as she came into that trembling pulse of her release. Gabriel prowled through his thoughts carefully: he suspected that Miranda's passions could tear away his leashes, his intentions to be gentle with her. Just there, with her tossing beneath him, fever hot, their bodies sliding, he'd held her, possessed her, dived in to take what was his. A controlled man, Gabriel had held her hips and lifted them— He closed his eyes, the primitive scene locked in his mind. And as he held her, she held him, a match for the fiery need. He shouldn't have handled her so roughly—cupping her hips, finding her breasts with his lips, tasting her…

His hand trembled as he sliced tomatoes for the bacon sandwiches. "I have the feeling you just counted coup—won a small victory and scored a point for your side."

"I love feeling like a woman. You make me *feel*, Gabriel."

He studied this woman who could seem so delicate and yet he recognized her inner and physical strength—she could be both fierce and sweet when making love.

Miranda stood on tiptoe to brush her lips against one corner of his lips and then the other. Gabriel held onto the counter to keep from floating as she slanted him a look and placed a strip of bacon into his mouth. "I drove your Jeep up here with one of your horses tied behind it. I'll be riding the horse back down."

Gabriel tensed, the image of the big cougar he'd seen slashing through his mind. "No, you're not."

"I'm staying in Freedom Valley, Gabriel. I'm not running away and I won't be pushed away. You're going to have to deal with me." Those clear meadow-green eyes searched his face. She skipped from the argument he was prepared to meet into another dazzling realm. "You either lock me out in defense, or run. And I want all of you. I don't want you to protect me, to think of my best interests, to feed me, or anything else, unless it's a policy that can be returned in kind. See that you let me carry my share now, will you? Are you going to let me court you?"

Miranda placed her forehead against his shoulder in the old, trusting way and Gabriel fought yielding to the sweet enticement. "It's a silly thing," he said finally, his senses reeling with the fresh scent of her. "A woman should not court a man."

Then Miranda lifted her mouth to his and the searing hunger drove all else away. Each time he touched her, the need rose more quickly. He couldn't resist looking down at the soft body resting against him, and unbuttoned her shirt. Her breasts came into his hands as if they belonged in his keeping. The taste of them curled on his tongue, demanding more.

His hands swept down the indentation of her waist and opened to lock onto her hips, the veed shadows of her womanhood beckoning to him. He thought of the woman in the smoke: Miranda softly curved with his child and he pushed the treasured dream away. She trembled, and worried that his obvious need frightened her, he scanned her expression. Miranda's smooth hands framed his face, her thumbs soothing the corners of his mouth. Her eyes were clear and green as summer grass. "Love me exactly how you feel," she whispered. "No pretenses, no logic, no fear of hurting me. In this, give me honesty, what your senses tell you is right."

He closed his eyes and her flowing Celtic symbols came to him, the strength and the curve and the endless need that had increased with each touch.

Later, he drove her to her home, met the softness of her lips, and then alone again in his barn, wondered what he had done. He rubbed the ache in his chest, and shook his head. Miranda's courting of him chafed, the roles reversed. Freedom Valley was based on women taking the lead in dating customs and that put him at Miranda's disposal. He wasn't certain if he liked that or not. It was only a temporary game, he decided, Miranda's mind and body coming alive... nothing could come of it and then she'd be gone. *Miranda....* "Maybe I am delicate," he admitted and wondered what her next move would be.

Gabriel blinked, the thought pinning him very still, wrapping around him. *He was the hunted. She made the rules.* "This is very unwise," he said to the airy barn and didn't like the uneven sound of his voice.

Eight

When Miranda's turn comes to court a man, she won't be wanting the easiest of the pack. She'll want one with all the little edges to explore and tame. Despite her orderly and ladylike appearance, she can be quite the hunter and needs a match to her game.

Anna Bennett's Journal

"Stop scowling," Miranda murmured easily. She glanced at Gabriel, seated next to her in her new red pickup. "You look like you're being hauled into Doomsday."

Gabriel sat with his arms crossed. The pickup was small; his knees bent sharply to accommodate the length of his legs. It was better than revealing his fear of Miranda's driving by holding on to the dashboard.

The next bump on the road leading from his house took his head against the roof and jarred his knees lightly against the dashboard. He refused to rub the slight injury. "I could have driven down the hill to your mother's house."

He hadn't liked waiting for her to drive to collect him—"collect him," as if he were a helpless... The reversal of roles called for by Freedom Valley's courting system chafed him once again. In waiting for Miranda, he had changed clothes several times and nothing seemed right. He was a hunter, bred to stalk his prey, collecting it, and now as a potential groom candidate, he was very vulnerable and uncertain. No matter what his feelings were, how contrary being placed on an inspection block, he wouldn't let Miranda down. At the last minute, he'd made a silly trip down the mountain, hurrying to purchase new jeans and a light blue·dress shirt. He'd shined his best boots and belt and buckle. Miranda's party was important to her, and Gabriel sensed that amid Miranda's family and friends, he would be inspected as a suitable match for her. *He wasn't.*

By using the old system of messages by homing pigeons, he thought darkly, he was safe, not aroused by the tone of her husky voice. Why then had he ordered a new telephone line? This uncertain fragile-male business did not sit well with Gabriel Deerhorn.

Gabriel inhaled and braced for the next rut, which she hit as surely as if she'd been aiming for it. She glanced at him. "Stop shaking your head. You'll live."

"I've got magazine photographers coming up to-morrow. They're staying for a week and I'm guiding

them in the high country. A concussion would make
that difficult.'' He resented his bad mood and grump-
ing. His life was no longer smooth and comfortable.
The next bump jarred her breasts, which quivered beneath a soft green material concealed by her long
coat. Her scent wafted to him, erotic, enticing....

She patted his knee. ''I'll be careful with you,
baby. I'll get you home in plenty of time to rest up.
About that guide trip. I don't suppose you'd invite me
along?''

''It's all men.'' *Baby.* She was teasing him, and
Gabriel refused to take the bait.

''What does that have to do with anything?''

He felt like a stag protecting his harem of one precious woman from intruders. How could he explain
that logically, even to himself? ''We're camping....
Bathroom facilities,'' he muttered and his mind
swung to another danger—Freedom Valley's Bachelor Club. ''Has Brody come around? Koby?
Fletcher?''

''Uh-huh, all of them. They're going to be at my
party tonight. I think Mom would have liked all of us
together in her house. I enjoyed the preparations—
good food, Mom's punch recipe, baking bread and
cakes... And I'm not buying that 'bathroom facilities'
logic.''

Gabriel settled into his dark thoughts of the potential poachers surrounding his woman. ''But your hope
chest is still at my house,'' he said, carefully reaffirm-
ing his temporary rights to Miranda.

''Yes, it is.'' She glanced at him. ''You look very
nice, Gabriel.''

"Thank you." The words were tightly begrudged and dark and unlike him.

Anna's house was already lit up, cars and trucks parked carefully so as not to disturb her yard. Gabriel braced himself as he followed Miranda into the house, filled with laughter and chatter and good friends. At the back door, she replaced her serviceable winter boots with his beaded moccasins, and a bit of his uncertainty dissolved. Gabriel tried to shake off his image as a territorial male, and failed the first time Miranda stood on tiptoe to hug and kiss each of her guests—which included all of Freedom Valley's known women-hunting bachelors.

With large gold hoop earrings and a matching emerald tunic and flowing slacks, she moved easily through the role of hostess. Little remained of the pale, hurt woman who had first come to his home. She didn't need him now, he thought whimsically. Miranda had always been very capable, very organized, and now amid her friends and family, she laughed easily. Her green eyes danced with a tidbit Tanner had remembered of their childhood, a time when Miranda and Kylie had surprised him and his friends while they were skinny-dipping.

"Don't even think about it," Gabriel ordered lightly to Dakota Jones, who was woman-chasing for a mother for those children he wanted.

"You're going to have to step out more often, old man," Dakota returned easily with a grin. "Miranda likes this—family and friends around her. Look at how she glows. She's all lit up and you sure as hell can't be the reason. You haven't said much all night, and everyone knows you prefer your mountains to a crowd like this.''

Koby Austin, who had lost a wife and son to childbirth, sipped Anna's aged blackberry wine and studied Miranda, then Gabriel. ''Too bad about her baby—your baby.''

Dylan Spotted Horse nodded. ''A real shame. If I'd been the one she wanted, I wouldn't have kept it a secret, visiting her away from Freedom Valley.''

Brody Thor, who had married at seventeen and had raised his daughters alone after his wife deserted them, nudged Gabriel with his shoulder. ''I have a hard time believing that story, because I know you. If that baby were yours, she would have been wearing your ring. You're an old-fashioned man, Gabriel. You'd have lassoed her into marriage right away.''

Gabriel closed into himself, shielding his thoughts. Apparently his friends knew about the lie told to protect Miranda. In all possibility, any one of them would have done the same. He tried to concentrate on Dakota's sister, Karolina, as she asked him questions about the old outlaw's grave, reputed to be in the high country he roamed. But he worried about Miranda, the way she placed her hand on Gwyneth's round body, feeling the child nestled within. The delight in Miranda's expression said that her own trial had slid somewhat into the past. She laughed outright as she placed her other hand on Kylie's as yet flat stomach.

Gabriel's heart stopped as she turned, green eyes sparkling. She found him in the crowded room and the rising flush on her cheeks told him that she recognized him as her lover. The moment danced between them, softly, sweetly, laced with a mixture of sensuality and tenderness and memories of a wild-flower bouquet between them and that first heavenly, sweet kiss. She moved toward him, and he went dizzy just looking at her. The conversation became a buzz, the people he'd known for a lifetime fading into the background. Then Miranda stood in front of him, her expression one of pleasure.

There was little he could do but lower his lips to her soft ones.

Five days later, Gabriel ignored the men grousing about the freezing mid-March wind on a high, rocky mountain peak—perfect for photographs of the big-horn sheep nearby. He settled into the warmth of Mir-anda's lovemaking, the taste of blackberry wine and happiness on her lips, and knew that he was no longer complete without her. His mind told him that she would soon leave, taking his heart with her. He braced himself for the lonely life ahead and for a time gave himself to the cleansing wind and the stars above, allowing his soul to flow to hers, twining to-gether like the campfire smoke. He felt her in his body, pulsing, the warmth of her embracing him, those grass-green eyes drowsy in the aftermath of lovemaking. His hand curled within his heavy glove, sensitive to a softer texture, her flesh cruising along his body, drifting in his mind.

He'd invited her into his home after her party and once inside, he'd tugged her to him, hungry for her, the fire raging between them instantly. That primitive need to claim her could not be restrained.

His body sprung to her touch too easily, leaving

him little resistance. Each time she came to him, she left him less complete than before.

She would leave soon enough, that brilliant mind needing challenges Freedom Valley could not offer....

Gabriel opened his eyes to the night, the men huddling around the campfire, cleaning their expensive camera gear. She belonged to their world, business-savvy, smart, brain crunching numbers, logic layering every thought. What did he have to offer Miranda?

With his teeth, Gabriel tore away a chunk of dried deer jerky and chewed it without tasting. He'd been right the first time—to set her free, and after a long week away from the sensual needs of their bodies, Miranda's laser-sharp mind would be defining reality. She would define her life apart from his, recognize the folly of any relationship between them.

Gabriel scanned the night, listened to the wind in the trees and the animals that were a part of him. She could never be a part of his world, and his spirit, the strength of his essence, could never live in hers....

The savage, deep bloodred pulsing fever her scent could cause in him, or even one look from those dark green eyes—the need to mate with her, to give her his child, made him uneasy. Now it lurked inside him, humming when he would have peace.

Fletcher was restless, pacing the camp with raised hackles, a sign of a dangerous animal nearby. A man lit a cigarette, killing it when Gabriel stared coolly at him. The "man" smell, carried by the wind, would drive away any animals.

Or attract the big cat stalking them.

The next afternoon, Gabriel's binoculars pinned the bright red jacket, the slight figure of Miranda, bent against the forceful wind. On a rocky ledge above her, the cougar was sunning and watching her. Suddenly the cat was on his feet, his body crouched to stalk.

Gabriel quickly told the men to stay put, to watch for the cougar, and that he would return. At a run, with Fletcher at his side and his rifle slung to his back, Gabriel plunged into the thick pines, fear icing his blood, pushing him to his limits. *Miranda*...

Terrorized that he would cause the cougar to react, harming Miranda, Gabriel closed the distance, motioning for Fletcher to be silent. They hunted together now, man and dog, trained to notice and interpret the slightest movement of the other.

In the clearing, Miranda stood poised, a rifle to her shoulder. Wind whipped at her blue-black gleaming hair, released from the coat's hood. On a rocky ledge above her, the cougar was poised to leap. Gabriel forced himself not to yell, and moved silently closer. He could miss the long shot, only wounding the cougar and Miranda would be in more danger. To distract the cougar, focused now on Miranda, was safer. He heard the noises of the approaching men behind him and damned them for the complication that could cost Miranda's life. Without distracting Miranda, Gabriel inched closer, and motioned for Fletcher to circle the cougar.

"Miranda," Gabriel said quietly and moved forward, rifle in hand, placing himself between her and the snarling, crouched cougar.

Her voice was an uneven thread, caught on the wind. "Gabriel. Don't—"

Everything happened at once: Fletcher barked, startling the cougar. It leaped on Gabriel, who was closer, and Miranda fired. Torn from him by the feline's impact, his rifle was useless. Battling the wiry, strong mountain lion, Gabriel protected his throat and the slash of claws burned his thigh.

He rolled with the cougar and heard a second shot; pain stabbed into his left buttock and the cougar slumped upon him.

Pinned beneath the wildcat and stunned, his thigh burning, Gabriel distantly heard the sound of clicking cameras, saw their glass eyes focus at him as Fletcher barked excitedly in the distance. Heart pounding, Gabriel pushed off the limp beast, struggled to his feet and caught Miranda, who flew into his arms. He tugged back her hair, read the stark fear in her face, the tears streaming down her cheeks. *She was safe.*

He dived into her kiss, locked onto it and forgot everything but the joy in knowing she was alive and unharmed. She tore herself from him, then bent to see his leg, the torn cloth soaked with blood. ''We've got to get him to medical help. I need a tourniquet.... Now!''

Gabriel's icy fear still held him. He didn't know if it was Miranda shaking, or his heart, trying to leap free of his body. He wrapped a fist in her collar and tugged her upright in front of him. His fear shifted into anger. ''You could have been killed. What are you doing up here?''

She dashed away her tears with her glove, her eyes fierce and green and lashing at him. ''Tracking that cat. His prints are all over your yard. Then I saw them heading in the same direction as your regular trail— it was muddy and the prints were clear—and I

couldn't bear to have him hurt your less than affectionate hide. You had no business placing yourself
between him and me. If you had only stayed out of
this, you wouldn't have gotten hurt. Now see what
you've done.''

Now see what you've done.... The words seemed
to echo in the distance and Gabriel shook his head to
clear the weak, drowsy feeling. Perhaps it was his
reaction to the shock of seeing Miranda facing the
cat. Perhaps it was the toll of fear—

"I'm sorry I shot you in the butt with that tranquilizer, dear heart,'' Miranda was saying somewhere
near him as his head went floating off into the wind
and his body sagged heavily into the men's arms. She
bent low to him and tugged the stinging dart from his
backside. "I was aiming for the cougar. We'd better
get out of here, guys, before that cat comes awake.
It's a pretty light dose, that's why I thought a second
one might be okay. Please be careful with Gabriel.''

"We've been with this guy for five days and four
nights, lady. He's made out of leather,'' one of the
photographers said in the distance. Gabriel tried to
make his mouth move, but his lips were thick and
useless, his tongue not obeying his command.

"Shush. He could hear you. You'll hurt his feelings. He's very sensitive about some things. Come
on, let's move. We'll use my sleeping bag to fashion
a stretcher for him,'' Miranda crooned from another
galaxy. Her voice came harder then, more determined
as Gabriel struggled against the heavy weight in his
brain and body. "An emergency medical kit? Great.
Whiskey? Great, the alcohol will disinfect the wound.
Make that stretcher—cut holes in the bottom of the

bag and put those two branches through the bag. Give me a knife, someone. I'll disinfect and wrap this.''

Cold liquid poured over his leg and pain seared through him, bringing Gabriel close to the surface, and he struggled to defend his pride and honor. ''I am not 'less than affectionate.' ''

The men's laughter angered him, but there was little he could do as he drifted off again. He was barely aware of the trek down the mountain, and then Dr. Thomas White, a frequent visitor to Freedom Valley, was bending over him. Dressed in slacks and a matching vest, Thomas's immaculate dress shirt was folded back at the cuffs. ''I was just passing through on the road to Freedom when the call came in from Ella, the sheriff. Seems like one of your photographer guests has more sense than you do and packs a mobile telephone. I was here when they packed you in like a big game trophy. Seems like you had a nice sleep down the mountain, except for rousing enough to spout some pretty romantic stuff—something about the grass-green of her eyes, the petals of her lips—''

When Thomas caught Gabriel's scowl, he paused, grinned and then continued. ''She's done a fine job, keeping you off that leg. The wound isn't bad and you've got a few minor scratches. You lost some blood and the exertion as you fought with the cougar—when combined with the tranquilizer—caused you to go night-night pretty quickly. Offhand, I'd say you'd been missing some sleep—probably working on those neat little romantic phrases, like 'the sunlight of my heart' and 'wild rose beauty.' You've got a few stitches and probably a scar or two—good bragging material for those children you'll probably have one day.''

"He's angry and pouting," Miranda said quietly. "He didn't want me to help him."

Thomas chuckled. "He's the old-fashioned type. He's brooding because you've stolen his thunder. He wanted to protect you and I would say that he did his job. That cat could have hurt you badly before falling asleep. Gabriel had the strength to hold it off, until the tranquilizer did its job."

Lying in his bed, Gabriel ignored Thomas, and found Miranda in the shadows. He had stoically managed to let her sponge his face and neck, because the unique sensation of her fretting over him, tending him with such care, was too enticing to resist. His adamant protest had died the moment she placed her hand on his forehead. "You endangered yourself. You could have been killed."

"Mr. Deerhorn thinks he's the only person who can lend a helping hand. He resents his current position of being the person who needs help. I chose to go up that mountain. I was safe enough until you entered the ball game. I read the directions for the tranquilizers that you keep on hand. I am sorry to have shot you, though."

"She's a highly intelligent woman, who can make do under the worst of circumstances. She stayed behind to tranquilize the cougar again when it started to come to—giving the men more time to get you to safety.... If you hadn't been wrestling with that cougar, she wouldn't have shot you in the butt, old man," Thomas murmured, his narrow, aristocratic face alight with pleasure.

The men's voices outside Gabriel's bedroom echoed in what seemed to be a toast. "Here's to Old Shot in the Butt!"

"I know where she hit me," Gabriel returned too sharply and resented his frustration as he slid once more into sleep.

When he awoke, it was to the sound of his tractor revving up the morning. The smell of coffee filled the house, his leg throbbed, and after his sponge bath, the bandage didn't fit well inside his jeans. Managing to dress in jeans and a flannel shirt, Gabriel limped to the kitchen and resented his weakness. Morning sunlight slashed through the windows as he poured the coffee, sipping it. At least the men were gone now, their taunting cheer still hovering in the silence of his home.

On the countertop was a stack of large glossy black-and-white photographs from one of the men. A note explained that he had developed them in the kitchen sink with a very adept student, Miranda. Several photographers had added their notes, thanking him for the best action shots they'd had in their careers. Bracing himself, Gabriel studied the photographs, one by one—just there, Miranda, looking small and helpless against the highland meadow, dotted with snow, the cougar poised on the rock above her. In black-and-white, Gabriel and Fletcher blended with the trees. Gabriel's profile was hard, a hunter determined to bring down his prey. Miranda's face was white with fear, her eyes rounded as he moved in front of her. The cat's fangs were bared, muscles standing out in relief. One photograph was of the beast flying in midair with Gabriel beneath its shadow. The nightmare of the attack had been caught, and then the still body of the cat.

He'd held Miranda so close—he could feel the shaking of her body still, the fear leaping around them. One photograph held his attention—Gabriel had tugged Miranda's head back. The mountain wind had caught his shaggy hair, her sleek silky mass, and tossed them together, framing her fierce defiance, his primitive emotions in stark black-and-white.

Gabriel pushed away the close-up of the dart in his backside and frowned at the pictures of Miranda working over him, the men loading him onto the makeshift stretcher. Outside his house, the tractor revved and Gabriel limped to the doorway. The sun told him it was midmorning, the long furrows in his front door told him that the cougar had come calling.

Miranda swung the tractor and set the plow's tines into the rich earth. Breaking ground for the new garden gave her something to do while Gabriel rested up for another round of arguing with her. Within her gloves, her hands were shaking on the controls of Gabriel's tractor. He was limping toward her, and just as she had expected, his expression was that of lightning and thunder.

He'd been so pale, the blood gushing from the long scores on his thigh, soaking his jeans. The image of the man and the beast rolling on the mud and the snow would terrify her forever.

In the bright sunlight, Gabriel's hackles were up, a scowl etched on his darkly tanned face. Clearly he was set on an argument. Well, so was she. She'd lain beside him, soothed him as he tossed in his nightmares and tried to place the quaking fear into the past. His wounds could have been much more serious, but perhaps Gabriel was part leather—at least he was strong and had protected himself as best he could. *He'd placed himself between her and danger without a qualm....*

This morning, his expression said she was in for a scolding. Gabriel's emotions were usually so tightly leashed that she wanted to tear them away into the fresh spring air, revealing the deep natural emotions of the man. Tranquilized, he had murmured the most romantic phrases she'd ever heard, and they were all for her. He spoke of his heart leaping like a rabbit at the sight of her, how her skin was pale as cream, her scent of wild roses, that she was his woman of wind and fire— *How dare he hoard all that from her?*

She turned off the tractor, leaped from it and marched across the plowed ground toward him. She whipped off the red bandanna covering her hair. "Feeling better?" she asked briskly.

Gabriel scowled down at her, erasing the image of the romantic, tranquilized man holding her hand, kissing it. Once she had bent close to hear him whisper how he felt in her arms, filling her, feeling her glove him, his body pouring into hers, the fire of his passion for her....

Now Gabriel's tone ripped across the crisp March morning. No 'sweetheart,' no 'wild rose of my heart,' no 'thank you very much' or 'I love you.' "When was that cat here?" he asked harshly.

Her temper simmering, Miranda could have flung herself at him. "Before it took off the mountain after you. You're going after it, aren't you?"

"Someone has to. The wildlife people will probably mark and transport it elsewhere."

"Just like you'd like to do with me, right?" *Oh, Gabriel. Take me in your arms like you did then, let me know how much you care and that you want me so fiercely that nothing can take me away....*

"I don't want you working my place."

"I'm plowing a garden, not logging. Though at this moment, I'm so angry with you that I could take down a forest and not even be winded."

"A man should take care of his woman." His deep, soft voice was ragged, though he looked off into the pasture where the horses were grazing.

"Cannot a woman take care of her man, Gabriel?" she asked softly.

His cold black gaze swung down to her. "You don't belong here. This incident just proves me right. You could have been killed."

She shrugged and nodded. "Mark another one of my choices up to your side."

"Be logical. You're a remarkable woman. You belong—"

She walked toward the house, leaving him standing in the field. She had her pride, too, and she wouldn't ask him to reconsider. She wouldn't argue. She wouldn't—

Gabriel caught the door she tried to slam behind her, just a brief release for the frustration, anger and emotions storming her. She wrapped her arms around her body, unable to move, to leave him, when so much of her wanted to hold him, to love him, to hear those dark lush whispers of his passion.

His breath was harsh behind her, then he was tugging her back against him, wrapping his arms tight around her. His deep voice was uneven and urgent against her ear. "You think I don't want you? You, the other part of my heart and soul? When will you hate me, I wonder? When will you see that I can give you so little?"

"Is it only for *you* to give, Gabriel? Are you only comfortable in that one-way street where you are the provider and the protector? I'm a complete package now, Gabriel, and it is not in my nature to be helpless. If you can understand nature, and live with it, why can't you deal with who I am now?" *He gave her so much, that intricate, delicate part of him that no one had seen, the beauty of his soul, the gentleness of his heart.*

He spun her toward him, his expression fierce and desperate. He cupped her face within his roughly callused palms, scanning her expression. "You terrify me," he whispered simply before taking her mouth with undisguised passion.

She understood the need to celebrate life, to grasp it and revel in the survival of a past danger. She opened herself to him, taking from him, meeting that burning passion as his hand found her breast and cherished it softly. The fever rose between them and suddenly Gabriel stilled, the sound of tearing cloth echoing in the room. He shook, his hand trembling as he lifted it away from the flannel shirt she wore, the buttonholes torn free to reveal the dangling strap of her lacy bra.

Gabriel paled slightly, shaking his head as if to clear it, and Miranda wouldn't let him retreat. She reached for his cotton shirt and tore it open. "I want you just as badly now. Let me know what you really feel. Tell me with your body, if not with words.''

He hesitated, seemingly caught between the wars of his logic, his heart and his body. The burning fever of his hand touched her breast, then with a tug tore the remaining lace away. Holding her eyes, he eased her jacket away and bent to unlace her boots, removing them. His hands skimmed up her legs, her hips, unbuttoning her jeans to slide them away with her briefs.

Then Gabriel was carrying her to his bed, his mouth hot and sweet and hungry and urgent. He placed her onto his bed, the rumpled blankets carrying his scent. His trembling hands, the way he fumbled with his clothing, told her that he was deeply moved, anxious not to hurt her and yet driven by his own need for completion.

This was the real Gabriel, she thought, the layers gone, his eyes burning down the length of her body, consuming her, taking away her breath with that hunter's hungry look. He came to her quickly, his hands smoothing her body, finding her intimately, and caressing her.

The rough gauze reminded her of his painful wound and she pushed away from him, bracing her hands against his shoulders. That quick, dark expression told her too much, that he thought she refused him. Miranda wrapped her hands in his hair, drawing his head down, feasting upon his mouth to leave no doubt of her need. In the shadows, she briefly noted his honed features, the flush on his cheeks and the hardness of his body arched against hers.

Then his mouth was moving over her skin, nipping,

tasting, kissing. She cried out as he reached her breasts, suckling and giving her exquisite pleasure. "You're burning," he whispered roughly, cupping her, his fingers invading her delicately. "Soft and tight and so sweet."

She dug her fingers into the powerful muscles of his shoulders, her hips stirring restlessly against his touch, her legs moving along his. "Please be careful of your wound."

His tender smile curved along her stomach. "You would ask that of me now?" he chided gently. "When all of me is dying to fill you? When my skin is bursting with the need to become one with you? To feel your body move against me? To know that you soar with me into the fire? That the song of your release is too sweet to describe?"

"You're teasing me," she whispered shakily, uncertain of Gabriel's mood, when she had expected him to take her immediately.

"The honey of your skin is not a taste I can forget. I'm honored that you battle to give me such joy." His tongue flicked her naval, his hand spanning her belly. "Woman of fire and wind."

"Is that how you see me?" She quivered as his warm face pressed against her breasts, nuzzling them tenderly.

"Maybe." His answer came too lightly, tormenting her. He studied her breasts, tracing a finger enticingly over the sensitized surface, the jutting of her hardened nipples. With that, Gabriel eased to his back, his arms behind his head, and shot her a sultry, burning look beneath his lashes. "Be gentle," he whispered in a deep tone that curled around her.

She hadn't suspected that he would play, when his lovemaking had been so consuming, so serious and driving. She smiled and moved upon him. She closed her eyes and gave herself to the wonderful sensation of Gabriel's desire filling her, his hands opened and locked on her hips, caressing her. She rocked gently, bracing her hands on his chest, giving herself to the pleasure. "Oh, I intend to be very gentle and very thorough. Statistics prove that men like—"

"Concentrate on this man, song of my heart."

Nine

There is a part of any man which resists the woman selecting him as her mate, for he would like to think he has made that choice. The man's instincts are still to hunt and bring the woman to his lair—and so it is that we sometimes let them have their way.

Anna Bennett's Journal

Gabriel sat on his haunches, studying Anna's house in the night. He was bone-tired from tracking and tagging the cougar with the wildlife agent. The animal was now in a holding cage and would be relocated.

Gabriel's hunting blood was too restless to settle for the night, and Miranda was not in his house. What had he expected? She was a woman to make her own decisions.

She was still angry with him, for the years they had lost, for taking away her choice. He had felt the fine, prickling edge of her temper, though they had made love. She'd wanted to go with him, was nettled when he refused. But Gabriel couldn't bear the thought of her near that beast again.

What drove him to run on foot through the night, in the old way, hunting what his heart must have for peace? Though he had only run five miles, taking the paths that would bring him more quickly to Anna's house, he would have crossed much more to have her this night.

"'Less than affectionate,'" he repeated, the phrase nipping at him. He glanced at the moon, pine trees spiking silhouettes across it. A fastidious man, he smelled of campfire smoke and leather and of battle. He should have stopped at his house, showered, rested and gotten his need for her under control. And yet, he couldn't wait to hold her. The wildfire in his blood was not in his experience, the need to capture the treasure that had escaped him.

Gabriel rubbed his jaw, considering the yellow squares of light shooting from Anna's windows onto the ground. The ache in his heart could not let him rest until he saw Miranda, despite the fatigue lodged in his muscles. Without turning from his view of Anna's house, he frowned at deer moving through the brush. He recognized their sounds, understood their ways, but not his own.

A woman's shadow moved across the upstairs windows and Gabriel wondered if she were packing, preparing to leave. He held very still, listening to the night and to the hard beat of his heart, focusing inside himself. Lying beside him, Fletcher panted, his pink tongue dangling, and waited for his master's command.

Fifteen minutes later, Gabriel frowned at the locked door separating him from his quarry. His knock unanswered, Gabriel circled the house, located a big tree and began to climb. Five minutes later, he shoved open an upstairs window and entered Miranda's bedroom. Moonlight shafted through the window's lacy curtains, laying patterns over the quilt on the single bed, the dolls' faces staring at him from their shelf. On the dresser were framed pictures, an array of feminine bottles and a braided rug cut from old clothing covered the wooden floor. The light rectangular place on the floor was where Miranda's hope chest had stood, and now it was in his home.

He noted the open laptop computer on a small wooden desk, small gold earrings gleaming beside it. Gabriel's senses stopped as he studied the electronic tool that she would use in her work. Did the challenges of her career call to that bright, quick mind? Was she feeling the need to step back into business? How soon would she leave?

How could he keep her? Did he deserve to have her now?

How could he keep her? his mind repeated, while his body knew that she was his tonight—if she would have him. *For he needed her like the air he breathed, like the sun that warmed the earth....* Already his blood was rushing into the fever that was Miranda.

Gabriel carefully removed his denim jacket and hung it on the desk's chair. The masculine clothing was at odds with the lace and ruffles, giving him the same pleasure as when he looked at their coats, side by side, her smaller boots placed neatly beside his. Those were images he would carry in his mind forever, having no need of a camera to hold them. In his mind, he was married, for he would never love another woman as he did Miranda. Pinned by a moonlit square, slipping through the window's lace, Gabriel considered his well-worn comfortable tracking moccasins. In his heart, he was coming home to the woman of his soul, because she gave him strength and peace. The sound of the shower drew him to the bathroom, and Miranda's body, blurred by the frosted glass, beckoned to him. Scented of her, the steamy air curled around him. Gabriel stood very still, the scent and the woman a seduction.

Caught in the mirror, his image was that of a hunter—that narrowed look, features honed within the rough cut of his long hair, body taut and prepared to move. Gabriel glanced at the feminine lace hung on the back of the door, crushed it in his fist, holding it tightly for a moment as he would soon hold Miranda—if she would have him.

He should have called—he should have waited.

He smiled briefly, mocking himself. But then he couldn't wait, could he? His need for her was too strong.

Miranda inhaled sharply, the glass shower door sliding open and a tall, naked man dipped his head to enter. "Gabriel!"

In the small steamy enclosure, he looked so drained and weary, lines deeper on his brow, his hair untamed and damp now against his throat. He needed care and rest, she thought, and noted with pleasure as she glanced lower, that Gabriel needed more— He filled the space, towering over her, and then shook his head as if dazed at finding himself with her.

"Have a nice hunt?" she asked lightly, as though he were just coming home from a day's work at the office, not the dangerous trek to hunt the cougar. He was uncertain of her now, and of himself.

He was safe. She could have leaped upon him, taken him, burned with him and yet, Miranda wanted to savor the moment—for he had come to her, placing all else aside. She squirted herbal shampoo into her palms, rubbed them together and lifted her hands to massage Gabriel's hair. He lifted his head, his expression disdaining the feminine scent and then he settled into her touch. His eyes closed slightly, and she sensed the easing of that taut, wary mood riding him.

Miranda smoothed his face and he sighed slowly, relaxing slightly. How wonderful, she thought, as this tall, powerful man gave himself to her touch. Using her sponge laden with shower gel, she slathered his shoulders, admiring the strength in them, the gentleness that came of his consideration and control. His heart pounded heavily beneath her soapy palms and Miranda smiled, working lower, caressing him, soothing that hard, taut body as she moved. She traced the healing scars on his thigh, mourning his pain, and the vision of Gabriel taking the cougar's charge shot icily through her for just a moment. Then rising, she came against him, sleek and soft. She held that hungry black gaze as she slid her arms around him to soap his back.

"You're enjoying this. That I would come to you

first,'' he whispered roughly as the shower hissed around them. He had not touched her, his hands curled into fists at his side. His unsteady mood swept through the steam, his wariness of her an excitement that drew her on.

''You've never bathed with a woman, have you, Gabriel?''

''No.'' The answer was curt and warning, yet telling her that he'd given her more intimacy than he wished.

She strolled a fingertip down his cheek and circled that grim mouth. ''Turnabout is fair play, you know.''

Gabriel reached behind her and turned off the water. ''But then, you've already had your shower, haven't you?'' he asked, before shoving aside the door and circling her with his arms, lifting her out.

She almost smiled at the hurried way he swished the towel around her, as if she were his prize to carry off, to claim. Just once he searched her expression. ''This is your mother's house,'' he noted unevenly. ''I would not want to dishonor Anna.''

''She would want you here—with me.''

He lightly tugged a damp strand of her hair. His words were an uneven mix of whimsy and need, as though he had dreamed of her. ''I had hoped you would be waiting in my bed.''

''I'm not a woman to wait, Gabriel. Especially not now,'' she whispered and locked her arms around his shoulders. He was warm and safe and strong against her. She'd been terrified for him, afraid that this time the cougar's fangs would find that muscled throat, tearing—

''You need me.'' The tone was arrogant, masculine

and pleased, and Gabriel's grin teased her. Then that dark, fierce hunger coursed through his expression, his arms tugging her close. In the next heartbeat, Gabriel dived in to take—just as she wanted.

Whatever instinct that caused Gabriel to come straight to her, to need her to soothe him, Miranda rejoiced in the truth of that wonder. She reveled in how his hands roamed over her, shaking and possessing as they caressed. She met the fierce hunger of his mouth, fused to hers, slanting for a tighter fit, tongues playing, suckling. Suddenly he lifted her higher, her toes inches off the floor as he carried her, kissing her all the while, back to her bed.

Fire and flash, skin burning, Gabriel came down upon her. There was that hard hunter's look as he studied her, his hands possessing her, tormenting her. She did not fear that look, but reveled in it. Shaking with passion, she lifted to kiss his throat, to taste that dark, mysterious exotic skin. He inhaled roughly as she bit him gently, kissing the small wound. When she caught that flat nipple in her lips, tugging at it, Gabriel let out a muffled shout, jerking fractionally away from her.

In the shadows, his narrowed eyes burned at her as she arched beneath him. Gabriel's trembling hand slid down her hip, then to her thigh, stroking her. ''You're a furnace, sweet Miranda.''

She smoothed his long, powerful back, his firm buttocks and slid him a look. She loved being desired, flirting a bit, a game she'd never played. ''Miss me, did you?''

Gabriel nuzzled her neck, her ears, her forehead and nibbled at her ears. He rubbed his chest side to side, looking as if he were luxuriating in the softness of her breasts, the hardened nipples etching his skin. There was that quick, hot look down at their bodies as if the sight gave him unexpected delight. "I feared for my backside every step."

She laughed at that, a wild, free joy soaring through her. Above her, Gabriel was too still, watching her and when the laughter faded, she met his hunger, his body coming sleekly into her keeping. The pounding hunger rose quickly, once, twice and Gabriel held her poised, tormenting her as the riveting pleasure tore her apart. "Beast," she whispered shakily, her heart pounding violently.

He moved slowly then, surely, fulfilling them both and leaving her limp and breathless within his arms. His mouth leisurely roamed her breasts, then he turned her to her stomach, kissing a trail down to the small of her back. She tensed as those white teeth nipped her bottom lightly, playfully. Then he moved to cover her, his face pressed into her throat, his lips tantalizing. "I think it is you who missed me."

"Smug, arrogant—"

Then Gabriel turned her again and this time the taking was sweeter, almost dreamlike, until he rested gently upon her. She listened to the night and to her heart, and smiled, for this time, Gabriel could not deny whatever burned between them. He hadn't argued about what was best for her, or made any choices other than following his instincts. She kissed his forehead and smoothed that wonderful back, and wondered how his child would look, lying as closely to her breast.

In the morning, Miranda stood fully dressed in her

business slacks suit, studying the man in her bed. Clearly exhausted from his hunt and from the love-making throughout the night, Gabriel slept heavily. The flower print of her sheets and pillowcases only emphasized the dark power of his body, those rippling muscles as he sprawled. She couldn't resist bending to kiss the small of his back, admiring the cords and muscles that quivered from the light touch.

He'd come to her, not taking time to control his need to see her. That gift alone was enough to cause her to smile all the way to Noah Douglas's Investment Service office.

Later that morning, Gabriel stiffened as Koby Austin walked along beside him on Freedom's unique historical street, lined with two-story buildings. Koby sniffed the air. "Smells like spring flowers or a woman's shampoo—uh, oh, that's you, isn't it, Old Shot in the Butt."

Gabriel's dark look caused Koby to grin. "A legend in your own time. Shot by the woman who is courting you. Helpless as a baby— Okay, I see you're not exactly happy this morning."

When Koby strolled down to the Wagon Wheel for his morning coffee break, Gabriel glanced at the men on the street. Every one of them grinned back at him. Apparently the whole town knew of Miranda's ill-fated shot. Koby was right, Gabriel wasn't in a good mood. When he'd awakened, he'd expected Miranda to…his expectations were wrong. Tanner had explained that Miranda had taken two part-time jobs and her pickup was now parked beside Noah Douglas's sleek black Mercedes. John Lachlan at the bank was her other employer. Gabriel frowned, uncomfortable with his dark, surly mood. Both men were known wife-hunters and Miranda would be a match to either one.

He entered the feed store, and filled a small sack with beans for the garden she had tilled. He studied the bag and knew that Miranda could have her own garden at Anna's. Which would she choose? Would she come back to him?

Gabriel rubbed his jaw, considering the bins of seeds. He had not taken time to plant a garden, but then he hadn't had a woman to please, either. In quick order, he filled other sacks with lettuce, corn and squash. He glanced at the sticks that would become berries and thought of how Miranda enjoyed serving homemade wine, remembering her mother's recipes for jams. He added those to his purchase and John, the clerk, looked over his glasses at Gabriel. ''Doing a little spring shopping before going hunting, are you? I see you're wearing those moccasins and you've got that sharp, eagle-eyed look as when you were tracking that renegade bear. Heard you got that cougar, and those photographers passing through town said the pictures of you tangling with it were going to be in the magazines. Reckon even celebrities take time to make spring gardens. You've never been in here buying seed before. It's a first garden for you, is it? Say, you never answered me. Are you going on another hunt?''

Gabriel thought of the woman he needed to see this morning, and nodded, then exited the feed store. He could have cooked her breakfast, tried for less head-on, demanding, possessive lover technique, immediately bedding her. Even a stallion might nuzzle a mare before mating.... He wanted to be affectionate, dammit. He opened the door to the office and removed his Western hat, holding it in one hand and his other arm filled with the sack of his feed store purchases.

Miranda stood next to Noah as they studied the paperwork columns on an ultramodern desk. Gabriel froze; they looked so much in tune, Miranda suiting the upscale look of Noah, her gray slacks suit expensive and fluid as she straightened. Her watch was slim and practical as was the dainty beaded chain around her throat. Her gray pumps said she liked comfort as she worked, the cream silk blouse completing the picture of a businesswoman not often seen in Freedom Valley. Her bright look, that rosy flush, reminded him of the passion they'd shared as he braced himself to— To do what? It was her right to choose her life, not his.

Would her former lover come for her? Would she take him again?

"Gabriel," Noah murmured, his gray eyes taking in Gabriel's clothing, his tracking moccasins, and the way his fist gripped his hat.

"Noah." Gabriel wished he had changed; Noah's three-piece suit was classy and expensive. His hands weren't rough and callused, and his financial resources were enough to buy Miranda anything she wanted. Gabriel's fingers tightened on the paper sack and it rustled slightly. Miranda seemed like a creature from another world—sleek, modern, efficient—moving toward him. He was stunned by her kiss as she stood on tiptoe, her hand curving behind his head to draw his lips down to hers.

Gabriel trembled, shocked that she would exhibit such affection so openly. Her lips burned his and—Had he imagined that playful nip of her teeth? His heart leaped, bursting with pleasure, and when she drew away, he resisted the urge to pack her over his shoulder and take her home where she belonged. He pushed back that old-fashioned instinct to claim her, for he would have to learn new ways if he was to keep her, to please her. "You'll wait for me, won't you, Gabriel? I'll be just a little bit longer here and then I'd like to buy you lunch, if you have time?"

Time? He'd already waited a lifetime. Yet the custom of the woman to provide for him rankled. "I have time," he said, and eased into a chair in the waiting area.

She is a warrior, he thought, watching Miranda punch keys on her laptop, showing the results to Noah. A printer began to purr, spitting out paper, and Miranda whipped the list from the machine, studying it. She quickly circled items, recalculated the statistics and showed the results to Noah. Gabriel sucked in his breath as Noah bent over her desk, nodding as she showed him the results of her study. "You've done it. You've pinpointed the best balanced retirement fund mix that I can offer my farming and ranching clients. Make this a full-time job, Miranda, and you can name your price."

Noah hugged her briefly, took one look at Gabriel and cleared his throat. "I'll just take these back to the office and study them."

After he had gone, Miranda tugged up her suit sleeve, glanced at her watch and smiled. "Time for lunch. Ready, Gabriel?"

She frowned at the blond man entering the glass doors, careful of the huge wrapped presents he carried, topped by a toy panda bear. Dressed in a stylish black leather jacket, his crisp waving hair was neatly trimmed, his black sweater and flowing black pants were obviously tailored and expensive. His loafers were "city" and highly polished. He moved toward her, smiling warmly, clearly at home in the office setting.

"Scott," Miranda murmured softly, and Gabriel tensed at her tone. This was her former lover, a man who propped his designer sunglasses above his head. Gabriel noted the sleek red sports car parked outside.

At last, the father of her child had come to make amends. Gabriel breathed quietly, aware of Miranda's flush as she glanced at him. Rough and wearing his hunting clothing, he must look shabby in comparison to the well-groomed man she had loved, arms brimming with presents. The sack Gabriel held rustled—his gift to her of garden seeds and blackberry starts.

As they stood together, Miranda and the man, Gabriel thought that they were a matched pair—stylish, businesslike, expensive.

Then she stared at the gifts, the reminder of her lost baby obviously sharp and painful, the man's voice was smooth and cultured as he talked to her. Though the words were indistinct, the plea was there, a man trying to recover a treasure he had tossed away. Gabriel noted the pale color of her cheeks, the way her fingers gripped the toy bear, her expression rigid. She shook her head, her mouth moving, but the office was silent.

Gabriel could feel her pain—leaping within her,

tearing at her. He hadn't realized he was standing, moving toward her to protect her.

"It's my baby. I want to see it. You can't deny me that," Scott was saying. "Look, Miranda. I made a terrible mistake. My mother and dad want to know their grandchild. We'll work this out—"

"Will we?" Miranda's voice was hard, cutting through the shadows. "You're a little late, Scott. I lost the baby."

"You deliberately—" Scott swung to look at Gabriel, taking in his rough appearance. "Who's this?"

Gabriel smiled tightly and placed his sack on the floor. He stood slowly, and Miranda's eyes widened at the cold, silent threat. "You're not in this, Gabriel. I'll handle—"

"Am I not?" Gabriel's words were spaced and extremely careful.

"You don't waste any time, do you, Miranda?" Scott asked harshly. "Was it really my baby? Or his?"

Five seconds later, Scott stormed out of the glass doors, taking the presents with him. His red sports car roared out of Freedom.

Noah leaned against the wall, his arms folded, and grinned at Gabriel. "Well, that was something you don't see every day—Miranda slugging a man."

Gabriel grinned back as Miranda paced back and forth, muttering to herself, gesturing wildly with her hands. "True."

"She's got a mean right cross," Noah said. "I'd remember that, if I were you, Gabriel."

"I…am…a logical person, a lady, and…I have never, ever hit anyone like that before," Miranda said, shaking her head as if to clear it. Her hand trembled as she stared at it. "To think that he would have the nerve—"

Noah chuckled. "I bet he won't again, whatever he did."

"Men!" Miranda continued to pace and mutter and then glared at Gabriel. "I was only defending you. He could have hurt you."

At that Noah roared with laughter, doubling over. Miranda turned like a gunfighter, eyeing him and Noah blinked, his laughter dying. "What did I do?"

She frowned at Gabriel and took his jacket in both her fists, trying to shake him. "Don't say one word. And do not tell Kylie or Tanner about this. Do not tell anyone. I can't believe I— Uh!"

"Sometimes you talk too much," Gabriel said as he patted the soft backside draped over his shoulder. He took the sack Noah placed into his free arm and strolled through the open door, carrying Miranda.

On the street, Gabriel placed her on her feet, let her straighten her clothing and search furiously for words. Then he took her hand and drew it to his lips, sucking her fingers one by one as she stared, stunned, at him. "Thank you for defending me," he said softly and tried to smother his grin.

"Arrogant, hardheaded, muscle-bound— You can't just pick me up and tote me down half a block, saying 'Nice day, isn't it?' to anyone you meet, and—" Miranda paused, licked her lips and the look she gave him all the way down and all the way up caused his blood to heat. In his mind, he saw her nestled beside him, her body pale against his. He saw her laughing up at him, the wind tossing her hair, her cheeks rosy.

Miranda shivered and said, "If you keep looking at me like that, we won't make it to lunch. I'll have to cancel my afternoon job at John's bank."

"You like working with numbers, don't you? It's a game for you, isn't it?"

"I do…yes. But there are other things I enjoy, too. Something I do not enjoy is having you look at me in an office and watching your thoughts cross your face. You think I'm leaving, don't you? That I'm off to some fictitious high-paying job, some penthouse, some world without you."

"It is not for me to say," he stated carefully, because she had captured his thoughts too perfectly. He wasn't certain he liked her ability to interpret his expressions, especially when he thought he had them hidden. "But I would come to you, my woman, my heart."

"You can say the loveliest things," she whispered, studying him with that sultry look that said she, too, remembered their passion.

At the Wagon Wheel Café, Gabriel nodded at Fidelity who was stealthily considering Luigi as he circled Willa. "I see you two are working at this relationship. Five points, Gabriel. I saw how you squired Miranda down the street and held her hand. I worried about the lack of affection—those little demonstrative hugs and looks that are unique to people in love."

"It is for Miranda that I allow myself to be courted," Gabriel said stiffly, ill at ease with the thought that she would be paying for his meal.

"Of course. You are endearing yourself to all the Women of the Council by the way you are allowing her to set the rules. We had thought that you might be difficult in accepting our traditions. You're very old-fashioned in your way, too.''

''I may change the rules, but it does not mean that they are less honored,'' Gabriel warned softly, and was unprepared for Fidelity's delighted chuckle.

''But of course,'' she said as if she had expected him to challenge the Founding Mothers' traditions.

When they were seated in a booth, Gabriel placed the feed store sack on the seat beside him. He stiffened when Miranda's foot slid up his leg and her toes rested intimately on his thigh. He reached for her foot, caressing it. ''Having fun?''

She grinned and his heart leaped again, filled with sunshine. ''More than you know. What's in the sack?''

''Beans…corn…blackberry starts…for you.'' He was embarrassed that he had not brought a gift more suiting a lover.

''For me?'' Miranda's delighted tone caused Gabriel to relax slightly. ''How did you know? Oh, I…'' She stood slightly, bent over the booth and reached for him. Her kiss left Gabriel shaking and dazed. He leaned back in the booth, tried to breathe and tried to stop from glowing as Miranda carefully unpacked the small sacks from the large one, lining them up on the booth's table.

''This morning, I emptied the rest of your mother's jars and washed them.''

Her eyes were shimmering with tears. ''You knew how difficult that was for us, how much we missed her.''

''It was a small thing to do.''

''No, it wasn't. It was very, very thoughtful.

Mother's jars were so special to her. She took great care with them. Some of them came from her mother. I missed canning with her, filling those jars. Every cucumber had to be standing upright, matched in size, for dill pickles, the bread and butter sweet pickles sliced exactly right. A handful of less than ripe strawberries added to the jam mix, to keep the taste more fresh. Green beans had to be snapped just so. Nothing was wasted, even the green tomatoes were pickled before the frost came. She had such a hard financial time after Dad died. But she raised us without a complaint.''

Gabriel took her hands and bent to place his face within them. The tenderness in the gesture was unreserved, for Gabriel was a caring man. She knew he grieved with her, understood her heart. She knew he feared for her passage, for the day when the world challenged her again and she would leave him.

Sally Jo, the waitress appeared to take their order, pad in hand. ''Oh, my goodness. He is just so romantic. I saw him carry you out of the office. I'd love to have a man come for me like that, leaving no doubt to me or anyone else that he wanted me.''

Gabriel straightened, still holding Miranda's hands in his. His smile at Sally Jo was devastating. ''I am certain that, as lovely as you are, you have many men wanting you.''

Sally Jo stared blankly at him, then she blurted, ''I heard you didn't like women. That you were a mountain man avoiding female companionship. But how you do sweet-talk.''

Miranda studied Gabriel's charming smile, and his dark, contemplative look at her. She didn't trust that secretive, pleased-with-himself look, or the too-innocent one that followed it.

That look lasted throughout lunch, and Gabriel didn't object when she paid the bill as she had expected. He walked her to the bank and her afternoon job, bent to kiss her cheek as though he were a friend, not a lover. She'd expected a kiss to match his tenderness earlier, and yet the brush of his lips was almost impersonal. He strolled off down the street without another look back at her.

Miranda watched him, her hands on her waist. Gabriel had his edges, his moods and his games. She wasn't certain she'd forgiven him yet, for all those years they'd lost. Or for not giving her that kiss.

That night, he came to her again, leaving no doubt of his wildfire passion for her. She met him out there on that naked, hot plane, where every touch seared, every pulse and heartbeat matched, riveting and devouring them. And in the morning, Gabriel was gone.

Ten

There comes a time when what was important isn't any longer, replaced by truth. If love is at the bottom of the barrel, then it must be freed and cleaned and polished and met and brought into the daylight.

Anna Bennett's Journal

Fully dressed for work, wearing a white short sleeve sweater beneath her black pantsuit, Miranda studied the sack of seedlings and packages of bulk garden seeds. Gabriel's gift said she could choose where to make her life and where to live it, as she wished—planting where she wished, or not. Her tiny tomato seedlings stretched toward morning sunlight, and her mother's pantry was neatly lined with clean jars.

It was April now, the earth bursting with promise,

sunshine dancing on the newly budded leaves in her mother's garden. Delicate small white Lily of the Valley blooms would soon appear, leading the way for the scarlet bleeding hearts. It was as if the earth waited for her to move forward, to know herself, and place the past behind her.

Miranda leaned back into the kitchen filled with memories, tears filling her eyes, her throat tightening with emotion. On the counter, the blackberry starts were no longer dried looking sticks, but had begun to sprout green leaves. Their roots needed to be set in firm, nourishing soil, just as she needed to set the foundation for her life.

Who courted whom? she asked herself, for Gabriel had come to her every night, the taste of hunger on his lips, the trembling of his hands telling her of his need. During the day, as she punched in numbers, calculated statistics and waited for the night, Miranda caught herself dreaming of him—the way he touched her, that dark closed look that said he had secrets of his own. Miranda placed her hand on her heart, listened to the beat, and knew that her time had come— Until now, she wasn't ready to read her mother's journals, too filled with mourning to bear the encounter.

But now it was time, and she picked up the telephone to call Noah and take the day off. Curling up on her mother's couch, Miranda opened the worn books, her mother's handwriting curving through them.

''Truth, above all, must be met, good or bad. When a woman chooses her path, a good man will wait for her decision. That is hard for the male species—waiting, when their very nature says to stake their claim.

But when a woman finds her truth, knows it in her heart, she should hold it dear and meet it full force. She will battle all odds to keep it safe,'' Anna had written. "I worry about Miranda, for she is trying too hard to please everyone, but herself. She has a bright, quick mind, and needs challenges. A woman's battles are not always in business and money, but sometimes she has to listen to her heart.''

Miranda held the journal close to her heart. She had watched her mother widowed, trying to provide for her family. Miranda studied so hard to achieve, to win those scholarships, to help her mother. She was a girl, fearing failure, pushing too hard. She'd dived into everything the community expected her to be— an honors student, witty, vivacious, filling her life with everything youth had to offer. At seventeen, she wouldn't have been ready for marriage, and her mother knew. Gabriel knew.

Two hours later, the midmorning sun slanted through the pine trees lining the road to Gabriel's ranch. She reached out her free hand and gripped the sack with the blackberry bushes and the seeds. Only Gabriel would understand how she needed to fill herself, just as she would fill her mother's canning jars. The need to see him, to tell him what she now understood, was urgent, but the eagerness of coming home leaped through her, too. It had been two weeks since she'd seen it, the log cabin nestled in the woods, the huge old weathered barn in the field. She'd been too intent upon getting back into the flow of work, mentally drained when she returned home. The weekends were filled with Gabriel, staying at her house, with family and friends, as she slid back into life in Freedom Valley.

The garden she had plowed had been tilled; the neat fence around it would keep it safe. In the field, calves played, and twenty of Gabriel's Appaloosa fed on the huge bales of hay—the new grass not enough yet to support them.

She had to tell him.

Miranda glanced at the framework of a new addition onto Gabriel's simple, but large log home. She parked her pickup and hurried inside, finding the house empty, his camera bag gone. Jessica didn't move from her couch pillow, eyeing Miranda. "I don't have time for catering to you now," Miranda said and stepped outside. In the distance, higher on the mountain, Fletcher's bark was faint but distinctive. She smiled briefly, recognizing the dog's sound as he played with his master.

She had to tell Gabriel.

The sun, high in the sky, signaled noon. She stripped away her light denim jacket, tying it around her waist and scanned the woods, pine and fir and brush shielding Gabriel from her. She opened the top buttons of her cotton blouse, and picked the briars from her torn jeans. On a high ledge, overlooking his ranch, Miranda placed her hand over her eyes, scanning the thick woods. Fletcher was quiet now, giving her no clues.

Birds darted over the high mountain meadow, with its yellow-green new grass. Coming up from the valley, warmer in winter than the mountains, a herd of deer bolted into the woods. Gabriel's tripod and cam-

era were set up near a blanket and she scanned the
dark, mysterious woods for him. "Gabriel?"

Then a tall shadow slid silently into the clearing
and Gabriel said, "Why are you here?"

She should have known he'd watched her; these
mountains were his home. She wanted the words to
come, willed them to her lips and failed. "I have to
talk with you."

"Talk." The order gave no softening encouragement, as if Gabriel braced himself for a hard blow.
He crossed his arms over his bare chest, the muscles
taut beneath his gleaming dark skin. One hard look
took in her blouse, her jeans and the moccasins he
had made, a feminine match for the ones he wore.

She knew he expected her to leave, to find a high-
paying job such as the ones she'd had, filled with
marvelous challenges to be met. Why were the words
so difficult?

"You've waited for me, all this time." Her statement was breathless with wonder.

He nodded slowly, his stance wary, his hair gleaming and tossed by the light April breeze as it crossed
the highland meadow. "You were my vision, the
woman in the smoke. I could do no less."

She scratched Fletcher's ears when he leaned
heavily against her, pressing his need for affection.
Miranda met Gabriel's dark, intense stare, his expression taut, those beautiful lips tightened. "You were
right all those years ago, Gabriel. I needed to prove
myself against the world. I needed to make the journey, and I needed to come home to you."

He inhaled sharply, muscles tightening across his
broad chest, the bright sunlight skimming those pow-

erful shoulders. Only the pulse running down his dark throat gave away his deep emotion.

"I would never have known who I was, the person that I am now, if I hadn't gone to college, succeeded at my career. Had you not made that decision, all those years ago, we might have married. All that talk from the school counselor and principal, the tests I'd taken to confirm my potential, might have haunted me later. It could have torn us apart. I might have resented what I'd never done or seen. Now I know, without doubt, that my path is with yours. Here, in these mountains with you."

He nodded slowly, watching her with that wary expression, those marvelous eyes shielded by his glossy long lashes. She walked those few feet to him. "You are a spiritual man, Gabriel. Your essence is here in these mountains. You gave me time, when you had none, letting me find my own path, leading back to you. Yet nothing has really changed between us since you gave me that wildflower bouquet. You tore away my heart, only to give it back to me stronger than before, more certain of my life."

He swallowed roughly, and she knew that he was waiting for her to finish. She placed her palm over his heart, and it leaped, racing into her keeping. "You are my challenge, Gabriel, my excitement that will never end."

"You will become my wife?" he asked unevenly, the shiver racking his tall body telling her of his uncertainty.

"Yes." She smiled up at him, bursting with joy and loving him. "Your grandmother, White Fawn, told you that long ago, didn't she?"

He nodded gravely. "She knew my vision would be true, and that my heart could belong to no other. But she knew that you were headstrong and independent and the pressures were on you to go to college and to succeed. She said a long journey awaited you and I could not influence your passage. I could only wait for you to make it. Then when you were so ill, I could wait no longer to claim you, to care for you. I wished it were true, that the child was mine and that he had lived."

She touched his cheek, skimming the rugged contours, those high, gleaming cheekbones, that strong jaw, his incredible tender mouth. "Tell me of the first time you made love to me."

Was it only a short time ago? Yet she remembered his trembling touch, the way his body hesitated, then those first still moments within her keeping as if he were uncertain. "Just now, you said White Fawn told you your vision was true. You are not an undiscriminating man, bedding any woman for your body's needs, and you have said that you tried. Then, I thought you feared for me, for my healing body. Now, I think it was that and something else."

Gabriel's expression closed, and she knew she had hit her mark. "That's quite some case," he noted darkly. "Cannot a man keep one secret, or must you have it, too?"

"Tell me, so that I have everything," she whispered, loving him even more.

His hands rose to stroke her hair, lifting the strands to gleam in the sunlight, blue-black as a raven's wing. Then he bent to her, his lips brushing hers. "I was already married, in my heart. How could I share my body with another woman, when it belonged to you?''

He kissed the tears shimmering on her lashes, brought by joy and love. ''You are my first and only love. That time was my first, and yet, I knew it could never be like that with another woman. I feared so that I would hurt you, that my body would bolt from my keeping. I will never forget that moment we became one.''

With the truth sweet upon the fresh mountain air, the sunshine dancing around them and in her heart, Miranda eased open the jacket's sleeves, knotted at her waist. ''Love me now,'' she whispered, suddenly shy of him, for he was new to her, this Gabriel, the man of her heart.

His fingertip skimmed the heat of her cheeks, then slid to her throat, and lower to open the buttons of her blouse. He undressed her solemnly, reverently, until she stood proudly before him, the woman that she had become.

Her hands moved over him, their gazes locked as his clothing fell to the meadow's new spring grass. His touch trembled, skimming her body, treasuring it as he bent to take her lips carefully, gently with his own. ''So long I have waited for you,'' he whispered unevenly as she slid her arms around him.

He swept her up in his arms, carrying her to the blanket he had used earlier, lowering her to it. He was her promise, her dream, her heart, coming to her. There would be other times, when hunger drove them to the crest, eager for the heat and fire. But now with the sunlight warming them, the scent of spring touching them, Gabriel entered her wordlessly, his body telling her of his love, of the truth running between them. Over her, his expression was tender. "The river of my love for you will never stop flowing."

She would carry those words with her forever, she thought before giving herself to the sweet taking.

Gabriel waited for Miranda to come to him. He leaned against his pickup, filled with items from Anna's house. Michael's and Tanner's pickups were also filled. The day had been long for Miranda, working with her brother and sister to separate her mother's things. It was a task each had placed aside, but the time had come to work together, each considerate of the other. Gabriel scanned Anna's two-story home, wrapped in the first of May sunlight; some of the contents had been divided among Tanner, Kylie and Miranda. It had been a hard day for each of them, memories swirling through the house, Anna's presence held close and dear. Anna's jars and canning necessities, her favorite pots and pans had been divided between the Bennett sisters and the jars would soon be in the addition's new pantry. Women's things, Gabriel thought, passed from mother to daughter, would be cherished in the Bennetts' new homes.

With the help of their friends and family, the new addition onto his home was more suiting a wife and a family. Miranda had worked beside him, though he disdained her helping, and each night she came softly to his bed.

She'd turned furiously on him once, when he tried to take a board from her. "My mother worked beside my father. You would expect less from me? Who do you think you are?"

He could think of no answer, except to tug her close and slant his lips over hers, igniting them both. "That's who you are," he'd managed shakily later, and for the sake of modesty took the board and placed it strategically in front of his hips.

"Okay," she'd said just as unevenly, her face flushed. "I'm taking a shower and I'm going to bed."

His mouth had dried, his body leaping into the fever that she had called forth. "Miranda. It is noon."

The air had sizzled between them, and Gabriel had forgotten about everything but carrying her off to his bed.

As he stood in Anna's driveway now, Gabriel tucked that memory away to savor later. Gently rounded with Michael's child, Kylie hugged Miranda. Holding Anna's patchwork quilt tightly, Gwyneth's small body was ripe with the baby that would arrive in another month. Tanner paused, carrying a box of Anna's clothing to be donated to charity. He glanced at Gabriel and at Michael, also caught by the scene.

Anna's three children had been through hardships, and had survived, returning to Freedom Valley, where she had found so much peace and love. Now that peace and love would go on in their homes, small memories of her tucked into each piece of furniture, each doily, each quilt.

Because Tanner had learned carpentry from his father, and as a boy had worked with his father's tools, they were now his. Gwyneth moved toward Tanner, leaning her head against his shoulder, the gesture said she understood his sadness. They looked so complete.

Michael's arm was now around Kylie, his head bent to hers. She leaned heavily against him, and he swept her up in his arms placing her inside his pickup. Kylie snuggled close to Michael, his arm still around her as they pulled out onto the main road.

Gwyneth's hand smoothed Tanner's back as he carried the tools into the new building where he built custom boats.

Then Miranda walked toward Gabriel, her head bent. He lifted her face and kissed the tears away. "She's always going to be with you and Kylie and Tanner."

"I think—when it is time, there will be a need for her house." Miranda's forehead bent and she came to rest against him in the old way, that told him her grief ran deep. "Take me home, Gabriel."

At the ranch, Miranda didn't go into the house. Instead she walked to the garden they had planted together, a row of bright green lettuce just beginning to sprout. Miranda was placing the past behind her, keeping the good and discarding the ugly, preparing to move on in her life. Gabriel came behind her, folding her tight against him in the setting sunlight.

"I want our wedding here," Miranda said quietly, turning to him. "And soon. What do you think?"

How could he refuse her anything, this woman of his heart? He nodded, meeting her searching gaze. "Are you finished courting me?"

"I've just begun," she whispered, and stood on tiptoe to brush her lips against his. "I've just begun," she repeated softly. "Your dad is loaning me his best wagon and four-horse team."

Gabriel frowned, holding her away to study her impish grin. "You're not handling his four-horse team."

"Your mother does."

He shook his head, rummaging for reasons why Miranda should not manage the powerful horses. He decided to retreat; images of Miranda driving a wagon with him sitting beside her nettled. She had paid for the tickets to the Firemen's Spring Ball and for the dinners at the Wagon Wheel, and for the drinks at the Silver Dollar. "I'd better start unpacking the pickup."

"It can wait. You're upset and have that closed-in look."

"I'm going to the barn," he said, and realized that he was being unfair. Miranda was only following the customs of Freedom Valley.

Moments later, Miranda stepped into the barn, finding him immediately. "Let's have this out. You're a beautiful, caring man, but you're growling about the Rules of Bride Courting."

"I have the book Fidelity demanded I read." This discussion was unpleasant, and Gabriel did not like thinking about how many men had chafed under the town's unique custom, which had protected pioneer women.

"I haven't asked you to marry me yet, Gabriel Deerhorn. *You* have asked me, but *I* have not asked *you*," she underlined.

That ungentle reminder that in Freedom Valley, women had always determined their fate and protected other women, caused Gabriel to frown. He walked slowly to her and Miranda's green eyes widened as he leaned down to whisper. "Ask me."

"Not under these circumstances. I have a candle-light dinner planned."

Gabriel tugged on a strand of her hair and placed his lips near hers, whispering, "Ask me."

She shivered and flattened against the wall and he placed both hands beside her head, corralling her. "Ask me."

He nudged his knee between her jeaned legs, and whispered against her throat, "Ask me."

He kissed her slowly, thoroughly, his hand unbuttoning her blouse. Her bra tore easily, freeing her breasts to his roaming touch. She shivered as his thumbs cruised over her hardened nipples, his kiss deepening, his knee lifted to nudge her intimate warmth. It was a new game he had grown to love, seducing her, testing her, waiting for her to ignite.

Miranda's fingers locked onto his shirt, her color rising, those dark green eyes sultry upon him. "You love doing this to me, don't you?"

"And you love doing it to me?"

"Maybe," she whispered lightly.

Still she resisted, driving him on, passion dancing between them. Gabriel bent to take her breast, suckling as his other hand unsnapped her jeans and slid into her briefs.

She came quickly into his passion, warm and throbbing and arching against him, her mouth hot with the fever driving them both. In his plan to seduce her, Gabriel had not planned to be taken so quickly, the fire igniting as he filled his hands with her bare hips. Her hands fumbled with his clothing and then released, he filled her slowly, fully.

She held him tightly, answering his primitive call, matching him for strength, taking his mouth, feeding upon him as he tasted her. He was flying now, Miranda breathing unevenly, her heart pounding him, her body greedy for his. He filled his fist with her hair, tugging her head back gently, watching her passion flow through her, and she took it inside, nourishing his own with that fierce, wild desperation.

She fought to contain her release, and he could not have that, pushing her, holding his own pounding passion.

Later, he would hold her still, uncertain of what she would do. He had taken her primitively, fed by his own hunger. Miranda's heart still raced against his own, her body limp and soft, draped around him. Humor filled her tone as she said, "Okay. If that's how you really feel about it, I'll ask you. In your way, you can be a real rat, but I love you anyway. You're getting very good at seduction, slow or fast."

He smiled at that, loving the exciting game that would continue all their lives. "What's that? I can't hear you," he teased.

He looked down at their bodies, hers pale and soft against his, a beautiful, wonderful sight. His body was already hardening, filling her again. "It seems I need to make up for lost time," he whispered in an apology.

She watched him carefully, a tender smile curving her kiss-swollen lips. "Will you marry me, Gabriel?"

Gabriel waited for his wife to come to him as the mid-May night sounds cruised their mountain campsite. At their wedding, Fidelity Moore had kissed him soundly, shocking him. "This is a fine example of a husband. You unmarried boys take note of how he accepted his love's courtship."

Miranda, dressed in the doeskin beaded shift that his grandmother had made for her long ago, had shot him a disbelieving look. For Gabriel had loved every moment, playing the game of seduction with his love, watching her blush and run and tease and love him wildly.

He sighed, taking his happiness into him to cherish. Soon his wife's body would change, her breasts becoming fuller, her body softening and rounding with their child. He would treasure each moment, each change, for White Fawn had said that their first baby would be created on their wedding night. He rubbed the fullness in his heart, and wondered how such joy could come to him, how Miranda could love so freely and openly, sometimes shocking him.

His smile grew as he studied the starlit Montana night. Some things were better not shared, he decided. Miranda would want to tell him in her own way of their child. White Fawn had held up four fingers, indicating the children that would carry on his blood and his father's father's long after he was gone. But each time, he would wait for Miranda to tell him, to bring him her excitement and joy.

Well, then, he thought, turning toward their campfire, studying their future in it, he would build a home office for her, enlarging their home once more. If her numbers called to her, she would have what she needed. If she needed to work away from their home, he would tend their brood. For he had waited for so long....

Then standing beyond the fire and the smoke, Miranda appeared. She found him in the night, and slowly removed the doeskin wedding shift. It pooled at her feet, leaving the firelight and the moonbeams flowing upon her face, her shoulders, her breasts. Shadows dancing within the firelight traced her hips and long legs, but he knew the strength of them, the beauty of those curves. He'd seen her without clothing, but his body stirred quickly, waiting to take her as his wife.

The smoke curled between them, drifting high into the night sky as Gabriel watched the Miranda of his visions, his wife, come to him.

He had waited so long....

*   *   *   *   *

Don't miss Cait London's next powerful love story,
A LOVING MAN,
included in a two-in-one volume called
Her Ideal Man

on the shelves in June 2002.

VICTORIA'S CONQUEST

by
Laurie Paige

LAURIE PAIGE

was presented with the *Affaire de Coeur* Readers' Choice Silver Pen Award for Favourite Contemporary Author. In addition, she was a Romance Writers of America RITA finalist for their Best Traditional Romance award. She reports romance is blooming in her part of northern California. With the birth of her second grandson, she finds herself madly in love with three wonderful males—'all hero material'. So far, her husband hasn't complained about the other men in her life.

Chapter One

"I'm terribly sorry. This meeting was totally unexpected," the secretary explained, excusing her boss's rudeness in keeping his next appointment waiting.

Victoria Broderick glanced at the clock—almost forty-five minutes past the hour of one. Her appointment had been at one. She smiled politely. "That's all right. I don't mind waiting."

Since she'd come specifically to meet with Jason Broderick, she had nothing else to do. Because she was a relative, so to speak, being the widow of Jason's second cousin, he probably felt he didn't have to pay her the courtesy of timeliness.

"He's usually very prompt," Susan, the secretary, continued in defense of her boss. "Would you like another cup of coffee?"

She seemed anxious to please. Victoria agreed and took her cup over to the desk. The younger woman was *very* pregnant, and Victoria didn't want to cause her any extra work.

Twice already she had heard Susan gasp when she bent over the bottom drawer of a file. The way the secretary had laid a hand on her extended abdomen made Victoria wince. She knew what it was to be pregnant. She knew how labor contractions felt—how fast they could come, how soon it could be over.

Susan poured the coffee. Victoria returned to her seat. She turned her gaze out the window.

The June day was one to bring the poets running with pencils in hand. A breeze rippled the line of birches along the creek, setting their leaves a-tremble.

The ring of the telephone jarred her thoughts. While the secretary wrote down a message for Jason, she thought over her reasons for being there for the hundredth time.

Raleigh, North Carolina, was a huge metropolis compared to her hometown, Paradise Falls, West Virginia. As mayor of the small town—population 4928—she had a responsibility to carry out her campaign pledge to build a secure future for the area.

She was determined to do just that. In fact, it was the sole reason for her trip. Jason's systems engineering company had recently won a new contract from the Navy. She wanted him to locate the assembly plant in Paradise Falls.

She wondered if any of her arguments for the move would appeal to a tough businessman like Jason. He was from the area so he already knew it was a lovely place to live.

With the mountains cupping the town on three sides, it was protected from the worst winter winds. Spring and fall were a riot of color, as dogwoods bloomed or maples turned crimson. At present the summer season was just starting. The weather was perfect for picnics by the river and for hiking, she would remind him.

And it was a good place to raise children, she added to her mental list, when Susan again drew a quick breath.

Eight minutes since the last one. Victoria held her breath as she waited for the secretary to resume breathing.

"Are you all right?" she finally asked, a stupid question since no one ever asked it until it was obvious that the other person wasn't doing well at all.

Susan opened her mouth and drew in a gulp of air. She nodded. Laying a hand over her rounded stomach, she smiled. "Junior is being rambunctious today."

Relieved, Victoria smiled in understanding. She knew how hard a baby could kick. She'd been almost six months pregnant when the accident had occurred. An icy road. A driver who hadn't been able to make the curve. John cursing and cutting the wheel hard. Then a confusion of sound and blur of motion while they went off the cliff, turning over and over....

Susan paused and grimaced. Victoria checked her watch. *Six minutes.* This was making her nervous. She drew four deep breaths, then continued her mental review when the secretary resumed work.

The town had a skilled work force, she would tell Jason...*if* she ever saw him. Hand-made crafts for the tourist trade over at the new resort were popular items. But, she admitted, they were too seasonal for most people to depend on them for a living.

She glanced at her watch at another gasp. *Five minutes.*

Not that the town was destitute. Far from it. The Clairmont Textile Mill was rebounding quickly from the recession in the apparel market. Adam Clairmont had recently expanded the company to include a new line of clothing—breathable rain gear that was all the rage with backpackers and outdoor types.

As a businessman, Jason would understand that diversity was important. When one industry was in a slump, the other would take up the slack. At least, that was the theory.

Four minutes. A nervous tremor ran over her.

What the heck was keeping him so long?

She continued the review of her arguments. They needed another source of revenue more reliable than the tourist industry and with less competition from foreign markets than textiles. It would have to be a "clean" industry, no smokestacks or noxious fumes. Thus her decision that something on the order of an electronic assembly operation would be perfect.

That was the reason she was waiting to see Jason Broderick. As CEO of one of the fastest growing privately owned corporations in America, he could help her reach her goal and fulfill her promise to her constituents.

Although Jason hadn't lived in Paradise Falls in years and she'd met him perhaps a dozen times in all, she considered kinship enough of a tie to justify her calling upon him with her problem. In West Virginia family was important.

She settled back in her chair and crossed her legs, pausing in her mental meandering to admire her new pumps of embroidered linen. They were blue like her summer suit and nearly the color of her eyes. Her silk blouse was smoky pink and crisscrossed over her breasts in a draped, pleated V. She knew she looked nice in the outfit. She'd spent a whole day searching for it.

"Dignified, as the mayor should be, but smart. *Voilà*, I give you...the modern woman." Her friend, Cara, had approved while they scoured the town during the shopping expedition.

One thing she had learned in politics: appearance was important. Sometimes it was everything.

She thought people voted more for an image than for any other reason. She knew she was seen as the All American sweetheart—spunky, bright, hard working and kind.

People gave her more credit than she deserved for putting her life back together after the tragedy. What else could one do?

She'd opened a casual clothing boutique and made a success of it. Last year she'd run for mayor and won. Life goes on.

Occasionally she felt she was playing a series of roles, and the real Victoria Broderick had gotten lost between the acts.

The buzzer sounded on the telephone. The secretary leaned forward with a grimace and picked it up. "Yes. All right. Yes. I know where it is. I'll bring it to you right away."

She hung up, gave Victoria a worried glance and bent over her files again. With a grunt, she pulled a file folder out and stood, her hand going to her bulging waistline. When she opened the door, Victoria got a glimpse of uniforms and suits.

The Navy brass must be meeting with Jason on the new contract. Victoria nervously clasped her hands together. She wished she could join them. The secretary returned to the outer office and gave her an apologetic smile.

"Meeting still going strong, huh?" Victoria asked in a friendly tone to let Susan know she understood. "Some of our town council meetings last half the night."

Victoria had used her official letterhead stationery to request the appointment. With a busy magnate like Jason Broderick, she'd suspected prestige of office might count more than kinship. She was prepared to use both in her efforts.

"Jason is probably ready to slit some throats. I'm sure he didn't expect the conference to go on and on like this. The Navy people insisted on talking to him after they finished with the manager and scientist in charge of the project," Susan explained. She sat down in her chair with an audible catch of breath and closed her eyes for a second.

"Are you okay?" Victoria asked again, a frown puckering her brow as the secretary held on to the edge of the desk.

"It's just false labor." Susan sighed as the pain passed. She relaxed slowly. "It's a month too early."

Victoria glanced at the young woman's rounded abdomen and thought it looked more like a month too late. A prickle of foreboding swept over the back of her neck. "Perhaps you should lie down for a few minutes."

The office was furnished comfortably with a short sofa and two matching chairs in heather shades of mauve and green, a color scheme she might have chosen herself. A copper sculpture on a wall and copper accents in lamps and vases added a splash of brightness.

"No, I'm sure it's nothing—" Susan stopped as another grimace crossed her face.

Victoria placed the coffee cup on a low table and tossed her purse into the chair when she stood. Her nurturing instincts surfaced. She went to Susan's side and held her hand until she relaxed again. "Come on. You need to get your feet up."

She took a file folder out of Susan's hands, placed it

on the desk and helped the younger woman lie down on the sofa. With a hand at her wrist, Victoria checked Susan's pulse. Steady and strong. She noted the time. *Three minutes.*

"I feel silly," Susan declared, swinging her feet to the floor. "Really, I'm fine. It was only a twinge."

Victoria remained doubtful. "Looked like more than a twinge to me," she protested.

Susan stood and started toward the desk. About halfway across the room, she stopped dead still, her body taking on a strained posture.

Victoria rushed to her side and grasped her arm. "Susan?"

"Oh, God," Susan groaned. She bent slightly and pressed her hands on her thighs as her body was racked with a strong spasm.

"One minute," Victoria stated, glancing at her watch. "I think you're in labor."

"Can't be," Susan gasped. "Too early."

"As if that makes a difference. Mine came—" She stopped. Her baby had come during the accident, hours before they'd been found trapped in the twisted steel. She'd delivered it alone—a little boy with dark, downy hair on his tiny, perfect head.

"You've had a baby?" Susan asked as the cramp eased.

Pain flicked through Victoria at the brief, poignant memory. She forced a confident smile to her face. "Sure have. The secret is to go with the flow."

"Right. I've had classes." A ripple of surprise crossed Susan's face. She stared at the floor. "I'm...I'm..."

Victoria looked down and saw water puddling on the carpet. "I think," she said, "we've run out of time.

Come on, get back on the sofa before the baby falls out on its head.''

The feeble joke brought a fleeting smile to Susan's face. "Oh, help. It's starting again."

"Easy now." Victoria held Susan for the minute it took for the contraction to lessen, then guided her back to the sofa. "Lie on your side with your knees drawn up. That seemed to help me."

"Get Jason," Susan requested through pale lips. She was apprehensive now that she realized the real thing was happening.

"Good idea. I'll be right back. Don't move."

Brilliant advice, Victoria mocked herself as she headed for the conference room. She opened the door without knocking and stuck her head in so the men wouldn't see Susan. Eight pairs of eyes stared at her with varying levels of inquiry. One pair, as blue as her own, she recognized right away.

"Jason...Mr. Broderick...uh, could I see you for a minute, please? It's urgent."

"Gentlemen, if you will excuse me," he said without further ado. She was relieved he didn't rail at her for interrupting.

He came around the long table, ushered Victoria away from the door and closed it securely behind him. "What is it?"

At that moment Susan groaned again. "Jason, get Ted," she pleaded in a ragged whisper.

His gaze, outlined by a lush curtain of black lashes, flicked to the sofa. He took in the situation.

He looked back at Victoria. For a split second, his face altered. An emotion, deep and unfathomable, etched lines between his eyes. It passed as swiftly as it had appeared.

Victoria paused, surprised. She thought she'd seen pain

in his eyes, but she must have been mistaken. He was all brisk, jovial efficiency now. After taking off his jacket and rolling up his sleeves, he bent to Susan and laid a soothing hand on her brow.

"Darned right we'll get him. He'll want to be in on the big event. First we'll call an ambulance, then we'll call his company and tell him to meet us at the hospital."

He sounded so cheerful and capable, Victoria was put at ease. He was evidently a man of quick discernment and action; that was what was needed at the present.

"Too late, I think," Susan wailed. "Oh, Jason, I'm sorry."

"Sorry?" he questioned, kneeling beside her and giving her a roguish smile. "For what? It's not often a man gets to welcome his godchild into the world at the first breath."

Victoria found herself smiling at his teasing.

His glance flicked to her. "Get that ambulance," he said.

"Right."

She dashed to the desk and picked up the phone. Seeing the intercom button light up, she impatiently punched another one for an outside line and dialed the emergency number. A man's voice answered. She explained what was happening. He promised to send help right away.

"It's on its way," she told Jason.

"Good. Now call her husband. What's the number, honey?" he asked Susan.

She gasped it out.

Victoria dialed. She noticed her hand was trembling. She asked for Ted and was told he was in the lab. "Tell him Susan is in labor and to meet her at the hospital." She heard a groan from the sofa. "Tell him to hurry," she added.

The woman on the other end of the line promised she'd get the news to him immediately. Victoria relayed the message.

"Great," Jason said, giving her a glance of approval.

Warmth stole over her. She hovered behind him, wondering what more she could do to ease the situation. Susan appeared a little frightened; her eyes held a pleading look.

"There, now, it's going to be fine." Jason brushed Susan's bangs off her forehead in a caring, gentle manner.

Victoria was fascinated. He was very different from her first impression when she'd opened the door and interrupted the meeting. Then she had observed annoyance in his probing glance, but now he was all calm tenderness—reassuring and in control, exactly what Susan needed.

She watched his hands as he stroked Susan's cheek and arm. His fingers were long and lean. His skin was tanned. She knew he liked to play tennis. On the occasions he visited his folks in Paradise Falls, he spent a lot of time at the country club, picking up tennis and golf games.

"Get those men out," he directed, his manner changing as he spoke to Victoria. "Take them out the other door and—" he paused to think "—escort them to the cafeteria and give them lunch on the house. They can meet with the VP of operations if they still want to talk after that. Get back up here on the double when you get them taken care of."

"Right," she said.

She went into the executive conference room. The seven men were still sitting around the table, discussing a series of graphs. They hushed when she appeared.

"Gentlemen," she said, "Mr. Broderick has a… uh…family emergency." That was certainly the truth. "He suggests you break for lunch and perhaps he can catch you later in the main conference room. Will you come with me?"

She ushered them into the hall, lining them up behind her like ducks in a row. "Isn't it a lovely day?" she commented as they rode the elevator to the lobby. They agreed it was indeed.

Fortunately she remembered seeing a sign pointing to the cafeteria on the first floor when she had arrived that afternoon. She led them to it. She passed Jason's instructions to the cashier and returned to the third-floor executive office.

"Get that pillow and blanket out of the closet in my office. And towels from the bathroom," Jason ordered the second she reappeared. "Not that way, the other door."

Victoria changed directions and darted to the door he pointed out with a tilt of his head. He was holding both Susan's hands as she moaned through a contraction. In less than a minute Victoria returned with the items.

Jason slipped the pillow behind Susan's head and the blanket beneath her. He searched out the fastenings on her skirt.

"Jason," she said, a flush of red rising over her cheeks.

"Relax, I'm an expert at undressing women." His grin was bold, but his touch was gentle.

With rapid skill, he removed the damp skirt and underclothes while Susan closed her eyes tightly as if denying she was there and that this could be happening to her. With impressive strength, he lifted and positioned her, then he draped the towel over her drawn-up knees. She was in the birthing position.

Victoria's breath came as rapidly as Susan's as the contractions pulled and eased, pulled and eased.

Jason spoke continuously, his voice soft but wonderfully resonant, like the full-throated bay of a hunting dog heard from a distance through the woods. A memory stirred. His voice was so familiar…as if she'd heard him speak like this.…

The timbre beguiled Victoria. It was a lover's tone, rippling deeply with unspoken thoughts, a longing of the soul.

She studied her cousin-in-law with renewed interest.

He'd always held himself aloof from the family fun, smiling and watching mostly from the sidelines. She'd thought he was cold—a distant, cynically amused man. She saw she'd been wrong. Very, very wrong. A tremor glided over her. She wrapped her arms across her chest, fascinated by him.

"Hold tight," he murmured once when Susan cried out.

He would be an extraordinary lover. Victoria was shocked when the thought sprang full-blown into her mind. It unnerved her, jarred her composure…and filled her with a longing so acute, so potent, she, too, gasped. He gave her a brief, intense glance.

"Jason…I'm sorry…for all this," Susan panted.

"Don't be. This is what marriage is all about—loving and making babies. Sharing. It's life with a capital *L.*"

His smile was the most beautiful Victoria had ever seen. Tears filled her eyes at his tenderly spoken assurance. She blinked and moved closer, not wanting to miss a moment.

He looked up when she sat on the edge of the chair beside the sofa. Their eyes met.

Victoria couldn't look away. She felt that she was being pulled into an unknown universe through his gaze. He was asking her to come with him…to take his hand and come with him.…

"What?" she asked, coming back to reality and realizing he'd spoken to her.

"Hand me that washcloth," he requested.

She put it in his outstretched hand. He swabbed Susan's brow and gave her an encouraging grin. When the next contraction began, he put his hand down and let her hold on to it again.

A knot formed in Victoria's throat. When Susan made a choked sound, she picked up the cloth, folded it and held it out. Susan grasped it between her teeth, using it to bite against as the labor deepened. Victoria sensed the end was nearing.

"Where is that ambulance?" Jason muttered with a fierce frown.

"The man said it should be here in ten minutes," she replied.

"How long has it been?"

She looked at her watch. "Six minutes."

Jason grimaced. He removed his hand from Susan's and laid it on her rounded abdomen. He rubbed in soothing circles. "Relax, now. Deep breaths. Rest up for the big one."

Susan managed a smile around the cloth. She took it out of her mouth and sighed. "This really is work."

"They don't call it labor for nothing, right?"

"I wish Ted was here." Susan got a little teary.

"Hey, is that an insult to my bedside manner? Aren't I rubbing your tummy? Ted told me that's what he did when you had a restless night." With bantering good humor and infinite patience, he coaxed Susan through each minute, one after another.

Victoria felt sweat gathering on her forehead and between her breasts as time stretched into an eternity. She saw Jason steal a quick glance at his watch, then peer out the window. Ten minutes had come and gone. The ambulance was late.

"Maybe you'd better not push," he advised at one point.

"Have to," Susan said, her tone querulous.

"Well, then, that's all right."

Seeing the beads of perspiration on his face, Victoria grabbed a towel from the table behind her and mopped his brow. He turned his keen gaze on her. She smiled, offering encouragement and support. Her mouth trembled when he stared at her lips.

"She's had a baby," Susan said abruptly, nodding toward Victoria. "She said she had."

She saw Jason's throat move as if he'd swallowed something hard, then he said, "I know. I know about Victoria's baby."

"How old—" Susan broke off with a gasp.

Victoria hoped Susan would forget her train of thought before the contraction ended. This wasn't a good time to discuss what had happened that snowy day seven years ago. Recalling her own ordeal, her heart went out to the young woman who was trying so hard to be brave as Jason encouraged her to "hold on just a little longer."

She studied Jason, her feelings for him tender and suddenly clear. He was a man who'd be easy to love, *if* a woman could reach the compassionate center he hid behind his devil-may-care grin. That woman would be lucky beyond measure.

Susan uttered a keening sound. She caught a breath and held it. Her face turned red with effort.

"Pant," Victoria ordered. "Don't hold your breath. You need the oxygen. Pant." She panted to show Susan the rhythm.

"Take her hands," Jason broke in. "Get behind her and hold her hands. I'm going to need mine free."

His gaze locked briefly with Victoria's.

A thrill rushed through her. She realized she'd never felt so alive, so in tune with nature, with life, with another person. She was one with Jason and Susan...with this moment of birth...this miracle of life!

Together they labored through the contraction until it eased. Victoria brushed sweat off her brow with the back of one hand when Susan released her and relaxed once more. Jason did the same.

"Get two more towels," he requested.

Victoria ran to his executive bathroom and returned in record time, her breathing as hard as Susan's. She gave him the towels. He laid one across his knees, one across Susan after pushing her maternity blouse out of the way.

"You're doing fine, love," he assured Susan. "Yell if you feel like it. Easy now. We don't have to rush. There, it's easing up a bit. Rest and get your breath...."

His gentleness caused tears to come into Victoria's eyes. Then Susan gripped her hands as the next contraction started.

Jason leaned forward, intent and focused, ready to help the mother and child. Victoria couldn't take her eyes off him. If she'd had him seven years ago, might her baby have stood a chance?

Not likely, she acknowledged. But this man would have been a comfort. He was...*wonderful* was the only word.

There was a passionate intensity about him, as if this birth was the most important thing in the world, as if the sum total of all life depended on the success of this one event.

Strange emotions arose in her, filling her throat with a need to cry out her feelings as she once had at the climax of passion.

Then she experienced the oddest sensation. It was as if she'd been enclosed in an enchanting warmth and swept into a magic realm. She breathed the very elixir of eternity.

This man, she thought, confused by the longing that poured over her. *This man brought life.*

She watched his hands—such gentle hands—move over Susan again, calming her with his touch on her abdomen, and wanted to lay her hands over his and move with his movements.

She felt pain in her fingers as Susan squeezed harder. Joy washed over her. She was connected to this lusty eruption of new life. She was part of it...part of the miracle.

"All *right*," Jason exclaimed, sounding like a Little League coach in a tight game. "Show us what you can do, sweetheart."

"Hit one for the gipper?" Susan managed to tease.

Jason laughed, a vibrant chuckle that sent shivers bouncing along Victoria's spine. He had a laugh almost identical to that of the other Broderick men she had known, warm and husky and pleasing to the senses. With Jason there was more, though—undercurrents that hinted of mysterious depths. Like the birch trees along the river, murmuring and chuckling in the breeze, keeping their secrets....

She looked out the window, feeling bereft and saddened all of a sudden. This moment belonged to Susan, not her. She no longer shared life in the fullest sense.

Stop feeling sorry for yourself, she chided.

A commotion at the door brought her head around. Three paramedics entered, carrying a medical kit and stretcher.

"Thank God," Jason muttered.

So, he hadn't been quite as sanguine as he'd led her to believe. He wiped his forehead against his sleeve after he moved aside and let the medic take his place.

"Well, what have we here?" the man said on a jovial note. He gave Susan a reassuring grin. "We won't make it to the hospital, but I think we can get you into the ambulance where we have a better birthing bed than this one."

The other two men positioned the gurney. They lifted Susan onto it, strapped her in and headed out.

"Jason," she called, casting a panicky glance back.

"I'm right behind you."

"Come…with me?"

"I wouldn't miss it for the world." He gave Susan a cocky grin that dipped right down into Victoria's heart.

At that moment she realized she'd fallen a little in love with him during the past fifteen minutes. She knew the feeling was due to the emotion of the moment, but it didn't seem any less real.

Jason Broderick wasn't the man she'd thought he was. There was more to him—so much more!—than the sardonic, raffish person he portrayed when he visited Paradise Falls. She wanted to know him better. There were depths to this man.…

He paused at the door, a frown nicking a line over the bridge of his nose as he looked back at her.

"Don't worry about me." She gave him a wobbly smile. "Take care of Susan. My business can wait."

He tipped his hand in a half salute, his eyes dark with some emotion she couldn't read, and headed off at a run to catch the men carrying Susan. From the window Victoria watched him climb into the ambulance and reach out to comfort Susan.

The receptionist came into the office. "Shall I set you up with another appointment?" she asked. "I don't know how long Jason will be gone."

Victoria grimaced as she considered her wasted trip. "I don't have anything else to do. I need to talk to Jason when he comes back, so I think I'll wait, if you don't mind."

The receptionist looked unsure, but Victoria was experienced in dealing with people. She took a seat and smiled confidently. The woman hesitated, then shrugged and left to resume her duties at the front desk.

Victoria selected a magazine and thumbed through it. After five minutes, she closed it and laid it aside.

She reviewed the recent exciting episode. She still couldn't quite comprehend the difference in Jason. Today she'd seen a side to him that he'd never shown his family, at least not while she'd been around. Of course, it wasn't every day that a person was in on the beginnings of a new life.

Tears clouded her vision. She was still wound up from the excitement, she realized as she patted her eyes with a tissue.

And from watching Jason, her late husband's enigmatic cousin, who had been John's best friend when they were boys and best man at John and Victoria's wedding. The friendship had drifted into an occasional meeting after the marriage.

She propped her chin on her fist and considered their mutual past. She had sensed John's hurt at Jason's stand-offish attitude, although he'd never actually complained about it. He hadn't understood why Jason wouldn't visit with them or go on their frequent fishing and camping expeditions.

She personally thought it was because Jason, a bachelor, had been bored with their married bliss.

He probably had, but bachelor or not, he'd certainly been wonderful during this birthing crisis. She envisioned his hands, stroking and soothing—slightly callused on the palms, she'd noted at one instant—but so gentle…so very gentle. It still amazed her that she'd never seen him like that, never even realized the potential in him for that kind of emotional depth.

A pulse came to life deep inside her. Heat seemed to radiate outward from the same mysterious point, warming her all over. She stirred restlessly and frowned at the tension that filled her.

The sound of Jason's voice came back to her, low and husky, demanding and coaxing. She pressed her fingertips to her temples as confusion washed over her. He'd never spoken to her like that, so why did she seem to remember that he had?

She sighed, deflated now that the emergency was over. She needed to relax and rehearse her strategy for persuading Jason to come to Paradise Falls. When he did, she and her two best friends were going to give him a sales pitch he couldn't resist.

However, her mind wasn't on the task.

With painful honesty she acknowledged the subject foremost in her thoughts. Jason. His incredible tenderness. His surprising warmth. The engaging way he'd teased and soothed and offered firm, steady support. She closed her eyes and pressed a hand to the burning ache that filled her chest.

She recalled his hands, his movements controlled and assuring. Did he touch a woman like that when they made love…?

Her breath suddenly uneven, she tried to turn her thoughts in a different direction. It was no use. She couldn't forget that appealing degree of intensity she'd witnessed in him. It had been almost passionate…not sexual…but passionate nevertheless.

So strange, the feelings that had stirred in her. Like a part of her had been awakened from a long sleep. It had been over seven years since she'd known fulfillment. Shocked, she realized she wanted it now…this moment…the touching…the caresses….

She opened her eyes and shot out of the chair. Agitated, she paced the room. Drawing upon her thirty-one years of experience, she forced herself to look at the situation realistically.

The emergency had been emotional and unsettling. It had engendered a camaraderie based on high feelings, the way soldiers in a foxhole became fast friends. Yes, that was it.

Satisfied with this reasoning, she returned to the chair. The phone rang just as she sat down. It rang and rang. She went to the secretary's desk. Looking at the buttons, she realized it must be Jason's private line. Perhaps he was calling with a message.

She grabbed it up and spoke rather breathlessly. "Hello?" She couldn't remember the name of the company. "Jason Broderick's office." There, that sounded sufficiently official.

"Let me speak to Jason," an imperious female demanded.

Victoria's spine stiffened. She disliked people who treated others without courtesy. "He isn't available. May I take a message?" She forced a pleasant note into her voice.

"Where is he?"

"He had to leave the office unexpectedly."

There was a dead silence on the line.

"He's supposed to pick me up at eight. Tell him to make it eight-thirty. My modeling assignment is going to run over."

"Your name, please," Victoria said with great efficiency. She pulled a telephone message pad to the center of the desk.

"He knows who I am," the woman snapped.

"But I don't," Victoria replied sweetly.

She tried to write the time down on the pad and found the pen didn't work. She looked in a center drawer for another and spied an engagement book. She opened it to the current day and studied the list of Jason's appointments.

"What time do you expect Jason back?"

"Well, actually, I don't know. There was an emer—"

"Just give him my message. Did you get the time correct?"

Victoria looked at the name written in the engagement book and noted the restaurant listed beside it. Her own name was the only afternoon appointment. She gave a disgruntled sigh.

Fate had cheated her out of her chance. Not only was she going to miss her interview with Jason, but she was going to spend a lonely evening at the hotel. Time, energy and money wasted, and not one whit closer to her goal, darn it.

"Well?" the woman demanded.

"Are you Delores?" Victoria asked, a wicked idea popping into her head. Did she dare act upon it?

"Yes."

"Oh, good. Jason said…uh…I was to tell you he's…uh…not going to be available for the rest of the day."

"What?"

The angry shriek hurt Victoria's ear. "He sends his deepest regrets, but there was a…a family emergency."

Guilt jostled with self-righteousness as she told this bald lie. Look at the facts, she thought, defending herself to her conscience. Her reasons for seeing Jason were much more important than one woman's dinner date. Other people's lives depended on her.

Besides, Delores would have many opportunities in the future to dine with Jason…and the model was probably on a diet, anyway, she added as a sop to her scruples.

An irritated huff came over the phone. It took little imagination for Victoria to picture the beautiful but plastic woman who was to have been Jason's date.

"What kind of family emergency?"

It was obvious the model didn't think anything took precedence over an evening with her. Victoria tried to think of some vital reason for Jason's missing the date. Nothing came to mind.

When all else fails, tell the truth, she advised with wry humor. "Actually a relative from out of town has arrived—"

"Tell Jason to send him to a show or something. There's no reason to break our date. He can say he has a business dinner."

Victoria frowned. Jason couldn't possibly have a serious relationship with this female Narcissus. "Well," she began carefully, "I think it must be important. Jason seemed rather intent when he left the office." That much was true.

Sounds of muffled rage sizzled over the wire. Victoria's conscience scowled at her for the continued deception.

"Was it a female?" Delores asked in a furious snarl. "It was, wasn't it?"

"Actually, yes," she said hurriedly before she broke down and confessed all. "I'm sure he feels he has to entertain her. She's from his hometown. Family obligations and all, you understand."

"What does this cousin look like?" Before Victoria could answer, the model supplied her own description. "Some frowsy bleached blonde, no doubt, with big blue eyes and no brain."

Victoria frowned at this description of herself. While she did have blond hair, it was natural. Her eyes were blue, but she didn't think that impeded her intelligence. She felt a bit less guilty for her subterfuge.

"Well, her hair did seem kind of sun-bleached. She looked like an outdoorsy sort of person—"

"I know what you mean," the model said. "I hate that type, but men seem to like them."

"Oh. Do they?" The discussion was getting interesting.

"It's all an act."

"What is?" Victoria asked, worried that she'd somehow given herself away.

"That type of woman. The cutesy blonde. She probably pretends to like all that athletic stuff while acting helpless as a lamb at the same time. I hate fakey people like that."

Victoria thought this sounded like the pot calling the

kettle black, but she made her tone sympathetic. "She's only going to be in town for the evening, so Jason'll be available tomorrow."

"Tell him not to expect me to wait around for him. I've had an offer for a weekend party, starting after the session this evening. I've decided to take it."

"I'll tell him," Victoria assured her, conscientiously writing the message down word for word. She read it back to make sure she'd gotten it right. "Anything else?"

"No." The model banged the receiver down in her ear.

Victoria winced and returned her phone to the hook. A movement from the door caused her to look in that direction.

Jason stood there, his smile cool, distant, sardonic, his thoughts and feelings hidden. This was the Jason she recognized.

Chapter Two

Victoria realized Jason looked tired. He was also incredibly appealing. His tie was loose, his shirt was open at the neck, and the sleeves were rolled back on his forearms. His hair was rumpled. She wanted to run her fingers through the coal-black strands and smooth them.

"So what are we going to do this weekend?" he inquired with deceptive ease. He gave her an appraising once-over. Without waiting for her response, he offered several suggestions. "Dinner. We'll go to my place afterward. A nightcap, perhaps. Then…"

He shrugged as if to say the possibilities were endless. His eyes narrowed as he let his gaze roam over her once more, lingering at the point where the material of her blouse crisscrossed. A tingling sensation dashed through her breasts, like little currents of electricity running wild over them.

"I…" She tried to think of some excuse for her conniving performance. Nothing convincing came to mind.

"Tell me…is this a kissing cousin relationship, dare I

hope?'' He lifted his eyebrows in a sardonic taunt. ''It must be since we're obviously close…family ties and all.''

So, he'd heard everything. ''Jason—'' She cleared her throat. Her mouth was dry. She realized she was very nervous. She took a deep breath. ''I'm sorry for breaking your engagement, but my plane leaves at eight in the morning. I really need to talk to you before I go. It's important.''

Jason kept his expression carefully neutral even as a flick of anger whipped at his self-control. He wondered why fate had chosen to send her to him. *His one weakness…*

Weakness, hell. Honey-blond hair, big blue eyes and a lush, womanly figure were hard for any man to resist. When she'd opened the door to his conference room and peered around it at him, he'd felt a surge of passion so strong, he'd nearly exploded.

He smiled, mockingly amused at his own predicament. He wasn't as cool as he pretended. In fact, he was burning up. At this moment, he'd give ten years off his life to make love to her.

That was something she would never know. He knew first-hand how susceptible that left a man to a woman's wiles.

Anyway, the desire was a natural reaction, left over from the drama of the birth. Most men, after an emergency or a smashing triumph, wanted sex—hot, wild and mindless. He was no different.

Shifting his casual pose in the doorway, he was aware of the heaviness in his lower body. He ignored it.

''It's always important,'' he replied to her statement, ''especially when people want to ask a favor.''

A tinge of red crept into her cheeks. Anger or embarrassment? He couldn't decide. What difference did it make?

"I do want a favor," she announced candidly.

She looked at him with a level stare, neither begging nor using her feminine charm to coax him into a better frame of mind.

He felt a reluctant tingle of admiration for her. Whatever she wanted from him, she wasn't shy or coy about it. "So what is this great thing I can do for you?"

Victoria frowned at his cynical tone. At present he wasn't in a very receptive mood....

Well, of course not. He'd come from a long meeting to an emergency—she knew how that could drain a person emotionally—and here she was, canceling his date and arranging his evening for her own purposes.

"I want to talk to you about Paradise Falls. If I could have a couple of hours this evening, I'll explain why I'm here."

She tried to stay calm, as a public official should. But too much was at stake. Besides, he made her nervous. She kept imagining things, like how his mouth would feel touching hers....

"From the conversation, I understand I'm free for the entire weekend," he reminded her, his voice becoming very deep and husky, sort of...sexy. "So...won't you join me?"

The soft tone didn't disguise the subtle menace she detected in every word. Nor the danger that lurked within those mocking blue eyes with their to-die-for lashes of pure black. An answering thrill of excitement danced over her nerves. He was issuing a challenge. Was she going to accept it?

She had a job to do for her community, she reminded herself sternly. This wasn't a lover's tryst. The weekend would provide an opportunity to talk to him in depth about Paradise Falls and its problems.

She needed a whole weekend to do that? Just the two of them?

Some part of her was thoroughly shocked. But another part, well, it was an intriguing idea. Besides, she was a grown woman. She hardly needed a chaperon.

She frowned. The fact that she was intrigued unnerved her more than a little. The events of the afternoon had already sent her composure into a topsy-turvy mode... making her think she was in love with him...making her want the touch of his strong but gentle hands on her. She shivered delicately.

"My charm must be slipping if it's that hard for you to decide." He gave a cynical laugh.

"This is serious."

"I assure you, I'm always serious about my companion for the weekend," he mocked her scolding tone. He waited a moment, then said, "Think about it." He shrugged as if to say her decision made no difference to him.

"How long do I have?" She was startled to hear herself ask the question. Was she really contemplating an entire weekend with him? She was.

"Until—" he glanced at his watch "—until six."

That meant she had almost an hour. She bit her lip in indecision. A weekend. But it was for the community good.

Be truthful.

She would like to explore the depths she'd sensed in him earlier. Perhaps she would find the things in him that John had liked so much, although she'd never seen them herself. Until today.

She'd had a glimpse of the inner man during his care

of Susan. Why did he keep part of himself hidden behind a mocking wall of amusement? The tender, caring side was enormously appealing.

"I'll do it." She lifted her chin and returned his look as if he'd questioned her courage.

"The entire weekend? You'll reschedule your flight?" He gave her a curious glance, half-disbelieving.

"I can book another one for Monday morning."

He watched her for an eternity—until her nerves were stretched as thin as a silk thread—before he nodded, then ran a hand through his hair.

"God, I'm beat," he said. "Delivering babies is hard work, not as hard as having them, but damned tiring all the same."

He lifted his arms over his head in a spine-cracking stretch. His torso was outlined by the white Oxford cloth of his shirt. He was all muscle and sinew, the type of man who could eat without a thought to gaining weight.

A startling thought came to her. If she walked over to him, laid her head on his chest and wrapped her arms around him, he would hold her, kiss her, make love to her....

She forced the vision away. "How is Susan?" she finally remembered to ask.

"Mother, daughter *and* father are doing fine."

"A girl," she said, once more swept into the miracle of birth. "Ted made it to the hospital?"

"About thirty minutes ago. He was in some obscure lab, working on one of his crazy experiments. They had trouble finding him. I stayed with Susan until he arrived."

Victoria smiled, feeling tender toward Jason as she remembered their earlier efforts to help. She glanced at his hands. How very gentle he'd been. Tears came into her eyes.

His gaze locked with hers. For a second she thought she saw something—a deep yearning, perhaps—in those azure depths.

"You were wonderful today," she said. Her smile wobbled, then disappeared. Why was she being so emotional about it all? Babies were born every second of every day.

His expression changed. A barrier silently slipped between them. It was as if a cold fog had crept into the room. He'd closed himself off, the way he did when he visited Paradise Falls.

Why?

She found she wanted to know the answer to the puzzle that was Jason Broderick. After watching him today, she knew she'd never be satisfied to take him at face value again. There was much more to him than that.

"I have some calls to make," he said abruptly. He stalked across the room toward his office.

The quiet in the building and the increasing traffic noises from the street alerted her to the time. Everyone had left.

"I should go to my hotel and get ready for this evening. I'll call a cab."

He paused at his door. "Don't bother. I'll drop you by as soon as I'm finished here." He continued into his office, leaving the door open.

Victoria called and changed her flight to Monday, then waited for him to finish. She heard him talking on the phone.

His words were muffled, but his manner seemed relaxed. After a few minutes of serious talk, he chuckled. His words were suddenly very clear. "I won't be in town.

No, not Delores.'' He laughed. ''You don't know her. What? Oh, to the cabin, I think. She's...umm, you know, the outdoor type.''

Victoria's spine stiffened. A cabin. Did he think he was planning on taking her to some remote cabin for the weekend? She hadn't agreed to that, not by any twist of the imagination.

It was twenty minutes before he was through with his calls. He came out, locked his office and nodded to her. ''Ready?''

''Jason,'' she began stubbornly. ''About this weekend, what, exactly, are your plans?''

''Rest and relaxation,'' he promptly replied.

''I heard you mention a cabin. I don't want to make you give up your weekend—''

''You're not. You can come with me.''

''No.'' She realized she'd spoken too adamantly. ''I don't want to ruin things for you. I realize now that I was unforgivably rude in changing your plans to suit my needs. I'm terribly sorry. If you called Delores, I'm sure she'd reconsider...''

She trailed off as he shook his head. ''I don't want her. I want...you. You said it was important. Since this is the first time you've ever come to me, I believe you.''

I want...you. Had she really heard a slight hesitation in that statement, as if he really meant *her* personally? What would he expect of her? Gazing into his eyes, she found no answer. His expression was remote, yet alert, as if he noted her every thought.

She hesitated. Perhaps she was letting her emotions get the best of her common sense. ''All right,'' she agreed. She smiled. ''If you promise not to toss me off the nearest cliff for ruining your love life.''

It was as if a wall slammed down between them. She

shouldn't have mentioned his love life. She'd been too personal. He stared at her without speaking. The moment stretched out. A throbbing began deep inside her.

"I promise," he finally said, his voice devoid of emotion.

A chill spread over her. She wished he would laugh with her as he had with the person on the phone. Frowning over her own unpredictable reactions, she picked up her purse and preceded him out the door. He locked it and took her arm to escort her from the building. A sense of turmoil enveloped her. It was like knowing a storm was coming and knowing she couldn't get out of its way. She wasn't even sure she wanted to.

Victoria studied the black linen sheath. She hung it over the door and perused the suit she'd worn earlier. Her friend Cara had insisted she bring the black dress, but maybe the suit would be better. With her lace blouse, it was elegant enough for dining out, yet it would lend a businesslike tone to the evening. After all, this wasn't a date.

She put on her stockings while she thought it over. She finished her makeup and combed her hair, clipping it back behind one ear with a rhinestone comb. Finally she stood in front of the dress and suit again. Vanity won. She chose the sheath.

After stepping into it and zipping the back, she slipped into her heels and surveyed the results in the full-length mirror. Her cheeks were too red. She fluffed some powder across them to dull the flush of excitement. Really, this wasn't a date.

The knock at the door caused her heart to pound with an uneven beat. She pressed a hand to her chest.

This was *not* a date.

The knock sounded again, a bit louder. Jason evidently was not a patient man. She opened the door.

He looked her over in a leisurely manner, then grinned in silent appreciation as she stepped back to let him enter. He closed the door behind him and leaned against it, his hands thrust into his pockets. "Very nice," he said. "The city gals won't stand a chance when the guys see you."

"Thank you. I think." She managed a carefree laugh. "Does that mean I look okay for a country mouse?"

"More than okay." His voice dropped to a husky level.

She searched his face and realized she was looking for the person she'd seen during the emergency. All signs of the tender, caring man were gone, wiped as clean as a murder weapon after the crime. She wanted that man for her escort, not the Jason who stayed aloof, watching the world from a distance, his view cynical.

There was an answer, she realized.

Once upon a time he may have fallen deeply in love. That love hadn't worked out for some reason, so he'd withdrawn. Now he kept people at a distance, refusing to take another chance.

What a terrible waste of a wonderful man if that was true, she thought, the aching, elemental sadness she'd experienced earlier that day sweeping through her. She wanted to take him into her arms and comfort him.

If she did, he would probably think she was issuing an open invitation for a seduction. After all, they were alone in a hotel room with a queen-size bed not more than ten feet behind her.

Concealing her instinctive sympathy, she looked him over with the same insouciant perusal he'd used on her. "You look nice, too."

He was dressed in a black suit with a blue shirt. His

tie blended the two colors and added a dash of red. The overall effect complemented his blue eyes and black hair. He looked very worldly, very cosmopolitan and very masculine, with the polish that only experience could give a person.

I'm an expert at undressing women.

Victoria believed him. The model she'd talked to on the phone was probably a good example of the type he preferred. For some reason she felt disappointed in him.

"Ready for our big night on the town?" he inquired.

She frowned at his tone. It was falsely jocular. "How kind," she said brightly. "The long-suffering bachelor resigns himself to showing the uninvited relative a good time."

His eyes narrowed, giving his face a dangerous cast. "I'm trying to be agreeable. You're the one who set this weekend up to suit your own purposes, remember?"

"I shouldn't have bothered you," she said, troubled by her reactions to him, which seemed to roam the entire range of human emotions. She tried to laugh it off. "Who am I, a small-town mayor, to intrude upon a busy tycoon like you?"

"Having second thoughts about staying with me?" he inquired. His tone implied he'd expected it. She hated it.

Stiffening her backbone, she assumed a cool nonchalance to match his. "Not at all. It's just that I have this inconvenient conscience that gives me a hard time when I tell falsehoods. I don't like feeling guilty."

To her surprise, he laughed. She was enchanted. Jason laughing or Jason being gentle was far different from Jason being sarcastic.

"Your conscience can rest easy. Since I heard most of your conversation with Delores, I could have stopped you at any time if I'd wanted to see her this evening,'' he said, giving a casual shrug. "Shall we go?"

He took her shawl from her, when she retrieved it and her purse from the bed. His touch was a gossamer stroke against her arms when he draped the silky material around her shoulders. He escorted her from the room and down the elevator.

The restaurant was on the same block as the hotel. They walked the short distance and were taken to their table at once.

"Impressive," she murmured, regaining her equilibrium.

"I come here often."

"And leave large tips?"

The corners of his mouth flicked up in his usual cynical grin. "Guilty as charged," he confessed. "You've heard the story—money is like manure…"

She couldn't help but smile, too. "Yes. Spread around, it does a lot of good. Allowed to pile up, it stinks," she completed the maxim. "Which is why I'm here."

Although his expression remained pleasant, she knew the curtain had closed on his feelings by the way his eyes narrowed slightly. He became wary.

She supposed it was inevitable. Magazines loved to print success stories about entrepreneurs like him. They extolled his acumen in starting his own business from scratch. She'd read how he'd poured every cent into the company, and had eaten hundreds of peanut butter sandwiches to save money. He'd made it on his own. Other people had read those stories, too, and knew he was rich. He was probably asked for money all the time.

For a second, something in her rebelled at being another of those people who asked for favors. She sighed. As mayor, she had a duty to her constituents.

"So tell me about it," he invited. The waiter appeared at their table. "After we order," he amended.

After consulting with the waiter and with her, he made their selections quickly. She liked that. Dithering drove her insane.

Perhaps she was too impulsive, but she'd rather decide and go on, even if the decision turned out to be wrong, rather than spend ages worrying over it. Jason, she suspected, was like her in that respect. Studying the handsome, but hard, planes of his face, she felt a return of that warm, tingling hunger that radiated from deep inside her.

There was no denying the fact—she wanted him.

It was such a surprise, this intense hunger. She'd have to be careful around him. She was confusing desire with love, an emotional experience with the emotion itself. That would never do.

Yes, there had been a sense of oneness with him as they'd shared the moment of crisis. And yes, it had been wonderful. Her emotions had run high, and she'd felt totally alive for the first time in years. But fifteen minutes didn't make a lifetime.

"Now," he said, turning his attention back to her after the waiter left. "What's so important that it would take the mayor away from her duties to the home folk?"

"I'm not exactly on a pleasure jaunt," she said defensively.

The sardonic amusement disappeared. "Don't worry," he told her in his cool, distant way. "I never thought that for a minute."

She'd hurt him. It was a surprising revelation. "I mean, it is a pleasure to see you, but that has nothing to do with why I'm here." She was digging her grave deeper with each word. She regrouped. "I want to talk to you about Paradise Falls."

"Umm-hmm," he said with no inflection.

"Oh, hell," she said.

That got his attention. "Is that any way for the mayor to talk?" he mocked. "Whatever would people say?"

She studied him. "As if you cared," she concluded. "You've always gone your own way. A loner, John said."

He gestured with his hand, its sweep taking in the space around them and beyond. "That's right. I like to forge my own path. That's best done alone, don't you think?"

She couldn't bear his sarcasm. She wanted the inner person. "You can miss out on the good things in life like that," she said slowly. "Like you said to Susan...loving and...and..."

"Making babies was the term, I believe."

"Yes, and sharing all of life." Just for the tiniest fraction of time, she thought of making babies with him. A terrible yearning came over her. Once she'd held a baby to her breast and tried to breathe life into its tiny body....

No, she couldn't think of that, not now. She stared at his hand as he ran one finger up and down the moisture on his water goblet. Control. She had to keep control.

But the longing grew, and all she could remember was Jason, coaxing and tender, helping to bring a new life into the world. She wanted that...with him!

"You were so gentle," she said, unable to hold the words in. She put a hand over her eyes to hide the tears. Dear God, she was coming apart right there in front of him. She breathed deeply, striving for calm.

"What did you expect?" he demanded. "That I'd yell at her like I did when you—" He stopped abruptly.

She lowered her hand and stared at him. He looked as if he'd been turned into the proverbial pillar of salt.

The scene came to her, as real as if it were happening this very minute. She'd been cold, so cold. Then she'd felt nothing. Sleep had stolen over her. She'd dreamed of a meadow bathed in sunlight. Instinctively she'd known if she but crossed the short distance to it, she'd find warmth. She'd taken one step, then another—she was almost there!—but something called her back.

A voice, angry and urgent, had broken into her dream, calling her name, forcing her to stop. Someone *slapped* her! The meadow had disappeared, and she'd been cold again...cold and frightened.

"What's wrong?" Jason asked, his tone low and tense, breaking into the memory...dream...whatever it was.

"Nothing," she said, "just a...I just remembered a dream."

Jason had never shouted at her. He'd never touched her, much less slapped her. Certainly he'd never held her in his arms and wept over her...warm, wet tears on her cold skin. She touched her cheek, almost expecting to feel the moisture. It had been so real.

She shook off the nightmare. "When I what?" she asked, going back to his unfinished statement. "When did you yell at me?"

"When you missed that easy net shot the time we were tennis partners," he reminded her.

"Oh. That was a long time ago."

"Yes," he agreed. "A long time."

His thoughts seemed to turn inward after that. She wondered what he was thinking of. Their first course arrived, dispelling the moody silence. She decided it was time to start her campaign.

"About Paradise Falls," she began.

Jason listened to Victoria talk, her voice like a sweet melody as she spoke of the growth potential and low labor costs of the small town tucked into the West Virginia hills. She was so earnest, so appealing, it did things to him. Like make him want to snatch her up and— Forget it!

"So, will you come talk to the town council?" Victoria said at the end of her long list of arguments.

"Maybe," he said. When she opened her mouth to argue, he held up one hand. "Let it rest. You still have two days to go."

She grinned happily. "I'll have you convinced by then."

Heat flowed into his body. He wanted to kiss her. He'd never known the taste of her, but he'd imagined what it would be like.

"You'll try," he said, groping for a lighter tone.

"I'll succeed."

They had finished their main course, refused dessert and lingered over coffee while she extolled the wonders of the town. It was time to leave. He glanced around the dimly lighted room. The tables were filled with couples, laughing and talking, or just gazing at each other with love in their eyes.

He glanced back at Victoria. She was watching the dancers on the narrow strip of hardwood flooring. He somehow knew she wanted to join them. "Let's dance," he heard himself say.

Victoria was startled by his suggestion. She had been longing to do that very thing. She felt very young and girlish all of a sudden. When he guided her to the floor with a hand on her back, her skin burned all the way from her neck to her feet.

They danced circumspectly, with an inch between

them, unlike the couples on either side of them who were so entwined there was no visible space separating them. But she was aware of his hand at her waist. A tremor rushed over her. His hand tightened.

The top of her head came about even with his mouth. She noted he gazed over her head as if at some distant universe he longed to explore. She wanted to be there with him.

He glanced down at her. Their eyes locked. For a heartbeat, she saw the hunger, hot and passionate, in him. She suddenly felt as if she were drowning. She caught herself in time to prevent her body from gliding into his. Her lips trembled as she imagined the feel of his mouth on hers. She wanted him to touch her. Dear God, she wanted him to make love to her.

"This is all so crazy," she murmured.

"Yes," he said as if he understood exactly what she meant.

She wasn't sure *she* knew. How could he?

"When do we leave for the cabin?" she asked, breaking the visual contact. If she thought on practical matters, perhaps she could control her more tempestuous thoughts.

"Early. Can you be ready by seven?"

She nodded.

"I'll pick you up at the hotel. We'll have breakfast there, then get on the road before the freeway becomes crowded."

"Where is this cabin?"

"On a lake about two hours from here. It's hilly. There are woods all around so you can't see the other cabins."

It sounded like a perfect retreat, the type of place she had loved to go for a vacation. She'd always liked the quiet and the sense of being alone with the person she loved.

She stole a glance at Jason again. Love?

No, not really. They'd shared a moment out of time, one that would always be special to her—the drama of birth, the revelation of this other side of him—but it was no more than that.

Jason was an interesting enigma, there was something about him that stirred her imagination, but that was all.

His hand tightened at her waist as if he knew of her troubled thinking. They looked into each other's eyes, their lips as close as a trembling breath. For a second she imagined she saw a need that matched her own, then it was gone. He smiled, and his expression turned sardonic.

She'd do well to be wary of him, she reminded herself. He was a man guaranteed to break the heart of a woman so foolish as to fall in love with him.

Chapter Three

The music drifted into a slow song of lost love. Victoria felt an ache in the vicinity of her heart. Why did love have to be so sad? It wasn't always like that, she recalled. Her marriage had been filled with a deep, quiet sense of happiness.

Being with Jason didn't make her feel quiet at all. He made her nervous, put her on edge, wrought a tempestuous longing in her that reached right into her soul—

She stopped the wild thinking. Really, there was no need to dramatize the day's events nor her reactions to him.

When the music ended, she sighed with relief. He hadn't spoken during the sad love song, and his face had gone blank. As if he'd wiped clean every thought and emotion, she mused while he paid their bill.

Once on the street and heading for her hotel, she fell behind as he set a furious pace. Upon realizing he'd left her, he stopped and spun around. "Sorry," he muttered when she came alongside him.

He took her hand and looped it over his arm, thus holding himself to her stride.

"I'm not sleepy, are you?" he asked. They were ascending the steps in front of the hotel. A porter opened the door for them.

"No," she said. Was she up to a nightcap in the dim lounge? It might be better, considering her state of awareness of him, for her to put some distance between them.

"It's only ten. We could be at the cabin by midnight."

"T-tonight?" she stuttered.

They stepped into the elevator. The doors silently closed. He pushed the button for her floor. "Have you anything you have to do tonight or in the morning?"

"No."

"Well?"

She sensed the controlled impatience in him. He'd made up his mind, now he wanted to be off. The tension in him was almost palpable. A return of her earlier sympathy had her agreeing to the change in plans.

"Shall I pack and check out tonight?" she asked, digging the key out of her purse and handing it to him.

"Yes." He opened her door and stood back to let her enter.

The first thing she noticed was the bed. The covers were neatly turned down to reveal pastel sheets. Her lacy nightgown was spread over the sheets, the waist pleated into intricate folds. A rose and two candy mints lay on one pillow.

The scene was deeply, romantically intimate.

Need rose in her. She longed for warmth and the closeness of lovers. From a long way off, she heard the door close behind her. She let her purse drop into a chair. Slowly, she turned.

Jason stood in front of the closed door, his hands thrust

into his pockets. His eyes, as dark as midnight in the glow of the soft lamplight, roamed over her. She saw the leap of raw hunger in him.

A sound, almost a moan, tore out of her throat.

He stared at her without moving. Ten seconds... twenty...

The silence became unbearable.

She didn't know who moved first. All at once, his hands were on her, gripping her shoulders. His mouth descended, closed over hers. It was a kiss that burned all the way to her soul.

After that first startled second, she found her response came naturally. When his tongue stroked her, she opened her lips to let him in. Deep inside, she felt a softening as heat flared. Needs long suppressed bloomed into life. She swayed toward him.

He bit out an oath and abruptly went to the window where he stood with his back to her. "How soon—" He paused, then started again. "How soon can you be ready to go?"

His voice was harsh, almost hoarse sounding. Its timbre caused a chill to rush along her arms. Like him, she had to clear her throat in order to speak.

"Ten minutes?"

"All right. Wear something comfortable."

She nodded, even though he couldn't see. Glancing at the window, she realized he could. He was watching her through the reflections in the glass. Another shiver shook her.

Choosing the outfit she'd worn on the flight to North Carolina, she fled into the bathroom to change. When she returned, she quickly placed her suit, black dress and blouses in the suit bag, zipped it closed, then stuffed her overnight bag with her toiletries, nightgown and shoes.

"Ready," she said.

He looked at his watch. "Eight minutes," he commented. "Pretty good for a female."

He'd apparently recovered his poise. She wished she could say the same. He picked up the two pieces of luggage and led the way out. In the lobby he went for the car while she checked out.

"Was the room not to your liking?" the desk clerk inquired. He was young and seemed anxious about her leaving.

"It was lovely. Housekeeping did an excellent job. My plans changed unexpectedly." She hesitated, not sure if she'd be back Sunday night or not. "Perhaps I'd better reserve a room—"

"We're booked from tomorrow to the end of next week," the young man apologized. "There'll be a convention in town."

"That's all right. I'm sure I'll find something."

When she walked out the front door, Jason was there in his luxury-model car. He'd taken off his jacket and tie and rolled his sleeves up. She climbed in. When she had the seat belt fastened, Jason lifted his foot from the brake and started forward.

They left the bright lights of town. The night enclosed them.

Jason realized he hadn't said a word the entire trip. He would have to play the polite host all weekend, so he'd better start now. He stopped at a restaurant. "What would you like—coffee, cola?"

"Nothing, thank you," she replied just as politely.

"Other than wishing you didn't have to deal with me?" He slammed the door and went inside before she could answer. When he returned, he was aware of her curious stare. He started the car and drove off. If she could see into his mind...

Images of them at the cabin came to him with the regularity of the telephone poles whizzing by the windows. He kept seeing her in that silky piece of pink lace. It was so thin and pale, it'd be like she wore nothing at all.

His body throbbed painfully.

He took a drink of coffee and licked his lips, remembering the taste of her when he'd kissed her. She'd been startled, then almost at once, her mouth had softened and started to open. He'd backed off and gotten away from her.

If he'd taken her mouth completely, he wouldn't have been able to stop. He shuddered, just thinking of it...of all the things he'd like to do to her.

Did she know how near the brink he'd been while they were dancing? She would have if he'd pulled her close like the other couples around them. If she'd pressed against him, there would have been no doubt in her mind where his thoughts had traveled.

Damn, a person would think a thirty-three-year-old man could handle something as simple as lust. Only...he'd wanted her too long to be sane about it. She'd always been his one craziness, the one desire he'd never been able to eradicate or control.

"It's a lovely night for a drive, isn't it?"

Her voice—soft, melodious, just a tad concerned—broke into his raging thoughts. He risked a glance her way and found her watching him, her eyes luminous in the light from the dash. A giant fist clenched inside his gut, making the ache worse.

"Yes," he mumbled, not remembering the question.

He stared at the blank ribbon of highway, boldly out

lined by the moon. The night seemed dangerous and unpredictable, the air like quicksilver. He shouldn't have suggested she come to his cabin. It was a damned stupid thing to have done.

"I don't have to go," she murmured. "You obviously don't want me..." Her voice trailed to a stop, a slight question at the end.

"What makes you think that?" He tried to maintain his amused aloofness, but failed. Nothing had been funny so far that day.

"Your eager manner?" she suggested dryly.

"Sorry," he said, "I'll try to be more congenial."

Victoria felt a flicker of anger. "Don't strain yourself," she advised in a tone of mendacious concern.

He gave a snort of laughter that wasn't in the least amused. "You don't know," he muttered. "You just don't know."

"Know what?" she exclaimed in annoyance. "Was it the kiss? I'm sorry about that. I...it shouldn't have happened."

She must have been the one to step forward. Yes, she was sure she had. That was why he was so wary of her.

He stared at her for a split second before turning his dark, moody gaze back to the highway. "Damn," he said.

"Look, just take me back—"

"We're over halfway there."

"If you didn't want me, you shouldn't have suggested it," she snapped right back at him.

His grip on the steering wheel tightened. "But that's the problem," he drawled with deceptive calm. "I do want you. I want you right this minute."

She gasped at his boldness.

He gave her a coolly amused glance. "Is that so sur-

prising? After all, you're a beautiful woman. I'm an ap
preciative male. What could be more natural?''

His shrug was all nonchalant self-control. She wishe
she had a little of it. Right now she felt as if she'd ru
through a mine field…and set off every batch of explo
sives.

"It was the kiss, wasn't it?" She was embarrassed. H
probably thought she was a man-hungry widow.

"Right." He sipped from his coffee cup, his mout
suddenly hard and thin-lipped. He seemed angry.

She pressed her lips together nervously. He couldn
possibly know about her restlessness during the after
noon, nor the thoughts she'd entertained of them.

"Relax, Victoria," he said. "Nothing untoward is go
ing to happen. We'll simply discuss the business pros
pects of Paradise Falls while we fish and relax."

"Of course."

She'd been wrong about the anger. He was laughin
at her. She had to explain. "About the kiss—" She ig
nored his throaty sound of irritation. "It was because o
this afternoon. I mean, after seeing you with Susan. Yo
were so gentle." She had to stop and clear her throa
when her voice became reedy.

"The emotion of the moment?" he suggested.

"Yes," she said, glad that he understood. "It wa
wonderful, watching you, listening to you. I felt a par
of life again. It was as if I were waking up after a lon
sleep—"

"Like seven years?"

She met his probing gaze. "Yes."

Jason felt the renewal of desire in his blood. Her softl
spoken agreement, a sibilant murmur on the cool nigh
air, stroked him like a caress. He imagined the soun
coming to him from a shared pillow.…

Yes, Jason. Oh, yes. Yes! Yes!

His body became uncomfortably hard. He had to stop thinking of her like that. No way was he going to get mixed up with her. She'd been the wife of his best friend, he reminded himself grimly.

"All afternoon, I thought about how…how it would feel to have you touch me like that."

He strangled a curse and tried to keep from coming unglued. She wasn't being provocative, he reminded himself. Her tone was too apologetic. She was trying to explain something about the kiss to him…about why she'd started to respond.

"So, when we were in the room, I…it just happened. I didn't realize what I was doing. I hope you'll forgive me."

He frowned. What the hell was she talking about? "Forgive you?" he repeated, looking for some clue.

"For kissing you. It was like you said—the aftermath of a very dramatic afternoon, the tension and closeness and all."

The light dawned. "You…you think you kissed me?" he ground out, not sure he believed his own deduction.

"Yes. I started it—" She stopped at his bark of laughter and turned a wary gaze on him.

"Honey, you haven't a clue," he managed to say, holding in the laughter that was aimed at himself.

Victoria crossed her arms over her chest. Really, he was the most maddening creature she'd ever met. She was trying to be open and honorable about the whole thing and her ridiculous feelings, and he was laughing at her!

"I'm trying to be honest about this," she informed him. "This afternoon, I…well, I imagined…" She took

a deep breath. "I fell in love with you—a little bit—
watching you."

He gave her one of his cold, remote smiles. "Did
you?" He finished the coffee. "Are you afraid I'll take
advantage of your feelings while we're at the cabin? Is
that what's bothering you?"

"Of course not! I was trying to explain what happened
in my room, why I kissed you—"

"You didn't kiss me. I didn't give you a chance. I
started the kiss. I stopped it. When your lips went all soft
under mine, I knew I had to back off."

"Oh." Victoria tried to relive the moment in her mind
in order to see who had moved first. It was hopeless. All
she remembered was the kiss—hot, tempestuous and
much too brief.

She decided they had moved at the same time, a spontaneous action. Spontaneous combustion might be closer
to the truth.

"If I'd once tasted you, I'd have kept going...until I
tasted you all over."

"*Oh.*"

"Yeah," he agreed cynically. "Oh."

The rest of the trip was made in silence. A few minutes
after midnight, they pulled off the winding, two-lane state
road onto a narrow, tree-lined drive covered with pine
needles rather than pavement. They reached the house a
couple of minutes later.

"Wait here," Jason ordered.

He climbed out, opened the front door and flipped on
the inside and outside lights. The yard changed from
dark, menacing shadows into a fairyland.

Baby spotlights in blue and red were hidden among
the shrubs and trees, shining up through the foliage in

intriguing patterns. She saw that rocks and pine needles had been arranged to form ground covers so that no grass was necessary. Very efficient.

The cabin was a simple rustic log structure with a porch all the way around as far as she could see. She got out of the car and waited for his next directive.

From this viewpoint, she could see the lake, the moon shining on its still surface and reflecting pools of molten pewter. The wind was playful. It ruffled her hair and glided through the cotton of her blouse and slacks. She tucked her purse under her arm and hugged herself for warmth.

He returned and turned off the headlights, then locked the car doors and retrieved her bags from the trunk. "After you," he said, indicating she was to precede him inside.

She entered the house, filled with curiosity to see what his home-away-from-home revealed about his personality. She blinked in surprise.

"Why, it's charming," she exclaimed, taking in the comfortable chairs gathered in front of the hearth, the ceiling-high bookcase overflowing with novels and "how-to" books, and the curtains of some nubby material in honey beige. The dining area was at one end of the living room. There was a pass-through to the kitchen in the wall.

"What did you expect—the all-American bachelor pad?"

"No, I assumed you saved that for your city digs. I was afraid you went for the really primitive out here."

"Your bedroom is this way." He walked past her into a short hallway, where there were three doors and a staircase that led to an overhead loft. One doorway gave access to the kitchen. Jason opened the door to the left. He carried her luggage in and put the small case on a cedar chest at the foot of a queen-size bed. The suit bag he hung in the closet.

"The bathroom is behind the other door off the hall. There's only one. We'll have to share."

"That's okay. I don't mind."

"I wasn't apologizing."

"Fine. I still don't mind."

He gave her a hard glance before going to a chest of drawers and digging a pair of jeans and a T-shirt out of the jumble of clothing she saw in a drawer.

"Is this your room?" she asked. "I can sleep somewhere else. Really, I'd rather."

"This is the only bedroom with a door. You'll need the privacy." His tone dared her to argue.

She saw that he was tired. It had been a long day. "We should have stopped somewhere for supplies. A bowl of cereal or glass of cocoa would be nice. Milk helps a person relax."

He walked to the door and stood there with one hand on the knob, the other clasping his clothing. "There's food in the kitchen if you're hungry." He walked out and closed the door behind him.

Victoria sat on the corner of the bed and ran a hand through her hair. She rubbed her neck and realized she was pretty tired herself. Grabbing her case, she opened it and pulled out the nightgown, then the robe tucked into the bottom under her clean underwear. She changed, put toothpaste on her brush and started to the bathroom. A knock nearly startled her into dropping the brush on the shiny oak floor.

"Yes?" she called.

"I made some cocoa. If you want some."

She laid the toothbrush on her case and looked at her

outfit. The robe was heavy enough, perfectly respectable, in fact. It had long sleeves and a modest neckline. She decided to join Jason for the snack. The time, she saw, was one o'clock. Twelve hours past the time she was supposed to have seen him in his office.

Opening the door, she peered directly across the short hall into the kitchen. Jason was in there. He placed two steaming mugs on the counter that divided the kitchen and dining area.

He turned and gave her a laconic glance. "Come on out, Goldilocks. There's only one bear and he won't bite."

His changing moods were totally unpredictable—one minute angry, the next seemingly amused by the whole attraction thing between them.

Attraction? Yes. She wasn't feeling these crazy yearnings all by herself. He was vulnerable, too. For some reason that realization made her feel more secure.

"You guarantee that?" she asked, returning his gaze.

Placing his hands on his hips, he took a few seconds to study her mood. "Is that a challenge?" he finally asked.

"Maybe." She shrugged, then gave him a deliberate smile.

His chest expanded in a deep breath. He let it out slowly. She watched, fascinated. The curl of dark hair at the open neck of his shirt tempted her to unfasten another button and slide her hand inside....

"Very funny," he said. "Have a seat. I'll be with you in a moment." He searched the pantry until he found a tin canister. He placed it and a couple of napkins on the pass-through.

Victoria took a seat at the polished maple table. Jason placed the mugs and the tin of cookies on the table. He laid a napkin and spoon next to her place, then took the opposite chair.

She selected one cookie and nibbled on it. He wolfed down four, finished his cocoa and poured himself another cup after topping off hers. A man with an appetite, she surmised.

"Do you ever have trouble with your weight?" she asked.

"No."

She gave him an envious glance. "Lucky you."

He set down the cup and looked her over. "Do you?"

"Heavens, yes. Especially since I took office. I go to so many Rotary luncheons and Chamber of Commerce functions that I sometimes dream I'm swimming uphill through a flood of mashed potatoes and gravy. I wake up five pounds heavier."

Jason laughed at her wry confession. The sound enchanted her. With the night surrounding them, it seemed intimate and sensual, pleasing to all her senses, not just her hearing.

The warmth crept out of its secret place deep inside her and stole along her nerves. The delicately sizzling tension of sexual awareness glided into her consciousness.

He became silent. The amusement left his face, and he stared into his cup, his thoughts on some distant place only he could see.

She, too, became introspective. Her friends back in Paradise Falls would probably be disappointed if they could see her now, sitting here silent as a bump on a log.

They'd coached her for a week about what she was to say to Jason to convince him to return to his hometown for the centennial celebration of the town's official incorporation. Once she got him there, they figured they could convince him to move a plant into the vicinity in case she didn't.

And here she was, alone with him—he was a captive audience, so to speak—and she couldn't think of a word to say.

From the corner of his eye, Jason saw Victoria lift her cup and drink the cocoa. He almost groaned. He knew exactly what she would taste like. Since that ill-advised kiss in her room—a bad blunder, that bit of business— he now knew exactly how she felt when her lips became soft and welcoming.

That was the surprise, he realized. That she'd wanted him, too. Raw, wild feelings ran through him at the thought. He fought them until he was once again in control.

The knowledge of her desire gnawed painfully at his resolution not to become involved with her. She'd loved his cousin, and he would never take second place to any man, not even John. Especially not John. His mood darkened.

He realized she'd spoken to him. "What?" he asked.

"If you're finished, I'll wash up."

"Don't bother."

"I don't mind—"

"Forget it," he snapped. He saw the flicker of surprise, then hurt, pass over her face. He regretted his outburst, but couldn't bring himself to apologize. "Go on to bed," he said in a gentler tone. "You're my guest. I'll take care of this."

Victoria thanked him for the treat and took herself off to her assigned room, feeling she'd been put in her place. She was a guest, not part of his inner circle. There was to be no easy camaraderie between them.

Why didn't he like her?

She realized he never had. Maybe he didn't like adults. On a few occasions at family gatherings, she'd seen Jason warm and friendly with children, but rarely with others, not even John.

But he'd been wonderful with Susan.

Sighing, she took her toothbrush into the bathroom and prepared for bed. A few minutes later, tucked into the comfortable bed under a light blanket, she turned out the lamp and tried to settle down to sleep.

After giving up on counting sheep, she let her thoughts drift back to her enigmatic host. After their shared experience, she would no longer be able to look at him in the same light as she once had.

One thing he couldn't deny, in spite of disliking her, he'd wanted her as much as she'd wanted him.

A noise like a squeaky floorboard directed her attention outside. A shadow crossed her window. A momentary fear brought her heart to her throat. Then she realized the person was leaving the house.

Slipping from bed, she pulled her robe around her to guard against the chill night air. At the window she pushed the curtain aside and watched Jason walk soundlessly down the steps and along a path. He wore dark trunks, and his body gleamed like marble in the bright moonlight.

He looked like a young, powerful god come to life.

Through the clearing in the woods, she observed his rapid stride to the lake. She saw the white froth of his splash as he dove off the end of a pier.

She sank her teeth into her bottom lip as passion rose in waves like the ripples of water that flowed from his movement across the lake. For one insane moment she thought of going out and joining him.

A frolic in the moonlight…as if they were lovers….

She couldn't, of course. Casual, mindless sex wasn't in her makeup. That's all it would be for him.

What would it mean to her?

There was no way she could judge that in her present frame of mind. All she knew at the moment was the indescribable ache of longing. She wanted to be young and carefree and wildly in love.

The need grew in her, painful in its intensity.

Seven years ago she'd lost a vital part of herself in a tragedy she couldn't reverse. But now…now she felt that life waited for her. It was as close as…

She stared out the window at the lake.

As close as a walk in the moonlight.

Chapter Four

Victoria woke slowly the next morning. She snuggled under the covers, reluctant to face the day. To face Jason, she admitted.

Turning her gaze toward the window and the early-morning sunlight, her thoughts flew back in time to the dark hours after midnight. She'd stood by the window for twenty minutes, watching the small white splashes that indicated where Jason swam.

He'd finally climbed out of the water and come back to the house. She'd stayed there, her pulse hammering, when he took the two steps onto the porch. He'd paused, then looked toward her window. She'd known the precise moment he'd spotted her.

He'd become totally still. Like a stag scenting danger.

A frisson had dashed up and down her body. She'd wanted to run away and never see him again. She'd wanted to go to him and lose herself in the passion she knew she'd find with him.

But she hadn't. There was the bright light of day to be

faced the next morning, and she knew she couldn't easily sleep with a man, then continue as if nothing had happened.

Life seemed unbearably complicated all of a sudden.

She wondered what she would have done if he'd come to her. Instead he'd turned away, entered the house and gone to the bathroom. She'd heard the shower come on. Later, when the house had grown quiet, she'd known he'd gone to his bed in the loft. She'd fallen asleep after that.

Grimacing, she rose and went to the bathroom. Freshened, she returned and dressed again in the blue slacks and blue-striped shirt she'd worn on the trip. After making her bed, she ventured into the kitchen. It was seven o'clock. She figured she'd had about five hours of sleep.

There was no coffee made. Was Jason still asleep?

She listened for sounds from the loft. Nothing. It was almost eerie, not being sure whether she was alone in the house.

Searching through the cupboards, she found the coffee canister and put on a pot to brew in the coffeemaker. She found cereal on a shelf and a basket of fruit on the counter. In the refrigerator was a supply of milk, a loaf of bread, eggs, and fresh vegetables.

Hmm, curiouser and curiouser.

After helping herself to cereal and toast, she took her coffee mug and went outside to survey her surroundings.

The clearing opened onto a shallow cove on the bedroom side of the cabin. A pier led into deeper water, then turned a ninety-degree angle and jutted into the main body of water.

Walking out onto the wooden planks, she discovered the cove was part of a good-sized lake. It wasn't so large that she couldn't see the opposite side, but it was large enough to cruise around in a power boat.

Plunking herself down on a huge round pier post, she sipped her coffee and visually explored her surroundings.

Along the shoreline, she caught glimpses of civilization. There were several boat docks, all with rowboats or canoes. Motorboats must not be allowed. The residents apparently wanted their peace and quiet. She approved the idea.

She spied cabins tucked in among the trees. A lone fisherman cast his line from a breakwater of boulders extending into the lake from the next cabin to the left of the pier. She watched him catch a fish. When he pulled it out of the water, he held it up so she could see it before putting it in a small cooler. She waved.

"Hello. Are you visiting with Jason?" a female voice called to her.

Victoria swung around in surprise. A woman in shorts and a pink top tied under her breasts walked along the path around the cove, then stepped onto the pier. She was taller than Victoria's five-four, with a willowy grace Victoria associated with professional dancers. She was very attractive.

As she came closer, Victoria realized the woman was probably a year or two older than her own thirty-one years. She carried a basket, which was covered with a cloth napkin.

"Yes, I am," Victoria remembered to reply.

"I'm your neighbor, Millicent Bryant. That's my husband, Douglas, out there fishing. Call us Milli and Doug."

Again Victoria was surprised. The fisherman, with his gray hair, seemed much older than his thirties. Perhaps the woman was a well-preserved forty.

"I brought some fresh-baked rolls for Jason. Where is that scoundrel?"

"Still in bed," Victoria said without thinking.

She saw the neighbor's eyes widen slightly in surprise, then a big grin spread over her face. Heat suffused Victoria's cheeks when she realized what she'd said, or rather, what it implied about her relationship with Jason.

"Did you find everything you needed?" Milli asked. "I try to stock up on the most obvious staples when Jason calls to say he's coming down for the weekend."

"Yes, everything was fine." Victoria could feel herself drawing back from Milli's friendly inquisitiveness.

"Are you from Raleigh?"

"No." Victoria smiled to soften the curt reply. She may as well explain the situation before Jason beat her to it. "Actually, I'm from out of state. Jason is a cousin—"

"Oh, a relative." Milli looked disappointed.

"Sort of. I'm a cousin by marriage."

She saw the woman glance at her left hand. She'd put her wedding band away years ago along with the anger and sadness.

"I was married to Jason's cousin," she clarified.

"But you're not now?"

"I'm a widow."

"Oh, I'm so sorry."

"That's okay. It was long ago. I flew over from West Virginia to talk to Jason about a business deal."

"Business." Milli dismissed that idea with a deprecating wave of her hand. "Jason needs to lighten up. This is the first weekend he's been up here since he heard about that Navy contract."

Victoria glanced around, almost expecting to find Jason nearby, smiling in his cool, remote way while he listened to their conversation. The porch and yard were empty. Was he sleeping?

"They won the bid. I guess he decided to relax."

"Good. Here." Milli thrust the basket into Victoria's hands. "Look, tell Jason we have a refrigerator full of fish. I'd consider it a favor if you two would come over and help us eat them tonight. Around seven?"

"I'll tell him," Victoria promised.

She and Milli discussed the weather for a few minutes, then the other woman returned to her house. After another half hour, Victoria headed for the porch. The sun was getting hot.

Going in the kitchen door, she looked around. No signs of life. She put the basket on the counter, poured another cup of coffee and turned the pot off. Going into the living room, she peered upward. The loft had a half wall, preventing her from seeing into the area. Was he up there sleeping?

Surely he wouldn't have left without telling her. She tiptoed to the window. No, the car was still in front of the house.

She supposed he could have gone for a long walk. Or perhaps he was out fishing and she hadn't spotted him.

Her questions were answered by a low moaning sound from above, then the creak of bedsprings. Then all was quiet again. So, he was still asleep.

Remembering how tired he'd looked when he'd let his guard down the day before, she felt sympathetic. Selecting a book, she went out on the porch and read the rest of the morning.

Shortly after noon she went inside to fix a sandwich for lunch. Getting out bread, mayonnaise and a package of ham, she carried her stuff to the counter. She tried to open the wrapping on the meat with her teeth to no avail.

After muttering several expressive comments on package wrap in general, she rooted through the drawers until she found a knife.

She shoved the drawer closed with a swing of her hips and started back to her work area, her thoughts on Jason. The knife slipped out of her grasp and skimmed across the hardwood floor with two distinct thuds then a clatter until it came up against the cabinet with another loud bang.

Immediately thereafter, she heard feet hit the floor over her head. In another second, Jason appeared, a ferocious scowl on his face as he stormed into the kitchen wearing briefs that fit him very precisely. He stopped abruptly upon seeing her.

An image of long legs, lean hips, a broad, hairy chest plus several other masculine details burned its way into her memory.

She turned her back. "Sorry," she said. "I was hungry and decided to make a sandwich. I didn't mean to wake you. Would you like something? To eat," she hurriedly added.

She realized her sentence order wasn't very logical.

"Or perhaps you'd rather have breakfast," she nattered on, her face on fire as she envisioned several scenarios, none of which involved food. She picked up the knife from the floor. "I could fry some eggs."

"Forget it," he growled.

She heard his footsteps retreat. Heaving a deep breath, she got on with her lunch. Her hands were trembling. Seeing him with so little clothing on did things to her that she didn't like. And his body...magnificent and very male... She felt hot and fluttery inside just thinking of how masculine he'd looked.

Jason cursed himself for the fool he was as he went

upstairs to dress. Waking to some racket he couldn't identify, he'd gone to check it out without thinking.

As soon as he'd reached the kitchen door, he remembered his houseguest. By then it had been a second too late. He glanced down at his body in disgust.

There was no doubt she'd realized what had run through his mind upon seeing her. He was hard and aching for relief from the flaming desire that plagued him like a sore tooth. What imp from hell had gotten a hold on him and prodded him to invite her to the cabin for the weekend?

The real question was—how was he going to keep his hands to himself for another forty-eight hours?

He pulled on the jeans and T-shirt he'd laid out last night, then headed for the bathroom. He only nicked himself twice while shaving. After his ablutions, he combed his hair and started for the kitchen again, wishing he'd developed laryngitis the previous day or quietly lost his mind.

He laughed silently. That was the problem. He *had* lost his mind...head, rather. That was the only excuse for his lapse. He'd never had a woman at the cabin. It was his private place.

Well, he was stuck with her for the duration.

The kitchen was empty. A quick check out the windows informed him Victoria was sitting on the back porch, eating her lunch and reading a book.

He drank a glass of orange juice, poured a mug of coffee, then investigated a basket of cinnamon rolls on the pass-through. Milli had been over. He cooked an egg and ate it with a couple of slices of toast, then polished it off with a roll.

After washing the dishes, he had no excuse for lingering inside. He got two fishing poles and his tackle box out of the closet and went outside.

"I'm going to fish for a while," he announced to the woods. "I have a spare pole if you want to use it."

From the corner of his eye, he saw her lay the book against her breasts. The swelling in his lower regions started again.

"Your neighbor, Milli, invited us to a fish dinner at her house at seven. I told her I'd tell you. She brought some rolls over, too. I put them in the kitchen."

"I found them. If you see her before I do, tell her dinner would be fine." He wouldn't have to be alone with Victoria for the evening. That was a relief.

Victoria stayed in the chair. She couldn't tell if he wanted her to join him or not. Well, actually she was pretty sure he didn't, but did he expect her to? She would finish her book first.

The afternoon waned into early evening.

Victoria went out to the pier. She could see Jason working the shallows around some reeds a quarter way around the lake. She picked up the pole lying on the dock, saw it had a fishing lure attached and decided to try her luck. She cast from the end of the pier into the deeper water near the rocks.

To her surprise, the cast was straight and true. She'd not fished in ages. After five or six tries, she got a bite.

Excited, she pulled and reeled, pulled and reeled, until she had the fish close in. A bass. A big one. He came out of the water fighting. When he ran, she let him, then started pulling him in again, careful to keep the tension on the line.

"Steady on," Jason called. "Let him run. Now bring him back. Easy, easy." He leapt to the pier and came to her.

"It's a big one," she panted, pulling the pole up to bring the fish in, then reeling like mad as she lowered it again.

"I know. I saw him when he jumped." He stooped at the edge of the planking and readied a net to catch the thrashing bass when she brought it close enough.

It took over ten minutes for her to work the large fish in close enough for Jason to scoop him up. When he had him securely in the net, she slumped to the pier, her legs dangling over the side. "Wow, that was work."

"Good job," he complimented. He started to take the hook out.

"I'll do that."

"I'll take care of it for you."

"No," she said. "My father taught me to handle my own catch. Give it here, please."

Jason took one look at the set of her mouth and handed over the large-mouthed bass. He sat back on his haunches and watched her remove the hook, then, using the filleting knife, expertly clean the fish.

Admiration grew in him. She was a small woman, delicate looking, yet she could hold her own. Businesswoman. Mayor. Fishing buddy. Lover.

The ideas flowed one into the other without stopping.

"Hey, good catch." Doug Bryant came down to the shore on the other side of the little cove. "I believe that's the lunker Jason has been trying to catch for three years."

Victoria grinned back when he gave her a big wink. She glanced at Jason. He was smiling, too. Her heart felt suddenly lighter. "May I add my part to dinner tonight?" she asked Doug.

"Sure thing. The way Jason eats, we'll need the extra."

"I can believe that," she agreed.

"Hey," Jason protested, standing. "I'm sensitive about my eating habits, in case you two don't know it. And that isn't my fish. He's bigger and meaner than that tame thing. Why, it was so eager to get caught, it nearly jumped into her lap."

"It did not!"

"She couldn't have brought it in without my help," he added to Doug.

"I could, too!"

Victoria couldn't hold her indignant pose when he looked down at her and laughed.

Doug waved and started back to his house. "See you in about an hour."

"Right. Come on," Jason said to her. "We'd better clean up if we're going to make dinner on time." He held out a hand.

She took it and let him pull her to her feet. Tingles ran from her hand and lodged in her chest. As soon as she was on her feet, she let go and walked quickly ahead when he indicated she was to go first. Once off the pier, he walked beside her across the clearing to the house.

His shoulder touched hers. They both drew apart, but not before their eyes had met and looked away.

"You can have the shower first," he said. He took the fillets and headed into the kitchen without glancing back.

The attraction between them was as strong as gravity, she thought, becoming pensive. In her room she grabbed her robe and toiletries and headed for the bathroom. With the warm water running over her body, she contemplated the sparks that seemed to ignite whenever she and Jason touched.

She hadn't been to bed with a man since her husband died. The few times she'd thought about it—she had met

several attractive men over the years—something had
held her back.

Thinking on it, she realized she was too fastidious to
share herself intimately with just anyone. There had to
be more to it than sexual relief or even companionship.

So why the need to share herself with Jason?

She wasn't sure he liked her as a person. She'd often
thought him a cold individual. So why?

She knew he wanted her, but so had others. She didn't
think she was responding only to passion. She also knew
Jason wasn't all that cold and remote. Not after seeing
him yesterday.

Finishing her shower, she turned off the water and
dried off, her mind still puzzling over their reactions to
each other. She was beginning to suspect that Jason used
his insoucient attitude to hide his vulnerable side.

She put on her robe and went to her room. "You can
have the bath now," she called. Jason was sitting on the
porch, his long legs stretched down the steps.

Looking at him, she felt a softening toward him, not
of desire, but of tenderness. Yes, he'd been hurt. That
was the only explanation. Again she was seized by a
strange need to comfort him. She shook her head and
went into the bedroom, closing the door after her.

Victoria looked over her limited wardrobe. The black
dress definitely wasn't appropriate for a fish dinner with
a neighbor. Her blue slacks were beginning to look
wilted. She decided on the suit skirt and the pink silk
blouse that crisscrossed in the front. There, that was the
best she could do.

She combed her hair, which was still slightly damp,
and put on a creamy pink lipstick. Her nose and cheeks
were pink from her time in the sun, so she didn't add

any other makeup. She slipped on the flat, comfortable shoes she'd brought in case she got to do any sight-seeing.

Jason was waiting in the living room. Her heart thumped like mad when she saw him. He was wearing dark slacks and a red polo shirt. Contrasted with his black hair and vivid blue eyes, he reminded her of an adventurer.

"If you had your ear pierced, you'd look like a pirate," she told him, forcing herself to assume the ease of friendship they'd shared while catching the fish.

"Look closer," he invited, his laconic smile to the fore.

She boldly walked over to him and inspected his earlobes. Sure enough, his left one had been pierced.

"Product of my younger, more rebellious days," he admitted when she looked suitably impressed.

"You should be wearing a gold hoop." She smiled up at him. As she took a deep breath, the scent of his cologne teased her senses. She felt dizzy.

"Maybe I will one day. For you."

Things seemed to be getting heavy. She quickly changed the subject. "I can see you as a stormy teenager."

"Can you?" He raised one dark eyebrow, his mood amused and definitely devilish tonight.

His tone had dropped to a lower octave. It strummed an answering chord to life in her. Resonance, she believed it was called. She and Jason caused vibrations in each other when they were close. It was an exhilarating phenomenon.

And dangerous.

"Ready?" he asked.

She nodded, suddenly worried about what the evening

would bring. Heavens, but she was becoming as darkly moody as Jason could be at times.

They walked around the worn path to the Bryant home. Milli and Doug were in the kitchen. They called out greetings when Jason and Victoria stepped onto the porch and told them to come on in.

Victoria saw the layout of the house was the same as at Jason's cabin, with the dining area forming one end of the living room and a pass-through to the kitchen. There were two padded bar stools at the pass-through counter.

"Have a seat." Doug indicated the stools.

"Here's my special kickapoo joy juice," Milli announced. "It's wine and fruit juice, if you drink wine?"

Victoria nodded that she did. She sat on one of the stools. Jason took the other. Their knees brushed as they turned toward the kitchen.

Sparks seemed to leap at the slight contact. She took a big sip of the punch through a red-striped straw to cover her sudden case of the flutters. This was getting out of hand, she decided with a frown. She was acting like a…like a…a woman who was alive and well and very much interested in a virile male she didn't quite understand, but who intrigued her nonetheless.

Doug set the table with colorful, inexpensive dishes while Milli battered and fried Victoria's fish, then added it to a platter already heaped with golden-brown fillets.

"We don't have fried food often," Milli explained, "but once in a while I just have to have some home cooking. You know what I mean?"

"Yes," Victoria said. "I usually have soup or salad for my evening meal, but occasionally I rebel and go to the Paradise diner for a huge hamburger with cheese and onions and mushrooms. Oh, and the cook does the best

French fries. They're cut thin like yours, with the skin left on. I just love them.''

Jason stirred beside her. She glanced at him and caught his gaze on her. Although his smile was harmless, there was something mysterious in his eyes—something wild and dangerous and barely controlled. It called with unbearable insistence to something equally primitive in her that she'd never even known existed.

Since she'd stood close and teased him about wearing an earring, the tension had hummed between them, as tangible as the electricity in a high-powered line. She felt suffocated by it, by their longing for each other.

What a fantasy! Jason might want her, but it wasn't anything as emotional as longing. At least she didn't think so. It was just desire and proximity.

''Dinner is served,'' Doug informed them. He put the platter of fish in the center of the table.

Jason took Victoria's arm and helped her down from the stool. Without releasing her, he guided her to a chair and seated her. He waited until their hostess was seated before taking the chair next to Victoria.

The food was delicious, their host and hostess were charming. Just as Victoria began to feel completely at ease, Jason asked Doug a question about his company. She discovered the down-to-earth fisherman was president of Home Industries, one of the most prestigious home improvement and decoration companies in the United States.

Oh, dear, and here she'd been so chummy, telling silly little anecdotes about her fishing and camping experiences so that she'd had them all laughing, including Jason.

''Victoria isn't quite the rustic she pretends to be,'' Jason drawled. He pulled a curl that lay over her shoulder, then continued to hold it, brushing it back and forth with one finger. "This country cousin is actually an accomplished politician. She's mayor of Paradise Falls."

"We should have been calling you Your Honor," Milli exclaimed.

"Oh, just bowing three times when I enter the room is enough," Victoria said modestly. That drew another laugh.

They talked until eleven, then Jason said it was time to go. "I want to get a head start on the fish tomorrow," he explained.

After they said good night and were walking along the path, she decided to do a little probing into his psyche. "You're different here, more friendly and outgoing. In Paradise Falls, you seem to withdraw. Why?"

She stopped and waited for him to come alongside her when she reached the clearing. He stopped, too, his face in the shadows of the pines along the path.

"Maybe it's the company." His voice was cool, like the night wind off the lake. The movement of his shoulders indicated a nonchalant shrug.

Her question had caused him to recede to his safe, remote distance. That was it, she realized. Safe—that was the key. He kept his relationships at a guarded distance from his heart.

He liked the Bryants, he was obviously friends with his secretary and her husband, but they didn't threaten the secret part of himself he tried to keep hidden from the world.

She'd been right. Sometime in the past, he'd been deeply hurt. She was as sure of it as sailors were of the pole star that guided their voyages.

Folding her arms across her midriff, she crossed the clearing and sat on the porch. Jason joined her, taking a seat on the other side of the steps and leaning his back against the support post.

"You were once in love," she said softly. Sometimes the night shadows could inspire confidences.

He said nothing.

"You were hurt, so you keep people away by being cynical and cool and distant with them."

The silence grew between them. She decided to wait him out. Finally he laughed. It was brief and without humor.

"There," he said, "you have my life all figured out."

"Talk to me, Jason."

"What's to say?"

"Tell me how to handle the attraction between us. Tell me where it came from, what it means, where it will lead."

He stood and paced down the steps. At the bottom he spun and glared at her, his face highlighted by the moonlight.

Nearly naked, he'd looked like a god last night, sleek and muscular and powerful. She fought the vision but it haunted her.

"Are you attracted?"

"Yes. Aren't you?" she challenged.

"Hell, yes. I told you that much when we talked about the kiss that almost got out of hand."

"What are we going to do about it?"

He muttered a curse. "Nothing."

She'd always been honest about her feelings, to herself at all times, to others most of the time. She wanted to be the same with Jason. She wanted to understand her feelings and his.

"Why don't you like me?" she asked.

Jason swore violently to himself. She was surely the

most exasperating female he'd ever known. Instead of being hurt by this realization, she sounded concerned...for him! Her worry touched a place deep inside that he didn't want disturbed. He answered with the flippancy her probing deserved.

"What makes you think I don't? After that kiss and what I told you about it—"

"That was passion," she broke in. "Or just plain, everyday lust. I don't think you have to like a person to desire them."

She seemed a bit unsure of the last statement. For her, passion and feelings would be mixed, impossible to separate.

A flare of emotion surged inside him. It would be easy to take advantage of her. She was vulnerable after the crisis yesterday. Her emotions were tender and confused.

He could take her, he realized. Right this moment he could sweep her into his arms and carry her inside to his bed and make sweet, mindless love to her all night long until they were both sated with pleasure.

He was tempted.

But then there would be tomorrow's regrets, he reminded himself savagely. He couldn't face her disappointment when she woke up and realized he wasn't John, but a man who superficially favored him. He'd seen that disillusionment in her eyes once. He never wanted to see it again.

"What do you want from me?" He spoke harsher than he meant to, but was gentler than the rage inside him demanded. "I can't turn back the clock. I can't erase the kiss. I can't deny the fact that I want you. *Like* seems a pretty tame word for the fires you ignite in me."

"Jason," she murmured, breathing his name.

Her voice came to him with the softness of a caress.

He sensed the quick urgency in her, the need that matched his. She wanted him. He wanted her. He had only to reach out....

Victoria leapt to her feet and stood there at the edge of the steps, poised for flight, either to him or from him, she wasn't sure which. "Maybe *like* isn't the correct word. Do...do you know any others?"

"Pretty words. Is that what you want, Victoria?"

"Yes. Everything."

He seemed to know what she meant. He sucked in a hard breath, then turned from her, facing the lake.

"Everything?" he questioned. "I can give you the night. That's all."

The lonely cry of a loon underscored the melancholy that engulfed her.

"Will that be enough?" he probed relentlessly.

"Will it be enough for you?"

He slowly pivoted and faced her. "We can always find out." He held out his hand to her.

Chapter Five

Victoria held herself still, refusing to give in to her first impulse and take his hand. Did she know what she was doing? More importantly, did she understand why?

Pity for Jason's past hurts wasn't cause enough to accept what he offered—one night and nothing more. For both their sakes, she had to be sure of exactly what she wanted from him before she took that step. The future depended on it.

"Thinking of tomorrow?" he asked, a smile touching the corners of his mouth.

She was no longer surprised at his perception. "Yes."

"Go to bed, Victoria. And lock your door." He walked past her up the steps. "It's going to be a long night."

Troubled, she turned when he held the door open and waited for her. She went inside and to her room, closing the door securely after her. She heard the outside door close, then his footsteps on the porch, going away from the house. Later, when she was ready for bed, she went instead to the window and gazed at the moonstruck night scene.

Jason was outside. He sat on one of the pier posts, his legs stretched out in front of him and crossed at the ankles. His hands were in his pockets. He looked…so alone.

Again she was overwhelmed by her need to go to him and hold him in her arms, to give him what comfort she could. She cared for him, she realized. She cared deeply about this man who held himself aloof from involvement, yet who, she sensed, was as full of yearning as she.

Was she…could she be falling in love with Jason?

The next morning Victoria knew Jason was up before her. She heard him in the kitchen when she went into the bathroom.

The aroma of coffee and bacon piqued her appetite. She hurried and dressed, grimacing at the navy-blue slacks and striped blouse as she put them on. She folded a blue scarf and tied it around her head to hold her hair back.

"Good morning," she said cheerfully, crossing the hall into the kitchen.

He was breaking eggs into a pan. "Hello." He glanced once in her direction and went on with his task. "How do you like your eggs?"

"Over medium."

He nodded.

She helped herself to orange juice and coffee. Seeing the toast had popped up, she buttered it and put it on a plate. In a couple of minutes, they sat down to eat. He didn't bother with polite conversation. Jason the inscrutable was back.

Victoria ate her meal and tried not to be aware of Jason. She didn't want to worry about him, or feel anything for him. "Life is much easier when you don't feel things too deeply, isn't it?" she asked on a philosophical note when they finished eating.

"Still wrestling with your conscience over last night?" he asked, apparently amused by her predicament.

"Nothing happened last night," she reminded him. "What's on the agenda today?"

"I'm going fishing."

No invitation to her.

"I'll join you."

One thing her mother had always told her—don't fall in love with a stubborn man. He'll make you consider murder many times. Victoria was beginning to understand her mother's impatience with her father.

Jason gave her a hard glance. "I'll leave you some tackle on the pier."

She could be stubborn, too. After all, she'd gotten half her genes from her father. "That's okay. I'll tag along with you."

She tried to dazzle him with her smile. He ignored her and finished his coffee. Without further ado, he picked up all the dishes and took them to the kitchen. He washed them and left them to drain. She didn't volunteer to help.

When he went outside without a word, she filled her mug, pulled on a baseball cap she spied on a hook behind the door, and ambled out, too. She found Jason preparing to cast a line into the middle of the cove.

"I think I'll try my luck on this side of the pier," she called out. He made a noise that could have meant anything, but which she took as assent. She picked up the pole she'd used the day before and cast to the right.

Within thirty minutes, the peace of the place invaded her soul. She was able to look with amusement on the situation between her and Jason. The gods must have been chuckling while she flew so innocently to her fate. To awaken her to the one man who didn't want any emotional entanglements was no laughing matter.

So what was she going to do?

"Tomorrow I'll be gone," she said aloud.

Jason spoke directly behind her. She realized he'd moved onto the pier and was working the reeds on the other side. "Tonight," he corrected. "We'll be on our way right after lunch."

"I don't have a room for tonight. The hotel was booked with some convention."

"Damn. Why didn't you tell me sooner? Instead of checking out, you could have kept your room. They can't make you leave."

His irritation dampened her contentment. "I can probably find something—"

"You can stay at my place in town. It has three bedrooms. With locks on the doors," he tacked on as if this was a selling point with a prospective buyer.

"Afraid I won't be able to control my wild impulses?" she asked. "I'll try not to force myself on you."

She was sorry for her flippancy when she met his eyes. He looked angry and frustrated.

"Keep pushing," he advised.

"I'm sorry." She laid a hand on his arm, silently asking his forgiveness. Their problem was no minor thing. They were adults. They had to temper need with the knowledge experience had given them. She knew loneliness. She knew anguish. Jason did, too.

He stared at her hand, then sighed. A half grin tilted the edges of his mouth. "So am I. I'm in a rotten mood and taking it out on you. I apologize."

"Thanks. Look, I've got a bite."

The tension eased after that. They spent the morning in companionable fun, giving each other advice and rubbing it in when a fish got away.

Doug and Milli came out to the shore. "You two want to have lunch with us?" Milli yelled.

A chorus of voices answered her. Victoria noticed that other people were enjoying the lake, sitting on porches or in the grass or on boat docks. After much laughter and casual planning, it was decided everyone would bring a bag lunch, meet on Jason's pier and eat there.

A half hour later, Victoria realized she was having a great time. She met the neighbors on the north side of Jason's place and those to the south of Doug and Milli. They were all a little older than Jason and herself. Their kids were either married or off on their own pursuits, she learned.

She caught Jason looking at her more than once as if concerned that she was having fun. He was being the congenial host.

On an impulse she wrinkled her nose at him, then blew him a kiss. He grinned at her, then turned back to his conversation with the man to his right.

When it was time to go back to the city, she rose reluctantly. It was nice to be part of a friendly group. With Jason beside her as they crossed the clearing, she realized it was nicer to be part of a couple. If they were married, they could make love before they returned to the city.

It was a thought that plagued her the entire trip to town.

His home was in a wooded neighborhood of modest houses, not an ultramodern bachelor pad at all. He led the way inside when they arrived, his mood unreadable.

"This is nice," she said, admiring the period reproductions that added interest to his contemporary furnishings. An ornate gold-framed mirror resided over an old-fashioned drop-leaf table. A dried flower arrangement decorated the table.

"Your room is this way."

He started down the hall with her suit bag and case. She followed, peering around with undisguised curiosity. It was a nice house…comfortable…perfect for a family.

The guest bedroom he gave her was decorated in blue with lots of white accents and touches of mauve. The adjoining bath was white with blue and mauve bath towels of all sizes used as practical yet decorative displays.

"How lovely," she exclaimed. "I love the colors."

He glanced around the room. "It's okay, I guess." He set her case on the bathroom counter and placed the suit bag in the closet. "Did you bring some sturdy shoes? I thought we might hike along the bluff this afternoon. There's a good view."

She shook her head. "But you go on. I think I'll read."

He'd obviously had all of her company he could take for the weekend. She would try to stay out of his way. Give him some space, as the current philosophy went.

"All right. I thought we'd go over to Durham about six and have dinner. There's an old tobacco warehouse that's been turned into a shopping and dining complex. Is that okay with you?"

"Fine."

He checked on the soap and other necessities in the bathroom, then left. She felt the brightness seep out of her. They'd…correction, *she'd* had such a good time at the impromptu picnic with the other couples, she'd assumed he'd felt the same. Wrong.

She used the bathroom, then went downstairs. The silence bothered her. Restless, she explored the house. It was U-shaped with a formal living room, dining room

and kitchen on one side. The master bedroom was behind
the kitchen. She glanced quickly in the open door and
retreated.

The other side of the house contained two bedrooms
and a large family room. The family room and kitchen
adjoined in a breakfast nook facing the backyard.

From this point she watched Jason exit through a gate
at the far end of the long, narrow yard and strike off
through the woods. She glanced at her watch. She had
two hours before it would be time for their gala evening
at the tobacco warehouse.

Finished with her wandering through Jason's house—
she realized she was looking for more clues into his personality—she returned to her room, took a leisurely bath,
washed and dried her hair, then lay down for a nap with
an afghan over her.

She woke in confusion some time later. A banging on
the door caused her to frown. The door swung open. Jason leaned inside, keeping his feet firmly planted in the
hall.

"You didn't answer my call," he said. "Are you all
right?"

"Yes. I must have fallen asleep."

She saw his eyes burn a path down her neck and realized the afghan was bunched at her waist and she wore
only her underwear. She pulled the cover to her neck.

A smile flicked across his mouth. "Too late," he said
softly. He shook his head. "Just when I think I have
myself under control, I see you in a new light. It's hard
on my ego to realize I'm as vulnerable to the perfect
female form as an adolescent hanging out on a street
corner." He closed the door. "It's time to get dressed,"
he reminded her from the hallway.

Victoria let the afghan drop. She paused on the way

to the closet and studied her figure. Perfect? Hardly. She thought her breasts were too heavy and her hips too rounded. But then, so did ninety percent of the women in America.

Tonight she chose her blue skirt again, but with the white lace blouse over it, belted at the waist. That was the most she could do to vary her three outfits.

The drive to Durham was accomplished to the beat of a popular rock station in the area. Victoria gave Jason a wry glance. She figured the purpose of the music was to prevent his having to talk to her. It worked.

The warehouse was larger than she'd expected. So was the crowd. She and Jason window shopped for an hour before their dinner reservation. She hooked her hand over his arm so they wouldn't become separated. Whenever they were jostled, he tightened his arm instinctively to hold her securely to him.

Tiny flames ignited within her. She felt safe with him, she realized. Safe from others, not from him, nor from herself. The yearning that had awakened while watching him during the emergency had grown stronger over the weekend. His home and cabin, his ease with his neighbors, his caring attitude toward his secretary and his gentleness toward children, all these indicated to her a man who should have had his own family long ago.

At seven, they went to eat.

The restaurant, with its subdued lighting and soft music, lulled her senses. She resumed her review of Jason as a potential lover, knowing she was drifting into a fantasy. Strangely, it didn't seem to matter so much at the moment.

"I should be convincing you to return to Paradise Falls," she told him at one point.

"Will the city council be angry if you don't?"

"No. They don't know the purpose of my trip. I didn't want to get their hopes up in case I couldn't persuade you to attend the centennial celebration." In case she failed, she admitted to herself. "I wanted to speak to you alone."

"And wear my defenses down?" He gave her a cynical grin. His restless gaze roamed her face and flitted across her mouth before he looked away. "You've done that."

"I have?" She laughed in delight. "Then you'll attend?"

"I didn't say that. Only that my defenses were down."

Their eyes met. For a second she saw darkness in him, as if she looked into his soul. Then she saw the desire.

She understood that she would have to be the one to set the mood, and the limits, between them. It was up to her how far they would go. Jason wanted her, and he was no longer fighting it!

The knowledge both frightened and enthralled her. She'd never felt this responsible for another person, she realized. She could give him what they both wanted, or she could withhold it.

The rest of the dinner passed with little conversation. On the drive back to his home, he seemed to have closed himself off. Victoria resisted an impulse to touch his arm and remind him she was there. She knew he was aware of her.

It was not quite eleven when they arrived. Once in the house, Jason asked her if she wanted anything before she went to bed.

You.

She didn't say it, but she thought he detected the unchecked response before she said no. "I think I'll call it a night. My flight leaves at nine. That's a terrible time to get to the airport, isn't it? Perhaps I should reserve a limousine.''

"I'll take you," he said tonelessly.

"Thanks." She hesitated. "Well, good night."

"Good night." He stayed in the entrance hall while she went to the room she'd been assigned.

The evening was ending on a flat note. After experiencing the invisible sparks between them, she found it difficult to relax.

Once in her room, she prepared for bed, but couldn't go to sleep when she was in it. She rose and paced the carpet, aware of the heavy beat of her heart and the emptiness inside her.

There was an answering void in Jason. He, too, knew the pain of losing a loved one. She didn't know the details, but the loss was etched in the bleakness she sometimes observed in his eyes. The ache in her heart grew...for both of them.

She couldn't go to him. There was no future in sharing one night of passion. The emptiness would return with the cold light of day. So would the distance he maintained between them.

She returned to bed, but her eyes refused to close. Finally, in desperation, she pulled on her robe and went to the family room for a magazine. Jason was there.

He sat in a leather reclining chair, seemingly at ease. The television was on, but he wasn't watching it. His gaze was focused on some far point deep in his own psyche. She sensed unhappiness in him, fierce and relentless. She couldn't bear it.

But...if she went to him, she knew what would happen.

She stood, rooted to the spot, while a battle waged inside her. She knew she should return to her room at once, and yet she couldn't. Just as she resolved to leave, he moved, rubbing his hand across his eyes as if a pain resided behind them.

She looked at his hands and remembered that he'd been ready to help bring a new life into the world. Suddenly a memory, or a fragment of a dream, came to her— Jason holding a tiny baby to his chest, his strong arms cradling it, his tears falling....

She thrust aside the old nightmare. Reality was now, and she knew the tears were still falling in his heart. The source of his grief was unknown, but it was there in every line of his body.

Her doubts dissolved. She wanted this night with him. She wanted all the passion they could share. It was important. She knew it instinctively, without knowing all the reasons why, the way a robin knows it's time to fly before the winter gale strikes.

Jason needed her, and she needed him!

She walked into the room. He looked around at her step, but he didn't speak. She came to him, stopped, then took one more step until she stood beside him. She leaned against him, her thigh touching his. With a steady hand, she stroked through his hair, smoothing the shiny black waves while her heart ached for the hurt in his past.

He stood, gliding upward against her. She laid her hands on his chest. For the longest time, they stood there. She began to be afraid that he'd reject her, then, with excruciating slowness, he put his arms around her.

She sighed and rested her head on his chest between her hands.

They stood there for several minutes, absorbing each other's warmth, letting the need build. Her heart matched the tempo set by his, hard and erratic, increasing with each beat.

Finally he turned her with a hand on her shoulder. They passed the light-oak breakfast table and entered his bedroom. He paused just inside the door. She waited.

He watched her without speaking for the longest time, then, "Are you sure?" His voice was husky, with no cynical overtones.

She wasn't sure of anything—his feelings, hers, the future. "No, but it doesn't matter."

"If you stay…" He left the warning incomplete.

She tilted her head to look at him. There'd be no going back for either of them, she finished his statement, wondering if her heart was going to be broken. "I know," she said.

Jason stood still another second, then he took the one step necessary to lift her into his arms. Common sense had deserted him. So had his willpower. He'd wanted her too long.

Tomorrow she'd be gone.

It was the price he'd pay, but he'd have the memory to go with the longing and the gnawing hunger. He would know her taste, her texture, the essence of her. For a few hours she'd be his.

He carried her to his bed, threw the covers back and placed her in it, a treasure not to be taken quickly, but savored. He was trembling with need, but he didn't give in to it.

When she smiled up at him, his resolve nearly slipped. Her eyes were luminous. They seemed to light a path to some secret place inside him, a place he'd kept locked away for years.

He'd stayed away from her, first because she'd belonged to his cousin, later because he'd refused to be a stand-in for another man, but now she'd come to him. Tonight would be theirs.

And tomorrow?

She was just a woman, he argued, trying to vanquish his misgivings—one that he'd wanted for years, it was true, but still, a creature of flesh and blood like any other. They would give each other mutual pleasure, and that would be it. She'd leave and he'd get on with his life, having at last satisfied a curiosity and a hunger he'd thought never to appease.

Having sorted this out, he began to unfasten his shirt. Still watching her, he peeled it off and kicked aside his shoes. Then he sat down and stroked her arm from shoulder to wrist. It was the first move toward fulfilling a dream. A sense of urgency came over him. Dreams rarely lasted the night.

Victoria realized the moment when Jason again put a distance between them. It was the instant before he touched her. Did he think to close her out during this most intimate of acts between a man and a woman?

Rising, she pressed against him and slid her arms around his neck. The warmth and strength of his masculine body almost shocked her, it had been so long since she'd known that pleasure.

She sought his mouth and found it. For a split second he remained still, then with a groan he pulled her close.

The kiss was harsh. She wanted gentleness. It was cool, exploratory. She wanted mindlessness, intensity.

She turned her mouth from his. "Jason, please."

"Please?" he repeated hoarsely, slipping his hand between them and caressing her lips with the tips of his fingers. A smile tipped the corners of his mouth. "I want to please you. Tell me what you want—"

"You," she whispered, desperate to reach him. *"You."*

She ran her hands over his chest as if she hoped to

find the secret door into his heart. But there was only the sleek, warm feel of him under her palms, nourishing her desire.

He caught her hands and pressed them to him. "You have me. I've wanted you too long to resist this taste of paradise."

Shaking back her hair, she studied the darkness in his eyes. "You hated admitting that." The rightness of coming to him began to dim. She'd been wrong. Aching with unfulfilled need, she pulled away.

"I hate admitting to a weakness I can't control. You're that weakness. God help me, but I can't let you go now."

He kissed her then, with all the passion, all the intensity she could ever have dreamed. A fever swept through her. She was on fire, a forest burning out of control. And loving it.

"Yes, yes," she whispered when he left her mouth.

She cradled his head against her as he kissed and nuzzled her breasts through the silky material of her gown and robe. Her body arched upward, wanting more of his touch, no longer under her command. It didn't matter. She would trust him with her life.

"Like that, do you?" he teased, looking at his handiwork with a pleased smile. There was no darkness in him now. She saw only the blazing light of passion.

Jason touched her shoulder, slipped his hand along her tingling skin to her neck and let the edge of one finger glide along her throat to her chin, then back. He found the tie on her robe and pulled it until the bow released. He pushed the robe off her shoulders, letting his hands flow over her.

Her skin reminded him of rose petals, except flowers were cool, having no internal fire. She was warm and smooth and delicate, the tips of her breasts a contrast to the softness he found elsewhere on her. She smelled of soap and powder and some exotic perfume.

He took her mouth again and felt her lips tremble. He was shaking all over as the need grew. "I have protection," he told her, thinking of this one last thing before it was too late.

Then he kissed her and kissed her and kissed her. She let him sample and taste her as much as he wished, giving her mouth to him without hesitation. He thought his heart would explode as he caressed her all over. When he slid her gown upward along her legs, she moved her hips so he could push it out of the way.

He stroked her thighs for long, mindless minutes before becoming more intimate.

Victoria shivered, then clutched him tightly. She could keep no secrets from him. She was ready, and he knew it.

The world diminished until it contained only the space that enclosed the two of them. She writhed against him, covered him with her kisses. Her lashes became too heavy to hold up.

"Oh, love," she whispered, her need too great to hide even if she'd wanted to. "Oh, love, come to me. Come to me *now*."

He jerked back from her, his expression fierce and angry.

Then he was gone, rolling away from her and off the bed. For a second he stood there, breathing hard. When he left, she was so stunned she couldn't move.

Jason grabbed his shirt, pulled it on and went out onto the private patio adjoining the master suite. He leaned against the Japanese maple and stared over the roofline at the night sky. It was full of stars, all twinkling as if

he world was the same now as it had been an hour ago.
He knew better.

Fool, he mocked himself. What had he expected? That
she'd say his name in the throes of passion?

Oh, love. The very words she'd used seven years ago.
He remembered every detail of the night....

The call had come in over the remote radio unit of the
pickup truck where he and an old high school chum, now
a deputy sheriff, were arguing over Paradise Falls's
chances of winning the state football trophy. His friend
had lifted a hand for silence and listened intently.

"There's an emergency," Bill said, cranking up the
engine. "Someone just reported car tracks over the cliff
near Vista Point. You want to ride along?"

"Sure." He had nothing better to do, except go home
and listen to his mother complain because he didn't visit
more often. Nothing he'd ever done pleased her. He'd
stopped trying long ago.

The deputy put on the light and siren, and they headed
out of town. At Vista Point, they pulled off the road.
Apparently they were the first officials at the scene.

"Here's an extra flashlight," Bill said, getting one out
of the glove box.

They walked back along the shoulder of the road, then
followed the car tracks down the shallow bluff. "Damn,"
Jason muttered to himself, seeing the twisted wreckage
below them.

"Yeah," Bill agreed. "Lucky if anyone's alive in
there. There's an inch of snow over the tracks. That
means it must have happened three or four hours ago.
Probably been to Beckley to do some Christmas shopping."

They made their way down the snowy bank. Through
the rear window, they could see two people in the front

seat. Bill went to the driver's side while Jason worked his way to the passenger.

"Oh, God," Bill said softly. "Jason, don't look—"

But it was too late. He'd already seen who was in the car. Through the broken side window, he gazed at Victoria.

Pain tore out of his soul and clawed at his throat. She was deathly still, and pale, except for the red streak of blood that had dried on her neck where the glass had cut her.

"Victoria," he murmured hoarsely, almost afraid to wake her, more afraid that he couldn't. "Victoria, wake up, sweetheart."

He wrenched the door open. One glance at the driver's side told him his cousin was beyond any help he could give him. He laid his hand on Victoria's throat.

"I'll go up and call for help. We'll need wreckers and pulleys to get them out of here. Is she…" Bill hesitated.

"I don't know," Jason said. "I can't find a pulse."

Bill uttered a fierce expletive and headed up the slope.

"Come on, honey," Jason whispered, patting her cheeks. He touched her hands which were clutched on the lapels of her coat, holding it closed over her rounded body. She was icy cold.

He spoke to her, coaxing her to wake as time passed and she didn't stir. Despair gripped him when he realized she was probably gone. Fury washed over him in its wake. Fate couldn't do this to him! He wouldn't let it!

He shook her. Her head rolled around like a rag doll's. "Victoria! Damn you, wake up! You can't die!"

Nothing.

He shook her again. He tried to find a pulse. There was none. "No," he said, fierce and low. Life had never been fair. He'd stopped expecting that long ago, but to take her…

"You won't die," he muttered. "I won't let you." He would defy death itself before he'd give her up.

In desperation, he slapped her. Her eyes snapped opened.

"Victoria," he said, clutching her to him in relief. Tears appeared on her cheeks. His, he realized.

An indescribable joy swept over her face. "Oh, love," she whimpered, her voice barely audible. "Oh, love, I thought you were dead." She stopped, confused. Then she realized it wasn't her husband who held her but merely a cousin who resembled him.…

Jason drove his fist against the maple tree. He'd never forgotten the look of disappointment that had followed that realization. It would haunt him as long as he lived.

So would the knowledge that it should have been him in the car. He should have died, not John.

His cousin had urged him to come with them, but he'd refused. Being around Victoria, knowing she was carrying another man's child, had become too much. Even though the man was his cousin and Jason loved him like a brother, he hadn't been able to stand their happiness.

If he could have relived that night, if he had been driving the car, he would have died, instead of the man she'd loved.

He started from his memories as arms closed around him. Then Victoria, soft and warm, lifted his arm, dipped under it, and snuggled against him as if it was the most natural thing in the world.

"Umm, cold," she complained. She kissed his throat.

He couldn't believe she'd come to him after the way he'd left her. "Go to bed," he ordered. He sounded harsher than he meant to. Damn. He could never seem to strike an equilibrium with this woman. He fought the need and the pain that rose to choke him.

She leaned against his arm and peered up at him. "You've gone all cold and distant again. Why? Why did you leave?"

"Why do women always feel that a few kisses give them the right to probe into a man's mental processes?" he shot right back. He stared at the night scene, then, drawn by forces he couldn't control, he looked at her.

Her face was upturned so she could study him. Her skin glowed in the moonlight like some magical substance. He knew how soft it was…all over. He knew how warm and pliable she was. She'd let him caress her in every way he wanted.

Like a bolt of lightning, the hunger struck, making him clench his hands against his thighs to keep from reaching for her, from taking her there in the moonlight.

Dammit. He'd kissed her and tasted her. That would have to be enough. The curiosity, the need that had haunted him for years, would never be satisfied.

It wouldn't even if they made love, he realized grimly. He'd never get enough of her.

Anger warred with desire. He wanted to walk away from her and be done with the turmoil she'd aroused in him from the time he first saw her, the week before she was to wed his cousin.

His cousin. She'd loved his cousin, who was handsome and charming and everything that any woman could want. John, good-natured and kind, had been the golden boy. Jason, rebellious and smart-mouthed, had been the black sheep.

He forced himself away from Victoria and the temptation to disregard wisdom. When she came to her senses, she would know he'd acted for the best.

Victoria tried to shake off the despondency. What had she expected from Jason? That he would fall madly in love and reveal his deepest feelings to her?

"For us, it's a way of connecting," she finally answered his question. "Women are big on things like that, you know."

Their lovemaking had been hot and wild and wonderful. They'd touched depths in each other...maybe nothing as profound as souls, but something more than a meeting of the flesh. Their kisses and caresses had reached inside and opened all the floodgates of feeling she'd ever experienced. She'd thought it had been the same for him.

He would never admit it, she realized. Jason had been hurt. He retreated from intense emotional involvement.

Who could blame him?

It was frightening to be that entangled with someone. It left a person vulnerable...the way she'd felt after the tragedy in her own life...the way she felt now.

Well, it was obvious there could be nothing further between them. The disappointment she felt was as intense as the passion had been a few minutes ago.

She summoned a smile. "How lovely this is," she murmured, perusing the intimate setting.

"Yes." He looked at her again, then away.

She liked room to mull things over when feelings pressed too closely upon her heart. She'd give him the same courtesy. "I once read that architects call this a tee-hee garden. It seems apt, doesn't it?"

"For the fun and games that go on in them?" he said, remote and cynical again.

"Umm-hmm."

She and Jason were back to square one. She found she wanted more from him. And for him. He deserved more from life than one-night stands. There had to be something more tangible to living than a moment's passion, sweet though it might be.

"Go to bed, Victoria," Jason said, breaking into her thoughts, his tone harder, darker.

He'd erected his defenses and closed himself completely off. The moment when they might have touched each other's souls had passed. She turned regretfully toward the door, then paused, unwilling to give up her vision of them.

Looking at his profile, she was moved by the cold, clear beauty of his face and the isolation of his soul. He had awakened her to the possibilities of life by his gentleness during the crisis. She wished she could do the same for him.

"Good night, Jason," she said softly.

She stepped toward him and kissed his throat. The tendons tightened beneath her lips.

She went inside and down the hall to the guest room. There, she climbed into bed. For the first time in many years, she was reminded of how lonely a place a bed could be.

Chapter Six

Victoria let the screen door slam behind her after she entered her home in Paradise Falls. The first thing she wanted to do was ask Sally Winetski Houston, her best friend and former campaign manager, about Jason. Sally knew everyone in town. Best of all, she knew everything there was to know about everyone in town.

Sally could tell her all about Jason's early life. After seeing the man he really was, Victoria wanted to understand the forces that had shaped him into the solitary individual he appeared to be.

She also wondered about the woman he'd loved. Perhaps Sally would know the details of that. The affair must have been very passionate, the breakup very bitter, for him to remember it with such consuming anger.

Victoria realized she intensely disliked the woman who'd done that to Jason. To ruin a man like him... He obviously had a huge capacity for love and tenderness that was untapped.

Not that she had a chance to be his love, but she wished he could have the happiness he deserved.

Tears came into her eyes. She acknowledged she'd been rather callous toward Jason from the moment she'd met him. During her marriage, she'd been too blissfully involved with establishing her responsibilities as a wife to pay much attention to John's cousin.

Actually, she admitted with total honesty, she'd been glad Jason had stayed away. Like most new brides, she'd been jealous of her husband's attachment to anyone else, even his best friend.

Later she'd been so busy playing the brave widow she'd never given a thought to him. She recalled it had been Jason who'd eased the way during the terrible days after the accident, soliciting her wishes, then quietly making the arrangements. She hadn't spared a thought for his grief.

For that, she was ashamed.

Having seen the depths in him, she knew he'd held his own sorrow in check, asking nothing from anyone while he took care of the rest of the family.

She touched her cheek as a faint memory came to her—tears falling on her while a dark-haired, blue-eyed man wept over her. She shook her head, not understanding the fragment of old nightmare that had haunted her of late.

Pausing in the living room, she dropped her luggage and picked up the phone. After dialing Sally's real estate office, she peered at the familiar room, her mind back in Raleigh.

That morning, when Jason had driven her to the airport, they'd been stilted with each other. He'd not said more than two words during the trip. When it had been time to board the plane, she'd asked if he was coming to Paradise Falls for the celebration.

"That probably wouldn't be wise," he'd said.

At his repressive tone, she'd dropped the subject, thanked him for his time and got on the plane.

When the receptionist answered the phone, Victoria asked if Sally was in. "Yes. Hold on and I'll get her," the girl said.

Sally came on the line. "Glad Your Honor made it back. How'd it go?"

"Not good," Victoria admitted. "Got time for lunch?"

"Umm, yes. Asher Inn in about an hour?"

Victoria agreed and hung up. She dashed up the stairs with her suit bag and case. Putting the dress and suit out to go to the cleaners, she tossed the rest of the stuff in the hamper. She changed into a tan linen skirt and a pink blouse.

Finished, she sat down on the window seat and gazed out at the town in its small scoop of land amid the mountains. The valley was three miles wide and eight miles long. On the opposite side of it, she could see the Clairmont Mansion, which was now an exclusive bed-and-breakfast resort. In the middle of town, she spotted the courthouse and felt a justifiable pride at the renovation being done at her instigation.

That had been one of her campaign pledges—to save the old courthouse from the ravages of age, if possible.

Finding the money had been the problem. The solution had been a value-added tax on each rented bedroom in town and on food at the restaurants. Her next task was to discover why the new highway hadn't gone through to the interstate highway. There was only one road into and out of Paradise Falls. Sometimes bad weather could shut in the whole town.

She rubbed a smudge from the windowpane with the heel of her hand. A sense of homecoming swept over her. She felt as if she'd been gone on a journey that had proven dangerous. Thank goodness she had returned safely.

Safety, security—here she had those. Was that the reason she clung to the old house so fiercely?

John had brought her there as a bride of twenty-two. The place had been in the Broderick family for a hundred years.

Letting her gaze roam the hills, Victoria admitted she loved the town. She'd been born there. At fourteen, she'd been sent off to boarding school in New York to prepare for college. Her parents had moved to New York shortly thereafter. It had taken her a long time to get over a sense of abandonment. Their apartment overlooking Central Park had never been her home. This house was.

Rising, she shook off the memories, checked her watch and went downstairs. She grabbed her purse and headed out the door. It was time to meet Sally for lunch. She drove to the Asher Inn.

Sally was waiting for her. They went inside.

At the table, Sally looked her over. "Well, you made it back in one piece."

"Did you think I wouldn't?" She managed a laugh.

"With Jason, one never knows. He can get quite fierce when he wants to." Sally frowned thoughtfully. "I thought you'd be back yesterday."

Heat rose in Victoria's face. She hoped Sally didn't notice. Her friend had an uncanny knack for understanding human nature and its foibles, also for ferreting out secrets one would rather keep to oneself.

"I changed my plans."

"So you spent the weekend with Jason," Sally concluded.

Victoria grimaced, then sighed. "How do you figure out things so fast?"

"I have a suspicious mind. Well? Are you going to tell me about it? Or shouldn't I ask?" Her gaze was shrewd.

The waitress came to take their order. Her eyes were as blue as Jason's, Victoria realized. Her own eyes were blue, although not as dark. If she and Jason were to have children, their eyes would be blue.

The thought jarred her. An ache started deep inside. For the tiniest second, she wished she and Jason had completed what they had started. She would love to have a baby.... She gasped as she realized exactly what she was thinking.

After the woman left, Sally leaned forward in her chair. "I asked you about Jason," she said. "How is my dear cousin?"

"Cousin?"

"On my mother's side. Her aunt married Jason's mother's uncle or something like that. In my family, that constitutes kinship. So, how is he?"

"Fine, I think." Victoria took a breath and plunged in. "We went up to his cabin. It's on a lake. Did you know he had one?"

"No. Slow down and tell me about it."

"Well, it's very nice." Victoria described the cabin, the lake and finally Jason's neighbors. "We had a wonderful time, fishing and visiting with people. Yesterday, before we left, we had a big picnic on his dock with several couples. It was fun."

"Good." A gleam appeared in Sally's eyes.

Victoria felt the ridiculous heat seep into her face.

"Jason needs to relax," Sally said. "I always thought he worked too hard, even when we were young. Our families used to visit a lot back then. Jason was always so serious under that mischievous banter, so determined to succeed."

Knowing it was hopeless, Victoria gave up her casual pose. "Tell me about him," she requested.

The two women gazed at each other for a long moment, then Sally nodded. "Let me think. There was some old gossip about his family. Oh, I remember." Her mood became pensive. "Jason's mother was in love with John's father at one time," she began.

"I didn't know that."

"It isn't the sort of thing you talk about at family reunions, but I heard my mom and aunt discussing it once. Naturally, I was nosy and asked questions."

"What happened?"

"Jonathan and Claude were first cousins and alike as two peas, naturally, since *their* fathers were identical twins. You've seen pictures of the grandfathers, haven't you?"

Victoria nodded. "They were very handsome."

"Those two cousins grew up here in Paradise Falls. Mother said she had a crush on both of them when they were young. All the Broderick men have that thick black hair and those incredibly blue eyes," Sally pointed out.

Victoria pictured Jason, his hair tousled by her fingers, his eyes filled with unconcealed hunger.

Sally pushed a wispy curl wafting over her forehead out of the way and continued. "Anyway, Jonathan and Claude grew up and went off to war. Jonathan brought a bride home with him."

VICTORIA'S CONQUEST 109

"John's mother," Victoria interrupted. "I know the
tory of how they met at a USO dance."

Victoria's mother-in-law had remarried a year after
onathan's death and now lived in Texas with her hus-
and. Victoria and John had visited them a couple of
imes during their twenty-eight months of marriage.

"Yes, but there was a girl he'd dated before he left.
he'd waited for him. When he came back with a wife
n tow, she married his cousin a month later."

"Oh, no," Victoria said, seeing the beginnings of trag-
dy.

Sally nodded. "Some people have wondered if Myra
ver got over her love for Jonathan. She had a son five
nonths after John was born. My aunt asked my mother
f she thought Myra had named Jason for Jonathan."

"What did your mother say?"

"She said Claude's middle name was Jansen and that
Myra was probably thinking of that when she named Ja-
on."

Victoria was relieved for Jason's sake. "Did Claude
now about his wife's feelings for Jonathan?"

"I don't know." Sally paused in thought, then
hrugged. "If he did, it apparently didn't bother him.
hey've been married for over thirty years."

"Yes, it seems to be a good marriage." Victoria stirred
neasily under Sally's narrow-eyed scrutiny. She had al-
eady given away more than she was ready to confess.

"When are you going to tell me what really happened
etween you two at that cabin hideaway?" Sally de-
nanded.

"Nothing happened."

Sally looked as if she thought of disputing that state-
nent, but she evidently reconsidered. "When our fami-
es used to visit, Jason would take the time to entertain

me," she said. "Did I tell you he taught me how to climb trees? I liked him best—" She pressed her lips together.

"Better than John?" Victoria asked, surprised.

"I thought they were both great." Sally picked up her fork and began eating the salad the waitress placed before them.

"But?" Victoria prodded.

"Well, John used to read to me, but Jason was the one who took the time to show me a bird's nest or the best apple tree."

Victoria envisioned a younger Jason showing a visiting relative his favorite spots. It didn't surprise her that he was kind to Sally. "Ah, now I understand," she said. "You and Jason were the rambunctious ones. He showed me his pierced ear."

Sally laughed. "I remember that. What an uproar that caused at his house! I'm sure Myra nearly had apoplexy. Claude finally put his foot down and told her to leave Jason alone."

Remembering Jason's father from the few times they'd met, Victoria said, "That must have been a shock."

"I'm sure it was." Sally smiled nostalgically. "Jason wasn't a mean person. Who wouldn't be rebellious if your mother was always comparing you to your cousin who, according to her, could do no wrong? John was just naturally good-natured. He never seemed to resent orders and, as far as I know, never caused his parents an anxious moment."

"Yes. He was always thoughtful…" Tears filmed Victoria's eyes. Was she sad for John, Jason or herself? she wondered. "John loved Jason. He missed his company. After we were married, Jason never came around."

Sally studied Victoria for a long minute. "Jason was

wise. Bachelors and married couples don't mix. Surely you're astute enough to realize why."

Victoria remembered the urgency of the desire between her and Jason. The way he'd touched her…it was as if he'd dreamed of doing so for a very long time.

"Yes, of course," she murmured.

"I'd like to see him find the happiness he deserves. It would take a special woman."

"I know. I learned a lot about Jason this weekend," Victoria admitted. "He has so much potential. He should have married and had children. Oh, Sally, I didn't tell you about the emergency."

"Emergency? An accident—"

"No, nothing like that." Victoria smiled. "You should have seen Jason. You'd have been amazed."

"What happened?"

"His secretary went into premature labor." She described the event in detail. "He was wonderful—so supportive and gentle with her." Emotion clogged her throat, and she couldn't go on.

"I always knew he'd be that way," Sally said in an approving voice. "There's a core of goodness in Jason. Some woman will find it and make him see it, too. She'll be a lucky woman, the one who catches his heart and teaches him to trust."

"Trust?"

"Yes, trust. Jason must have been hurt at some time in the past. I don't know that story. But he seems cautious about the loving and marriage business, doesn't he?"

"Jason did love someone once," Victoria blurted out. "He admitted it. He said it didn't work out."

"It must have been when he went off to college." Sally shook her head and sighed. "That explains it."

"Explains what?"

"Why, his standoffish attitude, of course." She gave Victoria a smile and stood. "It's time I was getting to baking that cake for the Historical Society. Sure you won't come to the meeting tonight?"

"No, thanks." Victoria stood. Emotions ran wildly through her, so mixed up and tumultuous she couldn't sort them. One thing she knew—she *hated* it that Jason had been hurt. She wished she'd been kinder to him.

The rest of June passed in a busy routine of meetings and luncheons as usual. The weather was sunny. With no rain in sight, Victoria watered the garden with the hose and talked to Miss Josie, her neighbor, who was doing the same and worrying about her winter supplies if the vegetables didn't grow.

"You might have to buy them," she teased the retired teacher who thought store bought vegetables had no vitamins.

July puffed in on a breath of hot air—ninety-two degrees. Victoria dreaded the town council meeting. Tempers ran shorter than dynamite fuses during the dog days of summer. The night of the meeting she entered the council chamber and spoke to the other council members wearily. She'd been putting in fourteen-hour days.

She called the meeting to order promptly at seven. The door at the back of the chamber opened. A man came in and took a seat on the back row.

Victoria blinked twice before she could convince herself it really was Jason. She drew four quick breaths as Miss Josie had taught her to do before making a campaign speech. In a husky tone, she asked for the first item on the agenda.

A resident stepped to the microphone and stated her

name and address. She was president of the PTA. "This is the third year I've been before the council with this request. We have the land for a park near the elementary school. The land was bought and paid for by the parents and children of the community, you might recall, through bake sales and car washes."

They listened to her plea for the playground equipment which had been promised if the land could be acquired. The woman finished and looked at the council with a determined gleam that said she wasn't leaving until she got a commitment.

"Thank you," Victoria said, smiling at the woman. "I think Mr. Wagner has a report on that."

Mr. Wagner, retired accountant for Clairmont Textiles and, at present, council member, explained that due to emergency repairs to other property, no funds were available to complete the park. However, it was still in the general plans.

The audience booed this announcement.

Victoria rapped the gavel against the table. When quiet was restored, she referred the item to the finance committee for a funding study. This brought another round of protests from the parents in the audience.

She banged the gavel until quiet prevailed. "The purpose of this meeting is to conduct the city's business. If there are any more outbursts, the bailiff will clear the room." She called for the next item of business.

As the meeting went into its third hour, tempers frayed more easily. Most of the audience had gone home, except for the few diehards who attended every meeting. Jason was still there.

Slouched in the chair, he sometimes seemed to be dozing. Then he would look up with a quick movement of his head, and she'd know he was alert to everything going on.

She assumed he was waiting for her, but maybe that was vanity on her part. Perhaps he was just curious to see how she operated as mayor. There'd been a lot of that the first months after she'd taken office.

Glancing at the agenda, she saw they were ready to discuss the last item. "Do we have a report on the Paradise Lake road?"

The attorney appointed to investigate the reason the new road hadn't been built for the past three years stated there'd been no decision in the state road planning department. "It's still being studied," he concluded.

"They been studying it long enough to score a hunnert percent if we gave 'em a test," one of the regular observers in the audience remarked. That brought a cynical laugh from the rest.

Victoria turned a stern glance on the retired farmer who'd made the comment. "The audience will please refrain from speaking unless recognized by the chair," she reminded him.

Glancing toward the back, she saw Jason was grinning.

After thirty minutes, they gave up the futile discussion and asked for a delegation to press the state legislature for passage of the town-sponsored bill.

"I think you should go and speak to them, Victoria," Mr. Wagner said. "In fact, I'll make it official. I move that we send Mayor Victoria Broderick as delegate for the Paradise Falls road plan to the state capital as soon as the legislature reconvenes."

"Second," the farmer called out.

Victoria glared at him. Several in the audience tittered. Jason hid a grin behind his hand.

Another council member seconded the motion. It passed.

"Just what am I commissioned to do?" she demanded.

"Find out why the new road hasn't been approved like they promised us three years ago. See if you can get it on the new highway bill," another council member suggested.

Victoria thought it would be a waste of time and money. "Any new business?"

A lean form unfolded itself from the back of the room. Jason ambled up to the microphone. He stated his name and address. "I'm a former resident of Paradise Falls." He grinned. "Some of you were probably glad to see me leave."

The council and audience laughed appreciatively.

Jason grew serious. "A small town is a great place to grow up. It gives a sense of values and of belonging that's often missing in city life. Of course, you can't get away with a blasted thing...."

Victoria realized Jason was a very good public speaker. He knew how to get a crowd on his side with wit and humor.

"If the council is interested, I have a friend, an architect, who designed a build-it-yourself playground for a school near my place. I think I can get the plans at no cost. I'll donate the materials if you think the residents would be willing to build it."

"Oh," Mary Beth exclaimed. "I saw a program about that on television. The architect designs the equipment, then supervises the community in putting it together. It saves thousands of dollars in labor costs."

"Right," Jason said.

A hum of conversation filled the chamber as everyone commented on this. Victoria banged the gavel and gave a questioning glance at the PTA president, who had stayed for the rest of the meeting.

Mary Beth beamed. "We'll back it," she said firmly.

"But," Mr. Wagner worried, "who would supervise the project? Do you think your friend would come here, Jason?"

Victoria observed Jason as he thought it over. "If he can't, then I will," he volunteered. "I helped with the other one."

"Well, durn, let's do it," the farmer called out.

There was a consensus.

"May I please have a motion to accept Mr. Broderick's offer?" Victoria asked.

The motion was made and seconded.

"Any further discussion?"

"We should have a liaison with the council," Mr. Wagner mused. "To coordinate everything. Isn't Jason kin to you, Victoria?"

Victoria saw where this line of thinking was heading. "Mary Beth is president of the PTA. She and Jason should work together on it."

"Yes, and you can help them with the red tape, if we have any left from our other projects," Mr. Wagner declared.

There was a verbal agreement from the council.

"If there's no further business, this meeting is adjourned," Victoria declared before she was handed another task. "Buck passers," she muttered loud enough for the other members to hear.

Mr. Wagner smiled and went to speak to Jason. So did the rest of the crowd. The farmer thumped him on the back as if he were a returning hero. Victoria gathered her papers, stuffed them in her briefcase and headed out the side door for her office. There, she filed everything neatly away.

Leaning back in her chair, she tried to still the emotions that thrummed in her. No matter how hard she tried, she knew there was no way she could have prepared herself for this meeting with Jason. Not in a million years.

The kisses they'd shared had blended into every dream she'd had for the past few weeks. How could she face him as if nothing had happened after the passionate way she'd responded?

It seemed harder now than it had the morning she'd boarded the plane to return home. She still didn't know exactly how she felt about him. Another thought came to her. Maybe he didn't know how he felt, either.

Maybe that's why he'd come home for the centennial celebration to be held in conjunction with the Fourth of July festivities. Maybe he'd fallen a little bit in love with her....

Her heart pounded so hard she could feel every beat through her body.

She was overreacting. Before she met him, she had to get herself in hand. She was the mayor, for heaven's sake. She handled crises every day. She could handle this, too.

A shadow appeared on the ripple glass of her door. She recognized the broad shoulders, the thick wavy hair, outlined by the hall light. She saw him lift a hand.

He knocked softly on the wooden frame next to the glass.

She rose and crossed the room. What, she wondered, did a woman say to an almost lover? Hello? How are you? Fancy seeing you again? Nothing seemed appropriate. She opened the door.

Dark blue eyes scanned her quickly, as if checking her

against a vision only he could see. Then he stood there and waited without saying a word.

Jason, the inscrutable.

Whatever she'd expected of this first meeting, it wasn' this, she realized. She'd hoped for the softer Jason…the one she'd fallen a little in love with. Instead, he was the hard, remote man he portrayed when he came home.

She saw the shields all in place, blocking his thoughts and emotions. Did he think she was going to make some claim on him because of their night together? She would set his mind to rest on that score, she decided, hardening herself against him.

"What are you doing here?" she asked.

Chapter Seven

"Is that any way to greet a benefactor?" he drawled.

Victoria managed a laugh. "It was rather abrupt. Your appearance surprised me, that's all. I saw your folks after church yesterday. They didn't say they were expecting you."

"I'm a big boy now. I don't ask permission for my comings and goings," he said, his smile sardonic.

She didn't respond to his taunt. If he was expecting a fight or recriminations about not contacting her after their one night together, he was in for a surprise. "Your gift to the town was generous. I keep expecting strings to be attached."

"You've turned into the cynical politician," he observed. He moved his shoulders as if impatient with her doubts. "No strings. With the new contract, the company's doing well, so I thought I'd give something back to the community where I started. I can take a tax deduction and be a hero at the same time."

"Hmm, would you pass that philosophy along to other

former residents? That would solve all our financial woes.''

"Sure.'' He paused. ''How about a cup of coffee?''

She hesitated just a fraction too long.

"Worried about what people would say if the mayor was seen with the town renegade?'' His smile became hard edged.

"No. It's my own reactions that bother me,'' she confessed, as forthright as he. ''I have a terrible weakness for rogues.''

The air sizzled with a sudden escalation of tension. She saw his chest expand as he drew a quick, deep breath. Somehow she knew instinctively that this was the correct way to deal with a wary individual like him.

She would treat him with respect, with gentleness and with as much honesty as she could, regarding her feelings for him. At times during the week, she hadn't been sure if she would want to hit him or kiss him when she saw him again. He had that kind of effect on her.

"I might be tempted to take advantage of that weakness.'' He grinned, but his gaze was dark and solemn.

"I'd be tempted to let you.'' She locked her desk and hitched her purse strap over her shoulder. ''Shall we go?''

"Is the diner okay? I'd like to avoid a crowd.''

The only other place in town was the Asher Inn. The city council and several others would be there by now, arguing over everything that had been discussed during the meeting.

"Fine,'' she said.

They stepped into the hall. He waited while she secured the bolt, then took her arm to escort her from the building.

She led the way across town in her car. He followed

in a rental vehicle with four-wheel drive. He hadn't forgotten the roads were narrow, winding and steep in the area.

At the diner they chose a booth and ordered coffee. When the waitress left, Victoria leaned forward. She wanted to ask if he was considering her proposal to move a facility here, but she refrained. First he needed to see the changes in the town and be convinced it would be feasible. She would give him some time to look things over. Meanwhile, she had a plan.

"You need a beard," she told him. "Otherwise you might be arrested and put in the stocks for indecent exposure."

"You've passed a law that all men must have beards?"

"Starting Wednesday everyone is supposed to dress in pioneer clothing or the finery of a hundred years ago."

"I suppose I'd better find some overalls and a straw hat."

"Right," she agreed. "We have some fun things planned every day through Sunday, five days of celebration for the Fourth and our town centennial."

"I remember you mentioned the festivities."

Their eyes met and exchanged other memories. Victoria tried to block them out, but it was useless. She could almost feel the way he'd moved his hands over her, caressing and exploring, giving her the most exquisite pleasure....

"Don't," he said harshly.

Her mouth had gone dry. "What?"

"Your eyes give you away," he accused.

The waitress brought their cups. "Cream?"

They said no in unison.

The woman put the check down and left.

"About the celebration," Victoria continued, returning to her topic. "We have lots of contests planned, old-fashioned fun and games"

He made a low sound, almost a moan.

She stopped abruptly, a relentless blush creeping up her face, then forced herself to go on. "All the industries that have been here will be represented in our parade on Sunday. Logging was first. Then a grist mill that failed. That was before Nathanial Clairmont came here after the Civil War and set up the textile mill using the old grist mill site."

Jason laid a hand over hers. He disliked the fact that he made her uncomfortable. "You don't have to be nervous with me, Victoria. I'm not going to embarrass you before the town."

"But I might embarrass both of us," she suggested wryly.

He tried to figure her out. He'd thought, given time and distance, she would regret their passionate hour together. Instead, he could sense the tension in her. She still wanted him.

More surprising, she seemed to want to be friends with him. Her eyes, when she looked at him, were warm and…inviting. But she wasn't making any demands. It was contrary to everything he'd learned to expect from women.

So maybe he would stay for the celebration and… The thought trailed off as he watched her take a drink, then lick her lips.

Her mouth was beautiful. It went soft in a kiss. She'd let him taste her as much as he'd wanted, her tongue playful and ardent against his. Heat poured over him like a flood tide. He'd better think of something else.

"What happened at my place won't be repeated. It was

an impulse of the moment. We're mature enough to handle it. I wanted to see you before we were thrown together in a roomful of relatives, to let you know I don't expect to conduct a full-blown affair in a small town like Paradise Falls."

"Why don't you let *me* decide where I want to conduct an affair?" she asked, eyeing him with something like distaste.

"Maybe I'm not saying this very tactfully," he began again. He was making a hash of it. "I meant, I realize I don't have any claims on you, or you on me, because of a few kisses."

"Thank you very much." She bit the words out.

Damn, the situation was getting worse. "Look, I'm trying to reassure you—"

"I don't need your assurances. I'm a big girl. I can handle my emotions and my libido without any help from you. And I've never been under the delusion that I have any claims on you, nor you on me."

He studied her expression. She looked mad enough to punch him one if he didn't watch it. "Well, how do you want me to act?" he demanded. "Like we're in the middle of a flaming affair?"

"Yes."

Victoria almost laughed at the shock that ran over his face. She'd gotten through to him at last.

"You don't let anything pass, do you?" he finally said.

"No."

"So what do you want to happen between us?"

"I want to understand why we can't have a normal life like other people. I'm single. You're single. Even the residents of Paradise Falls, backward as they may be to you city types, know about dating. Why can't we see each other if we please?"

He'd evidently thought that one out. His answer was swift and sure. "Because I won't get involved with you. You called it the first time—I'm a loner."

"But," she said softly, "you shouldn't be."

He gave her a cold appraisal designed to put distance between them. "It's the way I want my life."

She thought of the passion between them. She recalled how glad she'd been to see him when he walked into the city council meeting. Like a light had come on inside her.

There was a reason for that. She wasn't sure she was ready to acknowledge it yet. Perhaps the next few days would tell.

She realized she was tired. "I've got to go. Why don't you come over and have dinner with me tomorrow night? Perhaps Sally and her husband can join us. She confessed to a soft spot for renegades, too," Victoria added.

"Some women are soft in the head. Renegades can never be tamed." Jason smiled grimly. There, he'd given her ample warning. If anything further happened between them, she knew the score.

"Tell your parents to come, too. I haven't seen them in ages."

"I'm not staying with my parents." He stood when she did and picked up the check. He tossed enough money on the table to handle the cost of the coffee and the tip.

"You're not?"

"No. I find it's easier to come and go as I please by staying at an inn. I checked into the Clairmont. Adam and I went to school together. We used to sleep over at each other's houses when we were boys. I thought I'd enjoy seeing the old mansion."

"I didn't know that. My parents sent me to a girls"

academy for high school, so I lost track of the local people until I came back with John.''

He saw her to her car, said good-night and watched her until she drove out of sight. It was an idle thought, but he wondered, if he'd asked, would she have let him stay at her place?

It was just a thought.

The door to the old Broderick family home stood open to the July heat. The sun had dipped behind the western ridge, and the air was beginning to cool. Jason knocked on the wood frame of the screened door.

Victoria appeared in the hall. ''Come on in. We're having an emergency in the kitchen.'' She disappeared.

He opened the door and quickly walked to the back of the house where the kitchen was. Sally and Victoria were standing at the table, watching as icing dripped off a cake.

''I think it must be the heat, Sally,'' Victoria said.

''This recipe has never failed before.'' Sally turned to Jason. ''What do you think?''

He leaned down for a closer look. Swiping a finger through the frosting, he tasted it. ''Delicious,'' he declared. ''It's probably the humidity. Also, the cake is still warm. Coupled with the heat, it's melting the icing, I suspect.''

Sally conceded defeat to Victoria. ''I guess you were right. It was too soon to ice the cake.'' She turned with a smile to Jason. ''I wanted it to be ready for our town benefactor.''

Jason groaned. ''I've been hearing about that all day. If I'd known what a stir it would cause, I'd have reconsidered. The Lion's Club, the Rotary Club and the Chamber of Commerce want me to speak at their next meetings.''

''Welcome to the mashed potato circuit, to quote one of our country's presidents,'' Victoria said dryly. ''By the way, Sally will be eating with us. Her husband's out of town.''

Sally laughed and held out her arms. ''Come on, cousin, where's my kiss? When we were kids, he told me I could be a kissing cousin,'' she explained to Victoria.

''My *only* kissing cousin,'' he corrected firmly, giving her a kiss on the cheek. ''My mother always tried to make me kiss her two old maiden aunts.''

''I remember them,'' Sally sympathized. ''They smelled like moth balls and snuff.''

Jason felt the warmth of Sally's affection. She'd always liked him, he realized. At times he thought she'd preferred him to John when their parents visited. He'd liked her, too.

''Listen,'' he said, ''cake with chocolate sauce is my favorite dessert. Why don't we spoon the frosting on when we eat it?''

''Good idea. What do you think, Victoria? It's your party.''

''Fine by me.''

Jason risked a direct look at her. He almost groaned aloud. She wore a pink sundress with tiny straps that just barely held it up. The cleavage was modest, but that made no difference. He knew what she looked like, how round and firm and womanly she was.

From the moment he'd walked in the front door, one idea had chased around and around in his brain. A husband had the right to make love to his wife. Later, after dinner and the house was quiet, a man could take his wife to their room. He could strip her out of her pretty pink dress, her silken underwear and stockings. Then he could make love to her until they were sated with all the pleasures of the senses.

He silently laughed at his own musings. Any man who let himself get so carried away with a woman deserved whatever Fate handed out to him. He would not be that kind of fool.

Victoria tried not to be entranced with Jason during the evening. It was difficult. He praised the food until she blushed. He extolled the virtues of mashed potatoes and gravy until both women burst into laughter.

When the meal was over, he wouldn't let Sally clean up. "I can help. It's the least I can do. You take your glass of tea and relax on the front porch. That way you can keep an eye on the neighborhood."

"Are you implying I'm nosy?" she demanded.

"Let's just say the world is a better place with you here to keep it straight," he replied. When Sally departed with a fresh glass of iced tea, he started gathering the dishes. "I'll stack and rinse while you put the leftovers away."

"All right."

They worked in companionable silence.

"You know," Victoria pondered aloud, "you're really quite charming when you want to be. That cool distance you keep between yourself and others is a sham."

He gazed at her mouth, her throat, then swept on down her in an inventory that left no part of her feeling unnoticed. "You're right. Around you, I'm not cool at all, and distance is the last thing I want between us."

"Jason!"

"I thought you wanted the truth between us."

She wrinkled her nose at him. "Thus speaks the cynic.

You use the truth like other men would use a sword—to keep your foes at bay.'' Pausing, she considered, then added softly, ''I'm not your enemy, Jason.''

''You're my nemesis. I've often wondered what awful thing I did in a past life to deserve you in this one.'' He smiled, but the strain was obvious.

In spite of his amused tone, his words were serious. They indicated deeper feelings. She pressed her lips together, holding in the demand to know what he really felt toward her.

They were interrupted by voices on the front porch. ''Your parents, I think,'' she said. ''I invited them to stop by when they couldn't come for dinner.''

''Good. I talked to them briefly when I arrived in town. My father and I are planning a fishing trip up to the falls.''

''Oh, I haven't been up there in ages. I don't suppose you'd let a female tag along?'' She waved a hand, negating the request. ''No, it's a male bonding thing. Forget I asked.''

They went out to greet his mother and father.

Victoria observed Jason's parents with an interest that was new. Myra and Claude were in their mid to late fifties. She had dark brown hair and hazel eyes. He had thick, wavy hair, which was beginning to turn gray, and eyes that were as blue as the ocean at its deepest point.

''Isn't this weather terrible?'' Myra commented. ''The garden is full of weeds. I don't dare water it until Claude gets them chopped out.''

Victoria noticed the way Jason's mouth tightened at the mention of his father. She wanted to tell him it was okay, that his mother was making a social comment, not a complaint.

"What happened to the man you hired to do that?" Sally asked.

"Oh, he said he hurt his back." Myra frowned slightly as if she didn't believe that excuse.

"Maybe you worked him too hard," Jason suggested with his usual sardonic humor. "I remember the list of chores I had to finish before I was allowed to join my friends at the swimming hole on summer days."

"You used to rise at dawn and be done with them before those other lazy rascals got out of bed," Myra replied in a scolding tone. She turned to Victoria with a smile. "Then he'd pester me until I'd give in and let him go. The other mothers would call and complain about being roused out of bed."

Victoria caught the hint of pride in Myra's manner, but she didn't think Jason did. He remained polite but removed from the scene...distancing himself from emotional involvement, she thought.

"Myra always said Jason could do more work as a boy than any two men she'd ever seen," Claude put in. There was no doubt of his pride in Jason. It beamed from his eyes as he looked at his son. "That's why he succeeded when he started his own company."

Ah, Victoria mused, the peacemaker. The husband accepted the task of explaining his wife to his son. From what Sally had said about the pierced ear episode, he also took the son's side against his wife on occasion.

Victoria wondered if there were depths to the father that he kept from others just as his son did. Could a man live with a woman for over thirty years and not reveal the secrets of his heart? Of course he could.

She wouldn't want that kind of marriage. A husband and wife should be best friends as well as lovers.

Drawn by forces she couldn't ignore, she looked at

Jason. He rested casually with one hip propped on the porch railing, his back against the support column. His glance met hers, as cool and distant as he'd ever been, as if they'd never shared a brief hour of intimacy so wonderful she'd almost wept.

Pain hit her, right below the breast bone, like an invisible dart. She wanted to rise from her chair and peel the mask from his face until he let her into his thoughts. Pressing a hand to her chest, she remained still until the impulse passed.

"A neighbor told me some interesting news this morning," Myra said to Sally. "Did Jason tell you about his gift to the town?"

There was a hint of censure in the statement. His mother would have liked to have been in on the news rather than having it second-hand from a friend.

"I think it was an impulse of kindness," Victoria stated, giving Jason a teasing smile. "When he saw the mob ganging up on the council, he came to our rescue with his offer. He even volunteered to direct us in building the playground equipment." She went on to explain the donation in detail, adding her own ideas when she didn't have hard facts.

While the other three adults discussed the playground, Jason leaned close to her. "Laying it on a bit thick, weren't you?"

She grinned up at him. "You're going to be a hero, whether you want to be or not. Your picture will be splashed all over the front page of the weekly paper on Thursday. Several columns will be devoted to your impressive sports career at Paradise Falls High School as well as your later success in life."

"John was the quarterback. He made the team a winner."

"You were his best receiver. You made the touch-downs," she retorted. She knew all about every touch-down.

"I had other players for the hard situations," John had once told her. "Jason took care of the impossible ones."

John had been special, she thought. He had been the most lovingly generous person she'd ever known. Jason was special, too. He'd accomplished tasks others would have deemed too hard. And Sally. People like her kept the world on an even keel.

Victoria glanced from Sally to Jason. They were very much alike—both of them hardworking people and kind to others without being soft. Tenderness toward them crept over her.

Her thoughts were interrupted when Claude spoke to Jason. "Your mother is going to be busy directing the donations for the cake walk tomorrow. You want to get an early start on the fish?"

"About four?" Jason asked.

"Sounds right to me," his father agreed. "I'll come by the Clairmont place. We can cut through the back trail to the falls."

"You will be back for the box supper auction, won't you?" Myra asked. She frowned at the men.

"Sure we will," Claude answered. He patted his wife's shoulder. "I wouldn't miss the chance to get some of that fancy apple-brandy cake I saw you making last week."

Victoria realized the woman was afraid no one would bid on her supper box. Her husband had realized it, too, and assured her that he would. Jason's father was a man of perception. Remembering her dealings with Jason, she thought Jason was, too.

"Would you listen to those crickets," Sally commented.

Twilight had descended while they talked. A few fireflies winked from the grass while the insects and peeper frogs sang to them from the trees.

Jason reached over suddenly and fondled a strand of her hair. Victoria cast him a startled glance. He held out his hand to her, showing her the firefly. It had landed in her hair.

He lifted his hand into the air. When the bug didn't move, he blew across his palm, launching the firefly into the night. It turned on its light and glided across the lawn. Another firefly joined it, and they flew away together.

Jason glanced at Victoria. They smiled at each other. For a brief second she saw into his thoughts. Heat rose to her skin from deep inside. She felt both mellow and tense.

"Victoria, should we serve our guests that cake, or just give them some ice cream?"

Victoria grinned at Sally and stood. "Both. The cake will taste wonderful even if the icing is drippy."

"I'll help," Jason volunteered when his mother started to rise. He followed Victoria into the house.

They worked silently around each other. She cut the cake and put it on plates, then he dipped up the ice cream. He carried the first three out to the porch while she wiped the crumbs from the counter and washed the cake knife and ice cream scoop. He returned just as she picked up their plates.

"Forks or spoons?" he asked.

"I prefer a fork."

"Forks it is." He got them out of the drawer.

They returned to the porch.

Victoria was aware of Jason in an aching, breathless

sort of way. He sat on the top step, his shoulder only inches from her knee when she resumed her seat in the chair. She drifted into a fantasy in which she and her husband were entertaining guests. Later they would go to their room....

She was glad it was dark enough that no one noticed the tremor that nearly caused her to drop her fork. While the other three talked, she and Jason ate in silence, commenting only when directly spoken to. When they finished the dessert, Claude rose and took Myra's and Sally's plates.

"Come on, son," he said. "Let's show these ladies we can earn our keep. We'll clean up the dishes."

Jason took Victoria's plate, and the men disappeared into the house. Sally spoke to Myra. "I saw my mother earlier this afternoon. She was wondering when Jason was going to marry and give you and Claude some grandchildren."

Myra sighed. "He doesn't listen to me."

Sally laughed. "He has a mind of his own," she said, openly approving of Jason's independent nature. "I remember when he and John graduated from high school. Their grandfathers would have been so proud to see how their grandchildren turned out, with John becoming a lawyer and Jason having his own company."

"John stayed near his family." Myra sighed softly, as if resigned. "Jason was always one for going off on his own."

"It was brave of Jason to start his own business," Victoria put in. "With his inheritance, he could have lived the life of a playboy, or he could have taken over one of the family holdings."

"He was never interested," Myra stated. "I tried to get him to go to law school and become a partner—"

"Jason would have hated that. He needs the challenge of doing things." Victoria realized she was becoming too defensive. She forced herself to relax. "Even John got bored with the endless fine nuances of the law. He once said he'd like to solve a case by shooting the man and being done with it."

"I've often felt the same," Claude commented as he and Jason returned to the porch. "The law wasn't my first love—"

"What was?" his wife broke in, surprised.

"You," he declared, causing Victoria and Sally to laugh. To Victoria's delight, Myra laughed, too.

"But after me, what did you love most?" she demanded.

"I thought I'd like to be an archeologist."

"Ah, that explains all those boxes of arrowheads." Jason stood at the edge of the porch. He didn't resume his seat.

Victoria anticipated his next words.

"I think I'll go up to the big house," he said, using the local expression for the Clairmont mansion, "and hit the sack. Four o'clock is going to come mighty early."

"All that soft city living has ruined you," Claude teased.

"Your old room is available—"

"Now, Myra, give the boy some space. No man over twenty-one likes to be under his mother's eye. Jason might have a sweetheart he doesn't want to talk about yet."

Sally laughed. "A person can't have a headache in this town without fifty people knowing about it within the hour."

"Amen to that," Jason said wryly.

Victoria looked up in time to see him glance at her

then away. A frisson ran over her as she wondered if Jason thought of her as a sweetheart.

Jason gave his mother a kiss on the cheek, then did the same to Sally. That left only Victoria unkissed. His heart sped up as he turned to her. Quickly he bent down. He saw the flash of her eyes as they widened in surprise. Without letting himself think of the night he'd kissed her until they were both senseless with the pleasure of it, he gave her a peck on the cheek.

"Well, good night," he said to nobody in particular. "I'll see you at four," he said to his father and hurried to the rental car parked at the curb.

He cursed himself all the way to the Clairmont mansion. The more involved he became with either the town or the family, the more involved he would become with Victoria. That was the last thing he needed.

Hanging around her like a dog hoping for a pat on the head wasn't going to be his fate. A man would be a fool to fall in love with a woman who loved another.

I fell a little bit in love with you...

That had been the emotion of the moment speaking, not real feelings. And later, at the cabin?

Sex. That was simple enough to figure out. It had been a long time for her. The emergency had left her vulnerable.

He clenched his hands on the steering wheel as memories tumbled into his mind. Finding her in the wrecked car...her joy upon seeing him...

Oh, love.

She'd said the same thing when they'd nearly made love at the cabin.

Oh, love.

But she hadn't meant it for him either time. She'd

thought he was John when he'd found her at the wreck. When he'd kissed her, she'd probably pretended he was.

Pushing the thoughts into the dark corners of his mind, he parked and went into the mansion. The cool air was a welcome relief from the heat. He noticed the light on in the library.

His old school chum, Adam Clairmont, came to the door. "Jason, come join me if you have a moment."

Jason crossed the hall and entered the library where he and Adam and John had played checkers and taken turns playing chess against Mr. Clairmont. Adam's father had promised ten dollars to the first one good enough to beat him.

Jason smiled in remembrance. He'd won that bet.

"Have a seat. Would you like a drink?"

"No, thanks." He sat on the comfortable sofa. The fireplace was filled with ferns. He imagined a fire there, with snow falling outside the windows and he and Victoria lying on the velvet couch. "What's happening?" he asked with an effort.

"I wanted to find out how long you were going to be in town. I have some friends I'd like you to meet."

"Only to the end of this week."

"Good," Adam said, obviously considering that sufficient. "Do you remember Sally Winetski? She was behind us in school."

"I know Sally."

"Her husband is Riley Houston." Adam grinned. "We have a business proposition for you."

"What kind?"

"You ever considered being partners in a resort and a sort of working ranch?"

Jason leaned forward, interested in spite of himself. "

have a feeling I'm being a fool for asking, but what's a sort of working ranch?''

"Riley has bought the land in the valley down the ridge from here. He wants to start a ranch where city kids can have a chance to spend the summer, working for their keep and learning something besides gang fighting. We thought we'd combine the house and the ranch into a resort for hiking and cross-country skiing. We're both stretched rather thin right now, so…''

"I think I begin to see the light,'' Jason murmured. "You need an infusion of cash.'' Just what he needed— to get involved with another charity project in the area.

He wasn't sure why he'd volunteered for the playground. Seeing Victoria, working with her on the project…well, hell, he'd already made a fool of himself once by kissing her until he was senseless, why not twice? ''So what's the deal?''

Adam explained in greater detail. ''There'd be four of us,'' he concluded.

"Four?''

"Oh, Sally Winet…Sally Houston. She's in business with Riley. He says she's the brains behind their outfit.''

"Yeah, Sally's smart.''

"She and my wife are good friends with the woman mayor we have. Victoria Broderick is kin to you, isn't she?''

"A cousin by marriage. She was married to John.''

Adam remembered the tragedy. ''Sorry.''

"It was a long time ago.'' Jason stood. ''My dad and are going fishing in the morning. You want to come? We can talk about this idea you and your cohorts have reamed up.''

"Maybe I will. One problem we're having is getting ne new road cut through from the resort over on Paradise

Lake. It's the most frustrating case of bureaucratic bungling I've ever seen."

"That was mentioned in the council meeting last night." Jason's eyes narrowed as he studied his friend. "Do you suspect anything?"

Adam nodded. "Riley and I think some money has exchanged hands somewhere to block the road. We can't figure out why. Everyone would gain from the road being built. Who would want to stop it?"

Jason had a thought. "Victoria was appointed a committee of one to go to Charleston to check it out. Maybe someone should do some sleuthing behind the scenes while she plays the 'front man' with the state government."

"Great idea," Adam exclaimed. "When are you two going?"

"Wait a minute." Jason threw up his hands as if to ward off an evil fate. "I didn't volunteer that *I'd* do it."

"Yeah, but..." Adam grinned. "I don't think our wives would let me or Riley go with her."

"I don't have the time."

"You volunteered to supervise construction of the playground equipment, didn't you?"

Jason refused to be drawn into another commitment. They talked another hour before saying good-night.

After Jason went to bed, he found he couldn't turn his mind off this new problem. He realized he wanted to know who was blocking the new road and why. Victoria had mentioned the problem over the weekend she'd spent with him....

He sighed and tried to ignore the clamoring of his body at the thought of her. It was just as well that he'd stopped. Having her once wouldn't have been enough. Having her a hundred times probably wouldn't, either.

Damn.

The evening at her home returned to haunt him…the sweet look of her in her pink sundress…the scent of her shampoo and cologne …her fluttery awareness of the attraction between them. Yeah, it was still there. For both of them.

Another thought came to him.

His mother had wanted him to attend law school with his cousin. He'd refused. Instead, he'd taken a degree in physics and engineering, worked for three years—until he'd come into his inheritance from his grandparents—then started his own company at the encouragement of his boss, who'd given him his first contract.

If he'd gone to law school like John, if he'd been on the student council with John and Victoria, he'd have met her then.

One thing he'd always wondered—if he'd met her first, would she have fallen in love with him?

It was just a thought.

Chapter Eight

Victoria wrapped Cajun chicken cakes—baked meatballs of chicken and bread crumbs rolled in a mixture of spices—and put them in the gift bag. She added homemade rolls, marinated green beans and pasta salad. Saving the best for last, she put in two large slices of Miss Josie's chocolate cream cake.

"I like your idea better," Miss Josie commented, comparing a shoe box that she'd decorated in pale lavender paper and tied with a white lace bow to Victoria's gift bag of sunny yellow with white kittens chasing after a snarl of rainbow-colored strings.

Victoria smiled. "Your box looks lovely."

"Lavender is an old maid's color." Miss Josie sighed. "And I'm an old maid."

Victoria's smile faded. Miss Josie's fiancé had been captured and died as a prisoner in the Second World War. "Didn't you ever meet anyone else you could love?"

"No." Miss Josie paused while wiping up the kitchen

counter. "Well, maybe one man, but he loved another and never got over her."

"Who?" Victoria asked in surprise.

"Now that would be telling." Miss Josie bustled out of the kitchen. "I'll get my purse. It's almost time for the auction."

Victoria smiled again as her neighbor changed the subject. Love, she thought. People were elated, confused or hurt by the ridiculous emotion.

She'd gone over her own feelings last night after Jason and his parents had left. She had herself under control now. She wasn't in love with him. Her feelings had been as he'd said—a product of the moment, derived from tension and crisis.

Thinking of the fishing trip, she wondered if he'd be at the festivities tonight. His father had promised to be back in time.

"Ready?" Miss Josie returned, picked up her box and looked at Victoria expectantly.

"Yes." She walked to the door. "I hope I'm not called upon for a speech. I didn't prepare anything."

"Just take four deep breaths," Miss Josie advised. "Then tell everyone how pleased you are with the turn-out for the supper."

"Yes, ma'am," Victoria replied with a grin.

The two women left. They walked the quarter mile to the town square where the chief of police would auction the box suppers. The money was going to the library for new books.

They met other residents going in the same direction, all carrying boxes of home-cooked food. The picnic supper was a popular event on the Fourth of July. Later in the evening the Historical Society would enact the signing of the Declaration of Independence on the courthouse steps. After that, the fireworks display would begin.

The first person Victoria saw when she arrived was Jason. Her pulse sped up at once when he looked her way. His gaze dropped to the gift bag she carried. She hoped he wouldn't bid on it. Not that a person *had* to eat with the one who bought the supper like in the old days, but it was just that…well, it was customary.

She nibbled on her lower lip nervously, not sure what she was feeling. It was one thing to decide on her emotions in the dark of midnight and something entirely different when confronted with Jason and his cool smile.

"Hello," Miss Josie called, waving to friends right and left.

Victoria trailed after the older woman to the long tables set up to hold the box suppers. They were just in time. Chief Doan stepped up to the microphone, and the auction began.

Victoria saw her friends, Cara and Sally, with their husbands. Sally waved her over.

"Go join the young folks," Miss Josie encouraged. "I think I'll sit with Myra and Claude and the rest of the fogies."

Victoria laughed and went over to her friends' table, glad to escape Jason's company. To her consternation, she'd no more than sat down when he left his group and joined them.

"Miss Josie said you expected me to be your escort," he said, one dark eyebrow raised suspiciously.

Victoria started to deny the statement but thought better of it. Like Miss Josie, she'd seen Jason as an outsider to the group. He lived away while the rest of them mingled almost daily in the small town. She'd observed that he'd sat silently while his kin had exchanged local gossip

"Unless you have a date," she challenged in a light tone. "I certainly wouldn't want to interfere."

His eyes met hers. She smiled, sharing the private knowledge that she had interfered in his social life once before. A quickly hidden emotion darted over his face, too fast for her to read. She knew he remembered their weekend as vividly as she.

"Here, have a chair," Adam said, pulling a spare one over from a nearby table. He introduced Jason to his wife, Cara, and to Riley Houston, Sally's husband.

"Listen to the chief," Victoria advised Jason when he was settled next to her. "He always puts a secret message into his auction prattle. Whoever figures it out wins a prize, usually a gift certificate from a local merchant."

They listened to the melodious drone of the auction. Adam and Riley bid against each other for their wives' suppers, running the price up to an impressive figure.

"Fifty dollars," Jason murmured. "An expensive picnic."

"You don't have to bid," Victoria said quickly. "The diner sells hamburgers from a stand."

"Oh, I think I'd prefer a surprise."

Her brightly colored gift bag finally came up for bid. It was the only one of its kind. The chief sniffed at it. "Something smells mighty good. Might be chocolate cake." He gave the crowd a mischievous grin. "But then again, it might not. Do I hear five dollars for this dee-licious supper? Wella, wella, five, I got five, who's gonna give me six, I got six…"

Jason lifted his hand.

"And-a six, I got six…"

Victoria grew warm as Jason and two other men continued to bid for her supper. The price reached fifty, then sixty, then seventy.

"That's too much," she muttered when Jason bid seventy-five.

"It's for a good cause." He bid again.

By now, most of the crowd had caught on that the pretty gift bag belonged to the mayor and that Jason was determined to win it. So was one other man in the audience, a young pediatrician who had made his interest clear during the past few months.

When the doctor bid eighty, Jason called out, "One hundred."

A murmur of appreciation rose from the crowd. A flush crept into Victoria's cheeks when her friends grinned at her.

"One hundred," the chief sang out. "Do I hear ten—my Aunt Kate—a hundred ten—can roller skate—I got a hundred…a hundred and fifty." He stopped his rapid singsong. "A hundred and fifty dollars. Going once. Going twice. Sold." He banged the gavel.

The crowd burst into applause.

Jason rose and gave a slight bow. He smiled at the young doctor, who saluted him in a good-natured manner.

"Wow," Sally said when the men left to collect the food.

A neighbor from a nearby table yelled, "What'd you have in that bag, Your Honor—a slice of government pie?"

Victoria was glad for the distraction. She didn't want to answer the questions she could see in her friends' eyes. "A contract for road improvement," she answered, recalling a recent scandal in the county road department in which the supervisor had awarded the contract to his own corporation. That brought a laugh.

Adam, Riley and Jason returned with the food plus tall cups of iced tea to go with it.

"I hope Sally didn't fix turkey sandwiches with pickles," Riley said, giving his wife a threatening glance. "That's all we've had for the past couple of weeks."

"I'm thinking of switching to watermelon," she said. "I've had a craving for that since I woke up this morning."

The couple exchanged an amused, tender glance.

"Sally?" Cara questioned.

Sally grinned. "Yes," she confessed. "I'm going to look like I swallowed a watermelon in another month or two."

The others chuckled at this description.

"You'll look beautiful," Victoria exclaimed, thrilled for her friend. "Sally pregnant. The first baby in our group."

"But not for long," Cara confessed, a flush spreading into her cheeks. "At least, Adam and I don't think so." She gave Sally a friendly shove on the arm. "I can't believe you beat me."

Riley raised one dark eyebrow. "Did you know we were in a race?" he asked Adam.

Adam shook his head. "Cara never tells me anything," he complained with a woeful-husband expression.

Victoria joined in the laughter.

"Maybe we can have them together," Sally suggested. "Would the doc give us a break—two for the price of one, do you think?"

"He should," Cara agreed. "The way he was bidding on Victoria's supper, he must have money to burn."

Victoria felt the heat rise in her face again at the reminder of the bidding. As the conversation returned to the coming births, a poignancy crept over her. She realized she wanted to be like her friends—happy and secure, in love and expecting a child. She clenched her fist in her lap, fighting emotion.

A hand touched hers under cover of the table. She glanced over at Jason. Was that compassion in his eyes?

An odd sensation flooded over her. She felt dizzy, a little frightened and full of longing. Yes, she wanted a child, one conceived in love and passion. A child with this man. With Jason.

She turned from his intent gaze and stared at the fading colors of twilight. A star hung low on the horizon. A wish formed in her mind, but she didn't give words to it.

The sweet ache of melancholy stole over her. She turned her hand and clasped Jason's in brief gratitude. For a second he returned the pressure, then he withdrew from her.

"I hope you like chicken," she said, opening the bag and setting out the meal. She gave him a plastic fork and napkin.

"It's one of my favorite foods."

They ate and listened to the reenactment of the signing of the Declaration of Independence. The best performer turned out to be Mr. Wagner, who got a hearty round of applause for his role as Benjamin Franklin.

"Say, doesn't Mr. Wagner have a friend who works in the state highway department?" Sally asked, a speculative gleam in her eye.

"I don't know." Victoria frowned at the implication.

Jason cursed silently as the worry of running the town government descended on Victoria. He saw the way she twisted her paper napkin until it came apart in her hands.

"When are you going to Charleston to find out about the road?" Adam asked.

"Probably not until September. We want to get the playground built next month. Before school starts, we hope."

Jason was aware of her questioning glance. "A set of plans are in the mail," he assured her. "As soon as I get them, I'll order the material. All you have to do is set up the date."

"I'll check with Mary Beth," Victoria promised. "Unless you'd rather do it yourself."

Jason allowed himself a slow grin. "No, I've found you adept at arranging my schedule."

"Do I detect a gibe in that statement?" Sally inquired of Victoria.

Jason wished he'd kept his mouth shut as he intercepted a grin from Adam. He waited to see how Victoria would answer.

Admiration for her warmed him as she shrugged nonchalantly. "I canceled his dinner date with some model while he was out of his office."

"You didn't!" Sally obviously relished the thought.

Victoria nodded affirmatively. "I knew you and Cara would kill me if I came back without accomplishing my goal. Due to, uh, unforeseen circumstances, Jason couldn't keep our appointment. I decided not to be outdone. When the model called, I happened to be the only one in the office. I told her it was off."

"I caught her on the phone," Jason added, "making up a story about a visiting relative I had to entertain."

"So he had to take me to dinner and listen while I extolled the virtues of Paradise Falls," Victoria finished the tale with a deprecatory wave of her hand.

"And?" Sally demanded, looking at Jason.

He knew she wanted to know if he'd decided to move plant there, but he hadn't planned on stating the facts to an audience. He wanted to talk to Victoria alone, to tell her the idea just wasn't feasible. "I'm still checking into it," he said, looking at her.

He saw her eyes and knew she guessed the truth. She covered the disappointment with a light laugh. "I was sure our labor force of fifty knitting grandmothers would impress you."

"The mill's doing well," Adam spoke up. "I don't see a slowdown anytime soon."

"There's a New York designer interested in our new rainproof material," Cara put in. "Wouldn't that be something if she did a bunch of outfits in it?"

"You should look closer to home for industry," Jason suggested to Victoria. "What raw materials do you have here? Nature is one. Adam and Riley have a good idea for a hiking and cross-country skiing operation along with a ranch."

"Tourism," Victoria scoffed. "It's so unpredictable."

"So is life," he reminded her, hating it that she'd been hurt. From the moment he'd met her, he'd wanted to protect her from all disappointments. Why? It was a question he hadn't been able to answer in all the years he'd known her. It was just there—like air, like sunshine, like life.

Victoria knew she had to find another way to help the town. "So it is, but still, there must be something else," she muttered, determined to find it. "First we need that road. I'll get up a petition and take it to Charleston right away. I'll find out why it's been stalled in the planning office for so long."

Jason's father came over and told them he was taking Myra home. He would drop Miss Josie at her house.

"Perhaps I'd better go, too," Victoria decided.

"I'll take you later," Jason volunteered.

"Stay for the fireworks," Sally urged.

"I can see them from my porch." Victoria stood. "Miss Josie must not be feeling well."

Jason stood, too. "I'll drive you both," he said.

They said good-night to the other couples, joined the older woman and left after a few minutes of conversation with Jason's parents.

"Are you all right?" Victoria asked on the way to the car.

"A mite tired," Miss Josie admitted. "You didn't need to leave on account of me."

"I'm rather tired, too."

"Let me help you two old ladies in," Jason said with a grin. He put Miss Josie in the front and Victoria in the back.

At her house Miss Josie made them wait while she fetched two more pieces of cake. "You might be hungry after the fireworks," she explained, handing the wrapped slices to Victoria.

"Thank you. Good night," Victoria called. Jason drove the few feet to her house and parked in the drive.

Victoria tried to perform her duties as hostess. "Would you like the cake now?"

"No. I'm not hungry for food."

He waited for her to precede him onto the wide front porch. The first Roman candle burst into fiery trails across the sky. The fireworks had started.

Victoria sat in the swing. Jason chose his former place on the porch, his shoulder against the post. She looked at his back, the outline of his head and shoulders, and experienced a terrible yearning, so painful it almost made her cry out.

She wanted...she didn't know what she wanted. Life

seemed too harsh all at once. When was she ever going to find happiness?

Tears forced their way to the surface. She wiped them away as a particularly beautiful burst of red, white and blue pinwheel sparklers flew outward from a central explosion.

Jason sat with his back to her during the entire display. It lasted almost an hour, fifty-three minutes of silence, to be exact.

"Well, that was impressive," he said at last. "Who paid for the entertainment?"

Her throat was too tight to speak. She opened her mouth and tried to draw a calm breath. "The town," she managed.

He swung around and stared at her through the dark.

"What's wrong?" he asked after a tense second.

"Nothing." She gave a shaky laugh. "I always get emotional at holidays and celebrations. By the way, you forgot to let your whiskers grow for the pioneer days celebration."

He rose and came to the swing. Pushing his hands into his rear pockets, he studied her in the dim glow of the street light. "I don't have time to grow a beard."

"That's right. You have to get back to your life in the city. Do our local traditions bore you?"

"Dammit, Victoria," he began. He stopped, then sighed.

"I'm sorry," she murmured. "I'm being a grouch. You're not going to locate a company up here, are you?"

He hesitated, then shook his head. "The transportation costs alone are prohibitive."

"I knew that. I just didn't want to admit it."

Taking a seat beside her, he pushed the swing into

gentle motion. "Does knowing about your friends' babies make you sad?"

She swallowed as tears rose again. "I don't think so." She sniffed, searched out a tissue in her pocket and blew her nose. "It's just... Sometimes I expect too much of life, I suppose."

"Like a home, a husband and a child?"

"You're as perceptive as your father," she murmured, getting herself under control.

"It's natural to want what you once had."

Jason grimaced. It probably wasn't wise to remind her of what she'd lost. He himself was reminded of what he'd never had—the companionship of a delightful woman who loved only him.

He was intensely aware of the light fragrance of her perfume, brought to him on the mountain breeze. Although he didn't touch her, he could sense her body close to him. Memories of her satin skin taunted him with a need that grew stronger each minute.

He wanted to lose himself in her warmth—she welcomed him so sweetly—and take them both to—

"What?" he asked, realizing she'd spoken to him.

"It's natural for humans to want closeness with other humans," she repeated softly.

"Do you want that?" His throat was suddenly so tight he could hardly speak.

"Yes."

"Now?"

"Yes."

Flames exploded in him, as brilliant as the fireworks they'd watched. He tamped them down. She was missing her husband and the child she'd lost. It was comfort she wanted, not passion.

He closed his eyes briefly. To this woman, this one

out of all the millions in the world, he wanted to give everything he had.

He put his arm around her shoulders carefully, not sure whether it was her or himself that might break. He almost came apart when she settled against him with a sigh. The scent of her shampoo floated up to him. He hesitated, then laid his cheek against her hair.

The night closed around them, deeply intimate.

Gradually the ache inside Victoria subsided, then slipped away. She no longer had to fight the wild yearning that had bothered her earlier. For this moment, she was content.

When she felt Jason plant a fleeting kiss on top of her head, she couldn't resist. She lifted her face to him.

"Victoria," he said.

A protest, she thought. She parted her lips, ready for his.

"I can't hold you and not want you," he told her, his voice so low she could barely hear it over the whir of the crickets.

"I want you, too," she said simply.

He ground out a curse, then his mouth descended. His touch was tentative, as if she might disappear like a soap bubble. She lifted a hand and caressed his jaw.

With a moan, she snuggled closer, clutching his shoulders and turning so that she could wrap her arms around him.

He lifted her and sat her across his lap. She sighed against his lips when he kissed her. His warmth came through her cotton blouse and caressed her breasts. Yes, this was what she'd wanted.

When he lifted his head, they were both breathing deeply.

"It's no good, is it?" he asked.

"It's wonderful," she contradicted.

"But what's the point? No matter how modern you think you are, you're still the mayor. Every move you make is scrutinized by the whole town."

"So?"

He eased her back into her place. "So I don't want to cause you any trouble with gossip."

"You won't—"

"Ha!"

Jason stood and paced the porch. Coming to a halt in front of her, he studied her, trying to figure her out. She seemed to be waiting for him to see their situation in the same light she did. Which was through the rosy haze of desire.

"Jason?" she said softly, her voice a song in his blood, like a melody carried on the breeze from some far and wonderful place. He longed to go there with her.

He thrust his hands into his back pockets to keep from reaching for her again. With very little provocation, he'd carry her into the deep shadows at the far end of the porch and make love to her right there. "What?"

"I think I've fallen in love with you."

All the clichés regarding the human body happened to him—his knees went weak, his stomach dropped and his lungs stopped working. Common sense returned.

"It's warmed-over emotion, not the real thing," he informed her as coolly as he could with his imagination on fire.

She sat up straight. "What?"

"Because of what happened at the office. We shared tense moment with Susan and the baby—"

Her trill of laughter cut him off. She shook her head.

He had to clear his throat in order to speak. "Later, at the house, there was passion. I admit it was wonderful."

"Yes," she said in a dreamy voice. "It was, wasn't it?"

"Right, so now you feel gratitude for that. It woke you up to being a real woman again." He was having trouble with his breathing. Pictures formed in his mind as he remembered how it had felt to kiss her and caress her to his heart's content.

"And what do *you* feel?"

He detected a deceptive innocence in the question. He thought it over from several angles but could see no obvious trap. "I feel the same."

"You're a wonderful lover," she told him. "So tender, and considerate, too, especially when you realized it had been a long time for me."

Victoria smiled slightly when he made a rough sound and paced the porch again. She wanted to break through that cool control he kept locked around his heart.

He gave a snort of laughter when he stopped in front of her again. "I nearly came apart in your hands. Your response was so natural, so spontaneous, it drove me to the brink more than once."

She stood and laid her hands on his shoulders. "A man and a woman sharing life's most precious gift is a natural thing."

"You're confusing passion with love," he told her.

"Then you do know the difference?"

"Of course." Jason recognized the trap the moment the words were said. He'd let her lead him like a babe until she reached the point she wanted to make.

"Well," she said softly, raising herself on tiptoe so their lips were a whisper apart, "so do I."

He pulled her hands off him and stalked away, needing distance so he could argue logically with her. "Not in this case. You're thinking of John."

There was a moment of silence, then, "What?"

"You're confusing me with John. He was your first lover, right?" When she didn't answer, he repeated, "Am I right?"

"Yes, but—"

"It was my fault. I knew you were vulnerable after the crisis at the office. The birth brought back memories."

"No," Victoria corrected. "It let me see another side of you." She went to him when he stubbornly remained apart from her, his back stiff and unyielding. She laid a hand on his arm, needing the connection between them as she felt him emotionally withdraw from her. "Why, Jason?"

"Why what?"

"Why keep that part of yourself hidden? You were wonderful with Susan and later with me when we nearly made love. You have a rich store of tenderness and compassion—"

"You're letting your imagination run away with you."

"I don't think so." She rested both hands on his chest. "Is it so hard to believe I might love you for yourself?"

"For myself?" He laughed briefly, then clasped her wrists, removing her hands. "When we were in bed, Victoria, you called me by the pet name you always used for John."

A denial sprang to her lips. She tried to remember, but murmured words blended into the bliss of sharing her passion with him. "What name?" she finally asked.

"Love. You always called him *love.*"

The tension drained out of her. "Jason, I call everyone love by that—my parents, my cousins, my best friends. It's an endearment I use when I'm feeling especially affectionate toward someone." She paused, then said in a soft voice, "I'd never confuse you with anyone else."

The silence grew between them as he looked into her eyes. She willed him to see the truth in her. He released her and turned away. "It doesn't matter," he said. "If, for a few minutes, you were happy, who am I to complain? I reaped the benefits."

"Thus speaks the cynical Jason," she said, "but I know the other Jason, and a few kisses aren't enough for him any more than they are for me."

"Forget him," he advised.

"I don't think I can. He's the one I fell in love with."

"Then you're a fool." He bounded down the steps.

"I don't think so," she called the instant before he reached the rental car.

He left without a backward glance.

Chapter Nine

Victoria checked off the last item on her list. The new fall stock was in. Now all she needed to do was arrange it on the racks in attractive displays. Thank goodness the windows were done.

She stuck the bills in the accounts payable file and went out to view her handiwork. The scene in the big window at the front of the store depicted a family on a fall outing—father in a plaid wool jacket and jeans, mom in a gold turtleneck with a gold-and-red-striped sweater over it and dark brown cords, two boys in hooded sweat-shirts and stone-washed jeans with bronze studs on the pockets.

She wondered if it had been a subconscious gesture on her part to use a black-haired, blue-eyed father with a blond-haired mother. Gazing at the mannequins and arti-cial leaves in bright fall colors, she pictured Jason and herself with two sons. Heat gathered in her.

Turning from the revealing display, she stroked a hand nervously down her heather-toned pantsuit. It was almost six. Time for the dedication ceremony for the playground. She had to give the official speech thanking Jason and the volunteers who'd put the thing together. They'd done it in one day.

Jason, Adam and Riley had divided the work into three sections and the helpers into three groups yesterday. The work had evolved into a competition to see who could get done first. As mayor, she'd declared a three way tie when they'd finished twelve hours later. The three men had stayed to tidy up the loose ends.

She ignored the hurt she'd felt when Sally had suggested the three couples go for pizza and Jason had gracefully declined, saying he had another commitment. He'd left without a word to her.

Sighing, she got her purse, locked the door behind her and went out to her car. The town was deserted. Everyone, it appeared, had gone to the park. When she arrived she found she had been correct. The park was full, and so were all the parking spaces. She drove to her house and walked back.

"Victoria, it's about time," Sally called. "We thought we were going to have to send Jason to drag you away from your desk."

Victoria managed a cool smile when she met Jason' glance. She hadn't been alone with him since he'd left her standing on the porch after the fireworks, seve weeks ago. He'd had Susan send a letter to her with th plans for the play equipment. All she'd had to do wa alert Mary Beth, the PTA president, who'd done the o ganization for the event.

During the construction, she'd worked on Riley team. Under his direction, she and Sally and two oth women had put together the sections that were now crawl-through tube for tots. She turned and surveyed the playground.

"What do you think?" a deep masculine voice asked.

"It's incredible. I can't believe we did this in one day."

"A long day," Jason reminded her. "Riley and I went over everything again to make sure all the joints are secure."

The breeze brought the scent of his cologne to her. She wanted to bury her face against his neck the way she'd done the night they'd nearly made love. She looked at her watch. "It's time," she said. "Come with me. You'll have to say a few words."

Jason grimaced, but followed along beside her. He helped her climb the steps to the first level of the "tree house" to make her speech. He stood on the bottom step and watched her.

Her speech was simple, but it was saved from sounding hackneyed by the sincerity in her expression. She liked people, he realized. She believed in what she said about a community reflecting the attitudes of its citizens. She told them how proud she was to be part of a town like Paradise Falls, "a town that cares." She related other incidents to them that indicated their caring, responsible attitude.

Jason could almost see the chests swelling with civic pride and a sense of duty well done by the time she finished telling the crowd how wonderful they were as a group and as individuals. She singled out Adam and Riley, then Mary Beth and finally himself to lavish with praise.

"Now I'd like to turn the podium over to Mary Beth."

Victoria stepped aside and Jason helped the other woman up the steps. "Jason," the PTA president said,

"would you please join me?" She had a covered object
in her hand.

Resigned to his fate, he went up the steps and stood
between her and Victoria while he was presented with a
plaque. She also told him the park had been named in
his honor, which surprised him. He shot a glance at
Victoria. She should have headed this off, or at least
warned him. She smiled coolly.

He made the appropriate remarks, similar to those he'd
said when he'd made the offer to the city council, and
thanked them for the award and the honor. He stepped
down from the platform amid cheers and applause.

"Now," Victoria said when the noise died down, "the
volunteer fire department has chicken and hot dogs on
the grill. The PTA has all the fixin's, so let's eat."

That led to another cheer and a rush to the tables.

Victoria was detained from joining the line by two
local merchants who wanted to know if she'd heard anything about the road yet. "No, but I have a petition with
over two thousand names. The state legislature can't ignore us this time. I'll take our case to them in person on
Monday."

Before she could get away, someone else had a question. "Has anything been done about the child-care center that was brought up a few months back?"

Forty minutes later she was still answering queries
from her constituents. From the corner of her eye, she
saw Jason make his way through the group surrounding
her.

"Your supper's getting cold," he announced. He
smiled at the crowd. "If you'll excuse us."

Amid some good-natured teasing, he took her elbow
and guided her to a picnic table where her friends waited

"I didn't think you were going to get a chance to eat," Cara told her when she sat down.

"Who fixed my plate?" Victoria asked, looking at the paper plate stacked high with chicken and vegetables.

"I did," Jason answered.

"Thank you." She gave him a radiant smile. She was suddenly happy. Stealing a glance at Jason, she knew she shouldn't be. Nothing had changed between them. Yesterday he'd been all crisp efficiency. Friday night, at dinner at his parents' home, he'd been his usual standoffish self, amused and remote, without a flicker of emotion showing when he'd looked at her.

She and Cara and Sally discussed their plans concerning the new road while they ate. When her napkin fluttered from her lap, Jason bent and retrieved it before it could blow away. Their fingers touched when he handed it back.

"Thanks. Again." Her voice was husky, and he gave her a sharp glance as if warning her to keep her emotions under control.

She couldn't. His nearness created havoc with her senses. She wanted to lean her shoulder against his. More than that, she wanted to feel his hands gliding over her, arousing her to the passion that simmered between them in spite of his remote manner.

"With Victoria in Charleston, working on that end, Cara and I are going to comb the county records and find out who owns every parcel of land between the town and the resort over on the lake," Sally explained to Jason.

"If anyone's buying up the land and holding it, they'll let me know. It might give us something to go on," Victoria declared.

"You're going alone to Charleston?" Jason asked. He frowned at the other two men. Adam grinned.

"Of course," Victoria said, giving him an irritated look.

"When?" he demanded.

"Monday."

"I'll drive you there."

Victoria and her two friends were clearly astounded. Adam chuckled. So did Riley. Jason's ears became warm. He felt like a schoolboy caught passing a love note in class.

"I'm on vacation for a week," he hastily explained. "My father and I were going to do some fishing, but he's involved in a court case. So I have some free time."

He felt even more like a fool when Victoria kissed him on the cheek and exclaimed, "How wonderful!" as if he'd given her the sun, moon and stars, all tied with a dainty bow.

His eyes met Sally's. She gave him a solemn stare. "I'm glad you're not ignoring this chance—" she paused "—to continue your civic duty to your hometown."

That drew a laugh.

Victoria stilled the clamoring in her heart. "I'd planned on leaving early Monday morning."

"I'll pick you up at seven."

She didn't argue.

The storm swooped over the mountain peak and into the tiny valley on Sunday afternoon. It kept up a steady drone into the night. Monday was dismal. The traffic in town was a snarl of frustrated parents dropping the kids off at school and harried business people trying to get to work. The streets were slick, and tempers were short.

Victoria sneaked a glance at Jason after they crept past a minor accident that had Main Street backed up to the Beckley Road turnoff. Finally they made it out of town and onto the twisting road that led to the interstate highway.

When they were on the scenic four-lane highway and rolling along at sixty-five miles per hour, she asked, "Why did you volunteer to come with me?"

"I thought you might need help. If someone is holding up construction of the road, they might not want anyone nosing around and trying to find out who and why."

She scoffed at this cloak-and-dagger idea. He didn't argue with her. She remained silent as the rain poured down in torrents. Jason required all his attention for the road, which was hardly visible through the blowing sheets of water.

Once he cursed as a plastic bag loomed out of nowhere like an alien invasion. It hit the windshield and whipped past them out of sight. The trip, normally a bit more than an hour, extended to two. By the time they arrived at the capital, she was in no mood for her appointment with their district representative to present the petition from the citizens and the various business owners in the area as well as those from Paradise Lake.

"There's a coffee shop across the street from your congressman's office. We can meet there later. I don't know how long I'll be. I'm going to do a little checking on my own. I went to school with a guy who's an engineer with the road department."

"All right," she said. "I'll probably be invited to lunch, so it might be a while before I'm free."

"I'll keep checking the coffee shop. We'll meet up sooner or later. Sooner, I hope." He peered at the sky after he stopped under the portico of the office building. "I'd like to be home before dark. The road to Paradise Falls is treacherous enough without navigating it in a blinding rain."

"You shouldn't be wasting your vacation helping me with the town problems," she said, giving him a worried appraisal. "You're supposed to relax on a vacation."

"Let me worry about that," he snapped.

Before she could say anything, he apologized, then smiled. Her heart melted. "I'll see you later." She climbed out and ran inside before more than a dozen drops of rain blew over her.

As she predicted, the district congressman insisted she join him for lunch after she presented her petition and explained the situation with the town. He was sympathetic, but wouldn't make any promises. She smiled ruefully as she recognized the political ploy. It was one she'd used often.

At two o'clock she went to the coffee shop. There, she waited for Jason. He didn't arrive until almost five.

He slid into the other side of the booth and gave her a solemn look, which she couldn't interpret. Gazing into his eyes, she sensed controlled excitement in him. A nervous tingle went through her. She had a feeling she wasn't going to like his news.

"Any luck?" she asked when he continued to study her.

He nodded. "Bingo," he said. "My old friend gave me a clue. Together we traced it down."

"So what is it?" She twisted her napkin in her hands. "Maybe the question is—*who* is it? Someone has blocked the construction of the road, haven't they?"

He nodded. "We think so. Frank Wagner has been buying land along the proposed roadway for three years. One more parcel and he'd have had it all. The widow who owned it sold her acreage to Sally and Riley for that ranch they want to start."

"Mr. Wagner," Victoria repeated. "Are you saying Mr. Wagner is the one blocking the new road?"

"Yes. I met an old buddy of his, the brother of the woman Wagner was to have married—"

"She was hit by lightning shortly before they married." Victoria remembered an old bit of gossip Sally had once told her.

"The man works in the highway department. I met him this morning. He asked about Wagner when he realized I was from Paradise Falls. That got me to thinking"

"Mr. Wagner is on the city council," Victoria interrupted. "He's very much in favor of the road. You're mistaken, Jason."

"I don't think so. I called Sally. She did some checking and verified the information I just gave you."

She realized Jason had withdrawn behind his sardonic mask. "He's spoken for the road often," she told him.

"Oh, he's for it. On his terms. He probably thinks to make a killing from the state when the project is finally released from the planning committee...which his old friend just happens to head."

Victoria rubbed her forehead. "I can't believe this."

Jason looked out the window. "Let's eat, then head back before the storm breaks again."

They ordered soup and sandwiches and were on the road by six o'clock. Unfortunately the next wave of the storm didn't wait for them to make it home. It unleashed its fury as soon as they were on the highway. By the time they reached Beckley, night had fallen. The storm continued as if driven by fury at the humans who had to be out in it.

Victoria clenched her hands more than once on the trip up the winding mountain road. It was during a snowstorm that she and John had been forced off this very same road almost eight years ago. Right before Christmas, she remembered. They'd been shopping in Beckley and had stayed for a late dinner before returning home.

She stared at the blinding rain, then looked at Jason. Fear rose to her throat. "Jason, be careful."

He didn't spare her a glance, but she saw his jaw clench before he said huskily, "I will. Don't be frightened."

"It's just…I don't want anything to happen to you." She tried to explain, although she wasn't quite sure what she wanted to say. "I don't want to lose you before I've had a chance to know you. Before we have a chance to know each other."

"After that night at my place, I think we know each other quite well," he remarked.

"But not completely."

He cursed, but whatever else he might have said was forgotten as he turned a blind curve on the steepest part of the mountain. He slowed the car and stared ahead. "Where the hell is the road?"

All at once, Victoria realized the pelting on the roof of the car wasn't only rain. "Rocks," she said. "It's a rock slide. Jason, look out!"

It was too late.

The slide gathered momentum. An avalanche of mud, gravel and boulders crashed down on them. The car skidded sideways. A boulder glanced off the top, denting it. Jason threw the four-wheel drive into reverse, but fate was determined the mortals wouldn't escape. The slide followed their efforts to retreat.

Then they were swept off the road and over the edge. Victoria relived the nightmare of turning over in a vehicle careering down a mountainside. She and Jason were going to die.

She'd never convinced him of her love, she realized just before the world disappeared in an explosion of light. Then all was dark.

The voice came to her from a distance. She'd heard it before. She remembered the time clearly—she'd been cold and alone and afraid, but the voice had called her back. Back from where? Oh, yes, the meadow with the wonderfully soft light falling on it. The meadow where John and the baby played—

"Victoria, are you all right? Dammit, answer me!"

She opened her eyes, but there was only darkness. "Jason?"

"Thank God," he said. "Where are you hurt?"

"My head, I think." She touched the throbbing lump on the side of her head. "I bumped it on something."

"What about the rest of you?" he asked. His tone was calm now. She felt his hand touch her shoulder.

She moved her arms and legs, then her back and neck. "All present and accounted for. How about you?"

"I'm fine."

"It's so dark," she said.

She heard the click as he unfastened his seat belt, then felt him lean past her. He retrieved a flashlight from the glove box and flicked it on.

"My God," he said.

She saw their predicament at once. They had rolled over and come upright against a pine sapling, hardly bigger around than the calf of her leg. Beyond it was a straight drop of fifty feet.

"We're near Vista Point," she said.

"Yes."

"Near where John and I went off the cliff."

"Yes." He turned the light out. He slipped his arm

around her shoulder and pulled her to him. "Don't be afraid," he murmured. "I'll get you out."

"You got me out of the car the other time," she said. Her thought processes were taking place in slow motion, but she knew the nightmare that had haunted her had been real. "It was you. You found me. You called me back. I was walking toward a meadow."

"I thought you were gone," he said in a hoarse voice, "but you came back."

"When you slapped me."

"Yes," he admitted.

The memory came back to her. "You saved me, Jason. I didn't realize it at the time, but...you saved my life." She released her seat belt and reached for him, needing his warm living touch.

"But I couldn't save your husband or your baby."

She remembered he'd removed her cold numbed hands, opened her coat and found the child clutched to her bosom. He'd lifted it from her. His tears had fallen on her face.

"It's all right," she said, twisting around in order to hold him close, to comfort him. "You did everything you could. No one could ask for more."

"You thought I was John, then you realized I wasn't. But I wanted to be. I wanted to give him back to you. I would have if it had been possible," he said, agony in his voice.

"Oh, my darling," she whispered, aware of his pain. She whispered soothing, comforting words to him. Another insight came to her, but this wasn't the time to discuss it. She would save it for later, when they were rescued.

The wind rocked the car, and she was reminded of their precarious balance. The rescue might not come in time. She held Jason tighter. "I love you," she said. "Jason, I love you."

He moved away from her. "Another crisis," he said in a mocking tone. "You might feel differently in the morning."

"No." She sighed and prepared to wait out the dark and the storm. Dawn was a long way off. Who knew what tomorrow would bring?

Chapter Ten

With the dawn came the realization that they weren't likely to be rescued for hours yet. Victoria was on the cliff side of the precariously balanced vehicle. "See if you can get the door open now that you can see better," she suggested.

He'd tried to open the door earlier, but it was stuck. He tried it again. The car rocked back and forth. The small tree holding it in place bent a little more toward the edge.

Victoria had an idea. "Try the window."

He turned on the ignition key and tried the button. To their surprise, the window opened almost all the way.

"We can climb out," she said, relieved at being able to take action after the long dark night.

She bit her lip anxiously as Jason eased into a crouch on the seat. The car swayed. Several rocks skittered over the side of the fifty-foot drop. Jason waited a few seconds, then tried again.

He edged his body through the opening. Victoria held

her breath when she felt the vehicle shudder. The rocks shifted again.

When she felt the car slip, she knew it was going to go over the side. "Jump! Jason, jump!"

He froze. The car steadied. The pine tree held.

Very slowly, he eased down into the seat. When he was seated, she raged at him, "Why didn't you jump? You could have gotten out. Why didn't you go on?"

He gave her a look just as furious. "The front tire is right on the edge. If I'd jumped, the car would have gone over. You'd have been killed!"

"But you would be safe! At least *one* of us would have made it." Was he so dense that he couldn't see the logic of that? It made perfect sense to her. She simply couldn't bear for him to be hurt, and *that* was the unadorned truth.

Grabbing her wildly gesturing hand, he leaned close until his face was inches from hers. "What the hell would the world be to me if you were gone?" he snarled at her.

The silence crackled between them.

"Jason?" she questioned softly when she could stand it no longer.

He released her, laid his arm over the steering wheel and rested his forehead against it.

"Jason?" she said again. She placed her left hand on his shoulder and felt the tension in him.

"I didn't mean to say that," he muttered.

Happiness burst into being inside her. He loved her. She'd thought so last night, but now she was positive. "Oh, love," she whispered.

He whipped his head around and glared at her. A shout from above prevented any discussion of their feelings. The chief of police had arrived.

In a few minutes tow trucks were on the scene. The drivers hooked pulleys to the front and back of the rental car to hold it steady, then they forced the door on the driver's side. Jason and Victoria climbed out after ten hours of entrapment.

"Ah, the world," she said, standing on Vista Point and watching the officials do their job. She smiled radiantly at Jason, who stood near her, a scowl on his face while he explained the accident to the chief.

One lane of the road was completely blocked, the other was covered with rubble. The edge of the road had crumbled. An earlier slide on that side must have undercut its support, causing it to give way beneath the weight of their car.

It had been a close call, but now...now she felt safe and secure...and wildly in love. She wanted to be alone with Jason.

It was more than an hour before they finally climbed into the patrol car and were taken to town. The chief dropped Victoria at her house first.

After thanking him, she turned to Jason. A rush of tenderness invaded her. "Would you like to come in and have breakfast before we face the world?" They had so much to discuss, so many plans to make. She felt dizzy thinking of it.

"No, thanks," he said. "I'll go over and assure my parents that we're okay. The news is sure to have hit the grapevine by now." He gave her one encompassing glance before climbing into the front seat where she'd sat on the ride home. The chief drove off.

Victoria went into the house. For a second she stood in the hallway and listened to the emptiness echo in her heart. Then she went upstairs to shower and get some sleep.

She heard from Jason's mother later that day. Jason

had gotten his tent and backpack from the garage loft and gone off on his own for a few days.

"He said he needed some quiet to let his nerves settle after the accident," Myra explained. "He did look rather pale."

"I see," Victoria said. Her voice sounded hollow.

The meeting went against Victoria's belief in government in the sunshine—meaning all business conducted by the council was also the business of every citizen. In this case she'd called a private meeting. After everyone commented on the accident of the previous day and how lucky she was to escape with her life, she took her place at the head of the table—the signal that the meeting was about to convene.

"The council is now in executive session," she said when the others were settled.

The five council members were gathered in the private conference room next to her office. The recording secretary and the city attorney were the only other people present. She hesitated, wishing she didn't have to do this.

The other officials of the town government looked at her expectantly. Glancing at Mr. Wagner, she noted he didn't seem in the least suspicious that he'd been found out.

Humans. They were the oddest creatures on earth. She looked at her notes.

"We appear to have a problem," she said after swallowing her disappointment with her fellow beings. "I have conclusive evidence that a resident of the town is responsible for the road delay."

Mr. Wagner looked as surprised as the other council members. Her confidence wavered. Maybe she and Jason and Sally were wrong. She studied the dates of purchase

and deed recordings from the county records. No, there
was no room for doubt.

"Well, Victoria, don't keep us in suspense. Who is the
culprit?" one of the council, a surveyor by trade, demanded.

"First I'd like to present the evidence." She handed
out copies of the paper listing the property transactions
for the past three years.

There were several minutes of silence while the other
three studied the report. Mr. Wagner glanced at it...and
smiled.

The knot in Victoria's stomach grew to grapefruit size.
She clenched her hands in her lap to stop their shaking.
She hated confrontations. But she had a job to do.

"Why, Frank, you've bought several thousands of
acres along the old logging trail west of town," the surveyor said when he finished reading the page.

Mr. Wagner nodded. He seemed quite pleased.

"It has come to my attention," Victoria continued,
"that you have a good friend in the highway department."

He nodded, his eyes gleaming.

She thought she was going to cry. He seemed
so...innocent! Perhaps he was becoming senile. Maybe
he didn't remember what he'd done. Maybe someone else
was gulling him into this, and he wasn't even aware of
it.

With an effort she pulled herself together. She had a
duty to the town. She couldn't shirk it.

"The evidence indicates that the land purchases occurred after the deletion of the Paradise Lake road from
the construction plan three years ago. Since then, the
project has been tied up in the planning department." She

swallowed hard. "That department is headed by the brother of your former fiancée."

Insight dawned on the faces of the other council members. They stared at Mr. Wagner, who smiled and nodded.

"That's correct," he said.

Victoria pressed a hand to her aching head. "I think, before you say anything else, you should have an attorney present to advise you," she said, pity in her eyes as she looked at the old man who'd figured prominently in the town for fifty years.

"I didn't stop the road from going through," Mr. Wagner said. "In fact the idea to buy the land didn't occur to me until after I called to find out why the road had been delayed."

"Why was it delayed?" the surveyor broke in.

"Construction problems. The engineers discovered that a huge clay deposit ran directly through the road bed, which had previously been thought to be solid rock. They've been studying the land for a way around it."

"We know about the study. It's been going on forever," the other man on the council spoke up.

"What was your part in this? Did you think you could buy the land and hold out for a higher price when the problem was solved?" Victoria asked, bringing the conversation back on topic.

Mr. Wagner laughed. He shook his head. "I'm going to donate it to the state for the road."

She stared at him in disbelief. "That land must have cost a million dollars."

"More than that," he declared in a satisfied tone. "I bought enough to have a park on each side of it. I'm going to donate the extra to the county and the town. There's one section missing. Sally Winetski beat me to it. She and her husband want to do that ranch thing and have city kids work on it," he grumbled.

In the silence that followed this pronouncement, the attorney chuckled. In a wry voice, he asked, "Did you ever think of telling anyone what you were doing?" he asked.

"I told my attorney. It's all in my will in case I died before I could get it finished. After all, I am seventy-five," Mr. Wagner stated righteously.

All that worry and work for nothing! Victoria drew in an exasperated breath. "Mr. Wagner, why didn't you tell the rest of us what was going on? Do you realize the citizens of this town have worried over that road for years?"

"I wanted to surprise you. Planned on having it ready to present to the town at the centennial doings, but couldn't get that last tract of land."

"A surprise," she repeated, not sure whether to laugh or scream. Not that either would do a speck of good.

"It's my legacy," he explained defensively. "My fiancée was hit by lightning—before your time, it was—so I never had children to carry on my name. I have no family at all. I wanted something to go on after me. I thought…well, you might name the park after me…my legacy to the future, you see."

She did. For the briefest second, she remembered holding a tiny baby in her arms—her own hope for the future.

Compassion brought the sting of tears to her eyes. "A splendid idea," she said huskily. "Why don't we meet with Sally and her husband tomorrow and see if we can work out something about the land you need?" she suggested. She studied a map of the area. "Actually, you only need a small triangle along the creek to complete your plans, it seems to me."

"That's right."

"Well, that wraps it up, I think. I don't have any further questions. Shall we adjourn?"

She looked at the city attorney. He nodded. She looked at the other three council members. They nodded.

"This meeting is adjourned," she said.

The small conference room became as noisy as the playground right after school was out. Everyone had a host of questions to ask her and Mr. Wagner. By the time the room was clear, it was time to go to the store to help with the evening rush.

She heard nothing of Jason for the remainder of the week. She went through the routine of ordering clothes, checking invoices and attending to her mayoral duties, but every nerve in her body hummed with impatience while she waited for his return.

First, she wanted to tell him about Mr. Wagner—that they'd been right about what he was doing but wrong about his motives.

The second item on her agenda involved them. She loved him. If he rejected her, if he refused to admit his love for her, then she would have to write him off and go on from there.

It would be a confrontation unlike any she'd ever faced, she realized, one that would affect her entire future.

"Hey, boss, I'm off," Terri said, sticking her head into the office. "The stock is straightened, the front door is locked, the burglar alarm set. Anything else?"

Victoria looked up from the catalog of fall clothes and smiled. "No, you may leave. Is tonight the night?"

The businesswomen's club was sponsoring a series of Saturday-night dances for the young people in town. The captain of the basketball team had invited Terri to go with him. The teenager had rhapsodized about it for three days.

"You bet! The outfit you helped me pick out will knock his eyes out. I hope." With a cheerful giggle, she was off.

Oh, to be that young again.

Smiling and shaking her head, Victoria locked her desk. The week had been so busy, she'd hardly had time to eat, much less think about her dating life, or lack of one.

After leaving the empty store, she stood on the sidewalk for a few seconds and looked at the happy family scene in the window. Perhaps it was time to change it. If things didn't work out between her and Jason, she'd have to find a new dream.

First she had to find him. Apparently he hadn't returned from his trek into the mountains. She'd spoken to his mother only that morning and asked about him—

Her thought came to a screeching halt. Jason!

He was looking at her. When he realized she'd recognized him in his father's car, he nodded without smiling. The light changed and he drove off.

Victoria stood as if rooted to the pavement. He was back. And it was obvious he meant to have nothing to do with her!

She drove home in a turmoil of conflicting thoughts. She was torn between never speaking to him again, pretending a cool indifference to him in the future or going to him and browbeating him into admitting he couldn't live without her.

By the time she reached her house, she was exhausted. Taking the cowardly way out, she telephoned his parents' home and asked to speak to him. His mother said, in a disapproving voice, that he was staying at the big house

"You'd think he wasn't welcome in his own home, the way he acts," she complained.

Victoria was totally sympathetic to Myra. "Yes, one can't accuse Jason of clinging to his family."

They chatted about the weather and the new storm that was blowing in before hanging up. Victoria heated a frozen dinner and settled before the TV to watch a KQED special on wild turkeys. It was an informative show. She didn't hear more than three words.

Since seeing Jason on the street and realizing he was avoiding her, the anger had seethed in her. It bubbled to the foreground of her mind as she sat alone in her house and listened to the soft patter of rain strike the windows.

The more she thought about it, the angrier she became.

Trying for calm, she carried her tray to the kitchen, threw out the remains of her dinner and put the dishes in the dishwasher. She returned to the living room. The silence of the house, the moan of the wind, the chatter of the rain on the tin roof were getting on her nerves.

Standing at the window, she stared at the lights of the town below her. Across the narrow valley, halfway up the far peak, the Clairmont Mansion stood sentinel on its own turret of land. She could hardly see the brick structure through the rain.

Was Jason up there alone?

She knew Cara and Adam had gone to visit Cara's mother and stepfather, and, since the mansion had only recently been opened as an inn, there were few guests.

A chill swept over her. She rubbed her arms to ward off the cold seeping through the window pane. She thought of Jason, alone on his side of the mountain. And here she was, alone on her side.

The decision leapt into her mind. Without allowing time for reflection, she grabbed her purse and, on her way

to her car, dug out the keys. In less than a minute she
was off.

The drive up the winding road to the mansion wa
slippery from the rain. At one point the gravel ha
washed across the road in a miniature slide. She grippe
the wheel firmly and pressed on up the mountain.

What would the world be to me without you in it?

She had another question to go with that one. At th
mansion she parked at the side of the circular drive an
dashed to the front door. The chill mountain breez
seemed to whip through her thin summer slacks an
blouse when she paused on the steps. The birch trees
the edge of the lawn whispered and laughed as if the
mocked her hopes.

Fear gnawed at her. If Jason rejected her…

Clamping down on the useless conjecture, she opene
the door and slipped inside. The house was eerily siler
A light fell across the hallway carpet from the partial
open library door, there was no sound from within. Pe
haps she should go to the kitchen and find Mrs. Grove
The housekeeper could tell her which room Jason wa
using.

Her heart went into double-time as she walked dow
the hall. The thick carpet runner muffled her footstep
She paused at the open door of the library and peere
inside.

Jason was there!

A low fire burned in the grate, but he wasn't sittir
on the long, tavern sofa in front of it. Instead, he stoc
at one of the tall, narrow windows that gave a view
the hills beyond this one. He looked as cold and form
dable as a medieval fortress.

Another shiver went through her.

The urge to flee and not force this issue tensed eve

muscle in her body. She'd never known herself to be such a coward.

Although she didn't move or make a sound, something must have alerted Jason. All at once his head whipped around, and he stared at her without a flicker of emotion on his face.

"Hello, Jason," she said. She walked boldly into the room as if her heart wasn't shaking like a birch leaf in a gale.

"Victoria," he said, acknowledging her presence. He held a brandy snifter in one hand, the other was in the pocket of his jeans. He looked fit and incredibly handsome.

Like a breathing statue, she thought. His was a hard, remote comeliness, *made only to look at but not to touch.*

He isn't like that, she protested. He's a man. Inside him beats a living heart. A closed-off, lonely heart, but a heart.

"May I come in?"

He looked surprised at the formal request. "Sure. Make yourself at home." With a wave of the brandy glass, he indicated the cozy arrangement of sofa and easy chairs.

She came into the room. Another chill washed over her.

"The storm has dropped the temperature to about fifty degrees," he said. "Would you like a brandy to warm you up?"

"No, thanks. The fire is fine." She chose to sit on the broad hearth where she could warm her hands and watch him at the same time. The clock ticked the seconds away. "Are you the only guest in the house?" she finally asked.

"Yes." His smile was laced with a thin thread of sardonic humor. "The housekeeper is in the back some-where. If you came to see her."

A tremor pulsed through her. "No. I wanted to talk to you." She stopped, unsure how to begin. It seemed harder somehow, now that she was here. "Jason, help me."

His eyebrows rose in surprise at her plea. He gave a short laugh. "How? I can't even help myself." He took a long drink of brandy and gazed out the window.

She wasn't sure what he meant, but she thought it had to do with her, with them. "Last week, when we were trapped in the car," she said in a rush.

He gave her a quick, harsh glance, then looked away. She waited but he said nothing.

Anger rose in her. "You're not going to make this easy, are you?"

"I've never found scenes easy."

She leapt to her feet. "I am not going to make a *scene*. I want to know what you meant when you said…when you indicated the world wouldn't mean anything to you without me in it."

He became perfectly still. Then he shrugged. "I thought it was pretty obvious."

"You love me," she said softly, relieved that he hadn't denied the feeling between them.

He laughed, an ironic sound that bruised her heart. "Love? The word is too simple. You're a fact of my life, like the beating of my heart, like the song in my soul when I see you, like the hunger that never lets up. I've wanted you from the moment I laid eyes on you. You belonged to my best friend, but I wanted you. Funny huh?"

"No."

The sardonic smile left his face. "No," he agreed.

"I've been free for seven years, Jason. Why didn't you ever come to me during all that time?"

"You never knew I was alive, dear cousin-in-law. Until you needed a favor."

"I'm sorry for that. I was callous toward you," she admitted. "But you were remote with me. Until I went to you for that favor."

"Yeah, that was a mistake—"

"It wasn't." She went to him and laid her hand on his arm. "It opened my eyes. Oh, Jason, without that incident in your office... Would you have ever let me see the real man?"

He interrupted her. "You saw what you wanted to see. You think I'm like your husband. I'm not. I admired John. Hell, I loved him. But I'm not him."

"I know." She sighed and laid her hand against his shoulder. He stiffened under her touch. "I love you."

"For right now," he acknowledged. "But what happens when you wake up and see the truth?" He drank the rest of the brandy, set the glass on the windowsill, then took her by the shoulders. "What happens when you realize you've made a terrible mistake? Don't forget. I've seen the disappointment in your eyes when you realized I wasn't the man you thought I was, the man you loved. If I'd been with you that night—"

She laid her fingers over his mouth. "You couldn't have changed a thing. That fate wasn't yours to decide. You aren't God, Jason, only a man. The man I love."

He spun away, thrusting his hands into his pockets, his back to her.

"That was a long time ago, Jason. Let it go. I have." She took a deep breath. Like the night she'd gone to him and they'd nearly made love, she knew they were right for each other, but she wouldn't beg. "I love you. I think you love me. If you reject our love, I'll walk out and never bother you again. So tell me, Jason, what am I to do?''

''Dammit,'' he muttered, sounding like a man at the end of his rope. ''Can't we drop this?''

''Yes,'' she said. The sadness engulfed her like the night enclosed the valley. She forced a smile. ''I'll go peacefully.''

Everything in her told her this was wrong! She and Jason belonged together. But he wouldn't let himself see that. She drew four deep breaths and fought the useless tears, then she walked to the door. There she paused, unable to believe it was over before it ever began. He didn't speak or look at her.

''Goodbye, Jason. I wish you happiness.'' She ran down the hall toward the front door.

A hand closed over hers when she reached for the brass knob.

''Victoria,'' Jason said. He locked his arms around her and pulled her against him, her back to his chest. He pressed his face into her hair. They stood there while the grandfather clock ticked off a full minute, then another.

''Let me go,'' she whispered on a ragged plea.

''I can't,'' he muttered, pressing closer. ''God help me but I can't.''

She braced her hands against the solid oak door, fighting the longing that made her want to yield to his wild caresses along her body. ''Please,'' she whimpered. The tears seeped along her face.

''Stay.'' His voice was hoarse, as if the words hurt.

''No,'' she denied the request. ''I want more than a moment's passion. One night isn't enough—''

''I know.'' He sounded so anguished, it caused fresh tears to form in her eyes.

"If I stay, then…then we marry and do all the things normal married people do—quarrel, make love…have children."

She stated her position so there could be no doubt in his mind what she expected. To take less would be to demean their love.

His arms went rigid. He let her go. She turned to face him. The look on his face made her cry out. She pressed a hand to her mouth.

"You'd go through that again?" he asked in a barely audible voice. "Marriage…childbirth…"

She nodded. "I want a future, Jason. With you." The tension stretched between them like high-powered electric lines. She saw the doubts, the despair in his eyes.

"When we went fishing, my father said something," he began.

"What?" she asked, hoping for a clue to his thoughts.

"He advised me to take the reality. He said that sometimes people see what they lost as some kind of shining example of perfect happiness, but that it's never real. He said to take the moment and don't worry about the past."

"And?"

Jason reached out a hand to her, then let it drop. "I'll take the reality. I've wanted you too much and too long not to take whatever you're offering."

"Love," she said without hesitation. "I'm offering you my love. I want yours in exchange."

He shrugged and gave her a half smile. "You have "

When she leaned into him, he closed his arms around her and held her so gently she felt as fragile as a bubble.

"Say it," she demanded. Her heart began to sing.

He gripped her tighter. "I love you," he murmured.

She laughed and squeezed him as hard as possible. "I

love you, too. Oh, Jason, I love you *madly*. Don't you realize that?''

He studied her rapturous face. "I always wondered how it would feel to be loved by you. Back when I first met you.''

She heard the longing behind the lightly spoken words. She saw the darkness that lingered in his eyes.

"You're not the first man I ever loved—I can't give that to you—but you are first in my heart, Jason,'' she explained softly. "You have been from that day in your office. You always will be.''

He swallowed hard. She waited anxiously, praying that he would see the truth. Then she saw the darkness begin to break up, to fade. A light gleamed in his eyes, fathoms deep. "You'd better tell me again,'' he said softly.

"I love you.''

He caught her to him in a fierce hungry embrace. She settled against his heart, where she belonged, with a relieved sigh.

"Kiss me, Jason. I've been so *desperate* for you.''

When she tilted her face up, he took full advantage of the offer of her mouth. The kiss went on forever, until they had to draw apart to breathe.

Lifting her, he walked back to the library. There, he stopped by the sofa. He urged her to lie down, then he slipped off her slippers. After adding another log to the fire, he kicked off his shoes and joined her, his long masculine body partially over hers.

"I'll take the reality,'' he murmured, nuzzling her throat. "After once knowing the feel of you against me the dream is no longer enough. It doesn't fill the emptiness inside me.''

"But I do?'' She ran her hand over his shoulders an

back, needing the physical reality of him as he needed her.

"Yes. If you ever leave…" He raised his head and looked at her.

"I won't," she vowed. She touched his face tenderly. It would take time, but she'd overcome his doubts. She'd show him how good life could be. Love would win…but it would take time.

She caressed his brow, his nose, his chin. "I hate the woman who hurt you."

He gave her an odd look, a trace of his old sardonic self returning to his smile. "No one hurt me," he said, attacking her neck with ferocious kisses.

"Your first love did," she explained, sighing in ecstasy when he stroked a long path along her side, then cupped her breast. "I hate her for hurting you."

He caught her hand and kissed the palm, then placed it over his heart. "You can't hate her," he said gruffly. "It was you. It was always you."

"I know," she said. "I figured that out a while ago. I still hate it that you were hurt. Why did you love me? I never gave you a reason—"

He touched her lips. "From the first, there was only you. I don't know why. It just was." His eyes went dark again.

"Oh, love," she whispered, filled with remorse.

Jason stopped her with a kiss. The hunger grew in him, and this time he couldn't fight it. Whatever she felt, it didn't matter. He would marry her. He'd be the reality of life for her just as she would be the center of existence for him.

Sometimes, when life got tough, perhaps she would think of her first love and she'd wonder, for an instant, how things might have been. But when she needed reassurance, when she needed loving, he'd be there for her. He'd accept that. Pressing his face against her throat, he held her tightly.

"Jason?"

"Yes, darling." The endearment sounded right.

"Were you going to leave town without seeing me?"

He lifted his head, looked into her eyes and saw it was important to her. Slowly he shook his head. "I tried. An hour ago, I got as far as Vista Point, and it was like an invisible wall holding me back. I couldn't go on. I turned around."

"Good," she said, satisfaction in the word.

It seemed time for a lighter note. "There were a couple of things I was trying to work out." He groaned when she slid her hands under his shirt and caressed his bare flesh.

"Such as?"

He slipped his hand between them and caressed her, thinking of how sexy she looked when she was pregnant.

"I was working out this big problem," he murmured. "Like—how many children should we have?" It wasn't exactly the truth, but he realized it was what she needed to hear.

With a brilliant smile, she demanded, "How many do *you* want?"

"A half dozen sounds nice." He laughed as her eyes flew open. He kissed them closed. "I'll settle for however many you want to give me." He paused, then added, "Shall we live here until your term is finished? Let's keep this house for vacations…and for our retirement home."

She pressed her face against him. "Sounds perfect."

It came to him then that she was truly his and that the

future belonged to them. It made him feel humble…and blessed.

A half dozen kids? Well, two or three, anyway.

It was a thought. A happy thought.

* * * * *

0402/51a

DESIRE

AVAILABLE FROM 19TH APRIL 2002

AT HER SERVICE

HARD TO FORGET Annette Broadrick
Running into his ex-sweetheart, Elena Maldonado, again after all these years brought army intelligence agent Joe Sanchez to his knees. With white-hot desire demanding completion Joe accepted his one true mission—infiltration…of the heart!

TALL, STRONG & COOL UNDER FIRE Marie Ferrarella
Handsome Bryce Walker had thought family wasn't in his future until Lisa Billings swept into his fire station looking for her missing daughter. They made him long for the dreams he'd put aside and his body yearned to be completely at Lisa's service…

SPECIAL DELIVERY

PRINCE CHARMING IN DRESS BLUES   Maureen Child
Bachelor Battalion
Stranded single mum Annie Foster couldn't believe she was having X-rated thoughts about the perfect stranger who'd delivered her baby! But the more time she spent gazing into Gunnery Sergeant John Paretti's eyes, the harder it became to ignore needs that only he could satisfy…

A LADY FOR LINCOLN CADE BJ James
Men of Belle Terre
After one night of passion, honour had dictated that Lincoln Cade imprison his feelings for Linsey Blair. But no more! A deathbed promise had delivered tempestuous Linsey—and their secret son—into his protection. Now nothing could keep him from his son, his lady and her love!

RUGGED, RUTHLESS AND…READY!

TOUGH TO TAME Jackie Merritt
Loner Jake Banyon didn't want fiery Carly Paxton invading his hard-earned privacy. She was just the kind of woman Jake had vowed to avoid. But he hadn't anticipated feeling an unexpected desire to be tamed by love…

THE ROUGH AND READY RANCHER   Kathie DeNosky
Flint McCray needed a horse trainer—not some curvy vixen infiltrating his masculine domain. But Jenna quickly proved her worth—and a threat to Flint's control. But for one earth-shattering night with Jenna, this man would risk his emotions…

AVAILABLE FROM 19TH APRIL 2002

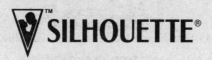

SILHOUETTE®

Sensation™

Passionate, dramatic, thrilling romances

HARD-HEADED TEXAN Candace Camp
DADDY WITH A BADGE Paula Detmer Riggs
CINDERELLA'S SECRET AGENT Ingrid Weaver
INTERRUPTED LULLABY Valerie Parv
IN CLOSE QUARTERS Candace Irvin
PLAIN-JANE PRINCESS Karen Templeton

Special Edition™

Vivid, satisfying romances full of family, life and love

BECAUSE OF THE TWINS... Carole Halston
THE CATTLEMAN AND THE VIRGIN HEIRESS Jackie Merritt
THE LAST MERCENARY Diana Palmer
AND THE WINNER—WEDS! Robin Wells
TEXAS ROYALTY Jean Brashear
COWBOY'S BABY Victoria Pade

Superromance™

*Enjoy the drama, explore the emotions,
experience the relationship*

MY SISTER, MYSELF Tara Taylor Quinn
THE UNCLAIMED BABY Sherryl Woods
JACK MURRAY, SHERIFF Janice Kay Johnson
AND BABY MAKES SIX Linda Markowiak

Intrigue™

Danger, deception and suspense

WOMAN MOST WANTED Harper Allen
CONCEPTION COVER-UP Karen Lawton Barrett
THE FORGIVEN Amanda Stevens
MARRIAGE: CLASSIFIED Linda O Johnston

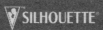

Welcome back to the drama and mystery of the Fortune dynasty

Fortune's Children: The Grooms—
five strong, sexy men
surrounded by intrigue, but
destined for love and marriage!

*The Fortune's Children legacy
continues in this popular continuity
series with two new books a month.*

THE TEXAS RANGER

He has a passion for justice

Published 15th March 2002

1 FREE

book and a surprise gift!

We would like to take this opportunity to thank you for reading this Silhouette® book by offering you the chance to take ANOTHER specially selected title from the Desire™ series absolutely FREE! We're also making this offer to introduce you to the benefits of the Reader Service™—

- ★ FREE home delivery
- ★ FREE gifts and competitions
- ★ FREE monthly Newsletter
- ★ Exclusive Reader Service discount
- ★ Books available before they're in the shops

Accepting this FREE book and gift places you under no obligation to buy, you may cancel at any time, even after receiving your free shipment. Simply complete your details below and return the entire page to the address below. *You don't even need a stamp!*

YES! Please send me 1 free Desire book and a surprise gift. I understand that unless you hear from me, I will receive 2 superb new titles every month for just £4.99 each, postage and packing free. I am under no obligation to purchase any books and may cancel my subscription at any time. The free book and gift will be mine to keep in any case.

D2ZEA

Ms/Mrs/Miss/Mr ....Initials...............................
BLOCK CAPITALS PLEASE

Surname ....

Address ....783........Deem T.U...................................

....

....Postcode...............................

Send this whole page to:
UK: FREEPOST CN81, Croydon, CR9 3WZ
EIRE: PO Box 4546, Kilcock, County Kildare (stamp required)

Offer valid in UK and Eire only and not available to current Reader Service subscribers to this series. We reserve the right to refuse an application and applicants must be aged 18 years or over. Only one application per household. Terms and prices subject to change without notice. Offer expires 31st July 2002. As a result of this application, you may receive offers from other carefully selected companies. If you would prefer not to share in this opportunity please write to The Data Manager at the address above.